HOMING

INSTINCTS

....

A NOVEL

KAREN GUZMAN

D1595622

Fiction Attic Press
Burlingame, California

Fiction Attic Press
P,O. Box 137
Burlingame, CA 94011
http://fictionattic.com

Publisher's Note: This is a work of fiction. Names, characters, places, and incidents are a product of the author's imagination. Locales and public names are sometimes used for atmospheric purposes. Any resemblance to actual people, living or dead, or to businesses, companies, events, institutions, or locales is completely coincidental.

Cover art by Roxanne Steed www.roxannesteed.com

Ordering Information:
Special discounts are available on quantity purchases by educators, associations, and others. For details, contact the "Special Sales Department" at the address above.

Homing Instincts/ Karen Guzman. -- 1st ed.
ISBN 978-0-9911499-3-3

For Ethan

ONE

....

I like to drive at night, something not many people understand. It's just a quirk I have. There are fewer cars on the road
at night, fewer jostling, glaring faces to contend with. On a
good night I could drive from Atlanta to Connecticut in fifteen
hours. This was barring crashes on Interstate Ninety-five,
traffic jams on the hideous Beltway around D.C., and idiotic
toll delays on the New Jersey Turnpike. My personal best was
fourteen-and-a-half hours. But that night in 2004 when I
returned home was not a good night. A misty drizzle started in
South Carolina and chased me up the seaboard. It slicked the
highway and fogged headlights in a gauzy haze. It streaked my
windshield as I crossed the George Washington Bridge,
melding into the cauldron of New York City. Time: seventeen
excruciating hours. Seventeen hours to ponder everything that
had gone wrong and the uncertainty of what now lay ahead.

Delia always said I drove too slowly. *The only man I've ever known
without a lead foot.* I'd taken this as a compliment, feeling it somehow distinguished me as cautious, as reasonable. Good things, I
thought. But it slipped through my lips that night in my car—*the
only man I've ever known without a lead foot*—clearly a put-down. *You
crawl,* she said one year as we were driving home for the holidays.
I'd laughed in response. Why had it taken me six years to realize

that wasn't mock disgust in her voice? *You know how to listen,* she once told me, *but you don't know how to hear.*

I was thirty-five that rainy night driving home alone, young at being old but not truly young anymore. This was before I understood the power of the things we tell ourselves, back when the words uttered to myself seemed harmless. It would take another year for me to see that the story I tell myself is the most important story of all. My father had died six months earlier, and I was returning to the town of my childhood, leaving behind the collapse of the life I had begun. Alone in my Civic, a cup of bitter, rest stop coffee in the cup holder, I followed the stream of red tail lights north. On the outskirts of Harlem and the Bronx, graffiti-splashed overpasses and chain link fences dotted exit ramps.

I pushed up through Yonkers, nipped the corner of woodsy Westchester County and crossed the state line into Connecticut. Here, zipping through the tony Gold Coast towns ringing Long Island Sound, my father began to seem real again. I could picture him, back when we were kids, switching lanes, tuning in his beloved golden oldies on the radio, chiming in with Frankie Valli. If "Can't Take My Eyes Off You" came on, he'd turn it up and take my mother's hand. My brother and sister and I would watch from the back seat, vaguely embarrassed.

In the dark, southeast Connecticut flashed by as the ribbon of highway drew me north. The lights and industry of Stamford crowded round. Then Bridgeport loomed, a sprawling, unwieldy jumble. Next came New Haven and all the Yale exits. I moved into the fast lane, pushing further north into the quiet coves and the modest corner of the state I called home. Another hour up the coast and I passed through New London, nearly there now. I crossed the Gold Star Bridge. Connecticut's Thames River flowed below, feeding into the scrubby wetlands and marshes, past the beach cottages, their wooden docks heaped with knotty lobster traps, and out into the vast, bruising Atlantic. Across the bridge, I guided the Civic into the exit lane and the familiar turn-off into the dark hills west, moving away from the water, onto the wooded roads of Ledyard.

I had not yet learned the secret of my father's happiness, of his ease in the world. Approaching middle age now, never married and unemployed, I still believed in geographic cures, in the power of landscape alone to heal.

My mother, in her sixties then, still lived in the white Colonial with black shutters. The red mailbox proclaimed "Hingham" in blocky, white letters. The house sat off a quiet road near the center of town, in one of those neighborhoods so common in Connecticut. It was an old house with a good acre of clear yard all around and dense woods behind. An aging stonewall marked the property's perimeter, setting it off from its similar neighbors. Stonewalls crisscrossed the town, popping up and disappearing, some more than two hundred years old and lovingly preserved, others disintegrating rock-by-rock. We had always tended ours. My father loved that wall. It dated back to the days of the Revolutionary War, when this was all farmland. It once marked the edge of a cow pasture. My father treated the wall like a museum piece, something precious and brimming with secrets.

Turning into the driveway, my headlights picked up a lump on the ground. At the end of the wall, where it met the driveway, a stone had tumbled loose and fallen. I parked and pulled the key out of the ignition. The Civic shuttered and sighed. It was a 1996—eight years old, survivor of three fender-benders and journeys too numerous to recall. I closed my eyes. A grainy loop of all the tired miles played out, that mind numbing, asphalt trek up the East Coast, through ports of industry and seats of power as the original thirteen colonies slide past.

The rain had stopped. The air was cool and awake, charged with the first stirrings of autumn, moving in a way the air in Atlanta never did. Lights glowed in the living room windows and upstairs in my parents' room—my mother's room now. There were no other cars in the driveway, and the garage doors were closed. My mother was awake, which was a good sign. It was only about nine o'clock, but since Dad died, she had been keeping strange hours, drifting off to sleep in the afternoon and waking around midnight to face the desperate, wee hours of insomnia. I'd had difficulty getting her on the phone.

I walked to the fallen rock, squatted down, lifted its crude, rough weight and placed it back on top of the wall. My father would have fiddled with it, wedging it down, tucking it in securely. But my father wasn't there. He would not open the front door and call, "Seth?" into the darkness. He did not know I was back. Still, I expected to see him, to hear his voice, the way some part of me kept waiting for the phone to ring long after Delia moved out. Only it never did, and now hundreds of miles lay between us.

I slid my key into the front door lock. We never locked our door when I was growing up, but alone here now my mother did. When I flew up for Dad's funeral six months earlier, I didn't really see the places or things around me. Delia came along, stiff and polite, perhaps sensing that she would leave soon but not having the heart yet to admit it to herself—much less to me. I probably should have seen it coming, but I am always lost in the details of things. I never see the big picture, the inevitable, coming at me. My father had lived in the big picture.

Inside, the warmth of the house welcomed me. A faint light glowed in the kitchen, filtering into the hall. I slipped off my jacket and dropped it on the bench against the wall, next to the wooden staircase with the banister that was draped with evergreen roping every Christmas. An imposing mirror, framed in rich walnut, hung over the bench. My face loomed. Gray half-moons hung beneath

4

my eyes. My skin looked fragile and pale. I could see the barest hint of the thin, white scar that clips the outer edge of my left eyebrow. The corner of my mouth twitched. Delia once said I had sensitive lips. "Thin and expressive" were the words she used.

My brother, Travis, and I looked a lot alike, though he was four years older. We both had wavy brown hair and hazel eyes, average builds, strong jaws, only Travis was a more imposing figure. He was solid and heavier. He took up space. Grandma Hingham had called me a "scrawny chickadee" when I was a child. I had filled out, but there was still a wiry, restless edge to my body at thirty-five. I hiked and skied, felt good most of the time. Delia had never complained about my looks.

"Mom?" I called, walking into the kitchen. No answer. The overhead stove lights lit a corner. A bowl of oranges sat on the center island. I moved soundlessly over the tiled floor. I found my mother in the small study at the back of the house, my father's old study, his unofficial retreat. His desk and bookshelves lined one wall. A faded beet-red, velvet loveseat sat beneath the window.

"Forget about me?" I said, stepping through the door. Mother sat on the floor, surrounded by boxes of photographs and albums. Her eyeglasses had slid down to the tip of her nose, and strands of gray hair had slipped loose from the bun at the back of her head. She wore an old pair of gray slacks and a rust-colored sweater that swallowed half her body—she was rangy like me—and sheepskin slippers. She looked up, blinked and stared a second, as if she were seeing a ghost.

"Seth, my God," she said, struggling to her knees to stand. I reached out to take her hand. With her hair slipping loose and the crazy big sweater, she looked a little like a bag lady, and the old anxiety stirred my gut. We shared a quick hug, Mother gripping my arms as she leaned in to kiss my cheek.

"Hey, Mom," I said. "No worries, okay? I'm safe and sound. How are you?"

"I've been waiting," she said. "What with the rain on the roads, and I hate that damn Ninety-five anyway. Did the rain ice?"

"It's too warm for ice," I said. "The drive was fine."

"In the rain with the traffic and all the lunatics racing about?"

"Yes, even with the lunatics."

She pushed her glasses up the bridge of her nose. "It's cold in here," she said. "I'm so submerged in these photos, organizing them before they all go missing the way so much does these days, I didn't even notice the chill." She went to the thermometer on the wall and fiddled with it.

I fought my usual impulse to counter my mother's anxious predictions, to dismiss her harbingers of doom.

"You must be hungry?" she said.

"A little. I had a sandwich at a rest stop."

She winced. "Seth, I saw a bit on the news just the other night—how filthy those rest stops are. The bacteria and viruses. It'll be a wonder if you live through the night."

I laughed and followed her into the kitchen. "You're thin," she said, turning the burner up beneath a cast iron pot on the stove. No non-stick or Teflon for Mother. She was convinced they gave you cancer, so she lugged around these pots that weighed a ton. My sister, Holly, once dropped a lid on her foot and broke her big toe. "Better a broken toe than cancer" was Mother's verdict.

"I may have lost a few pounds. It's been so busy with the move and everything," I said.

"When do your belongings arrive?"

"Middle of next week."

"But you left most of it behind, right? I mean, she took some things."

"Yeah, Delia took a lot."

"Sit," Mother said, taking a bowl from the cabinet and silverware from a drawer. "Seafood stew, your favorite," she said.

"Remember how Daddy used to make it? I've copied his recipe as best as I can remember it."

The stew was thinner, weaker than my father's. She'd done something weird to the tomato juice, watered it down somehow. But I drained my bowl. Mother sat, watching me eat. The clock ticked over the stove. I felt her grappling with what came next.

"So, Mom, are you seeing a lot of Travis and Holly? Or the cousins?" What I wanted to ask was: Are you lonely? What I wanted to say was: I'm lonely too. Only I couldn't. That was the kind of admission, of probing, that my mother would have scoffed at. Longed for, yet scoffed at.

She waved a hand. "God, they don't leave me alone," she said, though there was a note of satisfaction hiding in her tone. I was secretly, and shamefully, relieved. I would not have to carry her alone. "And you," she shifted gears and paused, her voice rising in a false show of nonchalance. "You have an interview set up? In Hartford, right? What did Jasper say? He believes you're a shoe-in, doesn't he?"

Now, we were getting down to business. Mother did not want to carry me, either. Not that I blamed her. Misery doesn't really love company. It loves sympathy.

"Of course, you know, you can stay here as long as you need," she said. "Permanently if you'd like..."

"I'm sure that won't be...

"It takes a lot of moxie to pick up and move without a job to go to," she said. "I never could have done it at your age..."

"But you were married with two children at my age."

"...still, and don't get me wrong, I admire your boldness—you have taken an enormous risk, giving up everything."

I swallowed. "Well, there wasn't much to give up, you know, Mom," I said. "I went to Atlanta for Delia, for her career. Emory has laid off practically my whole department. So there wasn't really a reason to stay, not a good reason."

"The promise of a job does not qualify as a good reason?"

"We've been through this, Mom." I put my spoon down and pushed away from the table. "There was no promise. I got laid off, remember?"

"Yes, but you could have stayed in Atlanta and reapplied for your position at the university when the funding comes back in."

"If the funding comes back in, and God knows how long that could take. It was a good time to make a clean break. I'll find another job. Please don't worry." I gave her a weak smile that wasn't enough to offset the insult I knew she had perceived.

"I'm not worrying." She jutted out her chin. "You may think I've turned into a wreck of an old lady, neurotically wiling away the hours without your father to reel me in, but I haven't. I've actually been exploring some new projects myself, some new directions I may take."

"Well, that's great, Mom," I said. "And no one thinks you're a 'neurotic wreck,' okay?" I took a deep breath. "So, yes, I've spoken with Jasper. Yes, I have an interview next week, and yes, it looks promising. Let's just keep our fingers crossed."

"Fine with me." She stood and carried my empty bowl to the sink. "I'm sure you're right. There's nothing to worry about." She ran the water and scoured the bowl.

"Mom, what I'm saying is you don't have to take this worry on, okay? You don't have to take *me* on. I've got it covered. What I'd really like to do is move further north, up into the mountains, New Hampshire or Vermont maybe, if I could just nail down a job up there. And listen, really there was nothing left to give up in Atlanta. I had already lost... It all slipped away so..."

"Whatever you say, dear," she said, flipping on the garbage disposal so its grinding whir drowned out my voice.

8

T W O

....

The next morning I went out and warmed up the car for Mother. Labor Day weekend was a few days away, and in New England this meant the nights were already growing longer and cooler.

"I didn't want to say anything last night," Mother said, sliding into the passenger seat, "but you need a haircut."

"Okay, I'll put it on my to-do list."

"I know you've had matters more pressing, dear."

I sensed that Mother was itching for a confrontation that I had vowed I was not going to give her—grief masquerading as hostility, a scenario custom made for her. A strong sun pushed out the clouds of the night before. Autumn's first dashes of gold and red touched the tops of the trees. My father's headstone had been delivered and installed at his gravesite overlooking the Mystic River. There had been a delay, something about an incorrect date and the stone had to be redone. It was Saturday, and the family was gathering at the cemetery to view the stone for the first time together.

I started the car, my mother's ancient, white Volvo wagon. It was the only car she felt "safe" in. We followed the circular drive past the porch, decorated with pots of yellow and lavender mums. Mother looked better in the daylight, more pulled together. She wore a brown skirt and matching sweater underneath a camel's hair jacket. I knew she bit her tongue when she saw my khaki pants and

9

fleece pullover. Only immediate family was going to be there—Holly and Travis and his wife and kids—so I thought this was good enough but I was beginning to regret it.

"You look nice, Mom," I said, edging up to the road.

"You'll get your hair cut before the interview, right?" she said. "Appearances matter. Wandering around in the woods all day, you may not appreciate that, but..."

"Mom, I don't wander around in the woods. I conduct field..."

"... other people notice. Delia always looked so nice, not that I'm saying that had anything to do with..."

"So we broke up, because I wander around the woods all day and I dress badly?"

"Not at all. The two issues are not connected, not in any way," Mother said, placing her had on my arm. "I'm the one who always thought that girl lacked substance, Seth. She wasn't your equal, not in the least way. I always had my doubts. I just kept them to myself."

I nodded, embarrassed by my outburst. "Okay, Mom, okay. I'm, ah, sorry. I misunderstood."

She squinted at me. "You're a little tense," she said.

"Maybe just a little." I laughed.

She patted my arm. "Let's get going. We don't want everyone waiting for us. Today is about honoring your father, not indulging our silly squabbles."

"Exactly." I flicked on my turn signal, glanced right and slammed the brakes, just as Holly's Volkswagen Beetle turned, way too tightly, into the driveway.

My mother gasped. "Dear God, didn't you see her car?"

"Sorry, no. I didn't. I couldn't. The wall hid just enough of the car."

Holly parked and strode towards us, grinning conspiratorially because she knew how our mother responded to slammed brakes.

I opened my window. "Nice driving, Holly."

"Oops," she said. Her long, glimmering platinum hair–it was dyed, she was really a light brown, like me—was piled on top of her head in a mass of curly tendrils with what looked like two chopsticks stuck through it. I was relieved to see that she wore faded blue jeans with a pink, heart-shaped patch at one knee and a chunky, green angora-type sweater. Holly was never cold. She skied in t-shirts. She had the soft, full face of a teenager and large, guileless blue eyes that lit with an unexpected shrewdness when you least expected it. She was thirty, five years younger than me, but she still looked like a college kid.

"Welcome home, Big Brother." She blew me a kiss. "Can I ride with you guys?" she said. "My car is making a funny thumping sound."

"I told you not to buy that clunker," Mother called.

"Ah, the sweet sound of regret," Holly said, rolling her eyes. "Thanks for reminding me."

"Hol," I said, kissing her cheek as she leaned into the window. "You're a piece of work, you know that?"

We followed the back roads to Mystic, because Mother hated the highway. Heading into the village center, over the drawbridge that spans the river, I saw again the sprawling homes and manicured gardens that line the riverbanks, the narrow wooden docks reaching out into the water. On this sunny Saturday morning, tourists and locals packed the outdoor cafés. They lingered over coffee and browsed the homey antique and gift shops. The bells in the Baptist Church on the hill tolled richly, and sailboats cut through the river's smooth surface.

Holly caught my eye in the rearview mirror. "You've missed this?" she said.

I wanted to appear blasé, in control. I was determined to show the world—if not myself—an untroubled face, a man who accepted and surmounted whatever came his way. If I kept the façade in place, I hoped, maybe it would eventually be true. My father was that kind of man. An accountant, he had a logical, orderly mind and a calm that deflated my mother's officious panic. But the truth was I had missed Mystic. I missed everyone and everything that reminded me of the person I'd been before Atlanta, and Delia leaving, and my father's eyes shut forever in that satin-lined box.

"Yeah, I guess I've missed some things," I said, but I could tell that Holly wasn't really listening. Her eyes followed the road. We pulled away from the village center, heading out towards the cemetery on a bluff overlooking the Mystic River. Holly had her own problems. She was having trouble with her live-in boyfriend, Bryce. We'd been commiserating through phone calls when I was in Atlanta, but after Delia left, Holly stopped bringing up the subject. Bryce was a poet, a thirty-year-old, college dropout, brewing coffee at Starbucks, dressed in black from head to foot, scowling over the cappuccino foam. I'd met him the year before, just after they moved in together. His real name wasn't Bryce. It was Bob. Bob Smith.

Black wrought-iron gates marked the cemetery's entrance, "I AM THE RESURRECTION AND THE LIFE" scrolled above them. I pulled into the tree-lined drive. Mother sat up straighter. "Do you remember where the plot is, Seth?" she said.

"No, I'm sorry," I said, and for one insane second, I thought that maybe this was all a mistake. Father was sitting on a bench near the river with the sun on his face. He would want to talk about the Huskies' basketball season or tax-deferred IRAs. He would erase all the misunderstandings we'd been laboring beneath. A cold, leaden weight filled my chest as we navigated the narrow road.

"Take a left here," Mother said. "Then at the end of the lane, turn right. The site faces the river, remember?"

Holly spotted the headstone first. "Weren't they supposed to wait for us?" she said.

Mother shook her head. "The workers place them as they come in," she said. "But it doesn't really matter, does it? We're here now."

I parked just past the plot. Holly jumped out and opened Mother's door. She held out a hand and helped Mother from the car. Mother really didn't need help. In fact, she'd always hated people trying to help her. But today she took Holly's hand. Her shoulders seemed somehow narrower, her body diminished. My mother had always been a robust woman—loud, florid, a real presence. Something, some essence, had drained out of her.

"The stone looks nice, Mom," Holly said.

"It should for what we paid," Mother said. "Your father would never have authorized such an expenditure."

"Yes, he would have. For you, for any one of us," Holly said.

"He was a practical man, a prudent old Yankee," Mother continued, as if she were explaining a stranger to us. "Your father knew what to do with money."

That was true. I was from a long line of prudent Yankees. Hinghams had been in this part of Connecticut since the Revolutionary War. We were never wealthy, never splashy, but we were comfortable. The headstone's flinty marble face sparked when the sun hit it: LEWIS T. HINGHAM, 1938-2004, *All Things in Moderation*.

"He would have liked that," I said. "What would he have said, Holly? An unexpected, little dividend."

Holly laughed. "He was always saying that. Remember when Travis and Rosemary found out they were having twins? It was the first thing out of Dad's mouth." She grew still. "He was so funny. We never appreciated how funny he was."

"It's the kind of thing you overlook in the bloom of youth," Mother said. "And children never, and I mean never, truly *see* their parents."

I wondered if she were right about that. Had I appreciated my father as much as I should have? Probably not, but regret like that were the sort of thing he would have shrugged off. "Fix your eyes on the horizon," he would have said. "Don't waste too much time looking over your shoulder.

Mother had brought three big pots of mums to place around the headstone. I walked back to the car to get them. I popped the trunk, and the bright yellow, bristling bouquets greeted me. They were ten-inchers, heavy and full. The pots were the rugged green, plastic ones from the nursery. They would look nice against the gray granite stone. It felt good to have something to do. I hoisted two into one arm, and the third into the other. I was slamming the trunk closed with my elbow, when Travis' big-ass SUV pulled up. I could see his wife, Rosemary, in the passenger seat, and the very tops of their twin boys' blond heads—Jeremy and Jason, age three—in the back seat.

"The prodigal returns," Travis said, slamming his car door. "How are you, Seth?"

"I'm okay, doing okay, yeah, fine."

"Good to be home?"

"Yeah, I, ah, guess it is."

Rosemary climbed out and gave me a jaunty wave. "Seth," she called over the car. "How was your drive up?"

"A little slow. The weather wasn't cooperating," I said.

"Ah," Travis said. "And which route did you take?"

Rosemary opened the back door and began unbuckling the boys.

"Ninety-five," I said.

"All the way?" Travis said. "I always find that detouring off the interstate once you're in, say, New Jersey, actually gives you..."

Jeremy charged around the car and plowed into Travis' leg. Travis winced.

"Daddy, can we go to the water now? Wanna see water," Jeremy whined.

"After we see Grandpa's new stone, remember?"

"No!" Jeremy scrunched up his face. "No stones. River!"

Jason sidled up to Travis' other leg. The twins were not identical physically or in terms of character. Jeremy was a real bruiser, while Jason was more tentative and cautious. "Is Grandpa here?" he said.

He clung to Travis' side. It was still strange, seeing Travis as a father. He was thirty-nine. All our lives he had never let me forget he was older and wiser, or so he imagined. I kind of enjoyed watching the twins badger him.

Travis was a chemist at Pfizer. He had a sprawling contemporary house in Mystic—all windows and angles. Rosemary had recently converted to some old-time, Bible church, according to Holly. She was supposedly as religious as a preacher all of a sudden. We were a family of watered-down New England Congregationalists, so nobody was much interested in Rosemary's newfound faith. I didn't believe in God, not the one you learn about in Sunday school anyway. I believed in cause and effect, though not necessarily in that order, and maybe in something else, something burning just out of sight, just beyond the wavy line of the horizon, that I could sometimes feel but never get a good look at. Holly believed in what she called a universal energy flow. "The great hum of all things" she called it.

"Hey boys," I said, and the twins threw me a glance. Jeremy stared, narrowing his blue eyes. Jason stepped closer to Travis. "Who dat?" he said.

"You know Uncle Seth," boomed Travis.

"Uncle Seth?"

"That's right." He turned to me. "How's Mom?"

"You'd know better than me really." I shrugged. "She seems okay." I squatted down before Jason and Jeremy and squeezed them together in a bear hug that made Jeremy giggle. "How are the monsters?" I said in a growly bear voice they loved.

"How is Mom *this* morning?" Travis said.

"She's holding it together as well as can be expected."

"That depends on what you expect." Travis winked. "You get a job yet?" He grinned and poked me in the side.

"Today? In the cemetery? No," I said.

"Smart ass," Travis said.

"Ass!" Jeremy shrieked and giggled. An elderly man and woman visiting a nearby grave threw us a dirty look.

Rosemary came around the car. She was tall and waspishly thin, with long brown hair and large, doe-like brown eyes. She wore dark slacks and a bright orange, knee-length jacket that made me think of pumpkins. "What your mother needs today is our support and love. And harmony," she said, stepping forward to kiss my cheek hello. She was a nice woman. I never understood how she ended up with Travis. He had our father's orderly mind, but he lacked Dad's easy touch, his way with people.

"Need me to carry a pot, Seth?" Rosemary said.

"No thanks, Rosemary. I've got 'em," I said, juggling the mums. "Good to see you again."

"Boys," Rosemary called, whipping around. Her mother's radar must have kicked in. Jeremy was climbing on top of someone's headstone. "Stop that! Jeremy, get down. Come here now."

"I've got him," Travis called.

Delia used to keep track of my family's squabbles. Every visit home, she'd wait for the first one and then critique it for me later. It had secretly annoyed me, Delia handing down judgment from her TV reporter's perch. Her voice even got on-airy when she described the fights, slow and crisp and exaggerated, as if I hadn't been there right next to her, watching it all myself. Once as we all sat on the patio on a summer evening, Travis and Mother argued about the best time of day to water the potted geraniums.

"Morning is optimal," Mother said. "I've always watered in the morning so they have a good drink before the heat of the day."

Travis, head buried in an issue of *Scientific American*, raised his eyes. "Actually sundown is preferable," he said. "The soil is more receptive."

"But they'll be parched by morning," Mother said.

"Not at all, Mom. Remember the dew of the early hours. Plants actually derive a great deal of..."

"I was growing geraniums when you were in diapers, and I think I know a thing or two about their care, Travis."

"Yes, but Dad was always the one with the green thumb, wasn't he?" Travis said.

Mother stalked off into the house.

In the car heading back to Atlanta the next morning, Delia giggled in the passenger seat. "The best part was the 'dew of the early hours,' wasn't it?" she said. Then she grew stone-faced, and her voice dropped an octave. "The mother rose and re-entered the home, leaving family members on the patio in an awkward silence. None would comment further."

I had laughed at Delia's little joke, grinding my teeth.

Jeremy and Jason took off racing when they saw Mother. "Grandma! Grandma!"

Mother stooped over and wrapped them both in her arms. "My darlings," she said.

I put the mums down at the foot of the plot. Some of the grass was already browning. I glanced around. No freshly dug earth anywhere. They must have rolled strips of sod over the grave.

"Well, what do you think?" Mother nodded at the headstone.

We stood silent a moment. "Nice work," Holly said. She was a graphic artist at a small ad agency up in Middletown. "Very clean, simple, succinct. Daddy would have approved."

"He does approve," Rosemary said. I glanced at her. She had a misty look on her face, as if she were beholding a great and awesome sight—the Grand Canyon or the peak of Everest.

"I thought we would group the mums around the stone," Mother said. "They have another good month of life in them. I always choose the late bloomers, you know."

"They're lovely, Mom," Holly said. "Trav, help me place them."

But Travis was frowning at the headstone. He looked like Dad, sort of, a beefier version, but the same high forehead and dark, clipped hair—though Dad was of course gray at the end. I remembered when his hair was dark. I saw us all raking leaves on a sunny, fall day. Travis and I were perhaps five and nine, and Dad was teaching us how to bag the leaves. Dragging my rake over the lawn, I hit something. A rock? No, a box turtle. It raised its cantankerous, leathery face and stared at me. Its spotted shell had been hidden in a leaf pile. It moved, and I shrieked. I was amazed that this thing on the ground was alive. Dad laughed. I looked up and saw his laughing face against the blue sky. His black hair gleamed. How vibrant and powerful he seemed. Now he lay beneath this ground.

"The headstone," Travis said. "The quotation is bizarre." Holly shot me an uh-oh look. A pleasure boat tooted its horn out on the river.

Mother looked over. "It was the quote your father requested. In fact, he left very specific instructions. He spelled out everything concerning his final resting place."

"It looks fine to me," Holly said.

"These were his wishes," Mother repeated.

Travis frowned. "Maybe so, but someone should have..."

"THESE were his wishes, Trav," Holly said, glaring at him. It was amazing the way Travis did not pick up on the signs that he had—in his typical, bruising way—gone too far. He rarely meant harm. There was no malice in Travis. He just suffered from some sort of social myopia.

"What does it mean?" he mused, his voice taking on a clinical tone. "That the deceased lived moderately? That he intended to exist moderately in the afterlife? That he was ready to die? That his life had been reasonably long and good enough? Whatever happened to 'Beloved husband and father?' That is at least clear."

Mother sighed. "I fulfilled his wishes," she said. "No one can say I let him down."

"No need to get melodramatic, Mother. I'm simply speculating," Travis said. "No one, by which you mean me, of course, is implying that you let him down."

"Not in so many words," Mother said. She lifted the pot of mums from Holly's hands and marched to the headstone.

"Ducks," Jeremy whimpered. "Wanna see ducks." He jabbed a tiny finger in the direction of the water.

I rubbed my forehead. "Oh, God," I said.

Rosemary whipped around. "Please don't say that."

"What?"

"God."

"God? Why not?"

"I find it offensive."

"I'm sorry." I lowered my head and mumbled, "Jesus." It just slipped out.

"Please!" Rosemary said.

"Why can't I say 'God' in a cemetery?" I said. "Or Jesus? It would seem the perfect place. The pastor said 'God' about a hundred times at the service here."

Rosemary ignored me. I had always liked her. It was unsettling to be on the receiving end of her annoyance.

"It's the way you said it, Seth," Travis said. "Believe me. I've been through this." Travis, last time I'd checked, was an atheist.

"Yes, it's the context," Rosemary said.

"Context is everything," Travis said. He paused. "Hey, *that* would have been an interesting headstone quote."

Mother placed her mums down and leaned over, her face inches from the headstone. Her hand traced the letters of Dad's name. Then she rose and began walking back to the car.

"What about the other mums?" Travis called.

Holly sighed. "God, Travis," she said.

Rosemary bit her lip. Holly brushed by her, striding toward the car. The little chopsticks on her head bobbed angrily. She looked like a blonde, avenging angel, swooping past the headstones. A slack, deflated look came over Travis' face. "I didn't mean anything," he said. The twins, spellbound by the tension for a moment, suddenly began crying.

Back in the cars, we snaked along in a gloomy caravan to a restaurant in the seaport for lunch. Sitting beneath a picture window overlooking the easy flow of the Mystic River, and further out the ripples of Long Island Sound, I had a bowl of real clam chowder—impossible to find in Atlanta. Delia and I had tried, in restaurants all over town. She would have liked this here today—the river, the creamy, smoky-sweet chowder and bud vases with yellow carnations on the tables. She would have shut out all distractions. That was what I needed to do. I closed my eyes for a moment and saw the dark silhouette of the northern mountains, the way they look when you drive toward them at night, pushing up through western Massachusetts into the quiet folds of Vermont, the soothing shadows huddled in the distance, waiting to envelope you. What I needed was a life there, unattached and unknown, tucked away from everything that had gone so wrong.

In the men's room, I splashed cold water on my face and stared, dripping, into the mirror. Time was rushing past. I was careening, crooked and flailing, into the future. I had reached none of the milestones or the achievements most people use to measure the passing of a life. I was drifting, unfettered. I leaned on the sink. My head grew light. I gripped the sink tighter and tried to draw a deep breath, thanking God that at least Delia couldn't see me now.

* * *

Lung cancer killed my father. It only took three months from diagnosis to death. I was in Atlanta. Mired in the unraveling of my own life, I heard the news the way you hear a faint sound, a tiny ping on the periphery of your range when you're deep in conversation with another person. You're not quite sure what it is or what it may become, so you just stay focused on the job at hand.

When Delia and I headed south six years earlier because she had been hired as a television news reporter for the local ABC affiliate in Atlanta, Connecticut fell into the background. Delia was from the Farmington Valley outside Hartford. We met as graduate students at the University of Connecticut. I was twenty-nine when we moved, and Delia was twenty-five. She rose steadily through the ranks at her station, until I could snap on the news almost any time and there she'd be, reporting "live" from the statehouse where the General Assembly was deadlocked on a vote, "live" from a wind-whipped beach in Savannah where a hurricane was drawing near, "live" from a charity 5K race through town, running alongside participants, puffing into her microphone, her dark ponytail bouncing side to side. It became a standing joke we had. I'd come home, for instance, and call out, "Delia, where are you?"

"Live on the toilet," she'd call. Delia had a sense of humor. She had it all, truth be told, and during our first couple of years together, I would occasionally stop and silently marvel that she loved me. I would watch while she was telling a joke at a crowded party or when she applied lipstick to her gorgeous mouth, staring into the mirror at the vanity table in the corner of our bedroom, and wonder how this could be true. I was a lucky guy, and it occurred to me after she moved out that perhaps I had lost sight of this one fact: Delia may have been too good for me.

I was working as a research wildlife biologist in the animal biology department at Emory University when Delia and I split. Wild turkey, black bear and deer were my most recent specialties. I've always found comfort in the fact that thousands of species besides us roam this planet. My Ph.D. thesis was "Water Resource Utilization Among Migrating Canada Geese." It was a big hit with the ornithology crowd.

Anyway, Delia was the glamorous one, the one people would say, "Really?" about when I told them who my girlfriend was. We were an unlikely pair, I realize that now, but early on when we were first stepping gingerly into the adult world, my quiet temperance and her vivacious energy balanced each other. And Delia made me proud. I wanted to marry her, and I was ready to do so when she became accidentally pregnant. That night was burned forever into my mind. I found her sitting on the edge of the bathtub in the fluffy, pink robe I got her for Christmas. She was inconsolable.

"It's not that I don't want children," she said, wiping her snotty nose on a tissue. "Just not right now and," she paused, "possibly not yours."

Possibly not mine? I stood there for a minute. My bare feet looked grungy on the bathroom floor. The toenails were too long. Delia hated "nasty" feet. Dark specs of mildew mottled the shower curtain behind her. Cleaning the shower was my chore, and I had let it go too long again. By the end, details like these were erupting into all night battles. Every minor transgression was magnified into betrayal: clothes on the bedroom floor, the stain inside the coffee pot, lint in the dryer trap, a litany of sins. I would promise to do better, but never quite make it. I promised again that night. I launched into a passionate plea.

"This is just what we need," I said, dropping to one knee before the tub and taking Delia's pale hand in mine. She sniffed, raising her teary eyes to mine. "A baby," I said, "imagine the difference this will make, Dee. With a baby—our baby—to focus on, we won't keep getting caught up in all the petty bullshit we fight about, right?"

She stared at the white, tiled floor.

"And you know I'll marry you, Dee?" I raised her chin so her eyes met mine again. "You know that, right?"

"I do," she said. "But Seth, I'm not ready. I mean, we're not. I don't know if we can do this."

I put my hands on her shoulders. "Look, what if I just ask you to think about it? Let's not make any decisions now, right this minute. Can we just think it over for a little while?"

Delia gave me a half-smile. "Yeah, we can," she said in a tiny, little girl voice. "Seth, I want to do the right thing..."

"Of course you do, and you will, Dee."

"...and I don't want to make a big mistake here."

Now she was talking, though as she had once so succinctly put it, I wasn't really *hearing* her. "Me either," I said. "Let's take a week, maybe two, to think things over?"

Delia sniffed, looking hopefully at me now.

I knelt on the bathroom floor and put my arms around her. Her head dropped to my shoulder, and I thought the issue was, more or less, settled. She'd come around. In fact I was so optimistic, the next day on my lunch break, I went to a baby boutique downtown and bought a cuddly, stuffed brown bear for the baby's crib. The bear wore a t-shirt that said, "Baby's 1st Bear." I picked up a book of Mother Goose rhymes, the same one I'd seen back in Travis's nursery in Connecticut. He had twin toddlers, and I remembered him saying something about Mother Goose being good for kids' language skills.

On my way out of the store, a crib mobile caught my eye. It was a large one—a lion, giraffe, zebra and monkey revolving slowly over a crib in the corner. The $110 price tag was a little steep, but wouldn't the baby love this thing? I left all the baby stuff in a shopping bag in my car trunk. I didn't want Delia to see it and feel pressured, but I couldn't wait to show it to her.

A couple of days later, I ducked into a jewelry shop and bought a platinum and diamond engagement ring I thought Delia would like. The salesman assured me we could exchange it, if she preferred a different style. She probably would. Delia had much better taste than me, but I needed a ring to slip on her finger when I asked her to marry me. This wasn't going to be a rush-job, shotgun wedding. Delia needed to know I meant it.

So it nearly knocked me over when about two weeks later Delia went and had the abortion. I cried like a slob when she told me. Delia just kept saying, "I'm so sorry. It's for the best, Seth. You'll see that one day, too. You will." She said this, staring at the floor, her hands trembling. I truly hated her in that moment, but on some buried level I suspected she was right. Delia saw things I didn't. She saw them first and more clearly. It had been that way our entire time together. Delia pointing the way and me nodding my head.

There is no way back to the place you were together after something like this happens. There are events, and then there is their impact. The first end. The second can turn you into different people. I returned the diamond ring, in its satiny box with the white ribbon on top, and never told Delia I bought it. I dropped the shopping bag with Baby's 1st Bear, Mother Goose and the mobile into a Salvation Army box late one night, drove back to the condo and got drunk. Delia had already moved out. My father had been dead three months. I slumped on the living room couch. A sense of detachment, of weightless confusion, came over me. It was as if I had turned a corner onto a familiar street, but all the landmarks were gone. The buildings I knew, the stop signs on the corners and traffic lights glowing in the intersections had disappeared. Without them, I didn't know what I was doing or where I was supposed to go.

Not long after, Emory announced its budget for the next academic year. Animal research took a hit. University administration, it seemed, was just not as concerned with the mystery of thinning wild turkey egg shells as we were. I could hang around and wait a year, in the hopes the university would increase funding and I would be rehired, or I could try my luck elsewhere. I chose to leave. In the end I departed Atlanta with the haunting sense that I was being chased out, rejected and cast off, deemed unnecessary in life's most fundamental endeavors—work and love.

THREE

....

When I was seventeen, I killed a classmate. I didn't actually murder him, but for a long time, it felt that way. Henry Apgar was the most miserable human being I had ever known. Just the sight of him, trudging down the hall in Ledyard High School depressed me. He was a big kid. Not especially fat, but big and bulky. Jumbo-sized. A lot of his trouble sprang from that fact. I'd known Henry since elementary school. He was a large little kid, too. He was teased, of course, but playground taunts paled next to the ostracism and utter rejection Henry faced in high school. I felt bad for him. We had played together in grade school, going over to each other's houses, building soapbox go-carts and camping in our backyards. This was before the misery of his adolescence, when Henry was still a spirited little boy. By ninth grade, I wouldn't know him anymore, and I was just enough of a shit myself to put some distance between us, lest he damage my own social standing.

But something else happened, too, that drove us apart. Henry soured. The older and bigger he became, the more awkward he grew. The more sullen, bristling and withdrawn he became, the more his classmates abused him. It was a vicious cycle. The roly-poly, pink-cheeked boy, who chased me in games of tag now stood six-foot-two in baggy jeans and over-sized flannel shirts, a permanent scarlet flush on his face and a baseball cap pulled low over his unruly mop of brown curls. He rarely spoke. I avoided him, and he appeared to have forgotten me.

Until one day in eleventh grade. The last bell of the day had just rung, when standing at my locker with Jasper, I saw Henry. He was shuffling up the hall, heading for the doors. A crush of kids stampeded to the waiting buses. Others headed off to the track or locker rooms, or classrooms where clubs met. God knew Henry wasn't involved in any of that.

Jasper and I were stuffing books into our backpacks. But when I glanced up and saw Henry approaching like a tired, woolly mammoth dragging itself home, something inside me softened. I suddenly saw him at ten at a Red Sox game at Fenway Park. His dad had taken us both that afternoon. It was a huge treat—something to lord over Travis—the drive to exotic Boston, the swelling cheers of the fans, the smoky baked pretzels and rubbery hotdogs.

It was an afternoon game, the sun high overhead, and the outfield glowing like an emerald, the players' uniforms dazzlingly white against it. Mr. Apgar was a big Sox fan, and he wanted Henry and me to follow in his footsteps. In Connecticut, you were either for the Sox or for the Yankees, a long-standing rivalry with absolutely no middle ground. Mr. Apgar worked at the Ledyard town garage. He drove a snowplow in winter and fixed potholes in summer. He saw the discipleship of new Sox fans as his personal mission. He always wore a Red Sox cap.

"Oh, for God's sake, Ump," he yelled at the field. "Are you blind?" It was the top of the sixth, and my attention had started to wander. From my aisle seat, I was studying the people around me. The candy apple guy passed by, climbing the cement steps higher into the bleachers. Henry's eyes followed him.

"I'd love one of those," he said. "This is getting boooring." Mr. Apgar glanced at us, and I poked Henry in the side.

"Hey, look," I said, pointing at a tiny stream of liquid running down the aisle, trickling over the stadium steps. "Gross."

"It's probably piss," Henry said.

"What?"

"It's probably piss. Someone drunk up there," he pointed to the bleacher rows up above, "is probably letting loose right now."

"You think someone's pissing in the stands?" I said.

Henry shrugged. "Could be. Doesn't it look sort of yellow to you?" He leaned lower over the trickle, wrinkling his nose and sniffing

A wave of hilarity surged through me then, the way it only does when you're a kid, when you laugh so hard, you can't breathe and your sides hurt.

Standing at my locker seven years later, watching Henry lumber along, a rush of warmth filled me. As he passed, I stepped forward. "Hey, Henry, need a ride home?"

Jasper spun around so fast, he whacked his head on my open locker door. "What?" he said.

Henry stopped dead. The little brown eyes buried deep in his flushed face met mine. For an instant, I thought he was going to blow me off, not even answer and just keep walking. But he must have seen a flicker of something on my face. He wavered. "Which way you going?" he said.

"Up Pine, past your road. Jasper's driving," I said, jerking my thumb at my baffled cousin. Jasper was a senior and had his own car. He gave me rides to school most mornings. We were close in high school, Jasper and me. I found him a prom date. He was horribly shy with girls back then.

"I've, um, got a lot of crap in my back seat," Jasper said, "books and papers and la crosse gear. There's not a lot of room, you know."

"Just shove that shit over, Henry," I said. "Or, you know what? I'll sit in back." I was too carried away by my gesture to stop.

Jasper would give me hell later, but who cared? We were giving Henry a ride home, and it *felt* right.

Jasper turned back to his locker. "Whatever. It's my car, but whatever," he said. He slammed his locker door. Jasper wasn't a mean kid. He was just afraid of the pecking order, as we all were. All except Henry, who had nothing to lose.

In the student parking lot, I clambered into the junked-up backseat of Jasper's old Mustang. It was an ancient heap he had pieced together. Henry dropped his bulk into the passenger seat, my usual spot, next to Jasper, who had retreated into stony silence.

Henry lived in a small gray ranch house across town from me, in one of the older neighborhoods a couple of miles from the high school. It wasn't so much a neighborhood as just a row of boxy houses with tiny front yards facing a broad cornfield. We used to tear up and down the cornfield rows when we were kids, playing "ambush," our version of hide-and-seek. Henry was never difficult to find.

"So, um, how are your folks, Henry? Your dad still a Sox fan?" I said.

"Yeah, he is," Henry said. The back of his head looked surreal in front of me. Once in seventh grade, I ducked into the boys' bathroom when I saw him coming down the hall. He'd been after me to go camping, but his growing outcast status had begun to trouble me. I hid in a stall, biting my lip until it hurt. I could barely meet Henry's eyes in class after that, I was so ashamed of myself.

For an awkward couple of minutes in the car, no one said anything. Jasper shifted into high, zipping up the main road toward the intersection where we had to turn onto Henry's street. The soft buds and shoots of early spring greened lawns and treetops.

"You doing anything over the summer?" I asked Henry.

"Working for my dad. He's got a lawn cutting thing on the side in summer now." He paused. "Last August I cut twelve lawns in one day."

"Twelve? Wow. That's, um, incredible."

"One of them was all hill, too. It was hard as hell, pushing that mower up hill, I'll tell you that much."

"Yeah, I cut my parents' lawn."

Silence. Henry didn't know what to say any more than I did. "Jasper, hang a left here," I said.

"Fourth house on the left," Henry said, shifting and creaking the springs in his seat.

"You know, you should have gone out for football," I said.

Henry grunted. "Yeah, imagine that. All those preppy douche bags and me out on the field together."

It was not a sharp turn onto Henry's road. It was a big, wide intersection with a blinking light dangling above. There was a clear line of vision that afternoon, no traffic in sight, and the pavement was dry—all things the police report would note later. The simple truth was Jasper cut the corner too fast and too tight. He didn't have good control of the car as we rounded the bend and I saw a flash of brown emerging from the cornfield. At first I thought it was a dog, but it was too tall—a deer.

"Deer!" I yelled as it ran for the road and tried to cut in front of us—a big doe with a bright white flag of a tail. Jasper hit the brakes and ripped the wheel to the right. I slammed into the door. None of us wore seat belts. Someone yelled. It might have been me. The deer was zigzagging all over the road. Jasper shouted. He ripped the wheel to the left, then to the right again, overcorrecting. We shot toward the woods and the six-inch culvert that ran along the road.

Then we were tipping, tumbling, rolling over. A shot fired through my arm, and my shoulder collapsed. I closed my eyes and heard a grinding rumble, a rush of air, screams and a great thud. Then, stillness.

When I opened my eyes, I was still in the car. Only it was upside down. I was lying on the ceiling. "Jasper?" I couldn't feel my body. A roaring filled my ears. "Jasper?" Someone moaned.

When the ambulances and fire truck came, they had to cut Jasper and me out of the car. Jasper had a broken sternum and ribs, and his left knee was smashed. He could barely breathe. I broke my right shoulder and arm, and a deep groove ran up the left side of my face, slicing through my eyebrow like a bolt of scarlet lightning. It was a miracle it had missed my eye.

They found Henry Apgar lying in the woods about ten yards from where we flipped over. He'd been thrown from the car. He was still alive. I used to wonder what he thought about, lying there. He died in the emergency room. My parents got a copy of the police report, which they tried to hide from me. But I found it, buried beneath tax papers in my father's desk. Henry died from "massive blunt force trauma," internal injuries, bleeding and shock too great to overcome. He broke through the windshield like a missile, ripped through the brush and crashed into a tree. The broken glass sliced wounds and great purple bruises all over his body. His liver was crushed.

I saw a therapist for six months, because I was afraid to get into a car and afraid to go into that section of town.

"Please listen to me, Seth," my father kept saying. "This is a terrible tragedy, but these things happen. When you're older, you'll understand this. You'll understand that there is no one to blame."

I couldn't hear my father then. I wouldn't be able to hear him all the years when Henry haunted my dreams. Jasper and I did not talk about the accident. We tried at first, a few awkward remarks a couple of times. Then he went off to college at Dartmouth in New Hampshire. A year later, I started at UConn, and we drifted apart. At family functions over the years, we avoided all mention of the topic. I always noticed, though, that Jasper drove huge cars, usually SUVs, despite the fact that everyone knew those things tip over all the time.

* * *

Jasper lived in Colchester, in one of those "big new monstrosities that are destroying the landscape," according to Mother. She had become a budding environmentalist, one of the new "directions" she had mentioned. Mother, who had never been the least bit politically aware, now decried—sometimes with a surprisingly pointed hostility—urban sprawl, wetlands protection, "the moron in the White House," global warming, whales, wolves, watersheds and the shrinking rain forest.

"He's in one of those subdivisions they've built where the old Keller Farm used to be. Remember the apple orchard there? I took you kids every autumn to pick apples," she said. She was watching me unpack in my old room. I had waited several days before unpacking. Living out of a suitcase preserved the temporary air, as if I was just here for a visit, a few days, maybe a week, not that I was unemployed and back in my mother's house until I pulled my life together.

"I remember," I said. I had loved that orchard as a child, the low gnarly arms of the apple trees, the cold, sweet cider that made your teeth ache and the crunchy cookies in the farm market. "Mr. Keller sold the place?"

"He died."

"Oh, I'm sorry." I arranged my good blue suit, my only suit, on a hanger in the closet. My old bedroom, a corner room upstairs, was largely the same—a comforting and yet somehow disturbing fact. The red, digital face of my high school clock radio still glowed on the nightstand. The wooden bookcase Travis and I carved our initials into stood in one corner, and the narrow twin bed, the boy's bed, I was now sleeping in.

"He died, and his children wanted nothing to do with the place." Mother threw her palms up in a surrender gesture, "Keller wasn't even cold, and they were selling out to the greediest huckster imaginable, a real stain of a man. Now it's McMansions, swimming pools and three-car garages. All the apple trees ripped from the ground. The meadow plowed under. It's just a crime."

"Jasper lives in a mansion? Geez, he's doing well with the state, huh? Maybe I should be taking this interview more seriously," I said, laughing. I lifted a suitcase overhead and pushed it back on the closet shelf. Hopefully it wouldn't be there long.

Mother cleared her throat.

I looked at her. "What?" I knew that little 'excuse me?' gargle of hers. Her eyes were wide with exaggerated astonishment.

"I suppose it isn't my place to say, but I had no idea you were *not* taking this interview seriously," she said.

"It was a joke, Mom."

"It seems to me a person in your position needs to take every potential opportunity seriously."

"Yes, thanks, Mom. You don't have to remind me. I am painfully aware of my position."

"Now Seth…"

"Look, Mom, I'm thirty-five years old, and there's an AC/DC poster hanging above the bed where I'll sleep tonight. How could I not take that seriously?"

She raised her palms. "Okay. Please finish up and come down for dinner. I have the apple pie you love. I made it just for you." With that, she retreated into the hall, and I felt a pang of guilt hearing her descend the stairs. Mother didn't want to tangle with me any more than I wanted to tangle with her. I'd become too touchy. I had to get a handle on myself. Mother's anxieties had bounced off my father. Off him and onto us, Holly once said. Maybe so. The truth was Mother could be impossible, but then she'd make you a pie or give you a hug, smiling hopefully up into your face, believing in your forgiveness. My father understood the importance of this forgiveness, of tolerance, and their power. I didn't know it at the time, but I was just beginning to.

I kicked off my loafers and sat on the edge of the bed. The mattress was too soft. I swung my legs up and laid out flat. My old room was the smallest of the house's five bedrooms. My parents' room and a guest room were downstairs off the living room. The kids' rooms were upstairs. It had always been our domain. As the oldest and the only girl, respectively, Travis and Holly snagged the biggest rooms. But that was always all right with me. There were tree branches just outside my windows, and I could hear squirrels running along the gutters at night. They're more active at night than most people realize. When I was a kid, I put peanuts and carrots on the windowsill to lure them. They would perch on the sill, holding a nut in their spindly little fingers, while I studied them from a nearby chair. I would hold still, breathing softly. I sometimes tried to sketch them, not that I could draw, but the fluffy, bristling, little acrobats fascinated me. Over a period of about a month, I managed to coax one to take a peanut from my hand. It stretched out its tense body, nose twitching, brushing my skin. Travis barged in one day, just as the squirrel was reaching for the nut. Travis yelled. I jumped, and the squirrel shot off. Mother made me get a tetanus shot.

I pulled out my cell phone and dialed Jasper's office line in Hartford. It was 2:27 p.m. He had to be back from lunch by now. It rang twice, and a woman answered.

"Department of Environmental Protection," she said. She sounded tired or bored. I had an urge to hang up. This was all a mistake—quitting my job in Atlanta, coming back up here to nothing, groping and begging now for any crumb I could find. If only Delia had kept the baby, maybe we could have gotten married, bought a house, worked it all out. Maybe we could have worked it out even without the baby...

"Yes, is Jasper Mahoney available?" I said.

"May I ask who's calling?"

"Seth Hingham."

"And this is in reference to?"

"To an employment issue."

"Sure, please hold a minute, and I'll transfer you."

I probably shouldn't have said 'an employment issue.' I didn't know what kind of rules the state had regarding nepotism. Of course Jasper would not be interviewing or hiring me. He just knew about an opening in one of the agency's other divisions, one, that according to Mother, I was "eminently qualified for." She was also convinced that Jasper had "pull" and could get me hired. Jasper to the rescue. God only knew what she had told him about my situation,

The line clicked. "Seth?"

"Yes, Jasper, hey. How are you?" I cleared my throat.

"Me? Good, real good. *How are you?*"

"Great. Back home, you know. I got in last night."

"Staying with your mom?"

"Uh, yeah, I am. You know, temporarily, while I get settled and all."

"She called me last week. She was pretty upset. Worried, I mean. It sounds like you've had a hell of a time, my man."

I forced a laugh. "Aw, you know mom. She overreacts to everything. You know how she gets."

Jasper chuckled. "Remember the time she burned down half the backyard at your house to trim back the brush so Lyme disease ticks wouldn't get too close to the house?"

"Yeah, that was some classic Millicent. She almost got arrested. And my father had to reimburse the fire department."

Jasper laughed again, and I felt my shoulders drop. "That's mom," I said. "There is only one, a true original."

"Ah, God. Good times, good times," Jasper said. "So, listen, we should talk about the situation here. The opening in the Bureau of Wildlife Management. I can e-mail you the job description, or you can look it up on the website. It's all there, hours, salary grade. I don't work for Wildlife Management, but this sounds like it's right up your alley."

"Yeah, absolutely."

'Working for the state, Seth, it's not a bad gig. The benefits are incredible."

"So I hear."

"Listen, I care about all that now. You know Chloe is pregnant?"

It felt like someone had punched me in the gut. "No, no, I didn't know. Wow, congratulations. How many months?"

"She's five months now, so we're feeling more confident. We had some, ah, miscarriage trouble earlier, and...

"I'm sorry."

"...so we kept it quiet a long time, only told a handful of people, my mom, Chloe's folks. But I guess the miscarriage risk is really low now, the doctor said."

"Oh, that's good." It was unlike Jasper to get so personal so quickly. I tried to shift the tone a little. "So you're going to be some poor kid's father?"

Jasper chuckled. "Yeah, the poor little guy."

"Better him than me."

"Well said. Hey, why don't you come out to the house Saturday? We bought a place in Colchester. Did your mom tell you?"

"She did. The house, the baby—your neck's in the noose now."

Jasper laughed. "Well we all end up here, sooner or later, Buddy."

There was an awkward pause, and I wondered what else Mother had told Jasper. Of course, she didn't know about Delia's abortion. No one knew about that.

"So, Saturday, then?" Jasper said.

"Yeah, Saturday's good."

We arranged to meet at his house around noon. I dropped my cell phone on the nightstand. The prospect of a job with the state, especially in Connecticut, didn't warm my heart—Delia's journalistic blather had made me suspicious of all government agencies, the bureaucracy, the waste, the politics. But what choice did I have? Jobs weren't exactly plentiful in the northern woods of New England, no matter how much I longed to slip up there. I'd been scouring the online job boards every day, and a sinking realization had come over me. Mother was right. I had taken a huge risk, a leap of faith that back in the place I knew best, I would find my way again.

"Seth! Seth!" Someone was calling from the backyard. Mother's voice. I snapped upright and bounded to the window. Locked. I turned the latch and pushed it up.

"Mom? What's wrong?"

She stood at the edge of the lawn where the woods began. "Look," she called, pointing down. I squinted. At her feet stood three sapling evergreens, just skinny twigs with tufts of pale green needles.

"I planted these as a memorial to your father, a living reminder," she said. "When I pass, I want you kids to sprinkle my ashes over them. I'm going to give myself back to the planet. It's the ultimate recycle." She laughed, a little too loud, a little too sharp, but I smiled anyway.

* * *

I wasn't naïve enough to bank on Jasper and the DEP. I had to conduct as broad a job search as possible, and the clock was ticking. To cast a wide job net, I contacted the biology departments of every university in northern New England, e-mailing and mailing my resume to them. I holed up in my father's old study. Unopened mail, magazines, *National Geographic, Scientific American*, addressed to him sat piled on one corner of his desk. Mother wouldn't throw them out. In his Rolodex, I found all the people he had known, all the faces from his funeral, including my own name with my Atlanta address and the word "Delia" in parentheses. A photograph of the house, taken at the height of summer with the flowering dogwoods and stonewall, was the screen saver on his desktop monitor.

I trolled the websites like a desperate man groping for a second chance. Mother left me alone, because I was working and she wanted me to work. It had become clear that the longer I remained adrift, the more anxious she would grow, so I had to get out. But I wasn't ready to give up on the North Country. Maine especially appealed to me. It was the furthest point north I could go without crossing into Canada. No one would know me. When my parents were young—with only Travis in the picture and me on the way—there was a fleeting period when they considered moving to New Hampshire where my father's sister had settled. Aunt Emily and Uncle Donald, a dentist, had carved out a nice life for themselves in the sloping valleys between the White Mountains. My father always sounded wistful when he mentioned them.

"It's wide open country up there," I'm told Grandma Hingham urged. "Low taxes, cheap land and people everywhere need accountants." Grandma Hingham was big on "open land." She hated crowds and traffic and "people swarming" around her. "Millicent and you should pick up and take off while you're still young," she told my father. He was all for the idea. Then Jasper's parents got involved. Why not all move to the mountains? The children could be raised in "God's green country," as Grandma put it.

Fervent activity ensued. Aunt Emily and Uncle Donald put everyone up for two weeks, so the adults could get the lay of the land and the employment picture. Grandma contacted a real estate agent and described in great detail the desired housing. Connecticut realtors prepared to list the Ledyard houses. Then everything stopped. Years later I would hear only that my mother began having second thoughts. Moving "way up there" frightened her. She could not be persuaded, or as my father in a rare bitter moment once put it, "even reasoned with."

By the time Holly and I heard this story, New Hampshire was a memory for my father. We hiked the mountains up there, he and I, every chance we got. Growing up, the North Country called to me, as I imagined it had my father. The glistening lakes and towering trees, the sleepy villages dotted with white church spires and the solemn, ancient stirrings of the forests running to the Canadian border. Something moved through the air up there, a silvery, eternal current, a spark off the water in a rushing stream, something that seemed to know me and something that I recognized. Waking in the night sometimes, I could almost smell the sharp, frosty pine of winter and feel the ponderous silence of a snowfall quieting the world.

"You're sure you're not just running away?" Holly asked, eyeing me over Father's desk when I told her I was job-hunting in the North Country. A dark headband held back Holly's mass of blond waves. Her blue eyes bored into me. She had taken a day off from work to come to the house and help Mother pack up Father's clothes for the Salvation Army.

"Moving on is not the same thing as running away," I said to Holly.

"To move on you've got to have something to move to," Holly said.

"And I will, as soon as the right job opens up."

"Okay then." Holly shrugged.

"What?" I said.

"Moving on is one way of looking at it."

I powered down and snapped off the computer. This was going nowhere. "What is it that you wanted to talk to me about, Hol?" I said. She had popped her head in the study earlier and whispered, "Seth, hang around. I have to talk to you."

She cleared her throat now. "It's Bryce," she said.

"What about him?"

"He won't leave. We broke up, you know. We broke up last month, but with Daddy and everything going on, I kept it to myself."

"I had no idea." Holly was a living contradiction. She'd pour out her broken heart over the phone for hours, because Bryce forgot her birthday, then say nothing when they finally parted ways. She was the one who had a knack for moving on. Once her mind was made up, Holly was finished. Case closed. She never looked back.

"I'm sorry," I said. "But, you know, I'm kinda glad, too."

Holly looked down at the silver rings on her fingers.

"You can do better, Hol. Seriously," I said. The truth was Holly had always picked zeroes for boyfriends, and for each one of these clowns, she had reinvented herself. It was like she was identity shopping. There was the motorcycle guy, when Holly wore a black leather jacket and had a small, red heart tattooed near her ankle; the triathlete, for whom she took up running and cycling and popped shin splints; the jazz musician who got her smoking pot every weekend, a habit she fortunately dropped along with him; and now the chronically underemployed Bryce. Holly had subscribed to about a dozen literary journals—none of which would publish Bryce's poems—and read them diligently.

"Well, we finally hit our Waterloo," she said. "Wanna hear the story?"

"Spill it."

"I won this award at work, okay? It's not a big deal. Just this plaque they give out twice a year to the employee who's brought the most energy and ideas to the place. They call it the Spirit of Success Award. Very corny, I know. I won it for a campaign I worked on for the chamber of commerce."

"Congratulations."

"So the company gives a little dinner, a simple thing in a steakhouse on Main Street. You get your plaque and everyone has an excuse to drink too much and cut loose a little on a Friday night. I wanted Bryce to come with me."

"And he couldn't?"

"No, he *wouldn't*." Holly sat on the edge of the faded red loveseat under the window. The sun was sinking low outside, throwing bars of hazy, dying light across the room.

"See, this is what we sank to," Holly said. "Any favor became too much to ask. That, and Bryce always was a bit of a selfish ass, don't you think?"

I raised my palms. "You're preaching to the choir. Why wouldn't he go?"

"That's the best part: He wanted to watch a movie he had rented."

"The movie couldn't wait?"

"No, he wanted to watch it then, that night." Holly shrugged. "That was the only answer I could get out of him. The next day I asked him to move out. Something just snapped in me, you know, and I was done."

I sat up. "You're right. It was over."

"He couldn't stand my success, however humble, when his poetry was going nowhere," Holly said.

"So what's the problem now?"

"Like I said, he won't leave."

"What do you mean, he won't *leave*."

"Just that. He hasn't left the apartment. He won't move out. He's sleeping on the couch, using my pots and pans, watching my TV. I don't know what to do."

"Is he looking for a new place?"

"He says moving just isn't in his budget right now. He has to wait for a more fortuitous moment, and until then I'm stuck with him."

I stood up and went to the window. A sleek doe was nibbling at the grass in the corner of the yard. I tapped the glass, and her head shot up, ears standing alert, eyes wide. Her dark muzzle glistened. "Where there is one, there are more," I said, rapping the glass again. The doe jerked toward the tree line, which shifted and erupted as two more leggy, brown bodies retreated, bounding into the woods. Had there been more than one deer in the cornfield the day Henry Apgar died? I couldn't remember seeing any others.

Holly turned to the window. "They'll dig up Mom's bulbs," she said.

"Has she shown you her saplings, the spot for her ashes to be spread?" I said.

"Oh, God, yes. She's gotten kind of morbid this past month."

"I suppose that's natural. Delia used to say she saw a lot of Mom in me. Do you?"

Holly leaned back, mock frowning, and studied my face. She had a small, dark mole on her left cheek like a Hollywood starlet's beauty mark, only it was real. "Kind of," she said. "Minus the intermittent hysteria."

I smiled. "Right." No one ever said they saw Mom in Travis, or in Holly for that matter. It had bothered me when I was younger. It was as if Travis and Holly had been spared some inherent weakness that I had fallen victim to.

"So how about helping me evict Bryce?" Holly said.

"Is his name on the lease?"

"No, he moved into my place, remember?"

"Then let's move his ass out. Pick a good time.

"I want to do it when he's not there," Holly said. "There's a storage unit in the basement of the building. It's never locked. We can put his things there. He doesn't have much, and he can decide where to go from there."

"Sounds like a plan," I said.

"And hey," Holly said, "hang around for the night, will you, just in case things get interesting."

* * *

Henry Apgar visited my dreams that night. He still popped up occasionally, tapping on the windows of my subconscious. I had passed a restless evening in Mother's house. In just two weeks, I had begun thinking of the house as Mother's house, not my home. Circumstance creates a home. A familiar building in a familiar place is not enough. I was not needed here anymore. Already I felt like the guest who had stayed too long. All through dinner Mother chatted about local children I'd grown up with: Where they were, what they were doing, the subtext of course being that none was thirty-five, unemployed and living at home. Why she wanted me out of the house as quickly as possible was something I didn't understand, and I suspected she didn't either. I think my floundering presence just made her anxious. She had invited me to stay with her until I was situated again, insisting I would be no trouble. "Why should you waste money renting?" she'd said. But if I had reminded her of this, she would have given me a mystified look and taken great umbrage.

In my dream, Henry Apgar was seated at a table—a dining room table, long, richly gleaming dark wood, the kind of table Grandma Hingham had. He was eating. The table was covered with plates and glasses, and Henry was not alone. But I was not surprised. It was as if I expected these people to be here. My father looked up from his plate. He appeared normal, so ordinary and everyday, gray hair combed back, eyeglasses perched halfway down his nose. I had been tricked. He was here. He had been here all along. He smiled vaguely at me, his dark eyes amused over his glasses. Then he con-tinued eating, unfazed, seeming to forget I was there.

"Dad?" I said. He dipped a spoon into his bowl of soup and brought it to his lips. "Dad?" He didn't acknowledge my voice. "I'm going to get hold of you now," I said. I had a terrible urge to grab his arm, to draw him near. But I didn't. This was forbidden. To grab, to insist, was to go too far. There were rules here. Somehow I knew this. I turned from my father, though I could still feel the weight of his presence behind me, almost pressing against my back.

Then I realized how quiet the room was. None of the diners was talking. Even their eating was silent, no clinking or scraping. Was I deaf? No, I could hear my own voice. I stepped through the silence. Delia sat on the far end of the table. I saw her plainly, clearly, but she didn't notice me. She was turned to her side, talking to a young child. Her smile was so tender and maternal, so gentle, my throat tightened. I could see the child only from the corner of my eye, in blinding flashes. I knew he was a boy, but I could not bear to look fully at him. Something terrible would happen. It had already happened. I was afraid. He was unfathomable to me.

I stepped on, passing other people, strangers I didn't know or couldn't recall, though some were vaguely familiar. A stocky woman with pitted skin conjured my seventh grade social studies teacher. A mustached man with oversized eyeglasses looked like the biology department chairman at Emory. They were engrossed in their meals and in one another.

At the very end of the table sat Henry Apgar. I was not surprised. It made sense, some kind of perverse, needling sense that he was here. What did you expect, he seemed to say. That we disappear? We never disappear. We're coming all the way with you. Henry looked as he did at seventeen: mop of brown curls, baseball cap, big flushed face. His thick fingers swallowed the silver fork in his hand. He glanced my way only for an instant, wearing the blank, blasé face he assumed walking the halls of Ledyard High.

He dipped a piece of crusty bread into a pool of red sauce on his plate and took a fierce bite. He chewed for what seemed like a long time. Then he looked at me. Directly this time, not a glance, but into my eyes and he spoke. "You didn't get this right either," he said. "You'll have to clean up the mess now. We," he waved his hand over the table, "have nothing to tell you." He tore back into the bread.

When I woke, a heaviness filled my chest. I turned to the window, blinking in the dark. The outline of the bare branches, the ones the squirrel had scrambled along, were silhouetted beyond the glass. Only the squirrel was long gone. I was alone here now. No voices called in the night. No doors closed or music played. My father's laugh would not ring up the stairs. My mother was no longer accessible. Emptiness hung like a shroud over this place, and out at the edge of the woods, the saplings waited.

FOUR

....

Jasper did not live in a mansion, Mc or otherwise. I pulled into his driveway just before noon. He lived in a spacious cape house with a wide porch and plenty of windows in the middle of a grassy lot. His neighbors had similar homes, some on bigger parcels, some on smaller. The old Keller Farm had not been entirely decimated. A grove of apple trees stood across the road from Jasper's house, though it didn't appear anyone was tending it.

A row of bright orange mums decorated Jasper's porch. He opened the door just as I lifted my hand to ring the bell. He must have been watching for me, which for some reason made me suddenly grateful.

"Look what floated up the coast," he said. "Seth, hey, it's good to see you." He grabbed my hand to shake.

"Good to see you, too," I said. "This is some spread you have here, huh? Really, really nice."

"Come on, let me give you the dime tour." He ushered me inside. I'd last seen Jasper at my father's funeral a few months earlier. I'd noticed then the way early middle age was thinning his sandy hair on top and broadening his waist. He still looked good, still the old Jasper: lips pursed in a wry comment, blue eyes wide with feigned shock over a stupid comment uttered by someone else, and of course, his telltale limp. Jasper hadn't escaped the crash that killed Henry Apgar unscathed. His shoulder healed, but his left leg, which had been pinned between the door and car seat, hadn't fared as well. There had been nervous talk of amputation, but in the end the screws and bolts held. Jasper was young—a big, strapping eighteen-year-old with his whole life ahead of him. So he limped on, some days worse, some better. On bad days, he carried a cane.

Jasper must have been having a bad day that day. He limped sharply ahead of me, leading the way to a bright and airy kitchen. A tray of cold cuts sat on the counter, next to a basket of deli rolls. "Beer is in the fridge," Jasper said, "let me show you the house first. Chloe's at a baby shower for a friend. They're pregnant at the same time. Only this woman is due any day. I wish she'd have the kid already. Every time the phone rings, Chloe jumps."

Jasper was clearly excited about his house, and I could see why. It was spacious and inviting and full of light, the kind of place I would have liked to own. I followed him from room to room, up and down the stairs, to the master bedroom, the living room with its stone fireplace and the nursery currently under construction with rolls of yellow ducky wallpaper border on the floor and a large stuffed bear standing in the corner. The bear reminded me of Baby's 1st Bear in Atlanta. During the weeks when Delia was "thinking it over," I'd driven furtive, roundabout routes to work every morning, exploring neighborhoods, lingering before homes with "For Sale" signs. The baby would need a room and a house with a backyard to toss a ball in. I jotted down the addresses I liked. That's how deluded I was.

"You really found a nice place," I told Jasper back in the kitchen. He shuffled to the fridge.

"We paid top dollar, I'll tell you that much," he said. "The market is pretty damn steep around here, Buddy. You're going to discover that."

"Well, it's not something I'm worried about at the moment."

"No, I guess not at the moment." He opened the fridge. "I found this amazing new microbrew out of Vermont. Try it."

"Jasper, I forgot what a piss-water expert you are."

He laughed.

"Sure, lay one on me," I said. Jasper fancied himself a beer connoisseur, and in fact, he probably was—more so than me anyway. He was always discovering new brews from the most unlikely places. I had discovered Sam Adams and New Castle in my twenties and never left them. The truth was, I had become a red wine man. I rarely touched hard liquor, never developed a taste for it. Delia teased me that this was the mark of an unsophisticated rube. No scotch on the rocks, no gin and tonic. She conveniently forgot that she loved zinfandel and wine coolers when I met her. She had moved on to dry martinis by the time we broke up.

Jasper placed a bottle and glass before me. We ate in the kitchen, at a little café table with two chairs overlooking the deck and backyard.

"Remember Keller's farm?" I said

"Sure, old man Keller is turning over in his grave right now."

"And his kids are counting their money."

We both laughed, and then Jasper eyed me. "So your girlfriend. I was sorry to hear what happened."

Mother, of course, had filled Jasper's ears, no doubt coloring things with her own special spin. "Yeah, what did my mother tell you?" I said.

Jasper laughed. "Nothing I accepted at face value. Dear Aunt Mil. I took it all with a grain of salt."

"A pound of salt would have been better, but yeah we called it off, Jasp. We just sort of hit this wall, where everything, every damn last thing, became so difficult."

Jasper chewed his sandwich, nodding. "I know that wall," he said. "It happens, my man. It happens."

"But you know, the weird part is I don't really know exactly what happened. We reached some kind of tipping point, and things just weren't fixable anymore. They weren't forgivable."

Jasper stopped chewing.

"So now here I am—homeless, unemployed and unloved," I said. "Nice, huh?"

Jasper swallowed. Then he decided I was joking. He laughed, and I let him. "Good Lord," he said. "Good riddance to her, I say. Hey, you're up here now, a fresh start and all that. Am I right? I bet it's great to be back?"

I told him it was great. "It'll be even better when I have a job," I said. "So the DEP, what's the deal with this?"

"I wish I could tell you more," Jasper said. "Scanlon's your man. He's head of Wildlife Management. You'll be interviewing with him."

"What's he like?"

"Typical state bureaucrat, cog in the wheel, everything by the book. Which isn't to say he isn't a decent guy. He is, and with your background, I'd say you've got a good shot. But do yourself a favor. Read up on the bureau's current initiatives. There's some stuff going on with birds on the shoreline, a deer overpopulation thing, coyotes killing cats. Go in there well versed. He'll be impressed."

I nodded. "You know a lot about animals for a lawyer."

"It's the secret of my success, Buddy. Every lawyer learns it. Know a little bit about a lot, just enough to bullshit your way through anything. You'd be surprised how far that gets you."

Candor had always been Jasper's best quality. "Where are you going to live?" he said. "I bet you're bucking to get out of Millicent's."

"You have no idea."

Jasper laughed.

"It depends where I land a job," I said.

"Well, if you end up on the shoreline, think about renting my condo in Norwich."

"In Norwich?"

"It would be convenient for you, for one thing, and that town is up-and-coming."

"Norwich?"

"Yes, Norwich. You've been out of the loop too long."

"Um, I guess so." Norwich was as stale and struggling as most of Connecticut's old mill towns.

"You remember my condo?" Jasper persisted. "In that revitalized mill? It's a great unit."

It was a nice unit, in a historic, refurbished yarn mill—high ceilings, exposed brick, tall windows. "I'll keep it in mind," I said.

Jasper leaned back in his seat and took a swig from the dark neck of his beer bottle. "I'm carrying both mortgages right now—the condo and this place. It's killing me and with the baby coming, something's gotta give," he said.

"When is Chloe due?"

"Early December."

"You've got a little time."

Jasper studied the label on his beer bottle. "We had a hell of a hard time getting pregnant," he said.

"Oh? I'm sorry to hear that."

"Two years. I had to perform on command. Not easy, let me tell you. And then we had the miscarriage."

I shifted in my seat. "I've heard it can be, um, difficult sometimes."

"The doctors had no idea why. When it finally seemed to take, to be lasting, I kept waiting for the bomb to go off. I kept looking for the red flag. You know? The tests were wrong. A nurse screwed up results or something malfunctioned. I still half-expect it to disappear, even now."

Jasper had never been the confiding type. At least not when we were younger, but that afternoon he wanted to talk. More specifically, he wanted to tell me things.

"Listen, this isn't easy, having a kid. Making this decision. I mean, you think long and hard," he said.

"I'm sure you have to," I said. *We're not ready*, Delia had said while the room spun around me in Atlanta.

"Hey, I know I'm thirty-six," Jasper said. "It's about time and all that, but that doesn't make it any easier. So much is riding on me now. And on Chloe, of course. Do you know what I mean?"

"I think so."

"What I'm saying is, just be ready before you take this step. Be damn sure. Because Chloe and I want this and we are ready, and believe me, it still isn't easy."

I raised my glass. "To you, Jasper, and Chloe and the baby. You'll make excellent parents. I have no doubt." We clinked glasses.

"And to the DEP," Jasper said, "for funding all our exploits."

"I've already sent my resume and portfolio into Scanlon. I fired them off the day after we spoke," I spoke.

Jasper raised his glass again. "To Scanlon then, who holds the keys to the future."

"You sound like my mother."

Jasper took another swig of his microbrew. "To dear old Aunt Mil," he said, "because there will never be another like her."

I left Jasper, standing on his new front porch. He was planning to paint the nursery and install the ducky wallpaper borders that afternoon. Ducks, he said, would work for a boy or a girl. They didn't know which they were having. They wanted to be surprised. Pulling onto the highway, heading back toward the coast, I wondered if I should have offered to help set up the painting equipment, to carry the cans and ladder up to the nursery. Jasper hadn't asked, but how was he going to climb a ladder with the limp so bad today? I should have helped. Delia used to say I had a tendency to become conveniently forgetful when it came to lending a hand around the house. Maybe she'd been right. But Jasper didn't seem to need me. He was deep in a world of his own making, a world where I didn't feel like I belonged.

On impulse, I flicked on my turn signal as I approached one of the Norwich exits. The old town looked pretty much as I remembered, though some revitalization efforts were going on in parts of the city: flower pots on traffic medians, a grassy walkway along the riverbank. Jasper's building loomed ahead, an aging complex of red brick and defunct smokestacks, one of the engines of the city's industrial past now trying to lure upwardly mobile professionals to live downtown. It was only three stories. Sunlight reflected off the tall windows. Jasper's unit was on the third floor, if I remembered correctly, a corner unit with a bank of windows overlooking the river. I cruised past and headed for the highway.

Just before the entrance ramp, a Dunkin' Donuts caught my eye. A hot cup of coffee sounded like a good idea. I parked around back, got out and was walking to the building when I noticed a few enormous seagulls standing vigilantly in a large puddle on the blacktop. They were big, herring gulls. One spread its wings like a great cape and flapped off. A lot of people don't like gulls, but I do. They are models of adaptation, the most elegant of scavengers; crafty and cunning but appealing, too, in their determination, their single-minded... a car horn blasted. I jumped. A black Datsun, an old compact with rust around the fenders, skidded to a halt right next to me. A shot of adrenaline tingled through my limbs. I stared at the driver. She eyed me back, and her mouth fell open. She ripped on her parking brake using both hands, jumped out and ran up to me.

"I'm sorry. My gosh, you're not hurt, are you? I didn't hurt you, did I?"

"I'm not hurt," I said. "You missed me." Her brown eyes were practically popping out of her head. She couldn't have been much older than thirty, small, petite in blue jeans and a jean jacket. Some kind of clip held a mass of curly, dark hair away from her sharp, little face.

"I didn't see you," she said. "You probably won't believe that. It sounds stupid, but it's true. I didn't see you. Sometimes stupid things are true, you know?"

She was like a wound-up Jack Russell Terrier, yipping around, jumping up and down. "That is true," I said. "But I'm fine, really. No harm done."

"Thank God." She heaved a heavy sigh and put her hands on her hips. "The last thing I wanted to do today was go out into the world and cause harm. Especially after the week I had."

I turned towards the Dunkin' Donuts. "Yes, well, don't worry. You haven't caused any harm. So, uh, thanks for asking."

"Let me buy you a coffee," she said. Her dark eyes brightened.

"Oh, that's not necessary."

She touched my coat sleeve. "No, really, I believe in repaying good for good. You didn't get all nasty and act like a jerk when I almost ran you over, and I'd like to thank you. You could have ruined my day, and you didn't. I believe in paying this stuff forward, in keeping the good energy flowing."

"Okay, fine. You're very kind, very, uh, nice to do this."

She stuck out her hand to shake mine. "Jenna Avacoli," she said.

"Seth, Seth Hingham," I said. "Nice to meet you."

"Likewise."

At the counter, she ordered a medium coffee with milk and sugar for herself. The pimply-faced kid behind the counter yawned taking her order. Anything else?" he said.

"And for my friend here," Jenna said, taking my sleeve again, "How do you take yours, Seth?"

"Black's fine," I said.

Jenna turned to the kid, who was stifling another yawn. "You heard the man," she said. Then she turned to me, smiling. She had small, even, white teeth and a nice mouth, good lips, full and soft looking. She wasn't wearing any makeup, as far as I could tell.

But unless a woman's wearing a lot of dark lipstick or blue colors around her eyes or something, how do you know?

"Black's the best way to drink coffee. You're a purist, aren't you?" Jenna said.

I shrugged. "I guess so when it comes to coffee."

The kid put the cups down on the counter and punched at the cash register. Jenna dug a few bills out of this huge, lumpy brown purse she carried. It looked like a little saddle, with all these buckles and belts.

"Are you sure?" I said. The pimply kid eyed us.

"When a woman's buying you a drink, you never ask her if she's sure," Jenna said. "A cute guy like you ought to know that."

"Right, ha-ha," I said. "Hey, thanks. Thanks again." I took my cup. "Take care." I turned for the door before she could answer, but I heard her anyway: "You, too, Seth. You take care."

In the car, I realized what an idiot I was. That was an invitation. I should have given her a witty, flirtatious response. Who knew where things could have ended up? We might have spent the night together. I'd been with Delia so long, I'd forgotten how to act with a woman—a different woman.

FIVE

....

"I want him to come home to the note taped on the front door. That's it," Holly said, standing in her kitchen. "He'll have a sleeping bag down there. At least he won't be out in the cold." She bit her lip. "Do you think this is too cruel?"

"Come on. The guy's a mooch," I said. "How else are you going to get rid of him?" I drove to Holly's apartment in Middletown the day after my visit with Jasper. She had asked me to meet her at six p.m. She must have said, "Don't be late" a dozen times. Bryce went to work at Starbucks at four-thirty and wouldn't get home until after ten. Holly estimated it would take us an hour and a half to haul his junk down to the basement storage locker.

She sighed. "I remember when we met," she said. "Seth, he was the sweetest man I'd ever known. I don't understand how it came to this."

"Yeah, well, it seems to be catching lately," I said. "Where's his stuff?"

She pointed to the living room. "In the boxes behind the couch. I gathered it all together. Did I ever tell you he once spent twenty minutes picking a splinter out of my toe?"

"No, that's one story I've been spared."

"It was during our first year together. Ever notice that's when all the nice things happen?"

57

I headed for the couch. Holly followed. She had stacked up maybe ten cardboard boxes—all sizes—behind her cat-scratched, brown couch. Claw marks ran down the upholstery on one side. "Never got Snowflake declawed, huh?" I said.

"I just couldn't." Holly stared at the couch. Tears brimmed in her eyes.

"Holly, listen..." I said.

"I picked up the splinter in the park," she said. "It was summer, and I was wearing sandals."

"Holly, trust me. Pulling the trigger with Bryce now is going to spare you a lot of pain later," I said.

"I hobbled back here, and Bryce sat on the bathroom floor, picking at that splinter with tweezers. He used rubbing alcohol and everything. He was so careful. You wouldn't believe it, Seth, but he was so careful with me back then."

Then she was crying. It was going to be a long night. We sat on the cat-shredded couch for fifteen minutes while she pulled herself together. Snowflake came sauntering out of the bedroom, pausing to stretch deeply—his white rump high in the air.

"Hey, Snowy-baby," Holly cooed. She sniffed. "Bryce never liked him, you know." The cat stepped delicately closer and rubbed up against Holly's leg. "He hates the white fur on his clothes. He tried to convince me to get rid of Snowy."

"Nice guy." I bent over to stroke the silky back. "I don't trust people who don't like animals. They lack something. I don't know what. Empathy or charity or curiosity. Something."

Holly sniffed. "Yeah, well, that's not all Bryce is lacking, right? Let's get on with this."

Delia didn't particularly like animals. She didn't dislike them either. She didn't care one way or another. She just wasn't interested. We rarely discussed my work in any detail, and when we did, I always had the sense she was half-listening, being polite. But I let it slide. That's what happens: You try to keep the edges from fraying, and the center falls away.

Bryce's boxes weren't heavy. I could handle most of them myself. The building was only two stories and a basement. It was a typical old high school, marble stairs worn smooth by generations of teenage feet. Holly had a one-bedroom unit with a bright, cheery kitchenette and tall school windows. Blue and gold butterflies decorated her shower curtain. I lifted Bryce's white, plastic hamper. He kept it tucked under the pedestal sink. Holly had forgotten it.

"There are still clothes in here," I called into the living room where she was taping up the last of the boxes.

"Are they dirty?" She asked.

I placed the hamper down with the other boxes. "I'm not touching them. That's where I draw the line. Does he keep clean clothes in his hamper?"

"Actually yes, since I took his clothes out of my bureau."

"Well, clean or dirty, they're going to the locker." I carried the hamper, topped by a shoebox stuffed with God-knows-what on the last trip to the basement. Holly lugged a large shopping bag filled with shoes. He owned a surprising number of shoes.

"He does have a certain style, a real fashion sense," Holly said. A little defensively, I thought.

"Maybe he can put it to good use in the locker."

"Don't be a jerk, Seth."

"Sorry." I resolved to shut my mouth. After Delia and I split, a couple of my Atlanta buddies tried to cheer me up by pointing out her flaws: her barky laugh, what a lousy driver she was. It didn't help. They meant well, but as Travis said in the cemetery, context is everything, and they didn't see the whole picture. They didn't know her the way I did. Delia could be a good friend when she wanted to be. She proofread every page of my thesis and had the finished thing bound in leather, like a little book, as a surprise for me. She was smart and funny and never at a loss for words, a talent I truly admired. I didn't event want to imagine what her friends must have said about me.

Holly and I trudged down the marble stairs to the basement with the last load. Storage lockers lined the walls, divided by wood partitions and chicken wire. Each apartment had a locker. Holly's was in the corner. A bare light bulb hung suspended from the ceiling. Cobwebs fanned out around it.

I stacked the hamper with the other boxes. Piled together in a corner, the sum total of Bryce's possessions looked pretty meager, and I felt an unexpected stab of pity for the guy. He was single again now, too, and homeless. He was a little too close for comfort.

"How old is Bryce, Holly?"

"Thirty-three." She pulled out a padlock.

Maybe we were members of the same lost tribe—Bryce and me, single guys in their thirties, growing ripe on the vine, chasing dreams of who we thought we were going to be. My stomach burned.

Holly hung the padlock on the door handle, but didn't snap it closed. Bryce needed to get inside. Holly didn't have much in the locker herself -- an old bicycle, a floor lamp and some ancient luggage. Even if the spirit moved him, there wasn't anything valuable that Bryce could trash or steal.

"Come on," I said. "Let's order a pizza. Are you up for pizza?"

Holly snapped out the light. I was spending the night, as she had asked. It seemed like overkill to me. Bryce probably already had another woman lined up to take him in.

I was sitting on Holly's couch and she was on the phone in her bedroom, ordering the pizza, when the deadbolt on her front door flipped. The door swung open and in stepped Bryce. Holly's superintendent apparently hadn't gotten around to changing the locks, as she'd requested.

I stood up. "Bryce," I said stupidly. He frowned at me, blinking in confusion. He wore black jeans, very slim and fitted around his weirdly skinny hips, and a black turtleneck sweater. His wavy dark hair was combed back straight from his face, so it rose in a poufy helmet on top of his head. Diamond studs glittered in his ear-lobes. What did Holly ever see in this guy? She stopped dead in the doorway coming out of her bedroom. Her mouth dropped open. A spasm of recognition and then a shrewd moment of calculation crossed Bryce's face. His eyes jumped around the room.

"Where is my sleeping bag?" he said. He turned to Holly. "It was rolled up by the TV. What is he, what is Seth doing here?" He glanced at me. "Hi," he said.

Holly looked like she was going to faint. Her face went bone-white.

"Holly?" I said.

She spoke up with surprising conviction. "We moved your stuff into the basement, into the storage locker," she said. "You can get in. You'll find it all there. You left me no other choice, Bryce. We can't, I can't, go on like this."

He took a step backwards. "You what? What are you saying? You carried my stuff, you removed my possessions from the apartment? Why would you do such a thing? I came home early, because I'm not feeling well, and you've been doing this behind my back?"

"Oh, get off it, Bryce. You know exactly why," Holly said.

Patches of splotchy red broke out on his cheeks and forehead. "I have nowhere to go." He pointed to me. "Did he talk you into this?"

"Leave Seth out of this."

He stood a little taller. "Right, now I see."

Holly shot me a look to keep my mouth shut. I bit my tongue. This was her fight. "He's got nothing to do with it," she said. "This craziness has to stop. I need to get on with my life."

"Your life?! What about my life? You're ruining it. You're *throwing* me out?" He stepped into the living room and Holly came forward, too. I could see Bryce's chest rising and falling. His pale, little hands curled into fists at his side. The audacity of this guy amazed me. His eyes narrowed, and his lips settled into a thin, tense line. "I'm not leaving," he said. "You can't *just do* this."

"Why can't she do this?" I said. "Why can't she *just* do this? It's her apartment. You've been given fair notice. You've had ample time. She wants you out. Now."

"This matter does not involve you," Bryce said. "Butt out, man."

Man? "Look, you've got options," I said. "You just don't want to exercise them. You want the world to accommodate you."

Bryce's eyes burned. "Why don't you exercise yours?" he said calmly, all smoldering control now. This must have been the tack he used fighting with Holly: turn soothingly cold and quiet but shoot to kill. "I know all about you," he said.

"You do, huh?" I said. "How fascinating, Bryce. Why don't you share your insights with me?" My hands were starting to shake. A tendril of fury was creeping up my body, something that I had held down too long now wanted out.

"Seth, please," Holly said. "Don't let him drag you in like this."

"Yeah, Seth, listen to your sister." Bryce was smiling now. "I know you're here to help her. Big Brother to the rescue. But from what I hear, it sounds like you're the one who needs rescuing. Running back to Mommy after your girlfriend walks out on you. Poor big brother Seth..."

Something in me snapped then. I lunged forward, caught Bryce by the shirt and ripped him toward me. He was surprisingly light. He weighed nothing. A twinge of shame shot through me, but I was too far gone. Holly yelled at me to stop. Bryce grabbed my arms, trying to wrench free.

"So, what do you know, asshole? Tell me what *you* know about me," I said. I could hear how loud I was, but it felt like my voice wasn't coming something outside me. I didn't know where it was coming from. I could see the fear on Bryce's face, but I couldn't stop. I hadn't been in a fight since junior high, and I lost that one, but a white rage consumed me. This was what I needed in my life: another critic, another self-assured jerk-off telling me what I already knew: that I was in trouble, that I had been foolish and weak and blind and that I was reaping what I had sown. I practically lifted Bryce off his feet, ramming him up against the wall, shouting in his face, "Tell me. Tell me." Holly grabbed me from behind, but I shook her off. "Come on. Tell me. You have all the answers," I shouted into Bryce's face. He sputtered. I let go with one hand and landed a punch, a solid popping crack, right on his jaw. Then I dropped him. He crumpled to the floor.

I backed away, panting. "You know nothing about me. Understand? Nothing," I said. Holly was gone. I stalked into the bathroom and slammed the door. A hot sickness filled me. I'd never knocked someone down with a punch in my life. Bryce was a featherweight when I grabbed him, stretching the fabric of his sweater. His panicky eyes were like a trapped animal's, like the eyes of the lab mice at Emory when they crouched in the corner of their cage, horrified by the groping human hand coming at them.

I turned on both of Holly's taps to drown out any noise, then I leaned over the sink, dry-heaving. It felt like I was trying to expel some poison, some damning toxin coursing through me, slippery as a glittering stream of mercury. I wretched until my throat was sore. Then I turned off the water and sat down on the edge of the bathtub. A few minutes passed, and someone tapped on the bathroom door.

"Seth?" Holly's voice, sounding remarkably composed.

I stood and opened the door.

She looked me up and down. Her eyes were wide, but she appeared calm. "Are you all right?"

"Yes. Where's Bryce?"

"Gone." She shrugged. "I don't know where. Maybe down to the locker."

I nodded.

"You didn't hurt him," she said. "I mean, he got up and ran off. How hurt could he be?"

"True." We went out to the living room and dropped down onto the couch. My hands were trembling. "Don't' tell anyone about this," I said. "Listen, I'm sorry." Holly held up her hand to silence me.

"Where's his key?" I said.

Holly dangled it off her finger, a little brass house key on a silver ring. "I grabbed it off the table on my way out the door. I couldn't sit here and watch you two go at it. I have my limits, too."

"I shouldn't have grabbed him," I said.

"He had no right dragging you into this, directing his wrath at you," she said. "That's the kind of thing he does. He twists conversations. He warps words. He ducks all responsibility. Believe me I've been on the receiving end, too. He's damn mean when he wants to be."

Then I remembered what Bryce had said. "Exactly what did you tell him about me, Holly? What was he alluding to? He knows all about me. What was that?"

She bit her lip. "You know how it is in a relationship, right? You share things," she said. "I told him a little about your situation."

"A little?"

"Just that you and Delia had broken up and you were moving back home."

"And that I was unemployed and living with Mom?"

Holly sighed and closed her eyes. "Yes, but I didn't make it sound like that. You're the one making it sound pathetic, Seth. You're the one who sees it that way. I said you were job-hunting and crashing at home for a few weeks. But Bryce knows how to twist things, I told you. He knows how to lob bombs."

"Right, you just gave him the ammunition."

"See it that way, if you want to. That's your problem, Seth."

"Oh, great, another diagnosis. I'm so glad everyone else knows what *my* problem is."

"Then you tell me. Exactly what *is* your problem?"

A knock came on the door. We both froze. "Yes?" I called.

"Pizza."

Holly sunk deeper into the couch, and then the tears spilled over her cheeks.

"It's been a crazy day, Holly. Let's just forget it, okay?" I said. She sniffed, nodding. I paid the pizza boy.

That night I dreamt I was back in Atlanta. I was downtown, walking toward Delia's television station, going to meet her. The sun baked the sidewalk and glared off office windows all around me. I rounded the corner just before the station, but the building wasn't there. The street wasn't there. Instead I was back at Ledyard High School, standing outside, surrounded by strange teenagers heading this way and that, to classes, to cars, to smoke in the woods behind the building. Everyone had some place to go. I walked quickly, certain that Delia's building would be around the next corner. Only I couldn't reach the end of the school building to round the corner. The school seemed to stretch on for miles, bricks and windows and cement steps leading to glass doors, on and on. There was no end.

This was the answer I wish I had been able to give Holly on the couch that night in her apartment: My problem was not that I could not see things correctly. My problem was that I couldn't see myself clearly. And the truth, I feared, would only condemn me, would only leave me forsaken. I couldn't have been more wrong.

The next morning, Bryce's things were gone from the basement. Holly and I stood in the locker, beneath the dull yellow of the cobweb light bulb. I was amazed that Bryce was able to move on so quickly, so seamlessly, without another word, almost as if he had expected this and he would never look back at all.

SIX

....

S canlon did not call right away, as Jasper had predicted. Waiting for the phone to ring, pacing the floors of Mother's
house, I slid into deep regret. The novelty of my return had
worn off. Holly was assigned to a busy new account at work, and
she was redecorating her post-Bryce apartment. Her phone calls
grew fewer, and she stopped popping in for dinners as often. I
didn't want to call Jasper and look like I was putting pressure on
him about the job.

Mother usually woke late in the morning, puttered in the kitch-
en, and then went about the many home improvement projects
she had devised—refinishing a bathtub that didn't need it, organizing the garage, alphabetizing my father's old papers and files.
Her anxious eyes followed me around the house, so I tried to keep
out of sight, surfacing only at dinner and to say good night, and
always with good news: an e-mail from a biology department in
Massachusetts with a research opening, a listing for a position at
the U.S. Department of Fish and Wildlife in Rhode Island. I left her
with the impression that my fortune could turn any day. The only
problem was I was making it all up. I had received no bites on the
dozen or so resumes I'd sent all over northern New England. I was
shouting into the employment void.

Another week passed, and I fell into a routine. I rose early each
morning, showered, and made it out of the house before Mother

was awake. Most mornings I headed to the town library, where I could study the Internet job sites at a leisurely pace and scan the newspaper classifieds. The library was an old stone building, drafty and quiet with a gaggle of elderly ladies gossiping at the checkout counter and a large community bulletin board filled with notices of town meetings and garage sales and kittens to adopt. I generally spent a good hour or so in the library. Then because I was in no hurry to return to the house and I had no place else to go, I began to roam. For three weeks, I roamed Connecticut, surprised by all that I had forgotten and by all that I remembered. I didn't drive too far south or west into the counties bordering New York; instead, I sought out the places I knew best.

I didn't know what impulse sent me out of the library's gravel parking lot towards Henry Apgar's house one morning. I had time to kill, but I hadn't intended to go to Henry's. Passing through the center of town, the Civic turned toward the high school. I thought I would drive by, see how it had grown and maybe tell Jasper. Cresting a hill on the serpentine country road that led out to the school, I saw the turn off to Henry's up ahead. I clicked on my turn signal. His parents still lived there. Mother had given me bulletins on "those poor people" over the years. She would run into Mr. or Mrs. Apgar at the grocery store or post office and draw conclusions based on the flimsiest evidence. Mrs. Apgar would be wearing a stained sweatshirt or a sweater missing a button, and Mother would conclude: "That woman has let herself go since that boy died."

I attended Henry Apgar's funeral, half my head bandaged and one arm in a sling. I felt like a mummy, swathed and wrapped, standing before the grave that sun-washed spring morning. Several dozen mourners ringed the gravesite, more people than I would have thought Henry knew. I was afraid to meet any eyes that came my way. The scent of fresh cut grass hung in the air.

Jasper was still in the hospital. My father stood behind me, both hands resting on my shoulders. They were the only things that kept me from floating away.

I couldn't look at the gleaming coffin or the bundles of sweet smelling flowers. I just stared straight ahead until by chance, I caught Henry's mother's eye. Standing across from me, the coffin between us, as the preacher droned on about "youth and time and questions that can't be answered in this life," she looked up, and our eyes met. At first I wasn't sure she saw me. Was she looking past me? Through me? Could she see at all? Mrs. Apgar was a tiny woman, petite with a thick braid of black hair hanging down her back. Her black dress was too big, hanging loosely off her bony frame. Her face was pasty white, her eyes, dark, blank orbs, like a doll's unseeing eyes. Then came a spark of some recognition, her brow creased with concentration. I mouthed a silent, "I'm sorry." If Mrs. Apgar understood, she gave no sign. She just continued frowning into the air. I looked away.

I had not seen Henry's house since the accident eighteen years earlier. His street, the doomed turn Jasper had rounded too quickly, too sharply, suddenly appeared. I remembered the drive as longer, as painstaking and fraught with towering moments. Time had magnified the details, real and imagined, of that terrible afternoon, and now I was shocked to see how short the distance truly was and how quickly it must have all happened. We were just boys, barreling along. Nothing could have prepared us for what was coming.

I did not slow down rounding Jasper's turn. I drove it the way I would any other turn, believing I would be all right. The cornfield loomed, still there, rows of short, yellow stubble, withering in the early autumn sun. Here was the spot where the deer had leapt onto the road. Further ahead was the edge of the road and the culvert we had sailed into, clogged now with browning leaves and a Pepsi can someone had tossed. Off to the side was the tree. I stopped and scanned the woods, but I never knew exactly which tree Henry's body slammed into. It could have been any one of them. There were no telltale tracks, no scarred tree trunks. Multiple shimmering seasons had erased the past. The trees kept their secrets, reaching for the sky just as they always had. They were all guilty, I thought, and all innocent. They were all the same.

Coming upon the house, I expected to see the simple, gray ranch I remembered, with its tin-roof carport, humble cement stoop and a Ledyard Road Department pickup truck in the driveway. Only that house was gone. It had been born again. A pristine white color with a deep scarlet front door and black shutters, the house now boasted a sunroom on one side, lined with flower boxes full of colorful blooming buds. I pulled over and slowed to a stop. A two-car garage had been added, along with what looked like a windowed, bonus room above. A studio or home office? Maybe Mrs. Apgar was into pottery now, or Mr. Apgar was creating a Red Sox memorabilia museum.

Not long after Henry's funeral, the Ledyard High School community decided to memorialize in death the boy who in life they had so sorely abused. It was June, right before graduation, when the principal announced a tree-planting ceremony to honor Henry. It would be held near the athletic track. The entire school was invited. Henry was two months in the ground by then. Jasper was still suck at home with his leg.

Henry's memorial tree was a white birch sapling. I saw it the morning of the ceremony next to the track fence, stuck in a pail, its roots wrapped in a burlap sack, waiting to be placed in the ground. I turned my head and went into the building to begin classes. The ceremony was scheduled for noon. A pious note of anticipation filled the halls. Cruising to first-period English, I passed a gaggle of preppy princesses in their premature pearls and headbands, sniffing back tears. For *Henry*? These were girls who probably never once said hello to Henry, who most certainly dismissed him as flotsam beneath their social radar. Now they were crying. The deadheads and stoners, as we called them then, appeared less troubled. They welcomed any disruption to an academic routine they despised. The celebrated jocks and brains of Ledyard were more difficult to read, but appeared mostly indifferent, which didn't surprise me. And the kids like Jasper and me, the minions who simply went to school, did the best they could and hoped to survive, had learned long ago to keep their true selves to themselves.

But it was the tears of the preppies that bugged me. They were more than I could stomach. So at quarter to noon, I got a pass for the boys' room, walked down the hall, past the classrooms and empty cafeteria, through a side door and out into the blinding sun of the day.

I started down the road toward town, and once out of sight of the high school, cut off into a dense forest preserve that ringed a deep reservoir. It was the spot where kids smoked pot and drank beer and clumsily groped each other, ever fearful of being discovered. I hiked about a mile into the woods and sat on a rock. I could not explain to my classmates or to anyone except maybe Jasper, who definitely was not listening now, how bad I felt and how crazily wrong things had gone when all I had wanted was to let Henry know that someone still saw him as a good guy. I watched the birds flit from branch to branch overhead. The ceremony at school didn't feel connected to me. I closed my eyes, listening to the sounds of the forest. When the sun began its afternoon slide, I walked back to campus to catch the bus home.

Idling before Henry's house so many years later, I saw a white sedan approaching in my rearview mirror. It was packed with teenaged kids, laughing boys in baseball caps. The driver tooted his horn as they zipped past me, and a boy in the passenger seat waved. I waved back, and they disappeared, probably headed to the high school. A breeze ran through the trees, sending a shower of golden leaves to the ground. I steered back onto the road, opening my window to let the cool air rush inside.

* * *

Some days I visited the little places, the spots I had forgotten and stumbled upon now by chance. Heading to Mystic one morning, I cut through the village of Gales Ferry on my way to the highway. The sole traffic light turned green as I approached, shifting the Civic into third gear. I flew through and a short way past it, glanced to the left where a faded yellow wooden sign read: "Go Kart Rides & Batting Cages." Behind the sign, I caught a glimpse of the little oval track Travis and I had raced around as boys, revving our go-kart engines, reveling in the heady power, determined to beat each other as our father sat on a bench outside the track waving each time we passed.

I pulled into the driveway and got out of my car. The place must have been closed for the season. The snack bar and batting cages were sealed tight. I walked up to the chain-link fence surrounding the track and hooked my fingers through the links. Travis always won our races. He was more courageous. He went through a phase at eleven or twelve when he was fearless, truly fearless, oblivious to all physical danger. He dove headfirst into lakes, threw rocks at every beehive he came across and rammed my go-kart with malicious gusto. The operator threw us off the track a few times when Travis got too rambunctious. My father shook his head on one such occasion, watching Travis and me skulk off the track.

"That guy's a wimp," Travis muttered

"You knew the rules going in," Father said. "No touching, no bumping."

"No fun," Travis said.

"Fun is what you make it," Father said. He winked at me. "One man's fun is another man's folly."

"Each fool to his own folly," I chirped. That was one of my father's favorite expressions, and he burst into laughter hearing me, at eight, repeat it.

Leaning against the chain fence now, I wondered what kind of fool he would consider me. Then I had to swallow over the lump in my throat because I knew he wouldn't consider me a fool at all. He would put his hand on my shoulder and assure me that I had done the best I could in a very difficult situation. Acceptance, he liked to say, is not the same thing as defeat.

Mother was weirdly animated at dinner that night. I made a pesto pasta meal, something easy, with a crusty loaf of French bread and a simple green salad.

"When you go to the DEP for your interview, keep your ears open," Mother said at the table. "This salad is delicious. Where did you get the lettuce?"

"At Stop & Shop," I said.

Mother cleared her throat.

"In the organic section, Mom," I said. Her organic kick was new, but if it kept her happy, fine. "What am I keeping my ears open for?" I said. Despite the fact that I had yet to hear from the elusive Scanlon, Mother was convinced I would be working at the DEP.

"It's a *government* agency," she said, "and it holds all the cards when it comes to protecting the environment."

"States don't hold all the cards when it comes to the environment, Mom," I said. "What, in particular, do you want me to listen for?" I poured myself another glass of wine and took a sip, savoring the gentle aroma, the way it sparked and then warmed my mouth and throat.

"There's a proposal to introduce deer hunting in one of the state-owned nature preserves near the Rhode Island line. They want to 'thin' the herd, as they say. Every year, if you can believe that, they're going to murder the deer who take refuge in those woods."

"Mom, you make the DEP sound like the Manson family. It's a humane solution to overpopulation. Hunting culls the stragglers. It's better than letting them starve in winter. Deer herd management is an issue in a lot of regions, not just here. Habitat is shrinking and crowding is a real problem."

Mother put down her fork. "Crowding? Just who is crowding whom, that's what I'd like to know. The deer aren't crowding humans. We're crowding them. We're gobbling up land like locusts and devouring everything around us. This is one issue where I can, and will, make a difference, Seth."

"Well, that's true," I said. "Development is getting out of hand in some places. The trick is balancing..."

"Please just keep your ear to the ground," Mother said. "Don't worry about all the arguments and rationalizations. I'm counting on you to do the right thing here."

I assured her that I would.

SEVEN

....

In the cool early hours of the next day, I e-mailed Jasper. Panic drove me. I had had no job bites. Someone from the University of Southern Maine had called about an opening. My hopes soared until I returned the call and found out that the position was temporary. Audubon in Boston sent me a listing for a field research position with a nonprofit salary so low I'd have to pitch a tent and live in the field. Even so, I sent Jasper an uneasy message: *Chief, how goes life in the house on the hill? I've been busy keeping Millicent under control and visiting some old stomping grounds. How's Chloe?*

I didn't mention Scanlon. I didn't need to. Jasper would hear the unspoken. I left out mention of my Henry Apgar house drive-by, too. Jasper and I had ducked the topic for so many years, hiding behind cleared throats and loud laughter. Did he even think about it anymore?

The first real cold snap had crept in the night before. Upstairs I pulled on jeans and a wool sweater, a navy blue crew neck Delia gave me for my birthday. I didn't brew coffee in the kitchen that morning, but I left Mother a note stuck to the pot, saying I'd be home late. I moved as quietly as possible through the house and out the back door. I wasn't going to the library. I was heading up to UConn, my alma mater tucked in the hilly northwest corner of the state. As an alum, I could pop into the career center and peruse the bulletin boards. I could rifle through the scientific journals in the library. It seemed as likely a way as any to find a job.

I chose UConn in the fall of my senior year in high school when I was still mired in the trauma of Henry's death. The campus was only a couple of hours from Ledyard, and my parents thought it wise to keep me close to home. It all worked out because I already knew I wanted to go into biology or zoology, and UConn had a great department. The school's rolling, rural campus also spoke to me. We called it a "cow college" back then. I didn't know what the students called it now, but driving through the central campus, cows seemed secondary. Growth had transformed the place I remembered. At each turn stood a new or enlarged building, columns of brick and cement punctuated with rows of windows; a four-way intersection with a traffic light; the domed Gampel Pavilion, where the famed Huskies played home basketball games, thundering up and down the shiny court, while the crowd roared in the stands.

Delia was a rabid Huskies fan, much more so than me. She had cheered them when we were on campus here together and then from afar in Atlanta, where, despite being surrounded by fanatic Southern sports fans, she remained loyal. When Delia fixed her mind on something, there was no dissuading her. Her overriding ambition was to make it to one of the major network stations before she hit her late thirties. Her heart was set on CNN, whose headquarters were in Atlanta, but she would have chased her dream anywhere.

I admired her ambition, but I was content enough at Emory, conducting research and sometimes publishing my findings. We once had a major fight, because I had forgotten to have my name included in the contributors' footnotes of a large-scale study Emory had collaborated on with a consortium of other universities. Dozens of researchers contributed to that study. I forgot to send my bio to the editor.

"That's the problem," Delia said, lying next to me in the dark in the oak-framed sleigh bed that we bought together when we—or at least I—believed we'd probably get married in a couple of years. "It doesn't really matter to you," Delia said. "Getting the credit you deserve isn't important. Getting ahead isn't important."

"Why is that necessarily a problem?" I said.

"What a strange question. What a Hingham-esque comment," she said. "It's like your brother turning down that promotion at Pfizer last year, because he wanted to keep working on the drug trial he helped launch. His wife wanted to kill him, and I don't blame her."

"Well, Travis was really invested in that research. You know how obsessed he gets."

"Yes, but who does THAT? Who takes it that far? Who turns down a promotion because he hasn't dotted all the I's and crossed all the T's on an old project?"

"Travis is thorough."

"Yeah, right." Delia rolled over so her back faced me.

"He's committed," I said, and then jokingly, "We Hinghams believe in the greater good." I retreated into jokes whenever Delia posed questions I couldn't answer. It pissed her off royally, and it was lame of me, but I didn't know what else to do. Staring into the dark that night, I thought maybe we weren't the most ambitious people, but ambition wasn't everything. I turned to tell Delia, but her breathing had grown deep and relaxed.

At UConn Delia was my salvation. The skinny girl with the bouncy ponytail and big, brown eyes. None of the guys in zoology, believe me, had a girlfriend as captivating as mine. The way her body curved and merged into mine, the surprising strength of her arms across my back in the off-campus apartment we shared. She helped me forget everything that had come before. One day early on, we drove to the coast and placed flowers on Henry Apgar's grave. It was Delia's idea. She said it would be therapeutic for me. I didn't know if it was or not, but I was in love.

But that morning years later when I went seeking job leads, I left the UConn campus as empty-handed as when I had arrived. Back at the house that night, I checked my e-mail one last time before going to bed. In my father's dark study, sitting in the glow of the terminal screen, I found only spam messages. I sat in the dark, feet propped up on my father's old desk, feeling night settle over the house.

A brilliant, glowing moon lit the yard beyond the windows. When we were kids, Travis, Holly and I used to play in the yard when the moon was full. Ledyard was a safe town, and as long as we didn't stray too far, our parents didn't worry. And we went only as far as courage permitted, crouching behind logs or in bushes, stalking each other in the ghostly twilight. I went to the window now, half-expecting to see our childish shadows still skittering among the trees. Did Henry Apgar play with us on those nights? Had we ever included him? Yes, on occasion when his father dropped him off to spend a weekend night with me, to "sleep over" as we used to call it. On those nights Henry was one of us.

I thought back and saw the dark tree line, the moths dancing in the porch light, and Jasper crashing through a hedge. The freedom of the night liberated us. The air was laced with dangerous possibility. I was eight, or maybe nine. I threw back my head and howled like the wolves in *National Geographic*. Then I lifted a long stick and threw it into the woods like a harpoon. Holly let loose a shrieking laugh, and Henry's voice called from the trees, "Seth! Seth! Over here. Oh my God. Over here. I found something, and it's ALIVE." He had lifted a rock and caught a slippery, little salamander. He was dangling the terrified creature by its tail, shining a flashlight into its stricken, unblinking face. "Check it out," Henry cooed, awestruck by his good fortune. He grinned at me as if we were sharing a great and monumental moment. I could still see his toothy little smile.

I turned from the window. The house had grown still around me. Mother was asleep. I turned for the door and the stairs up to my old bedroom.

* * *

I drove other places in Connecticut during the strange, restless weeks when I was suspended in time. Down the coast in Old Saybrook, I visited the Point, that swirling harbor where the Connecticut River, after its icy origins in Canada and long trip through New England, finally merges with the vast waters of Long Island Sound. The chalky white lighthouse still stood watch. I had learned to kayak off the Point.

Further up in the River Valley, I paused one afternoon, engine idling, outside a country inn in Chester, where I had taken Delia to dinner on our first anniversary as a couple. It was an elegant, white tablecloth sort of place set back in the woods. I was still working to impress her then. When had that ended? Some time in Atlanta. It died a hot, humid death, probably when Delia was "on assignment" and I was tracking black bear in the Appalachians or counting egrets on the water.

The next day I found myself sitting in a coffee shop in Mystic. Here I was, an able-bodied man sipping dark roast and staring out the window in the middle of a workday afternoon. I hadn't had this much time on my hands since high school, before that even, elementary school. My cell rang, probably Mother reminding me to swing by the grocery store on the way home. But the phone showed a Hartford area code.

"Hello?" I said.

"Yes, Seth Hingham please." A man's voice. A stranger's voice.

"Speaking," I said, clearing my throat. "This is Seth."

"Mr. Hingham, this is George Scanlon from the Department of Environmental Protection."

I almost swallowed my tongue. "Yes, Mr. Scanlon. Hello."

"Seth, May I call you Seth?"

"Yes, sure."

"I have your resume here. I'm sorry it's taken me so long to contact you. I wanted to call last week, but we've had some, ah, budgeting issues that seem to have been solved now. Are you still interested in coming in to interview for our opening in Wildlife Management?"

"Yes, I am. I definitely am."

"Good, what's your schedule like?"

My schedule of driving aimlessly around the state? "It's pretty open, pretty, ah, flexible at the moment," I said.

"How would ten on Thursday work for you?"

"Fine. Good. Is there anything more I can bring? I have some published papers and field research that touches on some of the issues here in Connecticut." I'd been boning up as Jasper suggested.

"Whatever you think is relevant, I'd be happy to look at. We'll see you at ten then, on Thursday," Scanlon said.

"I'm looking forward to it." It was Tuesday. I had a lot to do to get ready. But first I had to get Mother's coffee. She'd asked me to pick up a pound of these organic beans she was crazy about because they were "fair trade."

"No bean-pickers in South America have been exploited in the overbearing name of capitalism," she told me, "and it matters, Seth. I didn't always see that, but I do see it now."

On my way back to the house, I swung by my storage unit to get some research papers from my filing cabinet. I had rented a 10' x 15' unit in a facility off the highway, not far from Mother's house. A chain-link fence surrounded the grounds. A secret code opened the sliding, electronic gate after hours when the office was closed. I pulled in about three p.m. and headed straight for my unit at the end of one of the squat, steel buildings. I parked the Civic and fished the storage unit key from the glove compartment. Not a good place to keep it. *What if the car was stolen?* Mother's voice resonated in my head.

I unlocked my unit, twisting off the padlock and pushing up the squeaky, aluminum door to reveal the contents of my life packed inside. I hadn't realized how much Delia kept until I saw what was left stacked neatly against one side of the too-large unit I had rent- ed. My bureau (still filled with most of my clothes) stood in the corner. Books and boxes filled the other corner. My bike and kayak, my skis and hiking gear—tent, boots, poles, backpack—sat in the center. A pine coffee table with a dark, circular knot in the center was next to the wall, covered with small boxes loaded with kitchen stuff. The white floor lamp we had in the living room looked like an ugly metal branch rising out of a cluster of cardboard. Why had I never noticed how ugly that thing was?

"Hey," came a voice behind me. I spun around.

"Can I help with anything?" she said. It was a young woman, with a boy of perhaps five at her side. The kid, skinny and pale in too-big jeans hanging off his hips and a Red Sox t-shirt, darted into the unit and made a beeline for my bike.

"Cool, is this a ten-speed?" he said.

"Yes, it is," I said. "Do you like bikes?"

"Like them? He loves bikes. He's been begging me for a new one," the woman said. There was something vaguely familiar about her. Her curly, dark hair was pulled back in a ponytail. She had a sharp, angular face, a straight jaw line and pronounced cheekbones, and large, caramel-colored eyes. She also had a nice, trim, flexi- ble-looking, little body. She must have seen something cross my face, because all of a sudden she smiled, and I recognized her: The woman from the Dunkin' Donuts in Norwich.

"Seth Hingham," she said. "Imagine meeting you here."

"How do you know my name?

She rocked back on her heels. "You told me, remember? I never forget a name or face. I'd certainly never forget yours."

"Really? Um, okay. Do you have a unit here, ah..."

"Jenna. Remember? Jenna Avacoli."

She had the twittering appeal of a backyard songbird, a bluebird or goldfinch, something pleasant and approachable. "Are you keeping, I mean, do you have a unit here?" I said.

"I live here."

"You live in a storage locker?"

She laughed. She had nice, even teeth. Her mouth was small, but she had these generous lips, and it looked like she had some kind of gloss on them. They glistened in the late afternoon sun.

"I work here," she said. "And they throw in the apartment above the office. Have you seen it?"

"The office or your apartment?"

She frowned, and then smiled slyly. "The office, of course. If you had been in my apartment, I think I would've known."

Something crashed. I turned around. The kid had knocked a table lamp onto the floor. He stared at me with a stricken face and froze on the spot. I waved my hand. "Don't worry about it. I never liked that thing anyway," I said.

"I'm so sorry," Jenna said. "He's at that age—into everything. I can replace the lamp if it's broken."

I shook my head. "If it's broken, he did me a favor," I said. "It's just an old lamp."

Jenna smiled. The kid crept out of the unit and stood behind her. "His name is Andrew," Jenna said. "He's six."

"Six and a half," corrected the squeaky voice behind her.

"Six and a half," she said. "Say hello to Seth, Andrew."

"Hello."

"Nice to meet you," I answered. "I hope you get your new bike soon, Andy." Then I smiled and walked into my unit.

"Listen, let me explain, so you don't think I'm weird," Jenna said, following me into the unit.

"Um, okay."

"A lot of storage facilities have this kind of set-up. They hire you to hand out keys and be a sort of security person, some eyes on the ground, you know. They don't like to leave the place empty at night. And they give you a place to live. I mean, we pay a very tiny rent and utilities of course, but it works out perfectly for Andrew and me."

"Well, that's some deal. That sounds really convenient," I said, wondering why she was telling me all this.

"And I'm not just a security guard," she rushed on.

"Oh?"

"No, I'm going to the community college, to get my dental hygienist certification. I'm incredibly busy, between this place, Andrew, classes and my clinical work. You wouldn't believe all the stuff you have to know just to clean people's teeth."

"Really?"

She sat down on the arm of my sofa. "It's interesting, though." Andrew slid to the floor and pulled what looked like some baseball cards out of his pocket. "Do you know what I mean, Seth?" Jenna said. "You can tell a lot about a person by looking at his mouth. Teeth don't lie." She frowned. "Neither do gums."

"Yes, well. I'm just here to pick up some materials, and I really need to get going," I said.

Jenna jumped up from the sofa, as if I'd shocked her back into reality. "Oh, sorry. Sure, of course. Andrew's got his homework, and I've got mine, too. Never thought I'd be saying that at thirty-two."

"Yeah, I know how you feel."

She stopped. "Do you?"

I didn't know what possessed me to say that, except I thought I did know how she felt. I laughed. "Well, you know, we all end up in these places we never thought we were going."

Jenna stooped and lifted Andrew to his feet. "What do you do, Seth, for a living?"

"I'm a wildlife biologist."

"A wildlife biologist. You must love animals?"

"Yes, I guess I do."

She stuck out her hand to shake mine. "And they love you," she said. "You should come up to the apartment for coffee some time."

"I will," I said. "I'll do that. Take care. Bye, Andy."

He looked up from the baseball cards and gave a toothy, little grin. "Bye, Mr. Seth," he said.

"Just Seth," I said, and Jenna laughed.

Jenna Avacoli looked pretty good in her snug blue jeans. I couldn't help but notice. I'd been without a woman too long, but the truth was I didn't have much to offer a woman, any woman, at the moment. I made a mental note to come to the storage unit only early in the morning or during lunch, when Jenna and Andy were probably both at school.

EIGHT

....

Hartford was not a city I knew well. In its long ago heyday, it was a genteel town, home of the insurance industry—the nation's filing cabinet, as the joke went—broad boulevards, a green park downtown, Victorian homes with wraparound porches and immigrant neighborhoods teeming with industry and high hopes. That era, of course, had long since ended. Hartford now posted a shocking murder rate, gang violence, drug trafficking and a public-school system in perpetual crisis. I parked in the DEP lot Thursday morning, resigned to accept whatever came my way.

The DEP occupied a graceful brick office building with arching windows not far from the gleaming gold dome of the Capitol. State agency offices lined the surrounding blocks—transportation, consumer affairs, education, social services. Delia would have seen potential "stories" everywhere. She had a reflexive mistrust of authority figures, especially governmental ones. Was this really my life now? As I climbed the front steps of the DEP building, it felt as if I had stumbled, by calamitous accident, into someone else's.

Inside, the lobby was dim and cool with glinting marble floors. A heavy-set black woman sat behind a receptionist's desk in front of a bank of elevators. She was pecking away at a keyboard, but she looked up when I entered.

"Good morning, I have a ten o'clock appointment with George Scanlon. I'm Seth Hingham," I said. The woman watched my face as I spoke. Then she broke into a wide grin, as if she knew me. Her eyes skittered over the leather portfolio in my hand and my freshly pressed navy suit.

"Are you here for a job interview, baby?" She said. "Cause I just started working in this big, scary place myself." She laughed a hearty, amused chuckle. She was maybe in her mid-fifties with a round shiny face and striking white teeth that flashed when she laughed. Her hair was arranged in tight ringlets on her head and she wore enormous gold hoop earrings. The "baby" surprised me, but it was also familiar, as was her cadence. Her desk nameplate read : Glenda Jones.

"Yes," I said, "for the wildlife management opening."

"Mmm, mmm, mmm. Managing the wildlife," Glenda said. She shook her head. "You ask me, they the ones managing us." She burst into laughter again. It washed over me in a warm wave. Her accent clearly was Southern, and country, rural. She reminded me of the many kindly, older ladies I'd met in the South, the ones who saw me instantly as family, who took me under their wings to instruct and protect. The secretary of Emory's biology department was one, and Tina, my next-door neighbor, was another. After Delia moved out, Tina stocked my refrigerator with frozen casseroles and stews, as if someone had died. I had enough on my mind, she said, without worrying about cooking.

"Well, welcome Mr. Seth Hingham," Glenda said. "You can have yourself a seat right there, and I'll call up. I know George is expecting you."

"Thank you," I said. She punched some numbers into her phone, and I walked over to a small reception area near the elevators. A few chairs were placed around a table with newspapers and a couple of magazines scattered across it. As I sat down, Glenda's phone rang. I heard her answer, "Department of Environmental Protection... No, I ain't buying computers ... or access or Internet or whatever you selling... That's right. I'll put you through to purchasing, the office of purchasing. This is the government you're dealing with here, son."

I closed my eyes. I was an academic, a researcher. I didn't know anything about state agencies or politics, and I had no desire to learn. Good God, what was I doing?

"Seth, honey, George will see you now," Glenda said.

I stood. "Thanks," I said.

Glenda eyeballed me. Then she pushed herself up, came around her desk and walked over to me. "No need to be nervous," she said. "Meeting George Scanlon is nothing to be nervous about. Believe me."

"Do I look... I'm not nervous."

Glenda squinted. "You look nervous."

"Well, thanks for asking, but I'm fine."

"Maybe something else is wrong with you?" Glenda persisted. "Something troubling you?"

"No, I'm tired, but that's it. I've been pretty busy lately."

"Busy doing what?"

"Thanks again," I said. "What floor is Mr. Scanlon's office?"

Glenda smiled. "Third floor, last door on the left." She paused. "I know what you're thinking. Nosy old Glenda, sticking her beak in where it don't belong. Well maybe so. But you remind me of somebody, Mr. Seth Hingham. I can't put my finger on who, but somebody."

"Well, I'm glad," I said. "Third floor. Thanks again." I pushed the elevator button. The door slid open. I turned back to Glenda. "See you later," I said.

"Take a deep breath," Glenda whispered, because some other people were coming in the front door. "You're doing all the right things. I can tell." She hurried back behind her desk.

All the right things?

George Scanlon's office was a pie-shaped corner room with a bank of windows that overlooked the street. His desk sat in the center, flanked by packed bookshelves and chest-high filing cabinets. The door was open, but I knocked on it anyway.

He looked up from his desk. "Seth?" He gave a broad, gracious smile. A slight, slender man, with receding dark hair and wire rim eyeglasses, he was older than me, but not much, seven, eight years maybe. His skin was a warm olive tone. He took my hand and gave it a firm shake. "Have a seat, please."

"Good to meet you," I said, slipping into one of the chairs before his desk.

"How was the drive up from..." his eyes shot down to a paper on his desk, which I recognized as my resume, "Ledyard?"

"Fine. Rush hour was over by the time I got on the highway."

"Well thanks for taking the time to come up and meet us and learn a bit more about the opportunity here." Scanlon said. A silver-framed photograph of a perky-looking redheaded woman with two young children occupied one corner of his desk. A smaller shot of a sailboat sat next to it. Scanlon must have been a sailor. "I've gone over your material here pretty carefully. Can you tell me, why did you leave Emory?"

A clammy dampness broke out on my palms. "My department, zoology, had some cutbacks. The university had to shift more resources into this very high profile research in the medical school, and..."

"You were laid off?" Scanlon's eyes never left my face. His bluntness threw me, but only for a second.

"Sort of," I said. "Our whole research unit was suspended until the next fiscal year. There was a chance we'd be funded again but no guarantee, so I decided to move back and take my chances up here. I'm from Connecticut, you know? From Ledyard."

"Yes, a UConn alum. So am I," Scanlon said. "Atlanta wasn't for you?"

"Atlanta is a great town, don't get me wrong. I was just ready to make a clean break."

Scanlon nodded. "Welcome back," he said. "Do you have references at Emory I can call?"

"Absolutely."

He leaned back in his seat, the formalities apparently over. "Okay. Let me say this much, Seth. You appear to be qualified, more than qualified, for this position. Here's what we have. I don't know how up you are on some of the issues here and in the Northeast in general. We've been tracking a sediment contamination problem, mostly impacting run-off and the communities ringing Long Island Sound. We're concerned about the levels of a number of contaminants, metals mostly, getting into waterways and wildlife metabolism.

"Yes, I'm familiar with some of the issues," I said. "A good number of states along the coast have similar concerns, as I'm sure you know."

Scanlon nodded. "We need a field researcher to undertake a pretty wide-scale study. We want to get some baseline readings of stool toxicity in mammals—deer, coyote, raccoons, that sort of thing—and waterfowl in shoreline communities. Basically that means collecting and analyzing specimens. I know your work has leaned more toward the behavioral side, but this could help give us a new window into the health of waterways and the impact on local wildlife."

I cleared my throat. "I see," I said. "Of course waterways are an ecosystem key." My stomach clenched. "It is a step away from behavior, yes, but..." White lights flashed behind my eyes. I felt like I was stepping off a cliff. But I had no other options. "It's a step I'm ready to take."

Scanlon sat up. "Really? Good. I wasn't sure this would be up your alley. And, as I'm about to explain, I just don't have time to drag this out."

"Oh?" Here came the other shoe.

Scanlon leaned over his desk. The delicate red veins of his eyes were visible. "I'm sorry to put you in this position, Seth, but if you want the job, you're going to have to take it now," he said.

My heart skittered a beat. "Right now?" I could hear the stupidity in my voice. Now is now, not much room for interpretation there, but I wasn't ready to accept on the spot. I needed at least a night or two to think it over, to calm down. I cleared my throat. "Of course I'm very interested, as you know, in this position, and of course this is a generous offer, but I would like a day or two to think it over," I said. I shifted in my seat. "I can't decide something this big, just like *that*," I said. "I can't... I mean, it is customary to give an applicant a day or two to consider an offer."

At that, Scanlon slumped back in his seat. He took off his eyeglasses and rubbed his temples, and suddenly I liked him more. "Okay, Seth. Let me be straight with you," he said. "I'm not doing this to put the screws to you. I know this is odd. Welcome to the public sector. This is a budgetary issue. If I don't fill this spot today, the bean counters might yank the financing for next year. And if I don't have a warm body in this position, the Legislature could decide I really don't need one. Budget season is like that. Every year we hold our breath."

I blinked rapidly. "Oh, I see."

"Right, so unfortunately, there simply isn't any more time. The job is yours if you want it."

The bad choices of the past ten years all came back to me. Hanging on too long with Delia. With Atlanta, maybe not hanging on long enough. And now I was supposed to decide if studying animal shit on the Connecticut coast was a good career move. "A glorified shit scooper," I could hear Travis joke from the safety of his pristine Pfizer lab. And what about the North Country? Would it just slip away now, too?

I looked into Scanlon's eyes. "I'll take it," I said. He smiled a soft mixture of relief and sympathy, and I liked the guy even more. We didn't quibble over the salary. I already knew the range. It was advertised with the posting, and Scanlon offered me a figure near the top—not as much as I'd made at Emory, but not an insult either, and as Jasper had pointed out, the benefits were impressive.

"I don't think you'll be sorry, Seth. We're a good crew here at the DEP, though you'll surely hear otherwise, especially in election years."

We stood and shook hands. "You'll be based in Groton," Scanlon said.

"Groton?"

"Yes, since this has a coastal focus, we've arranged for some lab space at UConn's Avery Point campus, right on the water. Do you know it?"

"I took a summer course there when I was an undergraduate, marine ecology. It's one of my favorite spots on the shoreline. It's not far from my parents' place."

"That's what I call a shot of good luck," Scanlon said. "You'll be on your own, sort of camping out in a small space, but we have weekly staff meetings here in Hartford, and there's a lot of back and forth."

"Sounds fine," I said. The grayness lifted a bit. I saw the peaking waters of the Sound and the glint of the lighthouse at Avery Point, the broad, green lawn of the campus and the walking trail where lawn turned to tufts of sea grass, descending down a rocky slope to the beach.

In the lobby downstairs, Glenda saw my face as I stepped off the elevator. "I knew it. I knew it," she called. "I told you, Seth Hingham. I knew you were in the right place at the right time."

I stopped at her desk. "Looks like we're colleagues," I said, taking her hand to shake.

"I've been here a few months, moved up with my husband from Tennessee, cause he got family in Windsor Locks. You know Windsor Locks?" she said.

"A little."

"He's got a sick mama and our children are grown and on their own, so we come up here to be with her."

"How nice that you were able to," I said. "That's quite a move. I just moved up from Atlanta, myself."

"You ain't from Georgia, though."

"No, I'm from Connecticut."

"Son, I can hear that. And now you're in the right place at the right time, and that's half the battle, ain't it?"

"It's more than half, Glenda," I said. "And thank you for your, uh, reassurance, Glenda. You were right."

"We aim to please here at the DEP," she said, chuckling.

In the Civic, I slipped my favorite old Van Morrison CD into the player. Van was the man. I rolled down my window and turned up the volume. The highway ramp ahead seemed to loom with possibility. I may have been miscast and lonely, and groping for the threads of things I couldn't even name yet, but at least I wasn't unemployed.

NINE

....

"**N**o lease," Jasper said, standing in my new condo's living room, handing me the keys. "Not for family, and anyway I know where you work." He winked.

Chloe lumbered up beside him. "What a thing to say Jasper." She slapped at his arm. "Seth, we are so thrilled to have you here, and it's such a relief." She rolled her eyes. She was a petite, high-octane brunette with a way of looking you straight in the eye. She worked in public relations for Aetna in Hartford. She was the family's unofficial insurance expert, consulted when anyone bought a car or house, and she seemed to revel in the status.

"Yeah, no kidding," Jasper said. "This is a load off my mind." His limp was barely noticeable today. He didn't even have his cane. "You're going to love this spot." He went to the long picture window that ran along one wall and pulled up the blinds. Sunlight flooded in, hitting the wooden floorboards beneath our feet and warming the exposed red brick of the walls around us. Outside the river flowed past, the sun sparking off its surface. "It's a hell of a nice view," Jasper said.

I had to agree. The view, and of course the convenient location to Avery Point, were what sold me on the condo. Helping out Jasper made sense, too. Seeing him, silhouetted against the window, smiling because he wouldn't have to carry two mortgages now, a new respect surged up in me. Jasper had soldiered on admirably after Henry's death, shuffling some days, moving easily on others, finishing law school and marrying Chloe, struggling to have a baby, buying a house, snagging me to rent his condo, moving past whatever it was that had not worked.

"Hey, Scanlon was as straight-up a guy as you said he'd be," I said.

"George? Oh, yeah. With him, what you see is what you get."

"He a sailor?" I said. "There's a picture of a boat on his desk."

Jasper tapped on the window with his knuckles. "He'll show up down here," he said. "George spends a lot of time on the shoreline with that boat. He lives up in Glastonbury. Have you noticed his hands yet?"

"What?"

"His hands. Scanlon has these creepy little pale hands, like a child's hands," Jasper said, wiggling his own fingers. "Seriously, check it out next time you see him."

"Good Lord, Jasper."

"It's true." Jasper shuddered. "They give his department secretary the willies."

"Hey, do you know Glenda, the receptionist? She was so friendly at my interview. It was like she already knew me."

Chloe wandered towards the kitchen. Jasper's eyes followed her. He opened his mouth to speak. She stopped in the doorway, and without even bothering to turn around, said, "Don't tell me to be careful. Nothing is going to happen to me in the kitchen."

Jasper closed his mouth. "Huh?" he said, turning to me.

"Do you know Glenda?"

"How could I not? The woman's got something to say about everything, and no one dares to disobey her. Seriously, it's funny. She fussed so much one day last week when she saw Scanlon heading out the door without a jacket, he actually went back to his office and got one."

"She's kind of hard to tune out," I said. "But I got a good feeling from her."

"Sure, everyone does," Jasper said. "She kind of reminds me of Grammy. In a way, I mean."

"Hey, I never put it together, but you're right, Jasper. Glenda does remind me of Grammy, a lot actually now that I come to think of it."

"Ha," Jasper said. "Well listen, Buddy, enjoy your new home, and as dear old Grammy used to say, 'behave like a decent human being, for God's sake.' "

I laughed. That had been one of Judith Hingham's favorite expressions. *A decent human being.* Grammy Hingham had been a true believer in the power of the individual to set things right, in standing on your own two feet and "meeting the world head-on." But when her husband, Harold—known to us as "Grampy Harry"—died, Judith didn't last long alone in their riverside home in Essex. Two many ghosts, it seemed, and something about the serenity of the old slate-roof Colonial where the couple had raised their children—my father among them—irked her. The murmur of the river, its gentle trickle, at the edge of the yard grew insidious. Then it began to outrage her. Her husband was gone, altering forever the world she had spent a lifetime constructing, and the river took no notice. It altered its course, its flow and rhythm, not one bit. Such indifference in the face of grief had to be wrong.

The entire yard seemed to have joined this callous conspiracy. The grass grew in green and lush as ever, and songbirds twittered in the tree branches. But the Japanese maple in the center of the yard with its lacy, red leaves, must have particularly offended Judith. Its fate became part of the Hingham family lore.

Harry had planted the maple as a sapling. He tended it, loved it, wrapped it in burlap sacks to ward off winter's cold and watched it grow. Now in his absence, the tree stood tall and robust, and hateful in Judith's grieving eyes. After she took an axe to that beautiful tree, lopping off branches and gouging out great gashes of bark, so the maple bled a stream of sap, it was decided that she might do better living with Jasper's parents up in Ledyard. Judith left Essex and never returned. She did do better in Ledyard. There were more distractions and more situations to "straighten out" as she used to say. She was dead by the time Jasper and I hit high school, but she loomed as a powerful figure in our childhood—affectionate and critical at turns, frugal yet fawning, blunt to a fault and tireless in her efforts to make the world "behave appropriately." We loved Grandma Hingham with a misty reverence, and her death left a space in the family fabric that could never be filled.

I wasn't looking to fill spaces when I moved into Jasper's condominium in Norwich, and I didn't mind being alone. Peace was what I craved, and it had been impossible to attain in the mercurial, charged air of Mother's house.

Jasper and Chloe came with me to Mother's house afterward. Jasper's mother, Linda, was there, too. Mother had prepared a buffet of salads: chicken, Greek, Caesar and pasta. Holly and Travis showed up. Rosemary had taken the twins to visit her parents in Pennsylvania for a long weekend. Travis wasn't able to take the time off from work to go with her. Towards the end of lunch, Mother decided Linda should have a few of the books from Dad's personal library. As his only sister, Linda was entitled to his books, according to Mother, "to remember the life of his mind."

They disappeared into the study, and the rest of us went out to the patio. Mother had not stored the patio furniture for winter yet, so we flopped down on the wicker loungers and armchairs. A burnished mid-afternoon sun toasted the lawn, and the air carried the ashy odor of burning wood. Someone up the street must have been clearing out a stump or something. It was illegal, except on designated "burn" days, but people on the country roads away from the town center still burned whenever they wanted.

Lying on one of the loungers, I closed my eyes. I had broken to a new start, not the one I would have chosen and still a far cry from the North Country, but I was at least anchored by something real. The condo in Norwich was fine, even though I found the anonymous coughs of neighbors passing in the hall, the half-empty closets and cupboards and the bottle of aspirin the last tenant had left in the medicine cabinet vaguely depressing. I could not recognize myself in this new life yet, but I was at least on my feet again. An unlikely destination was better than no destination at all.

"So Seth kicked my ex-boyfriend's ass a couple of weeks back," Holly said. She was stretched out in an armchair, one of Jasper's dark microbrews balanced on her knee. She turned to me. "Did you tell them?" Glittering, butterfly-shaped barrettes perched in the blonde pile on top of her head.

"No, Holly. That's actually not a story I've chosen to share."

"He what? Shit, Seth, spill it," Jasper said. "I love a good ass-kicking."

"Thanks a lot, Holly," I said.

Travis perked up. "You got in a fight? A fist fight?"

"No, a duel with pistols at dawn," I said. "I defended Holly's honor."

"Hah!" she said, tipping back her beer.

"Look, it was stupid," I said. "We got carried away. I just lost my head for a minute."

"And he lost a few teeth, right?" Jasper said. "Are we talking about the poet dude you brought to Aunt Eleanor's for Christmas last year?" he asked Holly.

"Bryce," she said. "We broke up." She shrugged. "It had been coming for a long time. You know, unraveling. The final straw was when he refused to come to a dinner where I was getting an award from work. They were honoring me, and Bryce wanted to stay home and watch a movie. After all I'd done for him." She waved her hand as if to dismiss the subject.

Travis studied her, lips pursed in thought. "Which movie?" he said.

"What?"

"Which movie did Bryce want to see?"

Holly shook her head and popped on a pair of huge, owlish, black sunglasses. A good month after the breakup, she was sort of enjoying playing the jaded, bitter, victim of love. If the past held any indication, it wouldn't be long before the next boyfriend appeared.

Travis looked from me to Jasper. "Which movie could matter," he said.

"If you say so," Jasper said.

"The movie may have held great meaning for him," Travis said.

"He rented the DVD. He could have seen it any time," Holly said from behind her Hollywood starlet shades.

"Or maybe he's just a jerk," I said. "Why are you defending this guy?"

Travis studied the rim of his wine glass. "I'm not. I'm simply interested these days in what motivates people, in what they respond to." He looked up at me with this clinical, professorial expression he has. "What made you fight him? Did you start the fight?"

"He threw Bryce up against the wall and clocked him right on the jaw," Holly said.

"What did he do to provoke you?"

"Tossed him like a rag doll," Holly said.

"Let's not get into the details, okay?" I said. "He made some comments, some insinuations that didn't sit right with me."

"Bryce compared his own situation to Seth's," Holly said.

"Holly, come on," I said, but she had her cool, straight-talking shades on, and I could see she was going to steamroll ahead.

"I see," Travis said. "And you're very sensitive, Seth. You are the sensitive type."

"Thank you, Dr. Hingham," I said. Maybe a little sarcasm would end this.

Jasper laughed. "Ah, I bet the little jerk-off deserved it," he said. He glanced at Holly. "Sorry, Holly."

"Touché," she said.

"We're working on a new antidepressant right now, and the medical models are fascinating," Travis said. "The case histories, the personality types. I've been reading a lot of background on how they work and on whom." He pushed his wire rim glasses up the bridge of his nose. "It's amazing research."

"Well, thanks for sharing," I said.

"And you, Seth, are an interesting example. You take things hard. Remember that car accident in high school?"

No one spoke for perhaps twenty seconds. Jasper's eyes met mine and darted away. I cleared my throat. "Of course I remember it, Travis."

"That boy died, and you were pretty wrecked, if memory serves." Holly took off her sunglasses.

"We weren't sure, I mean Mom and Dad weren't sure, if you were ready to go off to UConn when you did. If you could handle it."

"Well, that was a *pretty* traumatic event," I said. Warmth flooded my face. I glanced at Jasper, but he was staring down at the gray slate of the patio.

Travis blinked. "I didn't say it wasn't. Of course it was traumatic for you."

"Well, for anyone, Travis. It would have been traumatic for *anyone*." Jasper sniffed.

"But to varying degrees," Travis said. "That's the interesting part. That's my point: We experience these things to varying degrees. We're impacted differently. Fascinating stuff." He tipped his wine glass so the sunlight caught it in a sharp sparkle.

Holly sighed, looked over at me, and ran her finger across her throat as if to say, *Cut it off. You know how he is.* She was right, of course. But something made me turn to Jasper. "What do you think, Jasp?" I said.

Jasper rubbed his bad knee. "To tell you the truth, these days I really don't anymore. I just do what I'm told."

"Spoken like a married man," Travis mumbled.

When I was younger, and not long after Henry Apgar died, I went through a phase when I believed, perhaps subconsciously, that Henry would haunt me. Not in a spooky, bump-in-the-night way, but as a more elusive force, a jinx. For years I waited for Henry to show up. Every time something good happened in my life: meeting Delia, finishing my dissertation, getting the job at Emory, I hesitated to embrace it, certain this good fortune would be snatched away. Sometimes in dreams I saw Henry's jowly face, flushed with outrage, brown eyes flashing with accusation: Why you? What right do you have to still be here?

"It was *Spellbound*," Holly said, breaking the silence that had settled over us. "The movie Bryce had to see that night. He was a huge Hitchcock fan, you know. I've seen *The Birds* a hundred times." She yawned, stretching both arms overhead so the golden bangles circling one clinked like coins. "He would only watch black-and-white movies. He despised color."

"Fascinating," Travis said.

TEN

....

I chose the weekend before I was to begin at the DEP to move. Even though I didn't have much in the way of furniture, I hired local movers—two self proclaimed "burly guys" and their truck—I found in the online Yellow Pages. The move was more than I could manage on my own, and I didn't want to ask Jasper or Travis for help. I wanted to slip quietly into my new space, alone.

"Don't throw out your back," Mother said, watching me fill the suitcase I had emptied with such misgiving a couple of months earlier. Something about Mother, sitting on my bed beneath the AC/DC poster, picking at a loose thread in the comforter, made me stop packing. We had visited Father's grave together the day before. She wanted to refresh the flowers. Now, in the brown days of early November, rushing toward Thanksgiving and the holidays, he seemed to be slipping further away. A panicked disbelief filled me at the thought.

"When I get settled, Mom, I'll have you over for dinner, okay?" I said.

"Sure, that sounds lovely," she said. "But you can come here, too." Her voice trailed off. "My goodness, this is your house, your home, and Travis's and Holly's, too. You can all keep coming here."

"And we will," I said, zipping up my suitcase. "Let's have Christmas here."

"Will it be Christmas without your father?" Mother stood and walked to the window. A diamond layer of frost coated the ground mornings now, and the tree branches reached like spindly, brown fingers against the changing sky.

"Of course it will," I said. "Travis will bring the twins. We'll do dinner and presents, and I'm sure Rosemary will make everyone go to church."

Mother shook her head. From behind, she looked small, wrapped in a long brown sweater. "That woman has gone off the deep end with all that religion."

"Rosemary means well, Mom," I said.

She shrugged. "Well, we never rammed religion down your throats, your father and I. We let you kids find your own answers. It's better that way, you know. 'Authentic,' your father called it."

"He was right," I said, going to the window beside her. She stared at the pine saplings she had planted.

"And believe me," she said, "nobody wants to believe in heaven more than I do right now."

I wrapped my arms around my mother and she leaned against my shoulder. The next morning I carried my bags over the frozen lawn to the Civic and drove back into my life.

* * *

The movers were waiting for me at Coastal Self Storage when I arrived. Their battered blue van was parked outside my unit, side doors open and ramp set up. I pulled in ahead of them. "Good morning," I called, closing the Civic door.

"Seth?" the tall one said.

"Yes, good to meet you guys. You beat me here."

The tall one nodded, but didn't crack a smile. "Rick Allenby," he said. "This is my partner, Rudy." Rick stood maybe six-foot-two, an immense, barrel-chested guy with a neck like a young tree trunk and forearms swollen with muscle and ropey veins. He wore jeans with a black T-shirt that said, "*If you can read this, you need another drink*" printed across the front in white lettering. He had flat blonde hair and a muzzle of biscuit-colored stubble around his mouth.

"We like to get at it early," he said. "We've been here maybe fifteen minutes already, but the woman who runs the place wouldn't let us in your unit."

"That's their policy," I said. "I'm sorry. I need to be here to let you in."

Rudy, the short one, grinned. "She wasn't budging, that girl. Mouth on her, too. Told us to 'back the hell up' when we tested the door to see if it was locked." Rudy wore white painter's pants and a gray, hooded sweatshirt. He was scrawny-looking for a mover. The woman he described must have been Jenna Avacoli. I unlocked the aluminum door and pushed it up.

"This is everything," I said. Sunlight hit the odd jumble inside.

"Travel light, don'tcha?" Rick said.

"Yeah, I guess I do." I stepped back and let them go to work, which they did methodically, loading up a wheeled dolly and rolling my stuff out of the unit, up the ramp and into the belly of the truck. A box teetered on top of a stack, and I jumped up to push it back.

"Thanks, but no thanks," Rudy said, grinning again, a little smugly this time, I thought. "You can't help us. Insurance rules. But any shit we break, we pay for, so don't worry, Seth."

He hit the 'Seth' in a drawn-out hiss.

I checked my watch. Nine-thirty. With any luck, we'd be through here by eleven, and I'd be at the condo by early afternoon.

"Hey, Seth," a voice said behind me. I turned around. Jenna in black jeans and a pink t-shirt, flip-flops on her feet.

"Hi, Jenna. How are you?" I said.

"Me? Just fine. Moving day, huh? I saw the truck roll in at quar-ter after. I followed them down here—I'm off school today—and said, 'You cannot attempt to enter a unit without the client present.' They gave me a dumb look."

I glanced over my shoulder at Rudy, spitting a gob of what must have been chewing tobacco on the ground. "Yeah, I can believe that," I said.

"God, that is the grossest thing." Jenna wrinkled her nose. "Movers are so crude. Believe me, I've met enough of them."

"Occupational hazard," I said.

Jenna cocked her head to one side and smiled. Her dark hair curled down around her shoulders. I have a weakness for brunettes.

"Where are you moving?" she said.

"Norwich. I'm renting my cousin's condo on the river."

Her eyes widened. "On the river, very chi-chi. My mom lives in Norwich. I grew up there. Everybody thinks that town is washed up, but it's coming back. Mark my words."

"That's what I hear."

"Maybe I'll be running into you at that Dunkin' Donuts."

"Which Dunkin' Donuts?"

"The one where we first met? Remember? I almost hit you with my car."

"Oh, yes. That one, yes. I guess maybe you will," I said. "Run into me, I mean. Not literally though, not with your car."

She laughed, and the curls danced. It was nice to hear a woman laugh at my dumb jokes. God knew I'd never been good at small talk. "Aren't your feet cold?" I said.

She looked down at her flip-flops. "Not at all." She raised her arms to the sky. "This isn't cold. You've been in Atlanta too long. You're spoiled."

"How do you know I was in Atlanta?"

She bit her lower lip. "Your paperwork, up in the office. I looked it up. I mean, I sent some of your bills and all, and I noticed you came from Atlanta. Why'd you leave?"

"It's a long story."

"That's the best kind." She smiled brightly, but something inside me froze.

"How's your son?" I said.

"Andy, he's fine. He's in school. He gets out at three."

"He's a cute kid."

Jenna's brown eyes glistened, and her mouth—those rosy lips dropped open. "And he's such a little trooper," she said. "You wouldn't believe this kid. He takes everything in stride. Hardly even knows his father. Gets shuffled back and forth between my mother and me." She waved her hand. "I don't believe all those statistics about kids from single-parent homes. Andy is the best-adjusted, sweetest natured child. Everyone says so." She stopped and took a deep breath. "Well enough of that, right? The point is he's a great kid. The love of my life."

"You sound like a great mom," I said.

A strand of tension around Jenna's mouth melted. She blinked. "Really?"

"Sure."

"Well, thank you, Seth. I need to hear that from time to time. All parents do. Do you have any, ah, kids?"

I swallowed. "No."

"Are you married or is there anyone special in your life?"

Nothing subtle about Jenna. "No and no," I said. "I'm a bitter, aging bachelor who's retreating from life."

She laughed, deciding as Jasper had at his house, that I was joking.

"Lift," Rick called behind us, and I turned to see him standing at the top of the truck ramp, arms full of my plaid sofa—the one

Delia hated—while Rudy staggered up the ramp, balancing the other half. He stumbled and dropped his end with a heavy thud.

"What the hell?" Rick scowled. "You numb-nuts. You forget what 'lift' means?"

I turned back to Jenna. "I better keep my eye on Larry and Curly here," I said.

"Hey, why don't I follow the truck over to your new place?" she said. "I've got the time, and two sets of eyes are better than one."

"Ah, no, Jenna. Thanks, really, but that won't be necessary. It's nice of you to offer, but I've got it covered."

"You sure? I don't mind at all."

"Yeah, really, it's okay. But thanks."

"Okay then," she said. She smiled, waved and turned to walk back to her office.

I stayed at my unit until Rick was back in the driver's seat and ready to go. Then I went to the office to turn in my key.

"I'll close out your account," Jenna said and offered me her little hand to shake. "Maybe I'll see you around Norwich?"

"Sure, probably," I said. "And good luck with everything, with school and all."

"Good luck with the animals," she said. "I've never met a wildlife biologist before, you know."

"Lucky you." I smiled.

"Maybe," she said. I caught the spark of mischief in her eye, and I just smiled again.

"See you around," I said.

ELEVEN

....

At night a sedating hush filled my new home. The air seemed to slow. Amber lights from cars passing on the street across the river drifted over the living room's brick walls. A sliver of moon peeked through the top of the high windows. I spent a lot of evenings on the couch that fall, watching UConn basketball games. My days fell into an easy rhythm, the flickering lights of the television, then bed, driving and work, the streets of Norwich a maze I slipped along unknown, the rocky coast outside my lab windows, a lone gull circling high above, and always the sensation of water, flowing beneath the apartment windows, lapping the beaches at Avery Point, carelessly marking time.

I began to slow down. Sleep came in marathon stretches, nine or 10 hours, deep and dreamless. I would wake rested and relieved. I realized then that I had never truly relaxed the entire time at Mother's house. With my father gone, her restless moods filled every corner. I called her a few times a week to check in and promised to visit soon.

My office at Avery Point was an empty science lab classroom with a blackboard up front and laboratory stations with sinks and microscopes along the walls. I moved my computer station near the windows that overlooked a slip of beach. I had a ton of research to do, getting up to speed on current pollutant patterns and staking out the region for the best specimen collection sites, before heading into the field. Scanlon came to see me my first day on the job. We walked the beach, discussing red tides and run-off. He bought me a lunch of fried clam strips at a local spot on the water and we set up a schedule to meet every Wednesday morning in Hartford. Later that week, my phone rang. I looked up from a map of the nearby Bluff Point nature preserve that I was dotting with locator pins.

"Seth Hingham," I said.

"You getting lonely down there, baby?"

"I'm sorry, what?"

"I may just pay you a visit." Hardy chuckling and a snort.

Glenda. The receptionist, of course. "Hi, Glenda," I said. "I'm doing fine, settling in down here. How are you?"

"Where they got you tucked away?" she said. "Where am I calling?"

"Avery Point on the coast. It's a small, UConn branch campus, tiny really, mostly for marine biology classes and summer sessions, things like that."

"On the beach? Sounds like you livin large."

I laughed. "You could say that."

"In that case, I am coming down. But in the meantime, I've got to give you some information and get some from you, Mr. Seth Hingham." She gave me the office's Federal Express account number and told me where to find mileage sheets for the driving I'd be doing. She double-checked my fax and cell phone numbers and arranged for me to get a UConn Avery Point parking sticker.

"Anything else you need, you give a holler," Glenda said. "And be sure you stop by and see me next time you're up here."

"I will, Glenda. I'll bring you a coffee."

"Cream and sugar, son."

"Got it."

An e-mail from Jasper came later that day. "*Welcome aboard,*" it read. "*You are now officially a cog in the wheel.*" A heart-warming thought. "*I'll be down your way next Thursday. Let's have lunch?*"

One night when UConn was down 7-21 against Tennessee, a tentative knocking sounded on my door. Tap, pause, tap, pause. Tap, tap, tap. I lifted my head off the couch. Someone was here? I sat up. Mother maybe? Or Jasper? I was so sure it was one or the other, I didn't bother peering through the peephole. I swung open the door, and Jenna Avacoli was smiling at me.

"Bet you didn't expect to see me tonight?" she said. At her feet was a straw basket stuffed with wads of fuchsia tissue paper. A big red bow adorned the handle. Andy stood next to Jenna.

"Hi, Mr. Seth," he said. "You have that cool bike."

"Uh, yes," I said.

"We just wanted to drop off a little housewarming gift for you," Jenna said. She heaved the basket up with both hands, and I stepped forward to take it from her.

"Oh, uh, wow, Jenna. You didn't have to do this. Come, ah, come in," I said.

Andy sailed by us into my living room. "Who's winning?" he asked, stopping in front of the television.

"You're new in town, and everyone deserves a housewarming, don't they?" Jenna said.

"Yeah, I guess so. This is so nice of you."

I placed the basket on the couch. Andy dropped down next to it and immediately began rooting through the tissue paper.

"Keep out," Jenna said. "Andy, don't. That's for Seth to open."

"He can open it," I said. Andy raised a questioning eye to his mother. He wore overalls and white sneakers. He was a spindly, skinny kid with a sharp, angular face like his mom's. He bit his lower lip, watching Jenna's face.

"Okay," she said, turning to me. "He helped wrap them, and he wants to explain them to you."

"Well, that's fine," I said.

"You know how kids are."

I smiled. "Sure," I said. "Can I, ah, get you anything? A drink maybe?"

"Thank you," Jenna said. "Maybe afterwards? I think the unwrapping has begun." She sat next to me on the couch, crossing one knee over the other. Her legs were encased in brown, suede boots up to the knees. A flash of skin peeped out between the top of the boot and her gray skirt. Her creamy sweater looked super soft to the touch. At the neckline, her delicate collarbones protruded. My eyes traveled up to meet hers, and I looked away.

Andy's little hand shot up in the air. "Candle," he shouted. He held a pink candle, one of those short, thick ones that smell. Delia always had one in the bathroom, a heavily scented, vanilla candle she burned when she took baths.

"Midnight Rose," Jenna said. "It's my favorite. I have one on my nightstand. You'll love it."

"Thanks, Jenna."

Andy stepped closer and put one hand on my knee. "It stinks," he said, looking me in the eye. "It smells like rotten orange peels. Don't breathe it in."

I laughed. "I'll take your word for it, Buddy," I said.

"It does not stink," Jenna said. "Andy, really. That's not polite. We would not buy Seth a candle that stinks."

Andy plunged his hands back into the basket.

"We just kind of threw together a bunch of little things here," Jenna said. "Things that help make a house a home."

"This was so thoughtful of you."

"Where did you live in Atlanta?" she said. "I mean, in a house or in an apartment?"

"In a condominium."

"Alone?"

"With my ex-girlfriend," I said.

Jenna grew still. "Oh, I see. I'm sorry. Not about the condo, about the ex-girlfriend."

I shrugged. "Don't be. It was for the best."

"Love gone bad? Listen, Seth, you don't even have to tell me. Okay? Really, nothing surprises me anymore. I can tell you some stories, trust me, about *his father...*" She silently mouthed the words, pointing to Andy "...and some guys I've dated that you wouldn't believe."

"Coffee," Andy said, dropping two bags of Dunkin' Donuts coffee beans in my lap.

"I know you like it," Jenna said.

"Yeah, great. I do. I'll bring one bag to work."

Jenna slid to the end of her seat, and I leaned back on the couch. "Listen, Seth, you're one step ahead of the game," she said. "You've already lived with a woman. That's good. You've been broken in."

"If you say so," I said.

Jenna laughed.

"African Violet," Andy said, handing me a small plastic pot with a little lavender flower looking out.

"Very easy to keep," Jenna said. "They require almost nothing. A little water, a warm spot. You can't kill them. I have a black thumb, so I know."

"I'll keep it on my desk," I said to Andy. "You think that's a good place for this plant?"

"At work?"

"Yes, my desk at work."

"Will it get lonely?" He frowned. His brown eyes were almost too big in his face, giving him a cartoonish appeal. He bit his lip.

"I'll get another plant for company," I said.

Andy smiled. "That's good," he said.

"Good call," Jenna said. "You handled that just right. Loneliness or pain or suffering of any kind is big trouble." She nodded at Andy. "He can't abide it. Anything suffering sets him off. Dying trees, sick people, lost animals. I can't tell you the conversations we've had over road-kill."

"Do you like animals, Andy?" I said.

He nodded. "Some of them, the ones that aren't mean or killers."

"Seth is an animal scientist, Honey," Jenna said.

"Cool." He peered at me with new interest. "I was a tiger for Halloween. We painted stripes on my old pajamas."

"Tigers are killers. They're predators," I said.

"Well, I was the not-killing kind."

"I see."

"Yes," Jenna said, "a special category of tiger all his own." She cleared her throat, and I glanced at my watch. I had turned down the volume on the UConn game, but from the corner of my eye I could see it was over. Fans were swarming over the court.

"Maybe you can visit Seth one day at work and see some animals?" Jenna said.

I swallowed. "There are no animals in my office, unless you count the students in the next lab."

Jenna laughed. "We'll count them, and maybe we can all have lunch afterward?"

"Uh, maybe," I said.

"If you've got a microscope, we can look at bugs," Andy said. "But we'd have to kill them first."

"We'll look around and find some that are already dead, that died of natural causes," I said.

"Natural causes?" Andy echoed.

"Bug old age," I said, and he giggled. I looked over to see Jenna watching me.

"I bet your parents are good people, nice people. They are, aren't they?" she said.

Abrupt segues, I was beginning to see, were part of Jenna's charm. "My mother is," I said. "My father was. He's dead. He died in the spring."

"Oh, I'm sorry."

"I was in Atlanta."

"Breaking up with your girlfriend."

"Yeah, I guess we'd begun breaking up. It took a long time."

"Sounds familiar."

"He had cancer, but still it came more quickly than we thought it would. My mother's house is incredibly weird without him. I half-expect him to walk in any minute." I felt myself going too far, but the words came in a torrent, undammed; I couldn't stop them. I am occasionally subject to these bouts of verbal diarrhea. Holly says it's because I keep too much bottled up inside.

"The kitchen is the worst, because I can so clearly see him there, at the stove, stirring something or chopping," I said to Jenna. "He loved to cook. He was good at it, too. I never told him how good he was. I probably should have."

Jenna and Andy were both staring at me. "He sounds like a wonderful man," Jenna said. "I'm sure he was proud of you. My dad has, ah, passed, too."

"Oh, I'm sorry. I didn't know," I said.

Jenna nodded. "I was just eleven. A car accident," she said.

"God," I said.

"Tough thing for a kid to go through."

"For you to go through."

"It was a long time ago."

"Grandpa's in heaven," Andy said.

"That's right, honey," Jenna said, standing to kiss the top of his head. "We should get going," she said.

"Can we visit Seth at work like you said?" Andy said. Jenna looked at me. I saw the flicker of hesitancy in her eye.

"Sure," I said. "I'm in the lab now most days. Pick a day."

"Should I call you?" Jenna said.

I gave her my office line. She punched it into her cell phone.

"Can we look at something gross under the microscope?" Andy said.

"If you look at anything closely enough, it's gross," I said.

"How true," Jenna said, flashing me a wry smile.

I sat on the couch a long time after they left. My heart had begun racing. I stretched out on my back to try to calm it. The ivory ceiling paint was brushed, or stamped on, in little swirling patterns. I'd never noticed that. I closed my eyes. Whatever happened to me from this day forward, my father would not know. There was no way to reach him now. Unless you're one of those people who believe the dead know all and see all. I never had been, but a silence, heavy with expectation—of what, I couldn't say—settled around me.

* * *

The Hinghams had a long tradition of agnosticism. My mother's side of the family did not originally, but she took to the death of faith with a strange gusto, declaring herself an outright atheist. Our agnosticism—my father's certainly—manifested itself mainly as a disinterest in organized religion, as a reasoned comfort with the unknowable, but with a tolerance for those who felt otherwise.

Given my lack of religious training, I was surprised when Jasper a week later asked my opinion on whether or not his unborn child should be baptized.

"Are you serious?" I said, fork poised midair on the way to my mouth. We were having lunch at the Captain Daniel Packer Inne in Mystic, in the low-ceilinged, Colonial era pub with its scarred wooden bar and smoky fireplace. "I'm not religious, Jasper. You know that."

"Neither are we," he said.

We sat at a table for two against the window, and in the daylight, I could see that Jasper, in his gray suit and royal blue tie, cut a pretty impressive figure. He was a great schmoozer, a great talker, someone who knew how to smooth over the rough spots. He was in Mystic today meeting with the developers of a proposed 20-unit condominium project on the water, not far from the historic district, right on the wetlands, abutting a residential section of town with traffic flow problems. The regulatory issues were numerous. I'd come over from the lab to meet Jasper. In my blue jeans and windbreaker, I felt like his little brother.

"For some reason, it's become a big deal for Chloe to get the kid baptized," he said.

The waitress came by with our bill. I grabbed it before Jasper could. "My turn," I said.

"I'm not lowering your rent, buddy."

I slipped my Visa card into the billfold. "You're a hell of a guy, Jasp," I said. "A prince of a landlord. Maybe you should just get the kid baptized, if it's what Chloe wants."

"That's what my mother said," Jasper said. He gazed out the window. "The mother's wishes, it seems, tend to dominate these matters. I dunno. Maybe it's for the best, in the end."

I shook my head. "Don't even go there, Jasper," I said. "The X-chromosome holds all the cards."

Jasper laughed. "So, what about you? Are you turning into some kind of celibate hermit?"

"Well, I haven't quite thought of it that way...Hey, get going if you need to," I said. "Beat the traffic back up to Hartford."

"I think I will. Thanks for lunch." He stood and pulled on his tan trench coat.

"How's the knee?" I said.

"Not bad. Some days it's like nothing ever happened. Others, damn, just getting around is all I can manage. You know how it goes." He clapped my shoulder. "See you later."

TWELVE

....

I'd been dodging Mother's calls all week. It was a crummy thing to do, but I could hear trouble brewing in her voice.

"It's Mom, Seth, calling to see how the new job is going," she said into my answering machine at home. *"I'm sure you're well aware that the shoreline deer hunt is coming up soon. And I know you hear things, tapped into the system over there..."*

The truth was I was privy to very little of the agency's policy machinations. The brass in Hartford handled that. I was a one-man outpost, miles from the nerve center where decisions were made. Mother couldn't seem to grasp that. In her mind, working for the state instantly made me "part of the system." And this deer hunt had taken on great urgency for her. There was desperation in her attachment to the issue, as if she were scrambling for her own lifeline.

The two-day hunt near the Rhode Island line, scheduled for mid-November, had become a political hot potato. Animal rights activists all over the region were protesting. Letters to the editor, lambasting the cruelty of a hunt on protected land, ran daily in the *Hartford Courant* and *The Day* of New London. Everyone had an opinion, but scientific types like me tended to come down on the side of common sense. Protected from natural predators and hunters, the deer herd on this swath of state-owned land had simply grown too large. Every winter a bunch starved to death.

Something needed to be done, and a bullet to the head, in some respects, was the kindest solution. The plan was for a handful of DEP agents to go in and cull a certain number of deer annually in order to maintain a healthy herd. This scenario outraged Mother and her compatriots.

On Wednesday I drove to Hartford for the staff meeting. Scouting for an empty parking space on the street, I passed by the DEP building. On the sidewalk out front a half dozen people—a clumsy little cluster of winter coats—marched in a tight circle. They raised signs high above their heads, their open mouths shouting. I slowed. "DEP: A LICENSE TO KILL," one sign read. Others proclaimed: "DEER ARE DEAR TO CONN." and my favorite, "WOULD YOU SHOOT BAMBI?!"

On closer inspection, the protestors were mostly women, ladies in their fifties and sixties with salt-and-pepper hair, fleece-clad do-gooders looking to right a wrong. I parked and made a beeline for the doors, keeping my head down. As I moved past them, one woman called out to me.

"There's blood on your hands," she said.

I turned around, and she stepped closer.

"You work for the DEP, right?" she said.

Stupidly, I engaged her. "Yes, I do," I said.

She was a solid, stout woman wearing a black beret with a rainbow-colored outline of the African continent stitched on the front and a black-and-red plaid, flannel coat that hung nearly to her knees. Dark sunglasses hid her eyes.

"Your agency is breaking the law," she said.

"It's not *my* agency," I said. The self-righteous pitch in her voice irked me.

"The deer have a right—a civil right—to be protected on preserve land," she said.

"Really? The last time I checked the Constitution, animals didn't have any civil rights," I said.

"Oh, sure, play your little word games. Be smart, split legal hairs, but we're here for the deer. Who speaks for them?" The woman's companions threw us curious glances.

"Who'll speak for them when they're dying a slow, agonizing death from starvation this winter?" I said.

She hesitated.

"Listen, I don't work on policy matters," I said. "You should contact the commissioner's office with your concerns. I can give you a phone number." It was the wrong thing to say.

She smirked. "Just following orders right, Sonny? That's what they said at Nuremberg. Well, it didn't fly then, and it's NOT going to fly now."

Before I could respond, she raised her sign high, threw back her head and shouted, "No to murder." Her shout roused her allies, touching off a chorus of "No to murder" and "Hey, hey, ho, ho, the DEP has got to go."

I climbed the DEP building steps, pulled open the door and stepped into the lobby. Glenda, sitting behind her reception desk, immediately waved me over. "You pass through those fools out there?" she said.

"Unfortunately." I stamped the cold out of my feet. For staff meetings, I spiffed up a bit: slacks and loafers, a blazer.

"I've never seen such lunacy," Glenda said, throwing up her hands. She wore a sunny orange blazer with a golden brooch as big as my fist on her lapel. "Back home, folks hunt and nobody says anything about it. Somebody has got to explain this to me," she said. "How come those women are out there, bleeding their hearts out over a bunch of deer, and meanwhile there's children stuck in foster care and homeless people freezing on the street and they don't say ANYTHING about it? How can you care more about a mangy animal than flesh-and-blood people?"

"And the biggest irony is the hunt will ultimately spare the deer suffering," I said.

"Some people got their heads so far up their asses, they forgot how to pull them out." Glenda glanced around the lobby. "Excuse my language," she said. "I'm fired up today."

"I don't blame you," I said. "I'd be fired up, too, if I had to sit here and stare out at them all day."

I rode the elevator to Scanlon's office. We met in a small conference room off it.

"As long as they stay on the sidewalk, I don't care what they say," Scanlon said, sitting at the end of the table. A dozen of his field staff surrounded him. "And you shouldn't either," he said. "The department is not in the business of making every member of the public happy. Our job is protecting and managing the state's natural resources. Somebody is always going to take a shot at us—no matter what we do. Let the commissioner's office handle this."

I'd grown sort of fond of Scanlon. There was a crisp honesty about him. You always knew where you stood, and you always knew where he stood. I'd come to look forward to the staff meetings. Scanlon's orchestration of the various field teams and their goals was interesting to watch, and I secretly enjoyed studying the other staffers. There was Jim, assigned to the beaver dams and flooding in residential areas issue, who amusingly enough had buck teeth; Sally, a few years out of UConn—round blue eyes, blonde ponytail—who took studious notes on everything Scanlon said; Trey, a waterfowl expert with the long neck of a goose. They were nice people from what I could see, and their genial welcome and interest in my research at Emory helped thaw me toward the DEP. Maybe this wasn't such a bad place to cool my heels until an opportunity popped up in the North Country.

After the meeting, I took the elevator down and waved to Glenda as I crossed the lobby. A group of men in suits stood around her desk. "Second door on the left," I heard her say to them. Then she turned to me. "So where's that coffee you mentioned, Seth Hingham?" she said.

"Glenda, I'm so sorry. I forgot. Completely forgot. Next week, okay?"

"Honey, recognize a joke when you hear one," she said. "I'll be here, and one week is as good as another."

"See you then," I said. "Coffee in hand."

The protestors were taking a break. A few milled around while others chatted in groups on the sidewalk. "What we should really do is call PETA," I heard one say.

A ceiling of moody, gray clouds had moved in overhead, and the temperature was dropping. A cold, still note of expectation laced the air. Snow weather. At least a flurry was on the way. Heading up the sidewalk, I spotted the beret woman. Her back was to me, but when she turned, I could see her profile. Maybe her heart was in the right place, but the heart, as I was coming to learn, needs guidance, and beret woman's head, unfortunately, was as Glenda had so aptly described it.

Back in my car, I called Mother before taking off. I'd promised her I would. "I'm in Hartford," I said. "I'm just leaving now."

"Drive carefully. It's looking very threatening here. Did you hear the forecast?" she said.

"It'll just be a flurry, Mom. It's too soon for real snow."

"You never know. Be careful."

"Hey Mom, Holly and I want to come help you winterize the house. What's a good day?"

"Whatever works for you two, of course," she said.

"Mom, are you alright?"

"Yes, I'm fine."

"You sound out of breath."

"I'm fine."

"You're sure?"

"As sure as an old woman can be."

"How about Sunday morning, say around ten?" I said.

"That's perfect, dear. I'll make pancakes."

"We'll see you Sunday then, Mom," I said.

"What's new up there at the DEP? I saw the protest on the news today." She chuckled. "I told you. We will not go quietly into that good night. This is an issue where I can make a real difference."

"Mom, I'll see you Sunday, okay? I need to go before the snow starts."

I wasn't back in my office at Avery Point for ten minutes when the phone rang. I assumed it was Mother, checking to see if I'd gotten back safely. I picked it up. "Seth Hingham."

"Seth, hi. How are you?" A woman's voice that didn't ring any bells. "It's Jenna," she said. "Jenna Avacoli."

"Jenna, hi," I said. "I'm good. Fine. Just fine. How are you?"

"I hope I'm not catching you at a bad time," she said.

"Not at all." I had a report to finish writing. UConn was playing Maryland that night. I wanted to take a quiet hike up the shoreline before heading home for the couch and the game.

"I'll make this quick," she said. "I was wondering if you'd given any thought to a good day for Andy and me to come visit your office. He hasn't stopped talking about it. You made quite an impression on him, I can tell you." She laughed.

Something inside me recoiled. "I'm sorry, Jenna," I said. "I'm just... it's sort of crazy busy right now. I don't have a lot of time to spare."

"Well I can bring lunch. Would that be better? You must get a lunch break, and we can eat while Andy sees the office. He's dying to look into that microscope."

The microscope. Oh, God. "That would be great, just not right now," I said. The words stuck in my throat. "I'm really sorry, Jenna. I'm just snowed under at the moment."

A heavy paused followed, and then she said, "Sure, of course. Hey, I understand. We all work, right? I know how it gets."

The note of false bravado in her voice killed me. "Maybe another time?" I said.

"Sure thing, Seth," she said.

"I'll call you."

"Sure."

"And thanks again for the basket."

We hung up. It was a shitty thing to do, but I knew that Jenna was interested in more than the microscope, and at that moment I just didn't have a whole lot to give.

THIRTEEN

My father always winterized our house. He took satisfaction in preparing for the coming cold.

"It's a 'protector' thing," Holly said to me one morning when we were teenagers, sitting in the kitchen eating cereal and watching Father seal the windowsills with plastic wrap between the storm windows and the interior glass for added insulation. He was whistling "Here Comes the Sun," singing the "do-do-do-do" part.

Holly and I sealed the windows my first year back in Connecticut. Mother greeted us that brisk November morning, the kitchen table laid out with pancakes and sausage, orange juice and coffee.

"You children are my saving grace," she said.

"Aw, Mom," Holly said, "You know we love you."

After breakfast, Mother disappeared into the study to "work."

"What's she working on?" I asked Holly when we were alone in the kitchen after clearing out the gutters.

"Something to do with that deer hunt," Holly said.

"Please tell me she's not involving herself in that."

Holly poured another spot of cream in her coffee and took a sip. She wore blue jeans and a sweatshirt, and her platinum hair was pulled back in a long ponytail. "I'm just glad to see her involved in something," Holly said. "Do you know about the trees?"

"What trees?"

"Those saplings she planted for Dad out back? One of them died. At least it looks dead. The needles are falling off. Mom took it hard. Didn't you speak with her last week?"

"Um, no, I...We kept missing each other. Maybe she needs help, Holly? I mean, counseling or something?"

Holly stared into her coffee cup. "Can you imagine Mom in a bereavement group? Anyway she seems better today. It feels like she's looking for something, some new thing to hold onto. Maybe she just needs to work through this in her own way?"

I shrugged. "Maybe. I hope so."

Holly placed her coffee cup in the sink. She gazed out the window to the backyard. "Are you?" she said.

"Am I what?"

"Are you working through it?"

"I'm working," I said. "Through what, I have no idea."

Holly turned to me and laughed. "Is the glass half-empty, Seth?"

I gave her a deadpan expression.

She poked me in the ribs. "Oh, come on," she said.

I grabbed her ponytail and yanked it.

"Hey," she said.

"Remember how we used to fight as kids?" I said. "You were tough, I'll give you that."

She flexed her arm. "Small but mighty," she said.

"Mighty, right. Hey, have you had any updates on Bryce?"

She slapped her forehead. "I meant to tell you. I passed him on the street last week. We walked right by each other on the sidewalk, and he didn't say anything, didn't acknowledge me at all. He just marched by like he hadn't seen me."

"Are you sure he *did* see you?"

"Oh yeah, I'm sure. We were the only ones on the sidewalk, it was the middle of the day, full-sun, and I was wearing a cute outfit with high boots. He saw me."

"I'm sure the boots clinched it."

"You know, it was strange at first after he left, but now I've gotten used to it. I mean, I think about him a lot. I do. But I also like coming home at the end of the day to peace. No more endless battles. I close my door. Snowy trots up to greet me and we settle in. I like being home again."

"But do you miss him?" I said.

"Yes." Holly answered immediately, so I knew it was the truth. "Don't you miss Delia?" she said.

"I don't know."

Holly rolled her eyes. "How lame. You can be so full of it, you know that, Seth?"

"I've been told," I said.

"Jeez, get in touch with your inner whatever, okay? Soon."

"It's at the top of my list."

"Good," Holly said. "Come on, let's get the outside water done."

At the circuit box in the basement, I turned off the outdoor water supply. Then we went out and circled the house, turning on all the faucets, draining the pipes so they wouldn't freeze and crack in the dead of winter. We watched the water gush, then dwindle to a thin stream, a trickle and drops. It seeped into the ground, disappearing.

The sun had passed the high noon mark and was beginning to sink through the trees at a shallow angle. The trees were mostly bare now, and morning frost coated the ground. This was one of the things I had missed about New England: these unmistakable signs that time is passing. Life is not one sunny, hazy blur, they insist. Pay attention. The hoarse cry of a Canada goose cut the air. They were soaring over the house, a flock in V-formation heading south. Those ragged honks and the sight of the flapping V against the autumn sky has always filled me with a sad restlessness, a sense that I am being left behind.

My answer to Holly, while lame, was also true. Did I miss Delia? She was receding along with the rest of my old life. I missed the familiarity of Atlanta. The pieces that were—or at least seemed to be—in place, the identity I recognized as my own. And, yes, sometimes on the couch in the evening, or driving home in the dark, I did miss Delia. If I conjured hard enough, I could re-create the feeling of her next to me in bed, the sheets falling in waves over her body, the gentle rise and fall of her chest, her dark hair splayed across the pillows. Yeah, I missed all that. Who was I kidding?

When we were finished, Holly and I found Mother in the study, tapping away at the computer.

"What great works are we interrupting?" Holly called as we entered the room.

Mother raised her eyes from the screen, fixing us in a stare over the top of her bifocals. "Do you really mean to say: What nonsense is the old lady wasting her time on now?" she said.

"Mom, no one meant anything of the kind," Holly said.

"Well," Mother said, slumping back in her seat. "No one would blame you if you had." She smiled weakly. "I'm just getting organized."

I walked over to look out the window to the backyard and the ill-fated pine saplings, scrawny, green tufts huddled together at the edge of the woods.

"Mom, the house is all set," Holly said. "The gutters are clean. The pipes are drained. We plastic-sealed the windows."

"And so we settle in for a long winter's nap," Mother said. "Thank you. Seth?"

"Yes?" I kept my eyes on the saplings.

"Maybe you can help me with something else then?"

"What's that?"

"I think you already know." Mother cracked a sheepish grin.

Holly sat down on the loveseat next to the window. I scanned the walls of Father's study, trying to buy time. His framed college degrees hung behind the desk. An aerial view of the house on a summer day, the green treetops plump and bristling like rows of broccoli, hung near the door. A buck-toothed Travis smiling in a Ledyard little league uniform, and a map of the world, blue oceans dotted with continents like ragged paint splotches, hung nearby.

"The deer hunt?" I said.

"Bingo." Mother's bright eyes fixed on me.

"I don't know how I can help you, Mom."

"I saw the protest on the news," Holly said. "In Hartford. Did you catch it, Seth?"

"I had the pleasure of walking right through it."

"We're planning another protest," Mother said.

"*We're?*" I said. "Do you know them?"

"I don't know those individuals specifically, but we're all over the region, Seth. I've told you."

"Who is?"

"Us, people who oppose the hunt."

I took a breath. "Mom, that's fine. It's your right. I respect that."

"So do I," Holly said. "I'm glad you're taking a stand for something you believe in."

Mother slid to the edge of her seat. "Good, wonderful. May I ask you a favor then, Seth? Will you find out how many DEP agents will be hunting and what areas of the preserve they'll be focusing on? What are the migratory patterns of deer in the preserve? I've been boning up on deer behavior."

With every word, she pushed me further into the corner of defending the DEP, of aligning myself with a place I'd wound up in only out of desperation. I held my palms out to her. "Mom, stop. I'm an employee of the DEP. I work for the agency. I can't leak information. I can't be your Deep Throat. What you're asking is probably illegal—and it's certainly unethical."

"Unethical? The only unethical thing here is the murder of those deer."

"Look, I know you feel that way, but please respect the position I'm in. I cannot get involved."

"Not even for a higher cause?"

"Whose higher cause? Who said it was higher? I think it's nonsense."

"I'm afraid you've swallowed the poison, my boy," Mother said. "You've drunk the state's Kool-Aid."

"Mother, just listen. I believe in responsible herd management. I always have—before I came back here, before the DEP job. It's a reasonable strategy used all over the world to ensure a herd's long-term survival. We don't live in Disneyland, Mother. And Bambi doesn't live in Connecticut. And remember, you pushed me to take this job. You were gung ho on the state and all its great benefits."

Mother's face softened. Her lip twitched. "That's true," she said. "I just wanted you back on your feet. It's a terrible thing to watch your children flounder." She sighed. "I won't bring this up again," she said.

"Mom," Holly said, "why does this mean so much to you? I mean, you've never particularly liked deer. You know how they dig up your tulip bulbs and spread Lyme ticks. They cause a lot of trouble."

"That may be true," Mother said. "But there has never been hunting in that preserve. Your father loved that spot. We took you kids every summer for picnics. Remember? And you swam and fished and hiked."

"I remember," Holly said.

"The land is disappearing. People are disappearing. We should be able to keep one thing the same, to hold onto it. I want to protect something important. Is that wrong?"

"Aw, Mom, no. Of course not," Holly said.

"It's not as if we don't see your point," I said.

"I just think that this one thing should not change," Mother said. She stood and snapped off the desk lamp.

"Mom?" Holly said.

But Mother left the room, closing the door softly behind her.

"Holly sighed. "At least she won't try to suck you in anymore," she said. "I'll go check on her."

"Thanks, Hol," I said, and Holly closed the door behind her.

Mother wanting to protect an animal was actually pretty ironic. Although we'd had pets as kids, she'd never been fond of any of them. When I was ten, I had a gerbil. Obtaining Theodore—or Teddy, as we called him—hadn't been easy. I had begged and wheedled and swore myself to a lifetime of servitude cutting the lawn, trying to convince Mother to let me have a gerbil.

"Jasper has two," I told her.

"Rodents carry disease," she said. We were sitting in the living room, around the wooden coffee table. Travis lay sprawled out on the couch, face buried in a chemistry textbook. The newly discovered Hanta virus, transmitted by mice, had killed a handful of people in Arizona and New Mexico that year. It was all over the news, and Mother was convinced that domestic gerbils in New England posed a threat, too.

"Hanta is a desert virus actually," Travis said. He was already a drug researcher in embryo, interested in the minute workings, the intricacies of things. "How would the gerbil contract it?" he said.

"Exactly," I said, happy for an ally, even Travis. "He's lived his whole life in a pet store. Pleeeeease can I get one?'

She finally relented. Father never objected, and Teddy became mine. I loved him with devotion. I watched him for hours. The wire whiskers and dark eyeball orbs, his delicate burrowing paws and translucent little ears fascinated me. I set up obstacle courses and mazes to test his intelligence—books, Kleenex boxes, empty coffee cans—on the floor of my room and urged Teddy through them. I placed my desk lamp over a corner of his cage every night for a few hours because he seemed to enjoy basking in the heat of the bulb, his little eyes closing in bliss.

I took Teddy out of his cage in my room and had him on top of my desk one afternoon. Holly wanted to touch him. I was pointing out his various features to her and letting her pet him, while Teddy scrambled around the desktop, little claws scraping the wood. I left to go to the bathroom, giving Holly strict orders not to take her eyes off him. But being five, she took her eyes off him, and when I returned Teddy was gone and Holly was crying.

Three days after his disappearance, my hope vanished, too. I had spent days searching under furniture and in closets. Finally I had to admit that either the cats had gotten him or he'd escaped outside. "In either case, he's toast," Travis pointed out.

"Of course Teddy could be stuck in the walls," he suggested one morning at breakfast. "Like a mouse."

"We'd hear him scratching," Father said. "But you know, I have an idea."

Late that night, when the house was dark and quiet, my father, flashlight in hand, appeared at my bedside in his white t-shirt and pajama pants. Something brushed my cheek and I opened my eyes. "Dad?"

"Yes, Seth. Ssshhh. We don't want to wake everyone. Come with me."

I followed him out to the hall. Two sleeping bags lay head-to-head on the floor, three or four open jars of peanut butter placed around them.

"Nice and smelly," my father said. "To lure Teddy."

My mouth dropped open. "Did you see him?"

"No, but from what I've been reading, gerbils are active at night."

"They're nocturnal," I said, pronouncing the word carefully. "He runs on the wheel in his cage at night."

"Exactly, and I bet that if we do find Teddy, it's going to be at night. So you and I are camping out. We can take turns watching for Teddy, and hopefully the peanut butter will draw him out of whatever crack he's hiding in."

Father took the first shift. I crawled into a sleeping bag and watched him shine his flashlight down the hall. The beam drifted slowly over the floorboards, down the corridor, past Travis's and Holly's closed doors, and stopped beneath the window at the top of the back staircase.

"Dad, what if we don't find him? What if we never find him?" I said, finally voicing the unthinkable. In the dark hall, so familiar in daylight and now a shadowy gauntlet that held Teddy's fate, the worst suddenly seemed very real. Tears flooded my eyes. I was too old to cry. I wiped my eyes with the sleeping bag.

"We may not find him," Father said. "But we will have the satisfaction of knowing we tried everything to find him. We did our best for Teddy."

My father knew people who had died, people killed in wars and Uncle Joshua who was MIA in Korea. He might know a thing or two about animals disappearing, too. I drifted to sleep and dreams of Teddy as an angel gerbil with little wings on his back, scurrying through a field in what must have been heaven.

Then something was shaking my shoulder. "Seth, Seth." My father could barely maintain his whisper. He was breathless, laughing.

I shot up in the sleeping bag. "What? What?" I said.

Father thrust his cupped palms into my face, opening them just a crack for me to see two beady eyes and a flash of brown fur.

"Teddy?" I cried. "Is it him, Dad?"

"I cornered him at the end of the hall. He squeezed under Holly's door. I saw a movement, and there he was running down the hall," Father said. "I threw this blanket over him like a net."

Teddy's head popped out between my father's fingers. "Teddy," I said. "Dad, you got him. You really got him."

We returned Teddy to his cage, and the miracle of his recovery filled the house for days. Father told the story again and again. Everyone wanted to hear it. Jasper rode his bike over to view the miracle. Henry Apgar stopped by. And I, possessor of the miracle, told everyone how my dad found Teddy, how my dad knew we should look at night, how smart my dad was. At the end of the week, my parents presented me with a second gerbil, to my great astonishment.

"A friend for Teddy," said Mother, who despite the Hanta virus, had gotten caught up in the drama, too.

"And a backup," my father winked.

I named the new gerbil "Carlton," after the Red Sox catcher Carlton Fisk, and later gave him the middle name "Lew," after my father. Theodore and Carlton Lew ran on the wheel in my bedroom for years. Mother never complained a word about them again and even refilled the little glass water bottle hanging in the corner of their cage whenever she noticed it was getting low.

FOURTEEN

··

J enna Avacoli called me again. Her housewarming bag of Dunkin Donuts coffee sat near the coffee pot at the lab, re-minding me every day of what a jerk I'd been not letting Andy come see the microscope.

"Seth, hi, it's Jenna Avacoli," she said, a note of reserve in her voice.

"Jenna, hey, how are you?" I said, shooting to sound friendly and warm.

She blew past the nicety. "I'm just calling to let you know that the automatic transfer of your security deposit into your bank account isn't working. You need to contact your bank. The problem's on their end," she said crisply. "Or we can just mail you a check. Your choice."

"That's strange," I said. "Hey, how have you been?"

"Fine. Would you like a check sent to your new address?"

"A check? Yes, sure."

"We'll cut you one this afternoon. Thanks, Seth. Take care. Bye."

"Jenna, wait," I said. I glanced at the Dunkin Donuts bag. "Would you like to go to dinner?"

She sounded hesitant at first, but she agreed to meet—her idea, not mine—at a bistro I knew in New London. She needed her own car to pick up Andy at her mother's house in Norwich afterwards.

"It's not like I don't want you to meet my mom," she said breathlessly, sitting across from me in a corner booth of the

135

dimly lit bar room. "She's just a handful, and I don't want to give her any ideas about you."

"You don't have to explain," I said. "I understand about mothers."

The corners of Jenna's shiny, rose lips ticked up. "I thought you would," she said. She sipped her martini, her moist lips closing delicately on the glass. She wore a silky-looking, cream blouse tucked into slim jeans that hugged her legs and ankle boots with pointy heels. Ropes of shining, silver beads circled her neck, lying inside her shirt collar, against her bare skin. Her dark hair was pinned up with some strands hanging loose around her face.

"So how is work going?" she said. "Andy is still after me about that microscope. That kid never forgets a thing. He was so excited when he heard I was seeing you tonight."

"He, ah, was?"

"Yes, it's funny how kids are, how they take a shine to some people but not to others. I swear he's got a sixth sense."

Just then the waitress, who reminded me of an older, tougher-looking version of Holly, brought our appetizer, stuffed mushroom caps.

"Smells great," Jenna said.

"My brother worked here as a waiter when he was in college," I said. "That's how I discovered it—a while back now. Travis actually got fired from his waiter job. He was so distracted, his mind going over a yeast fermentation experiment he had worked on the past semester, he kept screwing up dinner orders. My father called the job a 'bad fit.' Travis can only focus on things he cares about. All the rest just sort of washes over him."

"You have a brother?" Jenna perked up.

"And a sister—Travis and Holly."

"And you are?"

"The middle child."

"Of course. I thought so." Her eyes gleamed like a fortune tell-er's divining some long-buried truth. "I can always tell," she said, "even-tempered, easy-going, a peacemaker, a diplomat. Yep. Andy's dad, for instance, is a first-born." Jenna speared a mushroom and popped the whole thing into her mouth. "A Navy guy," she said. "I met him when he was assigned to the sub base in Groton."

"On one of the nuclear subs?"

"Fat chance. More like washing down the latrines. He was just in training back then. We were young...well, younger."

My curiosity got the better of me. "So you don't, ah, see him much now?'

"See him?" Jenna stabbed another mushroom. "We hardly *hear* from him."

"Where is he?"

She waved her fork, chewing. "Who knows? On a submarine beneath the Arctic icebergs maybe. Sometimes he sends us a check; sometimes he doesn't. In the end, I got tired of chasing him down for money. Do you know what I mean?"

"I can see how that would get old fast."

Jenna nodded, eager to be understood. "The craziest part is, his own son doesn't seem to matter to him," she said. "Every Christmas he sends a card with fifty dollars inside. So I go out and buy a couple more presents and tell Andy they're from his father. I mean we were never married or even engaged. We were only together for like six months when we broke up and I found out—oops—I was pregnant, so I can see how he's not so keen on me, but Andy?" She took a swal-low of her water. "Sure, the pregnancy was a mistake. I mean, at the time. But now? How can something you love so much be a mistake?"

Another mistaken pregnancy, only Jenna had gone through with it. "I don't know. There are so many personal variables involved in situations like this," I said. I heard the logical, insect buzz of Travis in my words. "But you're right," I said. "It couldn't be a mistake. It's sort of an ends-justifies-the-means thing."

Jenna furrowed her brow. "Yeah, that's what it is," she says. "I knew you'd get it, Seth."

I didn't know if I really got it or not, but it was nice having her think so. The entrees came—Jenna's chicken parmesan and my baked salmon. Grizzled Holly placed them before us and squinched her face into a smile. "Anything else I can get for you now?" she said.

Jenna shook her head.

"No, I think we're set," I said. After she left, I told Jenna, "She reminds me of an older version—a much older version—of my sister."

"Mmm." Jenna swallowed. "I have two sisters, Cindy and Mary," she said. "Cindy's younger, twenty-nine. She lives in California, in the desert. She's a yoga teacher. Actually she legally changed her name to Vinyasa. That means "flow" in yoga-speak. We call her 'Vinnie.' I miss her."

"It can be tough, living far from family," I said, though actually it never bothered me too much in Atlanta.

"Depends on whose family you're talking about," Jenna said.

"Ha, now you're talking," I said.

"Some families are, you know, better experienced at a distance." I raised my wine glass. "I'll drink to that," I said, and Jenna laughed.

"Take Mary for instance," she said. "Mary is the *good* one, the one who did everything *right*, according to Dorothy—that's my mom.

"You don't call her 'Mom?' "

"Not really. Anyway, Mary lives up in Simsbury. Her husband is an underwriter at Aetna in Hartford. They have the whole deal: big house, two kids, yard, dog. You know what I'm talking about, right?"

"Sounds like Travis, my older brother. He lives in Mystic."

Jenna pointed her fork at me. "I'm telling you, Seth, we have karmic connections just crackling and sizzling all over the place, don't we? You get what I'm talking about." She leaned over the table. "We connect."

I smiled and nodded.

She wagged her fork. "Think about it: difficult moms; dads not, uh, no longer in the picture; sibling rivalries, unlucky in love."

"Wow, what a couple of resumes we have," I said.

Jenna pushed the pasta around on her plate. "I hope you didn't mind the 'dads not in the picture' comment. It wasn't insensitive of me, was it?"

I was touched that she would notice this small thing and attempt to make amends for it. "Not at all," I said. "I understood what you meant." She smiled. Grateful again. "About the moms, though, you're right," I said, steering back into neutral territory. "Mine is what you might call 'difficult.' "

"Oh, please, I could write a book."

"My mother is eccentric. Maybe eccentric isn't the right word. Obsessive is better, and sort of anxious."

"Mmm, I know the type," Jenna said around a mouthful of chicken.

"Her latest fixation is this upcoming deer hunt near Rhode Island."

"The what?"

"The hunt on that state-owned preserve land?" Jenna's face was blank. "The one in the news? It's pretty controversial. My mother has taken on the cause."

"I don't watch much news," Jenna said, "but I wouldn't mind getting rid of some deer. There are way too many of them running around. I hit one last summer, and the thing totaled my front end. Dorothy calls them 'rats with long legs.' They're always digging up her flower beds."

"Well, the point of the hunt is to keep the herd at a self-sustaining level and prevent starvation this winter."

"Makes sense." Jenna sipped her wine. "I'm all for it. I'm on your side." Easy as that, her mind was made up. Then as if she had just read mine, she said, "Some things you don't need to know every last tortured detail about. Some things are obvious on their face."

"I think so," I said.

"You're like that, Seth. You're obvious on your face," Jenna said. She swirled the pale wine in her glass.

"Okay, but I'm just following standard practice here."

"Right, it's 'standard,' because it works."

"That's right."

"Then it's all I need to know. Your mom is grinding an axe over something else. People do it all the time. You know—kicking the dog when you get home because your boss yelled at you. That type of thing. Haven't *you* ever done it?"

Hadn't I? All those times I paused before leaving dirty dishes in the sink, knowing they'd piss off Delia. Part of me wanted to defy her, because I knew it wasn't only the dishes she objected to; it was me, my "quiet" career, my lack of desire to make a bigger splash in the world. Delia objected to me, and I objected to her objection.

In the parking lot after dinner, Jenna kissed me. Standing in front of her car, she stretched up and brushed her feathery lips over mine. "Thanks for dinner," she said, "and for a nice night. It's been a while since I had a date with a normal guy."

"Uh, thanks," I said. "It was a nice time. Get home safe."

"I will." The air stretched taut and charged between us.

"Tell Andy I said hi," I said.

"I will. Good night," Jenna said.

Then I spun around and headed for my car. My breath hung in vapory puffs in the cold, night air. We'd had a nice evening and now it was over. I could focus on getting my head on straight and getting, somehow, up to the North Country.

But in my car, skimming along the dark stretch of highway to Norwich, I relived Jenna's kiss, her upturned face moving toward mine, the way I bent my head to meet her—how could I not?—and then how quickly she was gone.

Nearing the condo, I drove by Sammy's Fish Shack in Groton. I'd worked there in the spring of my senior year of high school, one year after Henry Apgar's death. After school two days a week and on Saturdays, I cleaned and stocked fresh flounder, scallops and mussels at the roadside spot that was huge with locals because Sammy really did sell the "Freshest Fins Found in Town," as his sign proclaimed. An ex-Navy sailor from the sub base in town, Sammy left the service in the seventies but stayed around, first as a fisherman and then opening the Fish Shack after he hurt his back on a boat. A beefy six-foot-two with a head full of graying red hair and a matching beard, Sammy was a gabber, the kind of guy who told his life story to anyone who'd listen.

"Hiring local kids is half of why I opened this business, Hingham," he said to me when I applied for the job. "You screw up, and I know where you live." He chuckled. "No, seriously giving you guys a foot in the door is my pleasure." He always called me "Hingham," never "Seth."

I liked the job. After a while, the reek of fish wasn't so bad, and it seemed a small price to pay for a job where I could be largely alone, scaling and gutting fish in a shed out back, stacking the meat in neat piles, hosing down the floor afterward, throwing fish gut scraps to the gulls circling overhead and filling the display case inside. Plus the fish bodies were interesting to dissect and examine. Biology was my favorite class.

I saved the money I earned, or most it, for college. I had applied to colleges—along with the rest of the senior herd—in autumn, choosing them in a haphazard fashion my parents didn't dare criticize. My therapy sessions had ended, and I had reached a point where I was able to push Henry Apgar from my mind for stretches at a time, half a day sometimes. Jasper was up at Dartmouth. We hardly spoke anymore.

UConn accepted me first, and just to be done with the whole thing, I immediately agreed.

"You won't be far. You can come home any time you want," Mother said. She was still treating me like glass, fearful I was going to have a meltdown every time I frowned.

"And you can't go wrong with UConn. It's a top-notch school," Father said.

I didn't care if I did go wrong—or really if I went at all. As April slid into May, and the world erupted into emerald lawns and hills and flowering shrubs, I started getting nervous. Graduation was around the corner, and I would leave for UConn in August.

Dad came to pick me up at the Fish Shack one Friday night. I was working the late shift alone, closing up the place.

"Hey, Buddy," he called, stepping through the shop front door, the overhead bells jingling.

"Dad, I'm just wrapping up," I said. "Hang on." I punched a few keys and locked the cash register, then grabbed a rag to wipe down the display cases.

"What a night," Father said. "Summer is finally on its way. I thought we'd swing by the house, pick up your mom and Holly and head over to Mystic Pizza? Then maybe a walk by the river?"

In those years, Father was at his professional zenith. His accounting firm had flourished. He was a respected member of the community, a leader in the Chamber of Commerce, a family man and I realize now, a hell of a nice guy.

"Cool," I said. "But I've gotta close up the shed."

Father followed me around back. A soft breeze carried the fragrance of late spring—cut grass and tree branches heavy with buds and the fecund, damp stirring of life blowing in from the sea. "It's nice here, isn't it?" I said. "The Shack is a cool place. Don't you think?"

Father stood, gazing out at the marsh. "It is," he said. "And it's been a fine job for you. Your mother and I are both proud of how well you're doing, Seth. Sammy certainly seems to like you. I ran into him in the post office the other morning. He couldn't say enough good things about the job you're doing."

"He's a good boss," I said, closing the shed door and snapping the padlock in place. "I'm actually thinking of asking him if I can go full-time."

"For the summer?"

"For good. I mean permanently."

Father was quiet for a few seconds. A few of the gulls I often fed landed in the yard and watched us with beady, expectant eyes, cocking their sleek, gray heads to the side.

"You mind if I ask why?" Father said.

One of the gulls stretched its wings luxuriously, craned its neck forward and shook its tail feathers. "Well, I like the job here," I said. "I'm learning new skills." My voice floated into the evening air sounding small and foolish. "It's decent," I said.

"Yes," my father said. "It is decent. But is that all you want?"

It was. One year after the accident, I craved, more than anything, tranquility—no disruptions, nothing to conquer or reach for, just a reassuring flat line of days and nights running into each other. "It's also safe," I said, the words out before I could stop them. I was prone to bouts of blabbering even back then. "If I go up to UConn, anything could happen," I said.

The gulls, apparently tired of waiting, rose into the air and flapped off, dipping low over the marsh, crying in plaintive signals to each other.

"That's true," my father said. "But anything could happen here, too. It already has." He stared into my eyes, his face soft with understanding

"Yeah, it has," I said.

"I have an idea," Father said. "What if you talk to Sammy, but say you want to try UConn for a year. If it doesn't work out, you'd like to come back to your job here?"

Father said the right thing that spring evening. He gave me enough room to maneuver. Sammy agreed to the plan, though I'm sure he knew I wouldn't come back. He looked at me like I had two heads when I told him I wasn't sure about college.

"Why would you want to clean fish for a living when you can get an education?" he said. Then he shook his head. "Jesus, kids today. If my kid goes near a trawler, I'm gonna break his legs."

I turned onto the road leading to downtown Norwich, as my own old words came back to haunt me. *Anything could happen.* Only now, my father wasn't here to put things into perspective. Now it was up to me, and in some ways the prospect of "anything" happening still felt as overwhelming and fraught as it had when I was seventeen. Sammy would have shaken his head over that, too. I could just hear him: "You're a thirty-five-year old man, Hingham. Get a grip!"

FIFTEEN

··

The landscape of my little corner of Connecticut varies dramatically. Headed in the right direction on a daylong hike, you can roam from ecosystem to ecosystem. Hardwood forests turn to towering pine, the ground covered by a silent layer of amber needles which give way to undulating meadows of field grass dotted with bluebird boxes, then to reedy wetlands, nesting platforms for osprey rising like flagpoles from the mire, and finally to the beaches—narrow strips of sand or boulder-strewn coves—washed by the restless murmur of Long Island Sound.

As a child, I roamed these stretches, attuned to the shifting atmospheres—the air rippling through tall grasses, the deep silence of a mature grove of oak, the emerald moss coating the sides and crevices of beach boulders worn smooth by the sea. Above all, I looked for signs of life. What creatures made and defended their homes here? In my mind, they were all noble warriors. I scoured the pines, the open fields, the clumps of sea grass and the damp sand of the coast. I kept a journal, reporting all sightings. The entries were brief: *10/15/85 brown field mouse in hay field in Stonington; 7/12/92 hermit crabs on beach at Bluff Point; wild turkey flock, 1 tom, 7 hens, at edge of woods Ledyard reservoir;* and once thrillingly: *11/4/93 2 gray seals sunning on rocks off Avery Point, must have gotten lost and traveled too far south.* Even as a boy, I felt a kinship with these creatures.

My old journal entries contrasted sharply with the ones Jenna told me she wrote as a girl.

"I found it. I found it. Listen," she said one night. I was lying on my couch in the semi-dark, watching the passing lights of traffic drift in dull beams across the wall. "*Nov. 10, 1988.* I must have been in seventh grade," Jenna said, her voice breathy and amused coming through the phone. "*Mary Wallens wouldn't talk to me in the halls OR IN THE CAFETERIA today. What a little bitch.*" Jenna chuckled. "And this one," she said. "This is golden: *March 3, 1989. Eighth grade sucks. I don't even really need a bra. But everyone else does! Why not me??????* I'm not kidding. There are six question marks. Six. What a drama queen I was."

Jenna began calling me after our "date" once or twice a week "just to talk," she said. She called during the evening hours between dinner and bed, a time that had grown restless and brooding. The gossipy tidbits and stories Jenna shared distracted me, and it was nice to have a human voice in my ear after weeks of nights spent in solitude. Jenna had a bluntness, a way of labeling things for what they were and an eye for humorous detail. She was entertaining as hell.

I told Jenna about Delia—not much, just the little things: how we met, trips we had taken together, restaurants we frequented in Atlanta, and one or two of the long-standing arguments—they seemed stale and pointless now—we'd waged. Jenna listened without comment. She was so quiet sometimes, letting me rattle on, that I would pause, wondering if she were still on the line. Then I'd hear her breathing or she'd clear her throat, and I'd know she heard every word.

"You did have some good times together," Jenna said one night after I recounted in detail a trip Delia and I took to the canyons of Utah. "I mean, it lasted quite a while. I haven't had a decent—what you'd call a 'relationship'—in over three years, not since I broke up with this blackjack dealer from Foxwoods. Cute guy but he turned out to be a major boozehound. I just didn't have the energy to take that on."

"A blackjack dealer? Sounds glamorous."

"It kind of was for a while. And he was a pretty nice guy, sweet to Andy, fun to be around, not totally insane. He had a full-time job with benefits and a livable salary. You'd be surprised how hard that is to find. All the sane, employed men get snapped up young. They get whiplash, the women grab them so fast."

"Well, it was the dealer's loss. No pun intended," I said.

"Ah. I hear he's in AA now and doing fine," Jenna said.

"Well, you're not alone," I said. "My sister has had her dead-end boyfriends, too. Believe me."

"Really? Holly and I should talk some time."

"Maybe," I said. The thought of introducing Jenna to Holly, or Mother or anyone in my family, made my heart race. Meeting the family meant getting serious—or at least the potential to get serious—and I wasn't looking for that. I didn't want anything to complicate my escape to the North Country. Before we hung up though, I agreed to show Andy my office microscope after school on Friday. Jenna said she'd bring him by. It was no problem, she assured me, explaining that Friday was the perfect day, because no matter what happened, you had two whole days to get over it before life kicked in again. "That's why first dates are usually on Friday," Jenna said. "Recovery time."

* * *

Jenna didn't hang around while I showed Andy the microscope. "Would it be all right if I ran a few quick errands?" she said.

I didn't mind. I'd always liked kids around Andy's age, six or seven, when the screaming and crying stage is over. Delia had some nieces and a nephew who were a lot of fun.

In my office Andy looked up at me, brown eyes wide and curious beneath the fringe of his sandy-colored bangs. He wore brown corduroy pants with huge, folded-over cuffs at the bottom and a red sweater with a smiling snowman face stitched in white on the front. Little red lights flashed in the heels of his white sneakers every time he took a step.

"What are we gonna look at?" he said.

"How about a gull feather?" I said, whipping a long, gray one out of my back pocket. I'd walked out to the beach that morning to collect a few specimens for him: the feather, a bit of seaweed, a chip of shell. The animal feces specimens I'd begun collecting were staying in the fridge.

"I've seen feathers," he said, turning in a circle, taking in the room. "This is where you work?"

"Yes."

"Where are the other people?"

"Oh, they're scattered around. We have a bigger office in Hartford where most of them work."

"Somebody got shot there last night. In Hartford. It was on the news. My grandma says Hartford is 'a hell of a cesspool.'"

I laughed. The coarse language leaving his little mouth was fun-ny, even though I knew I shouldn't encourage it. Travis's frowning puss loomed before my eyes. Rosemary and he practically faint-ed when someone slipped and swore in front of the twins. Andy grinned, proud of surprising me.

"She's right," I said, "in some ways. Hartford is a dangerous place, but it has much more to offer. It's the state capitol, you know."

"Uh-huh. Don't you have a bug we can look at?

"As a matter of fact, I do. A ladybug. She was dead when I found her, so no one's killed anything here. We're just going to learn from her."

"Do bugs teach?"

I put my hand on his shoulder and guided him across the room to the lab station. I could feel his delicate, protruding bones. "They can," I said. "If you know how to listen." I lifted him onto the stool before the microscope. His hands, two restless little creatures, went immediately for the knobs. "Don't turn any yet," I said. "Let me get the feather in place." I had prepped a slide with a tuft of the feather's down. I slipped it under the lens.

"That's a feather?" Andy said.

"It's just a tiny piece of a feather. She how small this slide is? We can't fit the entire feather, but you'll be surprised how big this looks under the scope."

He accepted my explanation. I bent over the microscope and adjusted the lens to bring the feather into focus. Perfect—the delicate, fern-like patterns of the feather's edge and a couple of mites walking along it. "Take a look," I said.

His head brushed my arm as he bent over. At his age, I was pretty shy, living in the shadow of Travis and of the adored baby and only girl, Holly. Andy was not shy. He was a bold little guy, not afraid to be left here with me—essentially a stranger—and determined to have a go with this microscope. But when he lifted his large, wondrous eyes to me, he seemed scarcely older than Travis's twins. "What is this *thing*?" he said.

"It's the feather magnified—made bigger—many times. Think of it this way: You're looking at the feather way, way close-up, closer than we can see with our eyes."

He took another look and spoke this time without taking his eyes from the viewer. "There are tiny, squiggly things moving," he said. He lifted his stunned face to me. "Feathers aren't alive," he said.

I laughed. "Those are mites, tiny bugs that live on feathers. They live all over actually."

"Do they hurt you?"

149

"These ones won't," I said. "Take another look at how tiny they are." His head bowed over the scope. I poked him in the side. "How can something that tiny hurt you, chicken?" I said. "Are you worried that they're chicken-mites?"

He flinched and let loose a peal of giggles. "I'm no chicken," he sputtered.

"Maybe, maybe not," I said and poked him again. He shrieked, and there was a knock at the door. Jenna stepped in. She must have plowed through the errands. Andy's face was flushed red. It's always amazed me how kids can get so excited so fast. Their nervous systems go from zero to sixty in a blink.

"Half-chicken, half-mite," I said. "Maybe that's what you are. That's your species: a chicken-mite."

"No!" Andy howled, throwing his head back.

"Is something wrong?" Jenna said from the doorway.

"Not at all," I said. "Andy is just meeting his new mite friends."

"Oh."

"Seth is lying!" he giggled. "He's a mite, a chicken-mite!"

Jenna stared a second. "My goodness, Andy," she said. "I wouldn't have left you here if I'd known you were going to get so rambunctious. What did I tell you about behaving yourself today?"

"A rambunctious mite," I said, and Andy punched my arm.

Jenna looked from him to me. "What is this about mites?" she said.

I took them both to Mystic Pizza afterward and explained Andy's encounter with the mites to Jenna. We sat in a window booth, the sliced-up pie between us, as darkness fell over the street. Andy picked the mushrooms off his slice and piled them on a napkin. "Gross," he said, wrinkling his nose.

"Some people consider them a delicacy—a really special, delicious thing," I said.

"Delicacy," he said, mouthing the new word.

"Yes, they do," Jenna said. "And we all need to try new things, or else what is life about?" She sat up straighter, beaming a smile that was half hope, half disbelief. She gazed around the restaurant, carried away by the moment, daring everyone there to notice us.

* * *

"Chloe had her baby!" It was Holly's voice waking me at seven-twenty on Saturday morning.

"She has a baby?" I said.

"She *had* her baby. She gave birth last night," Holly said.

I opened my eyes. "But isn't it too soon?"

"Eight months. Premature, I guess, but she seems to be okay," Holly said. "The baby's in an incubator at the hospital. She has to stay there a while. It's a girl, Seth."

"A girl," I repeated. "How's Jasper?"

"I dunno. Okay, I guess. Mom filled me in. Aunt Linda told her."

I sat up. "Wow," I said. "Should we send flowers to the hospital or something?"

"Let's see what Mom is doing. I'm coming down there today to have lunch with her. Will you be around? Meet me at the house."

"I, um, I'm not sure I can make it."

"Why not? You got a big date or something?"

"No, I don't have a *big* date. I'm helping out a friend." I had told Jenna the night before that I would stop by the storage units and change her oil. Her car was way overdue, and she'd been complaining about how expensive it was to take it to a garage.

"You're kidding?" Holly said.

"You think I don't have any friends? I'm just changing someone's oil as a favor. Give it a rest."

"A woman's oil?"

"Yes, a woman's oil."

"A woman you recently met's oil?"

"Yes."

"Is she young?"

"Holly, you're as subtle as a B-52."

Holly gave an exaggerated sigh. "Have it your way," she said.

She was my closest sibling and I loved her, but Holly could be a real bulldog. Still, I met them for lunch. I hadn't seen Mother in a couple of weeks, and she'd start squawking if I didn't turn up soon. Andy had a YMCAs swimming class at noon, so I wasn't due at Jenna's until two.

Mother was in high spirits. She had just returned from her book club meeting at the library.

"We're reading Howard Zinn," she said. "*A People's History of the United States*. Fascinating stuff." She wore a gray dress, a silk scarf patterned with swirling vines of flower buds wrapped around her shoulders. We ate in the dining room, which felt unusually empty.

"What's missing?" I said.

"The small buffet table." Mother pointed to the wall it had stood against.

"What happened to it?"

"I've given it to Aunt Linda," mother said. "Paul and she came and took it away. It is an heirloom from your father's side of the family, and I felt Linda deserved it now."

"Linda always loved that buffet," Holly said, reaching for the bowl of chicken salad. "Remember that Thanksgiving when someone dripped candle wax on it, and she spent like half an hour, right in the middle of dinner, scraping it off?"

"The dog bumped the buffet," I said. "That's what spilled the wax."

"What's happening for Thanksgiving this year?" Holly said.

"Travis is hosting," Mother said. "Just the immediate family."

We ate in silence for a minute. The grandfather clock in the living room struck one. Holly's eyes met mine. "When do you need to leave?" she said.

"Yes." Mother turned to me. "What's this I hear about your new girlfriend?"

I coughed on the sandwich I was swallowing. "You've got a big mouth, Holly, you know that?" She widened her eyes in feigned shock. "I do not have a new girlfriend," I said. "I'm simply doing a favor for the woman who runs the storage unit facility where I had my stuff."

"That's nice," Mother said. "And have you seen this person outside the storage unit?"

"Well, yes," I said. "She's become a friend, as I said."

"A young woman friend who's also attractive," Holly said.

I felt suddenly and unexpectedly defensive of Jenna. "Yes, she happens to be attractive," I said. "She runs the units and is going to dental hygienist school and is from Norwich. And she has a young son."

A moment of silence, and then Mother said, "And no husband, I hope?"

"Mom," I said. "Of course not."

"Hah!" Holly said. "Gotcha! Why would it matter if she had a husband, unless you two are dating?"

"Very good, Sherlock, very impressive." I said. I turned to Mother. "Mom, any more news about Chloe and the baby?"

"You know everything I know," she said. "The baby's a preemie, but appears to be doing well. Jasper is beside himself. Called Linda in tears with the news. Tears of joy, that is. It scared Linda to death, though. She thought something had really gone wrong."

Jasper crying over a baby was a difficult image to wrap my mind around.

"We'll all go see the baby once things have settled down up there. Let's give them a chance to catch their breath," Mother said, standing. She collected the plates to carry back into the kitchen. "Besides," she said, "I've got a big weekend coming up myself, as you know." She shot me a sideways glance.

"Uh, let me help you with this, Mom," I said, collecting the salad bowls.

Holly stretched her arms overhead and yawned. "Me, too," she said. And then I've got to run."

"Oh?" I said. "Hot date?"

She grinned. "As a matter of fact, yes."

"Glad to see Bryce is becoming a distant memory."

"Bryce who?"

"Everyone is off and running these days," Mother said. "Hot dates, oil changes. I can't keep up with it." She headed for the kitchen, Holly behind her. When they reached the door, I said, "Jenna. Her name is Jenna." Holly threw me a smile over her shoulder. If Mother heard, she gave no indication.

* * *

When Henry Apgar died, Father insisted that I attend the funeral. Mother was dead-set against it. She wanted to minimize what had happened and get it behind us as quickly as possible. "Or this will change Seth's life," she warned. To which Father simply responded, "It already has." As I stood with my parents, staring at Henry's casket, I felt an odd, soaring sensation, as if I were rising up and floating over the rows of tombstones, over the iron fence surrounding the cemetery, skimming the treetops and heading into the hills. We come and go, I thought, and along the way things simply happen. This notion terrified me at seventeen. At thirty-five, driving to Jenna's that afternoon, the notion now felt so undeniably true—though maybe not quite as terrifying. And I recalled another thing Father said, seeking to reassure

Mother. "We don't always have the luxury of choice, Millicent, but a good reaction goes a long way."

Jenna led me around the back of the storage facility office to the parking space where she kept her car, an aging, red Toyota compact with rust-splattered fenders.

"It's nothing to look at, but these things run forever," she said, patting the hood. Standing in the sunlight, barefaced with her hair pulled back in a ponytail, she looked younger and more vulnerable. A wooden staircase climbed the back of the building to the second floor apartment she shared with Andy. Lacy curtains hung in a window. "Your place?" I said.

"Yes, but we don't plan on being here long, just until I finish school and get a job as a hygienist. Then we'll really get set up. This is a short-term thing, you know," she said.

"Sure," I said. "I've had plenty of short-term things myself." I never felt like I had to put on a show for Jenna, to make myself out as somehow better or smarter or richer or whatever. Jenna was too real for any of that.

"I'll make some coffee, okay? Come up when you're done?" she said.

"Give me twenty minutes," I said.

"Seth?"

"Yes?"

"Thank you."

"It's not a big deal," I said. "Twenty less minutes lying on my couch is all it cost."

Andy wanted to watch. He shadowed me, a little ghost in a UConn windbreaker. When I got on the ground and slid a pan beneath the body to catch the spent oil, he squatted beside me, observing like a studious, round-eyed owl.

"See how easy it is?" I said.

"My mom bought good muffins because you were coming over—the good ones that cost more money from the bakery in town, not the Stop & Shop cheap ones. Grandma said she's throwing money out the window," he said.

"Oh, that's nice," I said. "Is your, ah, grandma here?"

"No, she has her own house. I stay with her in the mornings sometimes when my mom runs errands. Like today."

"That's lucky for you and your mom."

"Yeah, there's a birdhouse at my grandma's house that I built. It's stuck up on a tree in the backyard. Last year a bird went in and had eggs there."

"I built bird houses, too, when I was a boy," I said.

"Maybe I can show you mine some time?" Andy said. "Unless you 'fly the coop.' That's what Grandma says you're gonna do."

The old lady sounded like a barrel of laughs. When I finished with the oil, Andy took my hand and led me up the wooden staircase.

Inside, the apartment wasn't bad at all. Small, yes, but tidy and bright and homey. I walked into the kitchen, but Jenna didn't offer to show me the rest. I caught a glimpse of a beige sofa in the adjoining living room, a crocheted, afghan-looking blanked tossed over the back. "There are a couple of bedrooms," Jenna said with a wave of her hand. "Nothing special, but it works for now."

The kitchen table stood beneath a window decorated with hanging stained glass birds—a watery, red cardinal, a cerulean bluebird, a sunny goldfinch perched on a twig. Sunshine blazed through them, warming the table in muted rainbow hues. Green houseplants crowded a shelf along one wall, vines dripping over. The plate of "expensive" muffins sat in the center of the table. An empty box from D'onofrio's Bakery in Norwich sat on the counter. D'onofrio's was the only place Grandma Hingham would buy Thanksgiving and Christmas pies. "The Italians know pastry," she used to say.

Jenna made the coffee too weak. But I drank it and made a big show of eating one of the expensive muffins. "D'onofrio's, my favorite," I said.

"Mine, too," Jenna said, sitting across from me. Andy milled around the kitchen a few minutes, then drifted into the living room. A few minutes later the unmistakable dings and beeps of a video game started up.

Jenna rolled her eyes. "He loves those things," she said. "My mother says he'll go cross-eyed staring at the screen, but what does she know? She's never played a video game in her life."

"And even if she had, it's highly unlikely that she, or anyone, would go cross-eyed from them."

Jenna smiled. "I love the way you talk. Highly unlikely," she said.

"It is highly unlikely."

"I know. I just like the way you put it."

I wasn't sure how to answer that. Jenna jumped up and grabbed a snapshot photo off the fridge. "My sisters and me," she said, handing it to me. "In high school."

Three girls stood side-by-side in the photo, arms draped over each other's shoulders. They were all dark-haired, like Jenna, grinning for the camera in front of a white brick fireplace. Jenna stood in the middle, and while her sisters smiled with adolescent swagger, her expression was different, thinner and more tentative. Something in the set of her lips suggested wariness. Not that I was anyone to comment. In all the pictures taken of me near the end of high school, after Henry's death, I look like I've just been shot out of a canon. In my graduation shot, I have a particularly dumbfounded look, tassel dangling from my mortarboard.

A flinty glint in Jenna's teenage eye, though, hinted at a fierce something beneath the surface. I tranquilized a mother black bear in the Georgia Smokies once, shot her with a dart gun, while her two tiny cubs clung to her legs. I was with two other researchers. We just wanted to put a radio collar on the bear. The tranquilizer was mild and would wear off quickly. The look in Jenna's teenage eyes reminded me of the one in that bear's eyes before I shot. *Do your best, it seemed to say, and I will match you every step of the way. I will fight to the finish.*

Before leaving that afternoon, I told Jenna I would call her. As the words left my mouth, I felt the situation slipping beyond my grasp. I wanted to call her, and I didn't want to call her. I enjoyed her company; maybe I was afraid to enjoy it too much. Getting involved with a woman is like being carried down river on a powerful current. At first, you lay back and enjoy the ride. But before you know it, you're swimming as hard as you can, and you can't reach the shore. You can't break free. And then when you finally do break free, you wash up on a distant beach where you recognize nothing, confused and bruised and struggling to breathe again.

SIXTEEN

···

The morning of the coastal preserve deer hunt sounded the first undeniable note that winter was coming. The golden tones of autumn had given way to the stark earthiness—the grays and browns and eventually the snowy white—that paint Connecticut's winter landscape. I had avoided my mother all week because she was in full-fever mode. It glowed in her like a great avenging moment on the horizon, at long last her chance to set things right.

"It is state land," she kept saying, "our land, PUBLIC property. I feel I have a duty to speak up."

Well okay, but maybe I had the right to dodge the whole thing? Mother had tried to recruit Travis and Holly to go with her to the preserve, but they begged off. True to her word, she had left me alone. The morning of the hunt I had planned to meet an old UConn classmate, Jim Hawley, for a hike on Bear Mountain, clear across the state, on the New York line. I'd also half-promised to take Jenna and Andy for ice cream that night. By Monday morning the hunt would be over, and I'd be back at my desk, no worse for the experience.

Then Scanlon called. I was making coffee, vaguely listening to the CNN morning show when my cell buzzed. "Hello?" I poured a mug of cold water into the coffee maker.

"Seth? George Scanlon."

"George, hey," I said, surprised to hear his voice on my phone on a Saturday morning. The number on my caller ID must have been Scanlon's home line. I didn't recognize it.

"I'm sorry to call you at home like this..."

"No problem," I said. "I'm not, ah, in the middle of anything."

"Good. Listen, I know this is short notice, but I've run into a situation, and I'd like to ask your help."

I put my mug down on the counter. "Of course," I said. Scanlon was such a reasonable guy and such a fair boss. I couldn't turn him down. I was also feeling a little guilty. The night before I'd stumbled across a research position posting at the University of Southern Maine. It wasn't the perfect fit for me, too heavily skewed toward marine work, but I thought I'd have a shot at it. I'd at least probably get an interview.

"Well, the problem is I need your help today, Seth," Scanlon said.

"Today?" My stomach sunk.

"Yes. I was planning to swing by the coastal preserve hunt this morning just to, you know, get a sense of things, but a personal issue has come up." He hesitated. "I've got to coach my son's pee-wee football game. The other coach came down with food poisoning last night, and no one else is available. We'd have to cancel the game otherwise, and it's a play-off game. Ah, listen I'm sorry. You know how it is with kids. Always some emergency popping up."

"Sure, George," I said.

"I'm asking you because you live so near. If you're not busy, could you just stop by and hang out for maybe an hour or two, tops. No more. Just get a sense of the mood. You never know with these things—and some of the radical animal rights groups out there," Scanlon said. "I don't expect any trouble. But it would just be good to have one of our people on the ground, sort of as a witness. Incognito of course."

"A witness? Yes, of course."

"I'll really owe you one, Seth."

"George, don't mention it. My morning is open."

"Okay. Can't thank you enough. And I pick up lunch next time I'm down there."

"I'll hold you to it, George."

The coffee maker was hissing and spitting. I walked over to the tall, narrow window that overlooked the river. Jenna's candle gift sat in the sill. I'd moved it from the coffee table where it got in the way of my take-out boxes. The river was placid. A line of cars moved slowly along the street lining the opposite bank—Saturday morning errands probably, grocery shopping and dry cleaners, parents taking their kids to soccer or karate. Delia used to attend a Saturday morning yoga class, and Jenna took Andy swimming at the YMCA two Saturdays a month. My errand would be a run by the coastal preserve. If the crowd was big enough, Mother might not see me. She'd be lost in the passion of the moment. She'd probably be the loudest voice shouting.

* * *

The parking lot was already a circus when I got there. Every space was taken, packed with cars and SUVs and, disturbingly enough, a few television news vans with satellite dishes stuck on their roofs. Scanlon could watch the highlights himself that night. A couple of state trooper cruisers sat parked at the edge of the lot, near a grassy area with picnic benches and the entrance to a trailhead network that wound into the forest and then out along the coast. A crowd milled about, standing three and four people deep, a wall of ski jackets and fleece. I couldn't see past them. I squeezed my car onto the sandy shoulder of the driveway, not a legal space, but hopefully I wouldn't be there long enough for it to matter.

An SUV immediately pulled in behind me. A woman sat perched behind the wheel. The troopers were sure to nab one of us. I saw one—a mountain of a guy, dark blue uniform and the hat with the little strap across the back of his head—glance our way.

"Do you have any tape I could borrow?" the SUV woman asked me as I stepped out of the Civic and she rolled down her window.

"Pardon me?"

She was maybe fifty, breathless and jittery, a little sparrow of a woman with graying blonde hair. "Tape," she said, "Scotch tape, or masking tape would be even better. It's for my costume."

"Your costume?"

"Yes, I have to change in my car." She sighed. "I'm running so late this morning. My husband took my car, and I had to hunt around for his spare set of keys. I hate driving this tank—so horrible for the planet. I feel so guilty. Every time I stop at a light, I'm terrified someone will recognize me."

"Um, no, I'm sorry. I don't have any tape."

She shrugged. "That's okay. I'll make do. The important thing is we're all here." Her voice was one of a woman accustomed to smoothing over rough edges and making people feel good. I suddenly wished I had some tape for her. She gave me a smile and disappeared back into the SUV, presumably to don her costume.

I made my way toward the edge of the crowd. Overhead the sky loomed a moody medley of gray and blue with sketchy, trailing white clouds. It would have been a nice day to hike in the preserve, to head out to one of the big, smooth boulders in the surf and watch the sea peak and lap all around. Instead I threaded my way through the rows of spectators, some of whom were jeering and cheering at whatever was going on up front. A chanting cut through the din: "WE'RE HERE FOR THE DEER!" Ripples of laughter skittered across the crowd.

"Hey, Rudolph," yelled a beefy, ruddy-faced guy in a baseball cap. "Hey, Bambi, watch out or they'll take a shot at you." He slapped the back of the guy standing next to him, who was dressed defiantly in green hunting fatigues. A few yards away a trio of what looked like college girls shouted in chorus: "D.E.P., NOT FOR ME!" Red peace symbols decorated their cheeks—painted or pasted, I couldn't tell. One wore a white sweatshirt with "Resist Oppression—All Forms, All the Time" printed across the front in bold, black letters. Every cause du jour appeared to be present. I'd noticed this sort of thing before. Delia once covered a rally at the Georgia state capitol when hundreds of people showed up to protest proposed education budget cuts. One guy carried a Tibetan flag.

Bob Dylan's croaky voice sang out over the crowd at the coastal preserve. The Palestinian flag flapped above the middle of the crowd next to the P.E.T.A. flag. A few "U.S. Out of Iraq" posters bobbed high.

"I didn't realize the deer had migrated here from Gaza," a woman behind me snickered to her friend.

"Or that the deer were against the Iraq war," her friend shot back.

The protesters—and their mockers—were restricted to an area at the preserve entrance. They were not allowed to enter the woods, where I knew a few DEP agents were already at work. I edged my way to the front of the crowd. Then I reached it. At first I thought the protestors must have been on break, and the spectacle before me was entertainment, some sort of half-time show. About a dozen people were marching in a circle, all dressed in full-body deer outfits—brown and furry with antlers, little white tails and black hoof-gloves. The mouths in their creepily human faces gaped in shouts, hooves raised overhead in blocky power salutes. They looked like a crazed herd of upright, mutant white tails. And then it dawned on me: They were the protestors. Was Mother among them? The costumes might have even been her idea. She'd always had a flair for the visually dramatic. The spectacle was more ridiculous, more *silly*, that anything I could have imagined. Fight public policy with Halloween costumes. The wind kicked up, tickling like cold little fingers at the back of my neck.

"Wouldn't it be karmic if it rained and they all got drenched?" a man standing next to me said. He was older, maybe sixty, clipped hair shot through with gray, a leathery, beach face and wire rim eyeglasses perched on a nose so boney I could see the faint glow of the white cartilage beneath his skin.

"Karmic?" I said.

"Yes, karmic." He pursed his thin lips. "They try to dictate to nature, and nature in turn pisses all over them. Kind of fitting, isn't it?" He peered at me over his glasses. "Oh, don't tell me you're one of them?" he said. His face puckered like he'd just bit a lemon.

"One of them? No, I'm not," I said, and then for reasons I didn't understand, I added, "but my mother is."

And there she was: Bigger than life, antlers perched atop her head and one angry fist-hoof raised high. Her mouth was wide open, her voice cutting shrill and bold above the rest of the herd: "HELL, NO! THE DEER WON'T GO!"

"That's her," I said.

Boney nose stared. "Is she afraid the deer will be shipped off to Vietnam?"

I laughed. "It's entirely possible," I said. Then I stepped backwards into the crowd. I ducked behind a couple of teenagers dressed in camouflage. I couldn't risk Mother spotting me. She was marching with a bit of bounce in her step, throwing her head back to call out: "ONE, TWO THREE, FOUR, WE DON'T WANT YOUR BLOODY GORE! FIVE, SIX, SEVEN, EIGHT, LET THE DEER PROLIFERATE!"

Mother broke rank and trotted to the edge of the clearing, where a pile of signs and banners lay on the ground. She hoisted one up to her shoulder and returned to the circle. "HUNTING= MURDER"the sign proclaimed. How would Travis pick that statement apart? He'd slide his glasses up the bridge of his nose and dissect, pointing out the flawed logic, the leaps in reason. But

Travis's logic only carried him so far. And Holly tended to gloss over the details. My father alone had gotten it right. He had embraced the good in Mother and somehow risen above the rest.

Mother broke marching rank again, only this time she stepped to the front and brought a bullhorn to her mouth. The brown fur of her deer head framed her pale face. Red splotches of agitation burned on her cheeks. She was going to make a speech. Sweet Jesus.

"I stand before you today on behalf of those who cannot stand here for themselves," she called.

"Nobody invited the deer?" a loud-mouthed guy somewhere behind me called back. Guffaws and giggles ripped all around.

"...for those who cannot speak for themselves," Mother repeated, her voice growing rich and resonant with conviction like a righteous pastor preaching from the pulpit.

"Hey, you're a deer, Lady, and you can speak, right?" Snort-snort, chuckle-chuckle. Loudmouth weighing in again. "Am I right?"

"Why don't you shut up and let her speak," a woman to my right said. I didn't dare turn my head.

"This is about more than deer," Mother said. "It's about a way of life, a whole way of life that's disappearing." The herd circled solemnly behind her.

"Yeah, whose life?" Loudmouth called.

Someone else groaned.

A conversation behind me: "How's shooting one of these tick-infested things going to end a way of life? They're giant vermin is what they are."

"You're asking me? I say let's do away with all of them."

"Hey, pipe down, please!"

The state troopers had moved in closer, tightening their ring around the crowd. Did they actually think this could turn violent? The local Fox News team had moved in closer, too. I saw one of the reporters who was on the evening news every night, the brunette with the shiny hair—Delia would have called her a "talking head tramp"—stretching up on her toes to get a better view.

"Oh, I've heard all the arguments," Mother called, raising one hoof like she was calling forth the multitudes. "My own son works for the DEP, my youngest son. I've heard the party line, the rationalizations for murder."

If she spotted me now, I was dead. I hunched down a little—ridiculous but I suddenly had visions of a mother versus son debate on TV—DEER HUNT TEARS FAMILY APART. I knew enough about TV news from Delia to know this would play big.

"So it's starve, don't shoot then? Starvation is the preferred means of death?" I glanced to my right. At the edge of the crowd, a man with a bullhorn challenged Mother. He rose head and shoulders above the crowd. He must have standing on something. He was a slight guy wearing a navy windbreaker.

Mother stared at him. "It's staying true to nature's way," she said, voice rising with conviction.

"Oh, *nature*. You want to get into that. Right, I see." The man snorted. "You liberals and nature. You cherry-pick the parts that suit your arguments and ignore the rest. I've got some news for you, deer-lady, nature makes mistakes all the time. Nature screws up almost as much as we do." He shook his head. "You praise all things natural," the man said. "Nature equals good. So I guess small pox is good then, huh? And cancer? And tsunamis and earthquakes and mudslides? And babies born with two heads?"

Mother's mouth dropped open. "You're not hearing me," she yelled, really yelled this time. The herd stopped marching behind her, puzzled in their hoof tracks.

"No, lady," the man called. "The problem is you can't hear yourself."

Mother hesitated. I could feel her mind racing. She glanced at the ground and then up into the sky. Seeking what? Clarity? Inspiration?

"We're here for the deer," she repeated into the bullhorn. "Plain and simple: for the deer."

The man waved a dismissive hand at her. She took this as a cue to return to the herd. "HEY, HEY, HO, HO. THE GUNS HAVE GOT TO GO!" she cried.

"Raving lunatics," the man said. "You're the one who's got to go, Lady."

That was enough. She may have looked crazy, but she was my mother. "Hey, why don't you take your own advice?" I called to the man. "Get out of here, if you don't like what you see." Then he flipped me the finger. He actually raised his middle finger at me, this middle-aged man at a public gathering. "Eloquent sentiment," I called back to him, but he was already turning away.

I made my way through the crowd. At the edge of the clearing where the protesters marched, I called, "Mom."

She hurried over. "Seth, is that you? What are you doing here?"

"Don't ask," I said. "Duty called. Listen, Mom, why don't you take a little breather?"

The crowd seemed to have lost interest, at least temporarily. Maybe the novelty had worn off. A fresh cluster of heavy gray clouds hung overhead. One of the news vans was pulling out of the parking lot.

"A break?" one of the other marching deer called to Mother. Up close, I recognized her, the lady from the parking lot, the one who asked me for tape. She must have found some.

"Fifteen minutes," Mother called, waving a hoof. She reached up and removed her deer head. Her hair was damp with sweat, her face flushed.

"Thanks for taking that off," I said.

She bit her lip. "The costumes weren't my idea," she said. "You think they're silly?"

I shook my head. "I'm not here to criticize, Mom."

"I know. I know." She exhaled. "Can we sit? This thing must weigh forty pounds." She moved toward the sidelines where the protesters had set up a little camp of lawn chairs and coolers. We sat side by side in two chairs, as the rest of the herd milled around, pulling off their heads and guzzling bottled water.

"You think we'll make it onto the news tonight?" Mother asked, pointing her water bottle at another departing news van.

I shrugged. "Maybe, if it's a slow day."

"Who cares?" Mother said. "Vultures. News business, my foot. It's nothing but sensation and scandal these days. I never told you, but I always disliked the fact that Delia was caught up in that business."

I smiled. "At least we're rid of that connection."

"I held my tongue," Mother said. "Believe it or not, I am sometimes capable of that. Just not today, right? I'm glad you're here, Seth, and coming to my side after that beast of a man attacked us."

"He's just a jerk, Mom."

"You know, every protester here is only here because they care. Their hearts are in the right place," Mother said. "Doesn't that count for something?"

I gazed over the crowd. My heart had been in the right place numerous times in my life, but that had certainly never guaranteed a happy outcome. "I don't know, Mom," I said. "It matters to us, and that's what's important, right? That's what I tell myself."

She patted my knee. "Intent makes all the difference," she said.

"I sure hope so."

"It's the only part we can control, right? Why we do what we do."

"Now you sound like Dad," I said. She did, too. That was the sort of observation he would make.

Mother smiled. "Almost forty years of marriage has to leave its mark. And you father was usually right about these things, or at least interesting to listen to."

"He was," I said. "He really was. Hey, you look kind of tired. Why not head home now? I'll help get your stuff into the car."

Mother shook her head. "No, I've committed myself here today, and I've got to see it through."

"Mom?" I hesitated a second. "Has it struck you as ironic that you're fighting for deer? The same animal that caused the accident for Jasper and me back in high school? And killed Henry Apgar?"

Mother grew still. She blinked. "You can hardly blame all the deer for that, Seth."

"I'm not blaming deer," I said. "But I can see the wisdom in having a few less of them around. Overpopulation is not a good thing."

"Your accident—that never occurred to me," Mother said. "I didn't realize this issue calls up all *that* for you, Seth. My God, if I'd known..."

"It's okay, Mom. It's not a big deal."

"I never connected the two."

"There's nothing to connect," I said.

"Nothing to connect? But of course there is. That was another of your father's great strengths, wasn't it? He used to tell me, 'Mil, you don't connect the dots. You think one thing ends and another begins, with nice clean breaks in between. It doesn't work that way.' It's a continuous stream, he used to say, one thing running into the next. Nothing is ever clean."

I looked away. Mother reached out and stroked the back of my head. "So much for the deer," she said. "My heart was in the right place, but it looks like maybe I need to find another place to park it? You know, after living a life where you know who you are and what you're supposed to do, how do you find something new?"

"Ha. If you figure that one out, Mom, please let me know," I said.

Mother stood. She pulled the clunky deer hood back over her head, and then her face was framed by brown fur. "I will. And I'll see you later, dear," she said.

"Mom, go slow," I said. "It's too hot in that thing."

She waved a good-bye hoof and turned to rejoin the herd.

It was easy enough to leave, melting back through the thinning crowd, out to the parking lot and into the Civic. There was nothing to report to Scanlon. I had to cancel my Bear Mountain hike, of course, so there was plenty of time to head home and apply online to the University of Southern Maine job. But marine ecology really wasn't my strong suit. What was the point of another temporary fix? I needed to settle into the right thing with the right fit this time, and Maine wouldn't be my last chance.

At the ice cream shop that night, I told Jenna about the protest, while Andy licked meticulously away at a double-scoop, chocolate-coconut cone. I spared no detail: the costumes; the jeers; the TV vans and Mother smack in the middle of it all. I didn't relay all the details of my private conversation with Mother. That would have felt like a betrayal somehow, but for the first time, I saw that Mother and I were sort of in the same boat, both of us fumbling around, trying to recover. When I looked at it that way, it didn't seem so bad. The things we did, the things we bumped into, didn't seem so unforgivable. Maybe that was how Father had handled Mother—he understood where *she* was coming from, not just her impact on him. Maybe that was what made him so good at handling all of us.

"My mother is, you know, still grieving. She's, ah, finding her way, you know," I said. "I mean, maybe we all are."

"Of course you are," Jenna said. She licked her fat-free yogurt cone. "I just wish my mother had as good an excuse when she starts one of her bullshit campaigns—which she does frequently. Andy, you didn't hear that, okay?"

She turned to me and silently mouthed "bullshit" again. "I try not to slip up in front of him, you know," she said.

"I'll watch it, too," I said, feeling a rush of gratitude. I could say almost anything to Jenna, confess the most troubling details or doubts, and she would just sort of nod her head and accept it all. She accepted me.

Andy looked up from his cone and gave us a grin. A chocolate smudge dotted his chin. "Bullshit," he said, and I laughed despite myself.

SEVENTEEN

··

J asper and Chloe named their tiny daughter Elizabeth. By the time she was a few weeks old, everyone was calling her "Bet." I concocted excuses when Holly and Mother made the first pilgrimage to Jasper's house in Colchester to meet Bet. I had a cold that I didn't want Bet to catch. I had to make an emergency run-off sample collection on the coast. "What, the animals won't be crapping next week?" Holly said.

Why did I avoid Bet? I think it had something to do with Jasper and the way he had forged ahead in life. He had a career that was on track, a wife he loved, a home and now a child, while I was scraping raccoon turds off the forest floor and eating take-out Chinese alone in front of the TV most nights. Not exactly where I had hoped to be at this point.

When I finally leaned over the crib in the nursery Jasper had painted pastel pink and green, like a giant Easter basket, Bet turned her wondrous eyes to me.

"She's filling out," Chloe said. "Preemies have some catching up to do. But look—look at her now." She reached to brush a finger over the baby's cheek. A trail of short, dark hair ran over the center of Bet's skull like a rooster's comb, or a baby mohawk. I touched it, the downy fuzz of all new hatchlings.

"She reminds me of a bird," I said. "A baby robin."

Chloe cocked her head to side. "She does?" she said.

"Yes, kind of puckered and wrinkly with a little fuzz on top of a big head and large, orbital eyes?"

Chloe cleared her throat.

"They're cute," I said.

"You have an interesting way of seeing things, Seth," Chloe said.

I hadn't meant to insult Bet. It was just an observation. That was the sort of defense Travis would launch. *Just an observation; sorry your feelings got in the way.* Chloe said she had to feed Bet then. I knew she meant breast-feed.

"I'll go see what Jasper's up to," I said and beat it back downstairs.

Jasper wasn't up to much. I found him in the kitchen, sitting on a stool at the L-shaped counter, drinking coffee. They had one of those fancy, speckled granite countertops the new houses have. Mother would have smirked.

I pulled up a stool. "Anybody ever tell you not to drink alone?" I said.

Jasper grunted. He needed a shave, and his eyes were a little bloodshot. "That person didn't have a new baby in the new house," he said.

"Yeah, how do you know, big guy?"

He looked at me, a deadpan poker face. "Because when you have one of these, crying night and day, waking you up, needing food or to be changed or to be held or God only knows what, you need all the coffee you can get."

I thought he was joking, so I laughed. But Jasper raised an eyebrow at me and rubbed his bad knee. "Never mind," he said. "You won't know until you get here."

I clapped him on the shoulder. "*If* I ever get here." I went over to the coffee pot and filled a mug for myself. "Well, you won't drink alone in my presence, old man," I said, slipping back on to the stool. "Why's it so dark in here?"

"Dimmer switch." Jasper pointed to the wall. "I installed it last week. Soothing, you know? Low lighting. We've been making all these little soothing tweaks in the house."

"Really?"

"Yeah, anything that might help. Chloe's put these scented candles—aromatherapy—all over the house."

I sipped my coffee.

"I've got these new vitamins, too, Stresstabs. That's what they're called. For stress. And believe me, *this* is stress. Stress like I've never known."

"I'm sure it's normal, Jasp," I said. "New parents, I mean you always hear about how fried they are."

He looked at me. "But that's not the worst of it. The crying is the worst part. I hear it in my dreams. I'm not kidding. It's nerve-wracking. It's like she's either crying, getting over a crying jag or gearing up to cry again."

"That's, uh, rough."

"But, you know, Chloe doesn't seem to mind," Jasper said. "She takes it in stride. Sometimes Bet will cry on and on, and you have no idea what's wrong or how to help her. She's not hungry or wet or cold or tired, but she's screaming her head off anyway."

"You just have to remind yourself that this is normal," I said, as if I had a clue what the hell I was talking about. "Babies cry; parents get through it, and you will, too. You just need to relax. You're a little, ah, overboard."

"You think so?"

"Yeah, just a little."

Actually I'd never seen Jasper so unglued. Not even after the accident, in the hospital when his knee was crushed and we told him Henry had died. He was lying in the hospital bed, and he sort of grunted and turned his head to me. We stared at each other for I don't know how long. I was sitting on the empty bed next to his. Out in the hall, my father was talking to the police. Mother was down in the cafeteria, crying with Henry's mother. When they came up to the room, Henry's mother stared at me, and the air left my lungs. She knew Jasper was the driver. But did she know that I was the one who had invited Henry along for the ride?

In the bleary years following Henry Apgar's death, Jasper and I had followed an unspoken code: avoid each other whenever possible. Of course Henry's ghost followed me anyway, but in the end it might have been my fault that Jasper and I drifted so far apart. I pushed too hard. A couple of months after the crash, I was in therapy twice a week with Dr. Haram, this kindly, bald Egyptian guy with moles on his scalp, who had a small office in Mystic. We talked, it seemed endlessly, about "grief" and "process" and "trauma." A big mole above his left ear was shaped like a little beehive with several, smaller mole "bees" buzzing around it.

"You could ask heem to talk, Seth. I think it could be benefeeshul for both of you," Dr. Haram said.

I shifted in the "patient" armchair. Dr. Haram's office resembled an intimate study—or reading room. It reminded me of Grandpa Hingham's old study down in Essex. Only Grandpa didn't have copies of "Conquering Depression" and "The Talking Cure" on his bookshelves. Dr. Haram had his work cut out for him with me. At seventeen, I was a man of few words.

"I don't think so,' I said.

"And why not?" Dr. Haram's enormous black eyes, magnified by thick glasses, blinked at me.

"Jasper's not a talker."

"Not a talker? Ah." Dr. Haram templed his fingers beneath his chin and stared at me.

"Anyway, the one *you* should really be talking to is my brother, Travis. He's totally nuts," I said.

Dr. Haram cleared his throat. "But Travis was not in the accident, yes? That is what we are here to discuss, yes?"

"If you say so."

"And what do *you* say?" Again, the big eyes.

I shrugged. Jiggled my knee. Glanced at my watch. The eyes kept staring until I couldn't take it anymore. "I say talking to Jasper about this would be sheer torture."

"Torture? Ah."

"Difficult. I mean, aren't things bad enough without me dredging all this up again?"

"It is painful to talk about, yes?"

"Are you kidding me? Yeah, painful. You could call it painful."

"Sometimes, Seth, where the pain is, the cure is also. We need to leesen to the pain."

Well, I was done listening. I wasn't really sure what Dr. Haram meant, but I pushed Jasper to talk anyway. The cast came off his leg a week later, and I went over to his house to visit.

Aunt Linda had ensconced Jasper in his own personal recovery suite. His bedroom upstairs had been outfitted with every amenity, all within arm's reach. A mini-refrigerator, stocked with cold drinks and snacks, sat next to the bed. A new television sat at the foot of the bed, remote control on the nightstand. His favorite magazines—Sports Illustrated (the swimsuit issue), Rolling Stone and Newsweek—Jasper was a budding policy wonk, even then—covered the opposite nightstand. Aunt Linda had even strung a waist-high system of ropes from the bedpost to the doorknob, then down the hall to the bathroom doorknob, so Jasper could hold onto something on his way to the toilet.

"What a wussy you've become," I said. "Your mom been wiping your butt for you, too?"

Jasper flipped me the finger. He was propped up on pillows, wearing a "Ledyard High" t-shirt and blue gym shorts. The leg with the mangled knee rested on a pillow. The knee still had an Ace bandage wrapped around it.

"Nice," I said, pointing to it.

"For support," Jasper grunted. "My physical therapy starts next week. This knee still hurts like hell. I don't know how I'm supposed to start moving it around."

A pair of crutches leaned against the wall near the door. They would eventually be replaced by a cane and then a series of canes as Jasper grew older. Unlike me, Jasper would always have a physical reminder of what had happened. Maybe if I'd known that then, I wouldn't have opened my big mouth.

"You back at school?" Jasper said, his eyes locked on the Red Sox game, minus the sound, flickering on the TV screen.

I sat in his desk chair. "Yeah," I said. "But it's been, you know, kinda weird."

Jasper turned to me. "Yeah? How so?"

"Well, you know, after what happened...and people knowing and everyone looking at me in the hall."

"That sucks."

"Big-time." I rolled the desk chair closer to the bed. "Hey, Jasp, do you think anyone, um, blames us?"

His eyes never left the TV screen. "For what?"

I almost laughed, and not because it was funny. "You know," I said.

Jasper shook his head. "No, I don't. What?"

He didn't *know*? I was staring at Dr. Haram's beehive moles two afternoons a week, discussing nothing but this shit, and Jasper didn't know what I was talking about?

"What? Come on, Jasper. HENRY. You know, Henry, the kid who died."

"Yeah, of course I know. I mean, it's too bad and everything, but there's nothing I can do about it," he said. At eighteen, flat on his back with a wrecked knee and the horror of the crash still fresh, this was all Jasper could muster. He was shell-shocked, too, something I couldn't fully appreciate at the time.

"I'm not asking you to do anything. It's just a question," I said. My voice must have gotten louder, because all of a sudden Jasper raised his.

"What's eating at *you*, Seth?" he said.

"Eating at me? What the..."

"Yeah, you come in here with your morbid bullshit and..."

"*My* morbid bullshit?"

"...and I'm trying to have a relaxing day. I'm trying to RECOVER, and..."

"Fine. Look, whatever, okay? Fuck it."

"I just need to rest. Can't you let me do that?" Jasper threw himself back on the pillows. "Do they blame us? Hell, if I hadn't listened to you that day at the lockers, we wouldn't be in this mess. You ever think that?"

It felt like someone had rammed a club into my chest, really into it, piercing it, crushing the tender things inside. I gripped the chair's armrests. Heat crept up the back of my neck. I couldn't speak for a few seconds, and then it hit me. Jasper wanted to pin this on me. The whole thing. Like I did it alone. *Like he wasn't the one driving.*

So I defended myself with typical, seventeen-year-old finesse. "Hey, dickhead, up yours," I said.

Jasper flipped me the bird again. Then he cranked the volume up on the Sox game. He stared at the screen.

"Jasper," I said.

The asshole cranked it up louder.

"You can't blame this all on me," I said.

The TV got louder.

"Hey?"

Jasper cleared his throat, his eyes never leaving the TV screen.

179

And then I lost it. I jumped up from the chair. A small card table was set up near the foot of Jasper's bed. His pain medication and water and some napkins were on it. I grabbed the table and hurled the whole thing across the room. It was lighter than I'd expected. Jasper made some kind of half-shout, just as the table crashed off the wall."

"What the hell?" I shouted. "I'm trying to talk you, and all you can do is act like…"

Aunt Linda rushed into the room.

"Seth, Jasp…What? What is it?" She was breathless. She must have run up the stairs. "What happened?"

Jasper and I were silent. Then he said, "Seth's gone psycho."

"WHAT HAPPENED?" Linda demanded.

We wouldn't answer her.

"Seth, I think it's time for you to go home," she said.

"Aunt Linda, I'm sorry. I…"

"Just go home."

I lunged for the door, not giving Jasper a second look. I flew down the stairs, through the entrance hall and through the front door. Their lawn, driveway and mailbox were a blur, and then I was heading down the road. I walked all the way to Ledyard Center, my breath rasping in and out, and tears clouding my eyes. The blossoming warmth of spring was buzzing all around me. Robins hopped across front yards. Squirrels chattered and scolded in the trees. The air was a soft breath across my skin, but I couldn't appreciate any of it, the way I usually would have. I had to get away from that house.

In a phone booth near the post office, I called my father. He was at work, but he promised to leave early and pick me up on his way home. He told me to get a Coke at the pharmacy and wait for him at the library.

"And don't blame Dr. Haram," he said. My father was the only one I talked to about my sessions with Dr. Haram.

"Jasper has to do this his own way," he said. "You just keep going. You're doing great, Seth. Just great."

I stared at the streaky glass of the phone booth.

"I'm proud of you," my father said.

I swallowed hard. "Dad?"

"Yes?"

"Don't be late, okay?"

I knew he wouldn't be. My father was never late. But he couldn't change the fact that now, on top of everything else, Jasper and I were no longer friends. Jasper had died to me, too, in way, and it would be years before he rose again.

Sitting in his kitchen now, with his newborn daughter asleep upstairs, Jasper said to me, "Yeah, you're right. It's just that this is so overwhelming. I had no idea. Everyone warns you; but I still had no idea."

I swallowed. "Some things are like that," I said.

"The fatigue, the sleep deprivation, is unreal. Half the time I'm so tired, I feel sick. The other half, I'm listening to her cry." Jasper took a sip from his mug. "And then there's something worse."

"Something worse?"

"Yeah, if something ever happened to Bet, if she got sick or had an accident and died, I don't know how we'd live without her. The thought of her gone makes me stop breathing. I never knew I could feel this way, be this way, about anything. I couldn't live without her, Seth."

"Jasper, just hold on a minute," I said. Were those tears brewing in his eyes? "Don't you think you're getting a little carried away?"

He sniffed. "Yeah, I don't know what comes over me sometimes. I was never like this before." He laughed. "What do they say? A child changes everything, right?"

I shrugged.

He hoisted himself up, limped to the coffee pot and poured more. Then he grew still. "Becoming a parent is just the strangest, most powerful thing that's ever happened to me," he said.

I didn't know what possessed me to say what I said next, but before I could stop them, the words were out of my mouth. "Stranger than Henry?"

"Huh?" Jasper said.

"Stranger than Henry Apgar being killed that day?"

Jasper stirred sugar into his coffee, keeping his back to me. "What a weird question," he said. "Why would you ask me that?"

"Uh, I don't know," I said. "It's just always stood out as the pinnacle of strange experiences in my own life."

"Yes, but why ask me now? I mean, the juxtaposition is a little off, don't you think? From having a child to the untimely, accidental death of a former classmate years ago. I don't see the connection."

I must have unwittingly put him on the defensive. The lawyer in him was coming out. "It's not such a stretch," I said. "Henry was someone's child."

Jasper turned to me. "So were we, Seth. We were all just children then."

Either parenthood had shaken something loose in Jasper, or it was the sleep deprivation talking, but he went on. "You've always had some sort of guilt complex over what happened," he said.

"Well, I wouldn't exactly say that..."

"You didn't say it; I did. And all I'm saying is this: however you've framed this in your head, Seth, remember we were all just kids. We didn't know our asses from our elbows back then. But we were trying. We were trying to get it right."

"Isn't that what we're still doing?" I said.

Jasper dropped back onto his stool and gave a tired smear of a smile. "I guess so."

I saw the fine etchings of grown-up lines around Jasper's eyes and mouth. "And how have you framed it, in your mind, Jasp?" I said.

"As the damnedest thing," he said. "The sorriest thing I've ever known. Regrettable in every way, but certainly no one's fault. And remember, I was the one driving, Seth, so if I can see this, you sure as hell should be able to."

I didn't have a response for that, but something inside me softened.

Bet cried out upstairs then, a sharp blast, louder than I would have thought her capable of.

Jasper sat bolt upright and struggled off his stool. "Hang on a minute. I'll be right back," he said. He limped out to the hall and to the staircase, his cane tapping along the tile. At the foot of the stairs, I heard him take a deep breath. Then he started climbing.

....

EIGHTEEN

Travis was hosting Thanksgiving dinner. He had the space, his big dining room with the picture window overlooking a quiet, reedy cove, and Rosemary was chomping at the bit to play matriarch. Mother offered no resistance.

"It's one holiday this country should not be celebrating," she told Travis, Holly and me the Saturday before Thanksgiving in the car on our way to lay fresh flowers at the cemetery.

"What do you mean, Mom?" Travis said. "You never said anything all the years we've had Thanksgiving."

"Yes, well, I never considered the injustice back then."

Travis, behind the wheel, furrowed his brow.

"We came over here and murdered the Indians—I mean the Native Americans—and stole their land, gave them small pox and alcohol, wiped out their cultures. It's disgusting," Mother continued.

"Who came over?" Travis said.

"The Puritans, sailing across the Atlantic,"

"The Pilgrims," Travis said.

"Yes, whatever, the *Euro-pe-ans*," Mother drew out the word. "And they had no business coming over here."

"Isn't it a little late to be worried about all that?" Holly said from the back seat.

"It's never too late," Mother said. It looked as if Native American rights had replaced deer hunting.

Travis cleared his throat and clicked on his blinker to make a right into the cemetery, where my father and Grandma Hingham—and scores of other Hinghams—lay.

"Rosemary embraces the religious connotations of the day," Travis said. "The religious freedom, you know. The Pilgrims came, at least partly, to be able to worship as they pleased."

"Nice fairy tale," Mother said. "Ask the Iroquois just how 'free' it all was."

"Mom, are you coming to dinner?" I said.

"Of course." She paused. "It is a day to be with family, and I would never let you all down." She turned to look out the window. Travis and I exchanged a relieved glance.

A week earlier Jenna had woken me from a dream of Delia. The phone rang just as Delia was reaching for my hand. We were sitting in the Civic, parked I don't know where, but a wave of warm relief was washing over me. There had been a misunderstanding, an enormous one. Nothing had changed; nothing was over. I was still the man I had always been.

Then the sharp blast of the phone, and I was groping, blinking in the glare of new daylight. Jenna wanted to know if I would have Thanksgiving with her family at her sister's house in Avon. I swallowed hard.

"The thing is, I know this is short notice, only a week before, and I know you probably already have plans..." Her voice grew softer, the way it did when she was struggling to maintain the phony nonchalance she sometimes hid behind.

"I'm sorry. I do actually," I said. Her family? I had to slow things down with her.

"This is the situation," Jenna said. "My sister Mary was supposed to have dinner with her in-laws, okay, and Andy and I were just going to head over to Dorothy's. But Mary's father-in-law has the flu or pneumonia or something, so she's not going..."

"Oh, I'm, ah, sorry."

"...but the damn part is Mary has decided to host instead and have us all to her 'fabulous' house with her 'fabulous' husband and honor roll kids. That's the word she uses, 'fabulous.' She's an R.N., for God's sake, and suddenly she's carrying on like the Duchess of Kent. I mean would you describe your life like that?"

"Probably not." I glanced at the alarm clock. I had to be at work in an hour.

"My mother says Mary is the one—the only one—who did things right. Vinnie is off her rocker out in California, she says, and—get this—she says this to me, right to me, 'Look at the mess you're in.' She says it right in front Andy, too, like he's deaf. She drives me crazy."

"I can see why."

"If you were with me, at least I'd have a date. I mean, they'd think I had a date, a decent guy, and well, you know, they'd shut up about certain things."

What could I say? I told Jenna I was sorry. She said she understood. She wished me a happy Thanksgiving and hurried off the phone. A few minutes later it rang again.

"Seth?"

"Jenna, yes?"

"Listen, I shouldn't have asked you to come with me. I'm sorry. That was a bit, uh, forward of me. It was kind of pathetic actually."

"Jenna, it's okay. Really, I'm flattered."

"I'll see you soon?" she said. "Andy made you a cardboard turkey. He wants to give it to you."

"Then we'll have to get together," I said. "No one's ever made me a cardboard turkey before."

Jenna giggled. "Bye."

I heaved myself up in bed. The sky outside the window was an uncertain gray. Any sort of day could lie ahead. I thought of the fierce glint in Jenna's eye standing next to her smiling sister in their old teenage photo. "Pathetic" was not a word I would ever associate with Jenna Avacoli.

* * *

We took off work early the day before Thanksgiving. Scanlon sent an email to the entire division: *Go home. Abandon all restraint. Enjoy the turkey-tryptophan high. Bill.* Scanlon had a wry sense of humor that crept into his manner usually only in emails.

Travis's house on Thanksgiving afternoon couldn't have been more picture-perfect. Set at the end of a narrow lane on the edge of a marsh, the house was a secluded nook, a private enclave with a wall of windows looking over the ripples and cattails, and a grassy slope of yard leading to the water's edge. A toothpick dock, weather-beaten and spotted with barnacles, perched over the water.

I was the last to arrive. Cars crowded the crushed stone drive-way: Mother's old Volvo, Holly's little Bug, Travis's Audi and a gray sedan I didn't recognize. I wasn't a big fan of cars. I barely gave them a second glance, but Delia loved them. She whizzed around Atlanta in a spiffy, lemon yellow, two-seat Mazda with a sunroof, leather seats and a GPS device with a creepy woman robot voice giving directions.

Knocking on Travis's door, I longed to stay in the yard. A blustery November wind was blowing, and moody clouds hung over the marsh. I've always enjoyed the mercurial skies of late autumn. Geese heading south could pass overhead any minute, sounding their lonely honks. Newly bare branches spread their crooked fingers against the clouds. I wanted to sit on the dock and watch the day pass. When we were kids and my father heard the geese overhead, he would point to the sky and say, "It won't be long now." He said this in a tone of expectation and a thrill always ran through me. He meant it wouldn't be long until winter settled in for its long, icy stay. Snow would fill the woods, crisscrossed with delicate animal tracks I could follow. Gusty winds would rattle windowpanes. Chimneys would send ribbons of gauzy smoke into the air. There would be snowball fights and snowmen and wet mittens and hats drying on the radiator afterwards, while Mother made hot chocolate. On dark, crystal nights, moonlight would shine cleaner and brighter than any other time. In Atlanta, people thought I was crazy whenever I mentioned that I loved winter. They didn't understand.

Rosemary answered the door. "Seth! Why are you knocking? Just come in. No one knocks today." A pink warmth flushed her cheeks. She wiped her hands on her apron, which was printed with tiny pies, and gave me a hug. She smelled of hot rolls and pumpkin spice.

"Happy Thanksgiving," I said. "Everyone's here already?"

"Your mom and Holly got here just a bit ago, and my parents drove up from Pennsylvania last night. They're all in the family room with the twins."

I handed her a bottle of pinot grigio, an Italian wine because Travis claimed they were the best. He wouldn't drink California whites. He claimed he could taste the acidity of the soil. "My meager contribution to what I'm sure will be a first-rate meal," I said.

"That remains to be seen." Rosemary laughed, and I remembered why I had always liked her—the easygoing smile and rea-sonable tone, her eyes rolling behind Travis's back and the way she smoothed over his rough edges. "But it is a blessing that we're all here together, and we can give thanks for that," she said.

"Absolutely." I made a mental note to watch my language, no swearing or "taking the Lord's name in vain," as Rosemary put it.

In the family room, Mother sat in the center of the big, ivory sofa that faced the windows. The house had an open floor plan, the kitchen flowing into the dining room, and around a corner into the living room in an airy arc. Beyond the windows, the waters of the cove winked, and I thought of the fish, the tough winter species moving silently through the cold currents, just below the surface.

Flames hissed in the stone fireplace at the far end of the room. A cardboard kiddie play house, painted like a haunted house—broken windows, bats on the roof, a "DO NOT ENTER" sign on the door, a Halloween leftover—filled the other end of the room. It vibrated with a sharp shudder and a howl rose within. "No turkey! Only pie, pie, pie. We want pie!" The house trembled again, almost toppling over.

On the sofa Mother had assumed a professorial air, gesturing broadly, lecturing Rosemary's unfortunate parents. Mother wore a black sweatshirt with "COLUMBUS WASN'T FIRST" printed across the chest in bold, red letters. Her Native American kick was apparently still going strong. Rosemary's parents sat in the matching ivory loveseat that faced Mother's sofa. A sleek, glass-top coffee table, loaded with chips and dips and a tray of crudité, separated them.

"The point is," Mother was saying, "the so-called 'New World' really wasn't new at all."

"No, I suppose it wasn't new when you put it that way," Rosemary's mother said in a tight voice. She took a sip of whatever filled the tumbler in her hand.

"But let's do our best to celebrate anyway," said her husband, a bearish, bald guy, whose name I couldn't remember. "History is all just water under the bridge anyway, when you think about it," he said, giving a big, belly laugh. His wife, who was rail-thin with steely gray curls and a raspberry-colored sweater, cracked a smile.

Mother pushed on. "So I'm here for my children today," she said. She winked at Rosemary's mother.

"Yes, of course," the woman said. "And for the twins. We drove up last night, and my stars, that traffic was..."

"The highway from hell," her husband interrupted. "Next year the twins are gonna haul their little hides down to Pennsylvania to see Grammy and Grampy," he said.

"Happy Thanksgiving," I said, stepping into the room.

Rosemary's folks turned to me. "Yes, Happy Thanksgiving," the woman said. "And you are...Seth, I remember. The best man at the wedding."

"Nice to see you again," I said. I'd actually forgotten both their names.

"Jillian," the woman said. "And my husband, Peter."

He reached to pump my hand. "Pete and Jill," he said. He had eyes like a calm sea and leathery, browned skin. "Call us Pete and Jill."

"You've been away. Your mother was just filling us in. Living in Atlanta?" Jillian said.

"Yes."

"How nice. Sorry to hear about your girlfriend." She patted my hand. "But these things happen for a reason. Always for a reason."

I threw Mother a look. "I'm, um, it's good to be home," I said.

Another hand pat. "Of course it is." Little silver crosses gleamed on Jillian's ear lobes. She must be where Rosemary got her religion.

"Hello dear," Mother said. "Would you mind poking that fire? It's about to go out."

I was glad to have something to do. I took the black iron poker from its stand and prodded the hissing logs. The end of one dissolved into a pile of ash.

"Of course the name 'Thanksgiving' is a misnomer," Mother said. Jillian cleared her throat.

"I did a stint in the South," Peter said.

"Really? Where?" I said.

"Camp Lejeune, Carolina, before shipping out to Korea. Summers hotter than hell. And the bugs, yeech. Nice people down there, though, huh? Friendly."

"Never been to North Carolina, but Atlanta is a great town," I said. "And the beaches on the Georgia coast are terrific. We rented a cottage every summer."

Peter pondered this a moment. "So, you head up to the Cape now, right? It's gorgeous up there. And plenty of night life. A single guy like you. You'll probably hit the town, huh?"

"You've got it," I said. I didn't tell him that I usually spend my time on Cape Cod bird watching. It's a birder's paradise up there, smack in the middle of a major migration route. Delia swore she'd never go to the Cape with me again after we sat in a birding blind in a swamp for four hours waiting to see the sharp-shinned hawk. Delia fell asleep. The sharp-shinned hawk never showed up, but a great blue heron put on quite a nice show for me.

"And who exactly are we giving thanks to?" Mother was saying to Jillian. "The Pilgrims? The poor turkey?"

"To God, of course," Jillian said.

"To God?"

I turned back to the fire and dropped on a new log. "Think I'll go see if they need any help in the kitchen," I said.

Jasper, Rosemary and Holly were sitting around the island in the kitchen. The luminescent gray of autumn filled the windows over the sink. The smell of roasting turkey infused the air. A blender full of what looked like tomato juice sat in the middle of the island next to a bottle of vodka and some celery sticks.

"...the fermentation process is key," Travis was saying.

"Seth!" Holly cried. "It's about time. We were all laying bets whether or not you'd show up."

"Oh, come on," I said. "When have I ducked out on a holiday? Though if I'd known Mom was going to hold a symposium on revisionist history, I might have."

"Is she still at it?" Holly shook her head.

Travis tapped the glass in his hand. "Bloody mary?"

"Strong," I said.

"Is Mom still rattling on in there?" he said.

"She's in fine form," I said. "Rosemary?" She was standing at the stove, sprinkling something over a glass dish of steamed corn. "I'm sorry for your parents," I said. "They're being bombarded."

"Ah, they're troopers," Travis said, raising his glass in a mock toast.

"Don't worry about them, Seth," Rosemary said. "My dad, you know nothing bothers him, and mom can hold her own."

"Seth?" Travis held out my drink—a deep ruby red with a stalk of celery poking up. "Cheers."

"Travis was just extolling the virtues of a good bloody mary," Holly said.

"Any alcoholic drink, actually," Travis said. "All alcohol must ferment properly."

"What an unfortunate name for a drink. Bloody mary," Rosemary said. A bubbly glass of seltzer sat on the counter near her.

Holly patted the stool next to her, and I slid onto it. "What we were really wondering was if you'd bring your new lady friend today," she said, smiling like a sweet-faced Cheshire cat.

"New lady friend?" Rosemary said.

In a moment of weakness, I'd told Holly more about Jenna. It was after a trip to Mystic Aquarium with Jenna and Andy. Andy wanted to see the beluga whales for a school project, and Jenna asked me to come along because I was an "animal scientist." The afternoon had stuck with me. Andy's hand felt like a warm little paw in mine as he led me around. The kid was growing on me.

"The thing is, Jenna and I are just friends," I told Holly on the phone that night. "I don't want to lead her on. Know what I mean?"

"Only a man would be stupid enough to spend a day with a single woman and her son and then wonder if he was 'leading her on,' " Holly said.

I didn't answer that, because I knew Holly was at least partially right. Only I didn't want to cut it off with Jenna. I didn't want to take things to a new level either, but I really did like her. Jenna was good company when she wasn't prying. She couldn't get enough details about Delia and my life in Atlanta. Once she asked, "How was the sex?" I pretended not to hear her.

"Lady friend is a little misleading," I said.

Rosemary chuckled. "What do you call her then?"

"Who?"

"Your friend who's a lady."

"Nothing. I mean, I don't call her anything. She doesn't have a title."

"Jenna," Holly said.

"Ah." Rosemary turned back to the stove.

"Titles," Travis mused. "We all have them, multiple ones actually. Father, husband, researcher, brother, son—those all apply to me, for instance."

Rosemary glanced over her shoulder at him. Then one of the twins cut loose in the family room—a full-blown wail. Rosemary wiped her hands on her apron. "Oh, boy, here we go. Let me see what happened. Holly, keep an eye on this?"

"A mother's work is never done," Holly said.

"Tell me about it."

"Hey, that's another label your lady friend has, Seth," Holly turned her little grin towards me. "Mother." I could see she was in one of her teasing moods.

"Really?" Travis said. He had taken a bowl of limes from the refrigerator and was arranging them ever so carefully on a cutting board.

"Hey, Holly," I said. "Why don't you give it a rest?"

"Sorry, Romeo." Holly went to the stove to stir a pot.

And then, for whatever reason, I thought, to hell with this. I had nothing to hide. "Yes, she has a son," I said. "Jenna has a son."

"And no husband, I presume," Travis said.

I stiffened. Over Jenna Avacoli's honor? To my surprise, yes.

Travis, in a rare moment of awareness, must have felt a spark come off me. He caught my eye. "Or she wouldn't be angling for you, Seth, right?" he said.

"She's not angling for me, Travis. She's a single mom," I said, and then I ran my mouth. "Her son's name is Andy. He's six. Jenna manages a storage facility in Groton. She lives above the office, rent-free, and she's studying to be a dental hygienist. Okay?"

"Okay what?" Travis said.

"Come on, Travis," I said. "Okay nothing, alright?"

"Hey, guys, let's drop it," Holly said. "I'm sorry I brought it up."

"A little late, don't you think?" I said. Holly was sorry, too. She wouldn't meet my eyes.

"Anyway," Travis said. "The point was just that maybe it matters very much what you call your lady friend, how you choose to label her."

"Thanks for that bit of wisdom. I'll file it away," I said.

Then Travis smiled that cursory little grin of his, the one that preceded one of his blind zingers. "Interesting," he said. He held a lime up in front of his eyes and scrutinized it. "How did she—how did Jenna—come by her son?"

I put my glass down. "How did she *come by* him? She gave birth to him, you know, the usual way," I said.

Travis chuckled. "Well, of course." He placed a lime exactly in the center of the cutting board and started slicing it with precise, even strokes. "That would be the usual way."

I rattled the celery stalk in my glass. Travis started whistling. I watched his careful, patient hands, his deliberate, controlled cutting here in his clean and orderly house. I cleared my throat. "Andrew's at the top of his class," I said.

"How wonderful," Travis said. "I would think that would be quite an accomplishment." He dumped the sliced limes into a blender.

"You *would* think," I said, or you *do* think."

He looked at me. "Huh?"

"You heard me. Andrew is at the top of his class. You apparently find it surprising. Why is that?" I faced him squarely, and he frowned.

"Who said I was surprised? I don't know what you mean. What are you saying, Seth?"

"Oh, come on. You said it yourself, 'a big accomplishment.'"

"Yes, it is a big accomplishment for any child, isn't it?"

"Especially Andrew?"

"Anyone." Travis gave me a dubious look and went back to the limes. "Maybe you're the one who's surprised," he said.

With that, Travis silenced me. I opened my mouth to speak, but nothing came out. Travis switched on the grinding whir of the blender. He nodded his head, counting the exact number of seconds the limes needed to chop. That was the thing with Travis. Innuendo or passive aggression weren't in his repertoire. He simply said what he thought. Maybe the damning echoes were all in my head, and why was that?

When we sat down to dinner, the mood was lighter. Mother had given up the podium, for one thing, and Jillian and Pete were visibly more comfortable. They sat side-by-side, the bank of windows and reedy waters of the marsh behind them. Travis was at the head of the table—the space Father had always occupied during holiday meals. Rosemary sat at the other end, with the twins in high chairs flanking her. Holly, Mother and I filled the remaining side.

The turkey, golden and glistening, with jaunty green sprigs of parsley tucked around it, commanded the center of the table.

"It's a magnificent bird, Rosemary," Holly said.

"Thank you."

"Your finest to date," Travis said.

"Maybe we should taste it before passing judgment?" Pete said.

Rosemary laughed. "Oh, Daddy."

Pete was the kind of guy who could say things like that, and nobody took offense. He was the opposite of Travis. He grinned and took a swig out of his Heineken bottle. He didn't want any of the wines Travis had assembled to complement the meal. He liked Heineken, and he liked it straight out of the bottle.

"Shall we say grace," Rosemary said, her voice lifting ever so slightly on the last word.

Holly, recovered from the Jenna conversation, kicked my leg under the table. "Of course," she said. "Mom, why don't you say a few words?"

"I believe I'll decline," Mother said, smiling tolerantly.

Jeremy, a pumpkin-orange bib around his neck, banged on his high chair tray. "Foodie, foodie, food," he said.

"I'll say grace," Travis said. "What's Thanksgiving without grace, right?"

"A celebration of imperialism and genocide," Mother murmured.

"Genside," said Jeremy, who apparently listened much more carefully than I gave him credit for. Holly snickered.

Travis grabbed my hand on his right and Pete's on the left and plunged on. "God," he said, head bowed, eyes closed. Travis, a confessed agnostic at age twelve, would say anything to please his wife. "Thank you."

Silence, five seconds, ten seconds, and then Travis continued, "For this food and family and all our blessings." Silence. "Thanks a lot, God. Really. Amen."

When we lifted our heads, Rosemary was staring at Travis. "Thanks a lot, God?" she said.

Pete snickered.

"If there is a God, I would think he'd favor sincerity over eloquence," Travis said.

"I suppose so," Rosemary said.

"Well, good, fine. Somebody pass me a slice of that bird," Holly said. "Mom, can I get you started?"

The twins had diced-up versions of the meal in little plastic plates on their trays. Rosemary kept turning from one to the other, wiping a chin, retrieving a fork or napkin from the floor, defusing trouble: "The beans are not funny looking! They're Mommy's special beans. We use forks, not hands. No throw. No throw. We sit nicely and eat like big boys."

The magic of the meal took over, the saucy aromas, the crinkly brown turkey skin. The eating began in earnest. The Bloody Mary had erased my own edge, and the wine I sipped was filing down the last sharp bits.

"I'm glad all my dental work is done," Travis said.

"What did you have done?" Holly said.

"Two crowns."

Jillian winced.

"Ugh," Holly said.

"Never pleasant," Travis said. "But, you know, dental work always makes me think. I feel a flash of mortality every time they tinker in my mouth, changing what God and nature installed."

"That's one way to look at it," Jillian smiled.

"Why couldn't God have installed a fluoride drip?" Mother said.

"Yes," Travis continued. "I've had some profound moments in the chair."

"Well, to the dentist then," Holly said, raising her wine glass in a toast. "Did I tell you my dentist had a Bryce sighting? That's my ex-boyfriend," she clarified for Jillian and Pete.

"She cleaned Bryce's teeth a couple months back. It seems he's moving to Vermont to take up the contemplative life."

"The what?" Jillian said.

"He's become a Buddhist."

"Oh, I see. How interesting."

The night of the punch came back to me: Bryce's pale face, red and inflamed where my fist met his cheek; the creepy click of his jaw against my knuckles. What an idiot I'd been, letting him get under my skin like that.

"You never mentioned this," I said to Holly.

She shrugged. "Slipped my mind. Anyway he's moving to some kind of communal farm—organic, Mom—and has relinquished all his worldly possessions."

"That mustn't have taken too long," I said.

"Say what you will. The man has apparently found peace," Holly said.

"Free-loading off the land," I said.

Pete barked a laugh and Jillian frowned, nibbling delicately at her lower lip.

"Well, I applaud his turn away from materialism," Mother said. "I want to move in that direction myself. We all should."

"Good luck to Bruce," Travis said.

"Bryce," Holly said.

"John actually. Remember, Holly?" I said.

She gave me a sour smile, and Travis said, "Who?"

"Oh my God, the carrots," Mother said, clapping one hand to her heart.

Jillian startled, her knee bumping the table leg.

Rosemary, busy spooning brown goop into a little mouth, turned her head at the word "God." She glanced from Travis to Mother. "Is something wrong?" she said.

"The dill," Mother said. "I forgot to sprinkle it on top before I brought the carrots over today. Your father always liked dill on glazed carrots. Do you have any dill, Rosemary?"

"Well, yes, but really Millicent, the carrots are just fine the way they are."

"Delicious," Travis said.

"Carr, fine," one of the twins trilled.

"I'll just run them out to the kitchen and sprinkle some on." Mother stood and lifted the carrot serving dish, a heavy-looking, pale blue ceramic bowl. "It'll just take a second."

"Mother, please don't bother," Travis said. "Sit down and relax."

"I've been preparing these carrots for Thanksgiving with dill for thirty years," Mother said. "They need dill. Your father would eat them no other way."

"Yes, but Dad's not eating them today," Travis said.

It was such a ham-fisted comment—even for Travis—the table fell silent. Even the twins seemed to pause.

"I'm aware of that," Mother said, jerking the bowl of carrots from the table. "Did you imagine that I'd forgotten?"

"Mother, of course not. I only meant..."

"Thank you, Travis. It's good to know you children consider me so senile, you have to remind me that my husband is dead."

"Mom, come on," I said.

"Mom," Holly said, but Mother stalked into the kitchen, carrot bowl held high.

"Nice going, Travis," I said.

"I only meant..."

"He was only trying to help," Rosemary said, "in his own way."

"Yeah," Holly said. "That's the problem."

From the kitchen, we could hear the carrot bowl meet the counter with a heavy thud. A cabinet door swung open and slammed shut. "Where is it? Where is it?" we heard Mother mumble. Another door creaked open, and Mother said, "the cheap dill, it figures."

Rosemary winced.

"Well," Pete said, winking. "Dill carrots *are* better."

"That's not funny, Peter. Not funny at all," Jillian said.

The twins, perhaps sensing an opportunity to add to the drama, chose that moment to melt down. "I pee-pee now," Jeremy said.

"Pee. Me," little Jason echoed, raising his blue eyes from the green mush he was grinding into his tray.

They were toilet training, as Rosemary had warned us. There were bound to be some interruptions today. "Now?" she asked them. "Go now?"

"NOW!" Jeremy howled, kicking to be freed from his chair.

Rosemary and Travis stood at the same moment, each to take a twin, and maybe that was what started the confusion. There were too many people shuffling about, too many chairs sliding, too many little arms and legs flailing. Mother didn't know what she was stepping into. Maybe that was why she didn't see Jeremy racing straight toward her legs. When they collided, Mother's knees buckled and she grabbed the table edge to break her fall. She also dropped the freshly dilled carrots. Airborne, the bowl—little orange carrot discs flying everywhere—came down with a thud, as Mother shrieked, slumping over the table.

"Millicent, oh dear, are you alright?" Jillian jumped to her feet.

"Mom?" Holly took her arm.

Jeremy must have been stunned into silence for a minute.

Breathing heavily, Mother managed to straighten herself. A big, slick carrot slice dotted her chest like a bull's eye. "Don't," she said, "make such a fuss. I'm fine. I'm fine."

Then the screaming kicked in. It began, dear God, and its ferocity obliterated everything else around it. We all sprang up and rushed to Jeremy.

"Jerry," Travis was saying, "hey, little buddy, you're okay. You're okay." He got down on his knees.

"Check his head," Rosemary commanded, rushing around the table.

Travis dug through Jeremy's floppy blond hair. "Oh," he said, pausing and glancing up at Rosemary. "I think this may need a stitch."

That's when Jeremy turned his head and we all saw the thin trickle of red running over his ear.

"Oh, God," Holly said.

"Now, it's just a cut," Travis said. "That bowl isn't heavy. It's just a deep nick." He tried to look the sobbing Jeremy in the eye. "You'll be good as new," he said.

"I'm sorry," Mother said. "I'm so sorry."

Rosemary hoisted Jeremy up in her arms. "Millicent, there's no need," she said. "He'll be fine."

"It was an accident, Mom," Travis said.

In the end, Travis and Rosemary took Jeremy to the emergency room. He needed two stitches to close the carrot bowl gash in his head. Rosemary's parents stayed with Jason and refused anyone's help cleaning up. I think they were anxious to be rid of us all. Holly drove Mother home, following her across Travis's driveway, throwing me a quick wave as Mother muttered, "I am so terribly sorry."

I went home to Jasper's condo on the river. On the couch that night, the flickering gray of the TV screen—some cooking show—in the background, the day settled around me. A bouncy brunette was frying garlic in a black pan, smiling rapturously as if it were the most exciting thing that had ever happened to her. I turned up the volume. *"...reduce the wine sauce and keep whisking. Scrape up all the good stuff on the bottom of the pan. That's your FLAVOR!"*

I punched the "off" button on the remote and let it fall to the coffee table—my coffee table, an upside down, wooden milk crate Jasper must have found at a dairy farm tag sale. I thought of Travis' smooth beveled glass, and of the oak table Delia and I had, the one with the whirling dark knot in the center. Delia called the knot "the eye of God." God trapped in a coffee table. I used to stare at it after fighting with Delia to steady myself. It sometimes felt as if the knot were staring back.

What I needed now was a good night's sleep. I had nowhere to go the next day, no plans for the weekend. A tepid ease came over me. To hide is a wonderful thing. To become invisible, even better. I felt it sometimes, melting into a forest, slipping away among the trees. Or driving alone on a country road at night, disappearing into the soothing dark, merging with the looming landscape and the shadows all around. I'd have plenty of time this weekend to hunt online for jobs in the North Country. In that whole region, something acceptable that paid a livable wage, had to break soon.

Bzzzzzz. Bzzzzz. Bzzzzz.

The front door?

Bzzzzz.

I sat up.

Knock-knock. "Seth?"

The voice. I knew it.

Bzzzzz.

I opened the door. "Jenna?"

She hesitated, watching my face.

"Hey," I said. "I'm just surprised, happily surprised. Come in, come in."

"I...thanks." Jenna gave a nervous giggle and stepped inside. "I'm not disturbing anything?" she said, glancing around.

"Huh? No, not at all. I was just unwinding. I got home a little while ago," I said.

"Oh." She sounded relieved. "I was on my way home from my sister's, you know, and I have this extra pie—pumpkin—and I figured, what the hell, might as well swing by Seth's and see if he'd like some pie."

My heart swelled. "That was awfully nice of you, Jenna, really," I said. "I had so much to eat already today. I'm kind of stuffed..." I just couldn't tell her no. "But maybe just a small slice."

"Great. I'll fix us some. You sit down, relax." She headed for my kitchen.

"Where's Andy?" I said.

"Spending the night with Grandma. It's something we do every Thanksgiving. Used to be because I worked the late shift at a diner—a little extra money. You'd be surprised the people in diners at eleven o'clock Thanksgiving night. Now it just gives me a break."

"Ah, good idea."

"Believe me, when you're a single parent, you need all the breaks you can get. Anyway it's like a tradition now, and Andy looks forward to it."

I started pacing the living room. Maybe Holly was right. I was leading Jenna on. I needed to be fair to her. I perched on the edge of the couch arm. A cabinet door creaked in the kitchen. Some plates rattled.

"Jenna, can I, ah, help out there?" I called.

Another creak and a clink. "No, I've got it." She sounded a bit too cheery. "Stay where you are and relax. This is my treat."

I picked up the remote control and pointed it at the TV. No, too rude. Music then? No, she'd think I was trying to set a mood. My mouth went dry. I turned up the lights, straightened the couch pillows and placed the newspaper on the coffee table. We could talk about the news, the tractor-trailer accident on I-95, the forecast for tomorrow. We'd chat and eat the pie and say good night.

Only that wasn't what happened. I blamed the pie. It was apple, and Jenna put scoops of ice cream atop each slice, something green for her and vanilla for me. The ice cream got to me. Jenna had remembered that vanilla was my favorite. I'd ordered it the day we had cones in Mystic. Delia hated that vanilla was my favorite.

"The blandest of flavors," she called it, "an empty canvass for the taste buds." She insisted I try new flavors, certain she could hook me on a more exciting one. We had a big fight at an ice cream shop once because I refused to order the key lime sherbet.

"At least try a sample!" Delia practically begged, and I shook my head.

"You're like an old man, Seth," she said. "Don't you ever get tired of yourself?"

Jenna came in from the kitchen, carrying a tray loaded with the pie and, sadly, a little cardboard turkey decoration, complete with a fanning crepe-paper tail and "Happy Thanksgiving" on a banner streaming from its beak.

She settled on the couch next to me, in her socks. She must have kicked off her shoes in the kitchen. She usually wore heels, I guess because she was so short. Her sudden drop in height made her seem vulnerable and, I had to admit, sexier.

I inched away on the sofa and tapped the turkey. "Nice touch."

"Andy's turkey," Jenna said. "Especially for you."

"Very festive," I said. "Tell him thanks. How was your dinner?"

She dug into her pie with gusto, breaking off a big chunk with her fork. "The usual." She shrugged. "We all admired my sister's 'charming' home—that's the word my mother used, like she'd never been there before—and her husband. Then at dinner, get this, my mother asks, about fifty times, if I'm dating anyone."

I swallowed. "Really?"

"Oh, yeah. She asks out loud, right across the table, and all these eyes turn to me, you know. It was hideous."

"Sounds it. What did you, um, say?"

"Easy." Jenna gave her toothy little grin, flashing the dimple on the left side of her mouth. "Andy," she said. "That's what I tell them: Andy is the man in my life. Everyone laughs, and my mother has to kind of let it go at that."

My blood pressure must have dropped twenty points. I don't know what crossed my face, but Jenna said softly, "I wouldn't do that to you."

Pie stuck in my throat. I forced it down. "You wouldn't do what to me?"

"You know, blab all around, talk it up like you and I are together, like we're...a couple or anything."

I cleared my throat and nodded at the newspaper on the coffee table. Why did she have to be so nice? I could mention the front page headline about the I-95 accident that had tied up traffic for hours the day before? No, too forced. The weather then? The weather was a good, neutral topic.

"The thing is, I have a new rule," Jenna said. "I don't discuss my romantic life with my mother. She's a snoop and she loves—I mean LOVES—to point out the flaws in my thinking."

So much for small talk.

"The flaws in your thinking?" I said.

"You know, she brings me down. Shows me why whatever I'm trying to do won't work."

"Sounds *charming*," I said. Jenna needed to vent. Might as well let her.

"Hah, hah," she said.

"So dinner wasn't so great?"

"It was about what I expected. You want another piece of pie?" She had already scarfed hers down.

"No, I'm okay."

"I'm gonna help myself," she said, "in a minute." She picked at the edge of the couch cushion. "The thing with these dinners is, I never have anything new to add. Anything good, I mean. My sister's kid is taking piano lessons. Her husband got a promotion. My mother won $200 playing slots at the casino. And I'm broke and living above a storage facility."

"Hey, Andy made the honor roll. I told my brother that today."

Jenna froze. I heard the elevator doors slide open and shut down the hall. The little bell dinged.

"You told your brother about Andy?" Jenna asked. She turned to me, and I was stunned to see tears sparking on her dark lashes.

"Well, yeah. I sort of mentioned it. It came up in conversation."

"You were talking about me?"

"Jenna, what's wrong?"

"Nothing. Nothing's wrong." She coughed, sat up straighter and tucked her hair behind her ears. That's when I saw her earrings— these little, plastic turkeys, tails fanned out like the centerpiece, dangling from her earlobes.

"Nice earrings," I said and smiled.

"I know. Dorky, right? Andy made them, too. These stupid, dime-store turkeys, he glued fishing hooks to them. I meant to take them off before I came over here tonight."

"Why? I like birds. All birds, even turkeys. I almost studied ornithology."

Jenna raised a skeptical eyebrow.

"Did you know Ben Franklin wanted the turkey, not the eagle, to be the national bird?"

"No, I didn't."

"He saw the turkey as a more 'honorable' bird..."

"Seth, I..."

"Yes?" I could feel the trembling edge of the sorrow she was trying to push down. She wasn't the only one pushing things down tonight. And maybe it was her tears or the little turkeys, or the vanilla ice cream, or just the way she'd come to visit me when I was alone, but something made me slide closer to Jenna. Something placed my hand on her knee. Then raised it to brush, ever so gently, the dangling turkey and rest on her warm cheek. When we leaned in to kiss, the rest of the room seemed to fall away. When I opened my eyes, my face was buried in the mass of her dark curls.

Jenna was so small and light, all angles and restless muscle. Delia was curvier, substantial and present. Jenna was like quicksilver, like mercury. She could slip away. Every time I opened my eyes that night, a rush ran through me that she was still there, gripping my back, rising to meet me, matching my yearning with her own.

In the morning bleary river light filtered through the vertical blinds that shaded the tall windows in my bedroom. I woke to the sensation of being watched. Turning my head, I found Jenna, brown eyes wide, staring at me.

"I used to organize closets on the side," she said.

"Oh, you...what?"

Jenna wrinkled her nose and smiled. "I'm sorry. Good morning," she said.

"Good morning."

"When Andy was little, I had this part-time job, organizing people's closets. It was a good job to have with a baby because I could take him along and he basically slept the whole time."

"People paid you to organize their closets?"

"Sure." She sat up and stretched, arching her back, arms overhead. She wore my white t-shirt and nothing else. "You wouldn't believe it. These wealthy people in Stonington and Old Lyme pay you to come in and clean up their mess."

I sat up.

"You should have seen the crap these people kept squirreled away. These big, walk-in closets crammed with old clothes and broken down shoes, stacks of papers—one guy had cancelled copies of every check he'd ever written. There was this one woman, a big executive or something, lots of suits and expensive shoes, she had a duffel bag full of empty nail polish bottles, all crusty and stiff. Bizarre. Another woman had a bag of old pantyhose, with runs in them. I mean, she couldn't wear them, so why was she keeping them?"

"I, ah, I don't know. Would you like some coffee?"

"Yeah, sure. Thanks. What made me think of the closets is today's Black Friday."

"Black Friday?"

"Yeah, the day after Thanksgiving, the biggest shopping day of the year."

"Oh, that's right. Are you going shopping?"

"No, are you?"

"I never shop."

"Never?"

"I buy through catalogues or online, and only when I really need something. I just don't, ah, need a whole lot, I guess."

Jenna thought about this for a minute. "I don't either," she said, and I wondered if she was just being agreeable.

"I used to love shopping, hunting out new stuff, bringing it home, showing everyone. But those closets cured me," she said. "People can get very strange about stuff. Do you know what I mean? Now I hate malls. Just the parking lots irritate me. Everyone looking to buy, buy, buy. There's something depressing about it."

We had coffee. She sat across from me at the round, two-person café table I hadn't used since I'd moved in. Jenna was rumpled and relaxed, her dark hair held back in a big, plastic clip, my old t-shirt hanging on her tiny frame.

209

I didn't have to hold up my end of the conversation. That was one of the good things about Jenna. She filled all the dead air. All I had to do was listen. The night before felt like a dream. Maybe I'd been presumptuous assuming sex would take us to a new level.

But later at the door, Jenna turned to me and brushed my lips with hers. "Will things change now?" she said.

I didn't know what to tell her. I'd never been good at predicting things or, for that matter, even recognizing them until I was up to my neck. So Travis took control of my mouth.

"Things are always changing, aren't they?" I said. Great, now I had morphed into a morning-after Confucius. Just what Jenna needed, but she let my stupidity slide.

"That's true," she said, smiling and turning to walk down the hall.

From the window I watched her car pull onto the street and pass along the river. She stopped at the corner, brake lights glowing red, and then she was gone. I pulled the blinds closed.

Jenna always left a deafening silence in her wake. Whatever space she occupied, she filled with bright, whirring energy, exclaiming over Andy, wrapping him in hugs, showering the top of his head with kisses; telling a story about her mother's latest outrage; punching me playfully on the arm. And last night, of course.

I drifted into the living room. The clock ticked on the kitchen wall. I dropped onto the couch, lifted the remote control and then put it back down. The elevator doors chimed open and closed. I exhaled. Delia was somehow more gone now. It felt like Jenna and I had snipped the last thread that connected me to Delia last night. A dull pain pressed in my chest, but the memory of Jenna's smooth skin next to mine eased it. *Things are always changing.*

The sun rose higher, warming the floorboards, bathing the walls in creamy light. The walls were bare. I looked around at them. I hadn't hung a single thing. How sterile the room suddenly seemed. Jenna's living room was a colorful, jumbled mess. But I had managed to ensconce myself here, leaving barely a hint of my presence. A visitor would be hard pressed to say who lived here or what he was looking for.

* * *

I went to Jenna's for dinner the next night. She boiled a mound of pasta and checked to see if the noodles were done by throwing a few at the wall. "If they stick, you know it's al dente, perfecto," she said, kissing her fingertips with flourish.

Andy buzzed around the room, bringing me things to look at: his books, his playing cards, a flat, black piece of shale stone he'd found in his grandmother's yard.

"I can find another piece of this rock for you, Seth," he said, "a bigger one." His eyes widened and then narrowed, darting conspiratorially toward his mother. "A sharp one," he whispered.

"I heard that," Jenna said. "No sharps, Andy. You know that." At the sink, she dumped the pasta into a colander. A wave of steam rose.

"No sharps!" Andy repeated. "Seth, no sharps!"

"That's right," I said. "Find me a smooth stone."

For some reason, this piqued his interest. "Like a marble?" he said.

"Well, marbles are glass, but yeah, sort of."

"I got marbles I can show you." And he raced off to his shoebox bedroom at the end of the hall.

"Andy, dinner is ready," Jenna called. "We're sitting down now."

"Let me help," I said. I placed the bowl of pasta in the center of the table. Turning around, Jenna took my hand and brought it to her cheek. She held it there and closed her eyes. I leaned in to kiss her lips. The nearness of her calmed me, quieting for a moment the scramble in my heart that begun the day my father died; the day Delia left; the night I drove up I-95 to my mother's locked house.

When we sat down, the three of us facing each other, I thought how normal and pleasant this was, how expected. Andy jabbered away, swinging his legs under the table. He filled dead air even better than his mother. Afterwards, I helped Jenna clean up, and then Andy showed us his handstands in the living room. The kid had amazing energy.

When he was asleep, tucked away in his room, I slipped into bed next to Jenna.

"You have to leave before he wakes up," she whispered. "I don't want him knowing you spend the night here."

"Of course," I said. "He won't walk in on us or anything, will he?"

Jenna laughed as she snapped off the light and snuggled up against me. "He's a pretty sound sleeper," she said.

Even so, I was careful to keep the noise down. I think Jenna did the same. So amid the whispers and muffled gasps, I lost myself in Jenna again. She was so vibrantly alive, pulsing and responding. I could almost feel her blood rush when I touched her.

That night I slept the deep, dreamless slumber of a man at peace, until I woke suddenly in the dark and for a moment didn't know where I was. The air of the little room hung heavy and silent. A watery bolt of light cut across the floor. Jenna stirred, rubbing her bare leg against mine. I sat up. The light on the floor was from the glowing "U-Store-It" sign in the parking lot. I was in a storage facility apartment in Groton, sleeping next to a woman I barely knew. I could hear the whir of the highway, the same relentless stream of taillights and high beams that had carried me north months earlier.

The world I had known had fallen away. My desk with the round, coffee mug stains at Emory, Delia's blue yoga mat rolled out on our bedroom floor, the creeping tendrils of the spider plants above the kitchen sink, Mother's voice on the phone reporting, "Dad is hanging in; he's as tough as they come." Now this: a new woman in a strange room. In the morning, the sun would come and throw fresh light on us all. The hard realities of a new day would begin, and the things that had been—both the good and the bad—would slip further away, until it was almost as if they had never existed at all.

I turned to the window. Something heavy, a truck, an 18-wheeler, must have been passing on the highway. The glass pane in the window vibrated. I felt tiny and transient, fleeting, a speck clinging to earth's surface. Jenna sighed in her sleep.

NINETEEN

....

The coastline in winter brims with secret, frozen life. I dragged Jenna, and sometimes Andy, up and down it those early weeks of December. It was cold, but not brutally cold yet. Stiff with frost in the morning, the beaches and marshland glistened. The rippling whitecaps of the sea were visible from roads. Sea grass lay, yellow and dormant, along the dunes. It was perfect hiking weather.

"And you don't have to worry about ticks this time of year," I said. Jenna was trotting along to keep up with me. I slowed down. Andy was way ahead of us, darting back and forth on a piney trail leading to a cove not far from Stonington harbor. The cove was a popular nesting spot for gulls, as I had told Andy. He raced up to us.

"Will we see a nest?" he said, breathless and red-faced beneath his Spiderman ski cap.

"Maybe," I said. "But more likely we'll see remnants."

"What's remnants, Seth?"

"Leftovers, bits and pieces. Sticks and feathers."

"No eggs?"

"Not until spring."

Jenna and I exchanged a glance. She wore a black and purple striped stocking cap with a pompom on the end. When I'd asked if it would be warm enough, she'd smiled. "We can't sacrifice fashion," she said, slipping into the Civic next to me. "Besides you'll keep me warm."

When the trail dissolved into a strip of sand ringing the cove, I took Jenna's gloved hand in mine and we walked to the edge. Silvery sheets of water ran up the sand. Andy immediately began throwing stones into the water. He was trying to skip them, angling his arm the way I'd shown him, but failing miserably. Each stone landed with a tidy plop.

"From the side, Andy," I called. "Move your arm sideways." He tried, his short arm, encased in a puffy red winter coat, jerking to the side.

Jenna squinted against the glare coming off the water. The sun was piercingly bright in the winter sky. "So, are you going to do his Career Day Show and Tell at school?" she said.

"Oh, yeah, didn't I tell you?"

"He'll be thrilled," she said. "Have you told him?"

"Not yet." Andy was halfway up the beach now, running at resting gulls, waving his arms. The offended birds squawked and rose over the surf. "Let's tell him now," I said.

"He wanted his dad, you know."

"Oh? Well, maybe then..."

"It's all about different types of careers, and Andy thought his dad could be the Navy guy."

"Well, that makes sense."

"The problem is," Jenna began walking again, "we're not really sure how to reach his dad these days. Email, phone, letters—I tried." She sucked in the cold air, then pointed out to sea. "So I told him his dad's boat is so far out right now, there's no way to know if he hears us." She turned to me. "So just watch what you say."

* * *

Kids Andy's age apparently didn't think twice about calling a grown man their "friend."

"We're friends," Andy told Mrs. Gibbon, his first grade teacher. "Seth is my mom's friend, but he's mine, too." He buried his warm hand in mine, as if to claim me. "We do things together."

It felt like Mrs. Gibbon stared at me a beat too long after that last comment. "Andy asked me to be his guest today," I said, smiling. "I'm a friend of his mother's."

"Well, of course. Everyone is welcome today," said Mrs. Gibbon, who looked to be in her early fifties. She had a broad, calm face and a long braid of graying hair. I thought of the gibbon monkey, of course. How could I not? Her skinny braid even curled at the end like a monkey tail.

"Mr..." she paused.

"Hingham," I said. "Seth Hingham."

"You'll see the children will have all kinds of friends and relatives here today. Why don't Andy and you take your seats. We'll be calling our guests up, one at a time."

Andy squeezed my hand and went off to sit at his tiny desk in the center of the crowded room. A row of folding chairs had been set up against the back wall for the visiting adults. I sat on the end, next to a heavyset guy wearing a white chef's hat. The kids buzzed, bobbing up and down at their desks. Mrs. Gibbon walked to the blackboard.

"I've got a crate of eggplant in my backseat," the chef said, leaning over towards me. He had black, caterpillar eyebrows and a hint of dark razor stubble. He craned his neck to look out the window. "I'm afraid they're gonna freeze. They're sliced and everything. You know, ready for parmigiana."

"Oh, yes."

"How cold was it when you came in?"

"In here or outside?"

He gave an exasperated sigh. "Outside. Did it feel *freezing* outside."

"Freezing? No. It's supposed to get close to forty today, I heard."

217

Beads of perspiration dotted his upper lip. "Two hundred dollars of eggplant." He raised his palms. "That's all I'm saying. If it freezes, I'm toast. I gotta crank out seven trays of parmigiana for a reception tonight. I'm just saying. And frozen eggplant—kills the whole thing." He rubbed his thumb and forefinger together. "The texture changes, like rubber."

Mrs. Gibbon clapped her hands. "Let's take our seats, sit down and quiet down," she said.

I'd never been in this elementary school. I'd gone to Ledyard schools. But I imagined they probably all looked pretty much alike—first grade classrooms anyway. The flag in the corner, the alphabet running above the blackboard and the goofy construction paper projects the kids make stuck on the wall.

It was early, before nine, the chef's eggplants may have been freezing. Career Day was scheduled first thing, so the parents could get to work. I glanced down the row of seats: a hot woman in a business suit, nice legs—whose mother was that? A guy—kid really, he looked about seventeen—wearing a white paramedic uniform, and on the end, a man who looked older than dirt still wearing the fuzzy red ear muffs he walked in with.

Andy was swaying side-to-side in his seat. Funny, the kid didn't look anything like Jenna. The floppy, sandy hair and hazel eyes must have come from the Navy dad. The Navy sperm donor. How had Jenna gotten mixed up with that jerk? She was probably in her early twenties when they met, and as Grandma Hingham used to say, "lacking the sense God gave a goat."

"Mr. Hingham?" It was Mrs. Gibbons, waving me to the front of the room. Andy was already there. I went and stood beside him.

"This is my mom's friend, Seth," Andy told the class. Some of the kids watched me, indifferent stares on their faces. One girl had her head down on her desk and appeared to be sleeping. A red-headed boy with freckles speckled all over his face stuck out his tongue at me. I wondered if the kid was a bully, and instinctively placed my hand on Andy's shoulder.

"He works with animals, and knows all about them. And birds, too," Andy said.

"Thank you, Andy. Please sit back down," Mrs. Gibbon said. "Mr. Hingham, tell us a bit about your job?"

I clapped my hands together. Showtime. "I'm a wildlife biologist," I said. "I work for the state."

The redheaded kid snickered.

I cleared my throat and gave a little spiel about my job, my typical day, animals I'd seen. Mrs. Gibbon nodded the whole time, and the kids, for the most part, seemed to be listening, except for the sleeping girl. Andy watched me with a worshipful look on his face. In the back of the room, the chef kept glancing at the clock over the door.

"Questions? Questions?" Mrs. Gibbon asked the class when I finished.

"Have you been chased by a bear?" a small girl wearing eyeglasses said. The other kids erupted into laughter.

"Did it bite your face, Mister?" the redheaded kid called.

Nice kid.

"Hands!" Mrs. Gibbon said. "Let's raise our hands and take turns."

A hand shot up, a buzz-cut boy on the end. "We have gooses at our house..."

"Geese," Mrs. Gibbon said.

"...geeses," the kid continued, "because we have a pond, and they crap all over the place, and my dad wants to shoot them. Dead."

"Crap" inspired more hilarity, of course, and Mrs. Gibbon clapped her hands sharply. "Enough," she said.

"Your dad needs a permit," I told the kid. He gave me a blank stare.

Then Andy's hand shot up. "Ask good questions," he said, his voice surprisingly firm, a tone I'd never heard from him. "You're wasting our time."

The redhead stuck a pencil up his nose and grunted at me.

Andy shook his head. "Moron," he said.

And then, despite Mrs. Gibbon's tsk-tsking, I laughed. Andy Avacoli was truly his mother's son. He was not the kind of kid who retreated. He must have gotten it from Jenna. She seemed to deal with whatever came at her and then move on. She let herself off the hook. She was generous with the world, and with herself, in a way that I had never been. Maybe that was why I liked her so much.

After the last guest—the anxious chef—gave his presentation, I shook Mrs. Gibbon's hand and waved good-bye to Andy. I closed the classroom door behind me and headed down the empty hall-way. In the parking lot, the sharp air hit my lungs with a jolt and I raised my face to the indifferent sun.

* * *

We ordered take-out Chinese that night. Andy tore open his egg roll and ate the vegetables inside with a fork, because the roll part was too "crunchety." Jenna spooned some of her chicken and broc-coli onto his plate, and he poked at it.

Jenna talked non-stop: the clinking noise her car made when she accelerated that morning; the guy with filthy molars she had to 'scale' during clinical training—"I can't think about it while I'm eating"—the computer screen that kept freezing down in the rental office. She wore old jeans and a big red shirt that came practically to her knees. Her dark hair was piled on top of her head with two chop-stick looking things stuck in it.

"Why doesn't that old man brush his teeth?" Andy said when we were clearing the table.

"I don't know, but it's about time for you to brush yours," Jenna said.

After he was in bed, she flopped down next to me on the couch and swung her legs up so they fell across my lap. "You made his day," she said.

"My pleasure."

"Want a drink?"

"Nah, I'm done."

"Want a backrub?"

"Now that, I could use."

For a small girl, Jenna had these terrifically strong hands. She attacked the knots in my neck and shoulders. It felt so good, I groaned. She dug and stretched, and a tight-fisted tension I didn't even know was there unwound. I exhaled and inhaled, and the breath seemed to move more deeply into my lungs.

"You get tighter than anyone I've ever known," Jenna said. "You gotta relax." She leaned over and kissed my neck.

Later, lying in her bed in the dark with the glow of the storage sign falling across us, I told Jenna about Henry Apgar. She listened to the whole story—the accident and Dr. Haram and the kids at school eyeing me, Jasper retreating into silence, Henry haunting my dreams—in ponderous silence. When I finished, she took my hand in hers.

"So, you've had your cosmic crapper," she said.

"My what?"

"I'm sorry. It's crude, I know. It's an expression of my mother's—big surprise, huh? Cosmic crapper. It basically means a disastrous event that's cruel and completely unfair and changes your life forever."

"And it's cosmic?"

"Yes, and everyone has one in life."

"Just one?"

Jenna nodded on the pillow next to me. "The rule is one, but you know, there are no guarantees."

"No guarantees."

"Nope. That's Mom's theory, anyway, and she's not one to sugar-coat things."

We lied awake a long time that night, holding hands. Jenna's fingernails were painted electric blue. I'd noticed them at dinner. Delia had usually worn a clear varnish, nothing more. "Understated," she called it. "Saying more with less." But that night I wondered if sometimes less is not enough. If sometimes you need to say things loudly and clearly, especially to yourself.

TWENTY

....

"This time," Holly said, "he's someone with a real life—a job, a decent living, a place of his own. You know, a grown-up."

I'd gone to Middletown to help Holly put up her Christmas tree. She put up her tree as early as possible each year, because she loved the holidays. As kids, we had to keep the tree up into February every year for Holly. I was on the floor and had just wedged the seven-foot monster she'd dragged home into its stand in her living room. The tree filled practically half the room. Good thing Holly's apartment had high ceilings. I rocked back on my heels and looked up into the spreading green branches.

"So what's this guy do for a living?" I said.

Holly had a new boyfriend, some guy she was all atwitter over, some guy who had her wearing pearls and sensible shoes. Holly was famous for tottering around in these spiky, high-heeled things she could barely walk in.

"He's an engineer. At Pratt in East Hartford. He works on planes."

"At Pratt & Whitney?"

"Yes. Why, what's wrong with that?"

"Nothing, just don't tell Mom. About Pratt, I mean. They do military work, you know? They supply military aircraft. You know how big she is on the 'military-industrial complex' these days."

"Oh, God." Holly laughed.

"Hey, you hair looks good," I said. She'd cut it shorter, so it just grazed her shoulders, and it was straight and shiny, and darker, too.

"Thanks." She touched the ends. "I decided to tone things down a bit."

"What's Romeo's name?"

"Michael. Michael Jordan."

"You're kidding, right?"

"No, I'm not. Ha-ha. Yeah, I know, just like the basketball player."

"Can he sink a mid-court three-pointer?"

Holly sighed. "How's Jenna, by the way?" she said.

"She's fine. You know Mom's not getting a tree this year?"

Holly sat on her couch, folding one leg beneath herself like a flamingo. "She told me," she said. "The 'silent scream of the trees.' Christmas trees aren't eco-friendly, she said, so I suggested she get one from the tree farms that plant a new tree for every one they harvest?"

"Good idea."

"Well, not to her. She said she's hanging some of the old ornaments on the trees in the backyard, and we can look out the window when we want to see them."

"There's the holiday spirit," I said.

Snowball strolled over to the tree, tail aloft. He sniffed a branch. I stroked his silky back. "I oughta get one of these," I said.

"Not too fast," Holly said. "Michael's allergic, and if things go the way I'm hoping they do, Snowball may need a new home."

"Holly, go slowly with this guy, okay?"

"I know, Seth. I know. I'm going to be thirty-one years old. I'm not a child."

"It just seems to me we've had this conversation before," I said.

"Well this time it's different," Holly said.

"Uh-huh."

"It *feels* different. And I should know. I'm not like you, Seth, with one person—Delia—all these years. I've been out there. I know when something's different. This time I'm onto something real."

Jenna had said almost the same thing to me that weekend, as we were driving down to the Peabody Museum of Natural History at Yale. A new exhibit featuring wild bird eggs of the Amazon had just opened. I really wanted to see it, and thought Jenna might be interested.

"They're like jewels," I told her, as we cruised down I-95. "The colors, the shading and speckles are just brilliant. When I was a kid, nothing thrilled me more than finding a nest of eggs."

Jenna's eyes followed the road. She shifted in her seat. "If I were still smoking, I'd light up right now," she said.

"When did you quit?"

"You didn't know that I was once a smoker, did you?"

I glanced at her. "No, I didn't."

"I quit when I got pregnant. Of course."

"But I know people say the craving is..."

"Did you think I was the kind of person who would smoke while she was pregnant?"

"Did I...What? No, of course not."

"Glad to hear it."

"Is something wrong, Jenna?" I took one of the exits for downtown New Haven.

"There's something I've got to make clear," she said.

"Um, okay."

"I am moving. I mean, my life is moving in a new direction now. People see me, and I know what they're thinking—crazy life, stupid job, rushing to school and back, canned soup for dinner three nights a week. I know."

"Well, your life is about much more than..."

"The point is things are going to be different. I can *feel* it coming. The pieces are falling into place, Seth," Jenna said. "I finish school next spring, and then we're talking a good job. We're talking medical benefits and vacation days and a bigger apartment. Dental hygienists are in demand, you know."

"Sure. They're the ones who do all the work. Sometimes you don't even see the dentist, just the person cleaning your teeth."

"EXACTLY. This is a career, Seth, not just a job."

"I know it is."

"Your brother and you are scientists, right?"

"I guess you could say that."

"And your sister, a graphic artist, and your ex, a TV reporter, right?"

"Yeah, well, she's no one for you to compare yourself to."

"I'm not comparing." Jenna's voice rose a little. "I'm just saying that I'll be a professional person soon. And it's going to be a whole new chapter for me. And for Andy."

"And you both deserve it." I pulled into a parking space in a lot right next to the museum. "Ready?"

"Seth?"

"Hmmm."

"Are you proud of me?"

"Proud? I...yes, sure."

"Are you glad to be with me?"

"If I weren't, I wouldn't be here."

"Or I wouldn't be here. You'd come see these eggs anyway."

She was right of course, and then it hit me. Was I doing with Jenna the same thing I'd done with Delia? Dragging her to see bird eggs that she probably didn't give a damn about? Marching her up and down frozen beaches?

"I've got a question for you," I said. She turned to me. She looked calmer, as if she'd gotten something off her chest that had really been bugging her.

"Do you want to be here?" I said. "At the Peabody? Was there something else you'd have rather done today?"

"Listen, Seth, I've been stuck in a lot of places," she said. "And if I didn't want to be here, believe me, I wouldn't be."

I let it go at that. But in the Peabody, Jenna surprised me. "We need to come back and bring Andy," she said as we passed by the dinosaur skeletons. "He'd go nuts over this."

She seemed genuinely interested in the eggs, too, or at least charmed by their delicate colors and by how tiny some were. "Imagine a life coming out of that little thing," she said, tapping on the glass case displaying a rose-tinted shell no bigger than my thumbnail. "Makes the whole pregnancy and live birth thing seem sort of inelegant, doesn't it?"

I almost launched into a spiel about the evolutionary advantages of mammalian live birth, but I stopped myself. This was a fun outing, not a tutorial.

Afterwards we drove back to Jenna's mother's house in Groton to pick up Andy. Dorothy lived in a boxy ranch house on a dead-end side street in a neighborhood of low-slung ranches and carports and grinning garden gnomes in front yards. Dorothy had a nice backyard, fenced and sloping towards a wooded lot. A collection of bird feeders, dripping with corn and seed, stood in the center, and a swing set filled one corner. Andy loved it.

When Dorothy opened the front door, she took a look at us and jerked her thumb over her shoulder. "They're out back," she said.

The front door opened to a small, tiled foyer and then the beige carpet of the living room, where a brick fireplace dominated one wall and a framed Monet—that beach scene everyone knows—hung over the couch. Matchbox cars were scattered across the floor.

"Ma, this is Seth," Jenna said, eyeing her mother steadily. "He's gonna give Andy and me a lift home."

"So you're the mystery this one has been hiding," Dorothy said, winking at Jenna.

"Ma," Jenna said.

Dorothy laughed to show she was just kidding. "Hiding you from her own mother. Imagine that?" She gave my forearm a playful squeeze.

Standing before me, Dorothy didn't seem half as monstrous as Jenna made her out to be. She looked tired mostly. She had that frosty blonde hair ladies her age seem to like, with a grayish hue down at the roots. It was short and stiff looking and puffed up on her head. A shimmery swipe of something shone on her lips. She was neither fat nor slim, just solid with age. She smiled again, and her eyes half-disappeared into fans of wrinkles. "I'm glad to finally meet you," she said. "Everything I've heard so far has been on the up-and-up. And, goodness, Andy never shuts up about you. Seth this and Seth that, Seth, Seth, Seth."

"Well he's a great kid," I said. "And nice to meet you, too." I shook her hand.

"And he's a smart little guy, let me tell you," Dorothy said. "So if Andy likes you, you must be alright, certainly nothing to hide anyway."

"Ma, please," Jenna said.

Dorothy gave a laugh, a back-of-the-throat chuckle that turned into a barky, ex-smoker's hack. She must have read my mind, because she said, "I quit a year ago, but sometimes, God help me, I don't think the coughing will ever end. What can I get you, Seth?" She shifted into a velvety smooth, generous tone. "Coffee?"

Dorothy worked as a hostess at the Norwich Spa, this very ritzy retreat place for women. I once bought Mother a gift certificate for a facial at the space—Delia's idea—but Mother refused to use it. She didn't want anyone looking at her "that closely," she said.

Dorothy apparently knew how to soothe all those high-strung, high-paying customers. "She's like a different person when she's there," Jenna had told me. "She answers the phone there some-times, and I don't even recognize her voice."

"Did Andy have a good day?" Jenna said, dropping her handbag on the couch.

"He always does," Dorothy said, "Mary and he built a teepee in the yard."

"Mary's here? I didn't see her car."

"In the garage. She came down for a visit. Randolph took the kids up to Boston for the day to visit their *other* grandparents. Mary begged off."

Mary? The older, "perfect" sister with the insurance exec hus-band and two kids? This could be interesting.

"I'll go round him up," Jenna said. "Seth?" She reached for my hand, just as her mother hooked her arm through my other arm.

"Don't go dragging him," Dorothy said.

"Ma, I'm sure Andy wants to see Seth." Jenna tugged on my hand, but her mother held firm.

"I promised this man coffee, and he's gonna get it," Dorothy said.

"It's not a big deal," I said. "I can ..."

"Nonsense." Dorothy gave a big tug, and we were heading arm-in-arm to her kitchen.

Jenna muttered as she headed down a staircase to the basement and then out to the backyard.

"I know, I know," Dorothy said, delivering me to a chair at her round kitchen table and raising her palms in surrender, "she's pissed at me."

"I, um..."

Dorothy went to the sink, to the cabinet for two mugs and then to the glass coffee carafe, already full. She'd been waiting for us. Steam rose as she filled my mug and sat down opposite me. A sliding glass door looked out on a wooden deck and the backyard. Jenna, Andy and a woman who must have been Mary—taller than

Jenna, heavier too with short, wavy, dark hair—were circling a lop-sided, makeshift tent. It looked like a bed sheet held up by long sticks. Andy jumped up and down.

Dorothy wagged a finger at the three of them. "I can only imagine what she's told you about me," she said.

I stirred my coffee. "I'm sorry?" I said.

"We don't have to pretend, Seth," Dorothy said. "One thing we've always been in this family is honest." She shook her head. "It was hardest on Jenna, losing her father like that. I dunno know why. Maybe because she was the middle kid? Mary has done great of course, and Vinnie—in her own kooky way—has at least established herself in California, teaching yoga or t'ai chi or whatever voo-doo it is she does out there. She just moved in with her voo-doo instructor boyfriend, too, so maybe that'll go somewhere."

She paused to sip at her coffee. Outside, Andy had Jenna by the hand and was pulling her to a corner of the yard. Jenna was laughing.

"At least," Dorothy lowered her voice, "neither of them was dumb enough to go and have a kid on their own."

I cleared my throat. "I don't know if 'dumb' accurately describes what Jenna has done," I said.

"How cute, you're coming to her defense." The surrender palms flashed again. "Don't get me wrong. Andy is an angel, and I can see he's brought some direction to Jenna's life..."

"We don't have to talk about this," I said. "I mean, no explanations are necessary, right? How long have you, ah, lived here?"

"...and God knows she needed it." Dorothy took another sip of coffee. "I'm not saying it was easy—me and the girls here alone after their Dad passed. Jenna was only eleven, you know, when he passed, and she was never the same."

Jenna didn't talk much about her father, and I never brought it up. Fathers were a topic I preferred to tiptoe around.

"Jenna sort of came unhinged when she hit high school." Dorothy shrugged. "Maybe it was my fault."

I cleared my throat and stared into my coffee.

"I did the best I could," Dorothy said.

"Of course you did," I said.

"This is the part children don't understand. Parents get heartbroken, too. You're heartsick, yourself, and no one sees it. You gotta hide it. A woman in my position certainly had to hide it. I had to pull myself together, find a job and raise these girls. I had to hold *everything* together. And I was dying inside, I tell you. Just dying."

Andy ran across the lawn, flapping his arms like a huge bird.

"So you hide it," Dorothy said. "It's what the world demands. And well, you know, maybe I got a little too good at hiding. That's all I'm gonna say. You put on a brave face too long, and it takes a toll." She sat back in her chair. "God, I wish I had a cigarette. It's just the urge—every now and then. Some things keep coming back, no matter how hard you beat them down."

"It's the toughest habit to break," I said.

"You a smoker?"

"No."

"I didn't think so." She patted my hand. "You got your head on straight. You're a nice guy, huh? I could see that straight off."

"Thanks."

"I can't believe Jenna's luck this time—provided you stick around."

Was there no way to stop this woman? Funny thing was, what she said next stopped me.

"Listen, I'm not gonna pry, okay? Not gonna be the prying, old bat making your life hell. All I'm saying is be careful with Jenna. She acts real tough. A tough chick. But underneath, I got a suspicion that she's a lot like me."

I never repeated these words to Jenna. I didn't even respond to Dorothy, because I didn't know how to, and mercifully right then the back door opened and Andy charged up the stairs and into the kitchen. Mary and Jenna followed.

"Seth," Mary said, taking my hand. "Jenna didn't say how handsome you are."

"Why don't you embarrass him more?" Jenna said.

But Mary just laughed. "Oh, I'm sorry. Am I embarrassing you?"

"No, of course not. I'm flattered," I said.

"Like he'd admit it," Jenna said.

"Well in any case, I am glad to meet you," Mary said and she gave me a little hug. She had a bland, broad face with no resemblance to Jenna's sharp features. Her smile oozed reassurance and calm. She was probably a good nurse. I could imagine her turning that smile on nervous patients.

"Don't smother the man, Mary," Dorothy said. "He'll never come back. Course he may not come back anyway." She winked at me. "Poor Seth, we're just busting on you."

"Okay, this is our exit cue," Jenna said, taking my hand. "Ma, thanks for watching Andy."

"Any time. I'm always here, you know that."

"Good to meet you both," I said.

"You'll have to come up to the house for dinner," Mary said.

"I'd like that," I said. "I know the Farmington Valley well."

Dorothy nodded. "Yep, his old girlfriend lived up that way."

I managed a smile. "See you soon."

* * *

"For someone you're not close to, she seems to know a lot about us, about me," I said.

"I do tell her things," Jenna said. "I mean, she's my mother. I tell her what's going on in my life."

Andy had gone to bed, and we were stretched out on the couch, feet propped up on Jenna's coffee table.

"She zoomed in on me," I said.

"Why do you think I kept trying to get us out of there?

I glanced at the television, CNN on in the corner of the room with the volume turned down. CNN: Delia's brass ring.

"Actually, she wasn't that bad," I said.

"Ha! Just give her time. Remember, just because I tell her things doesn't mean she understands them. You can be close to someone without being *close*. Know what I mean?"

I lifted her cool, pale fingers in mine. "Not really," I said. "But it sounds true." I brought her hand to my lips and began kissing down the length of her spindly strong arm. Her words sounded like an epitaph for Delia and me, a slogan carved on the tombstone commemorating the last six years of my life.

TWENTY-ONE

....

Jasper stopped by Avery Point in early December. The campus was emptying for the holiday break. Students were wrapping up final exams, and most professors had already locked their office doors. I'd fallen into an easy rhythm at Avery Point, which is easy to do when you're working alone. Scanlon and I checked in two or three times a week, I sent him my research data, answered questions and hoofed it up to Hartford for the weekly staff meetings. Working for the state, while not my ideal, had turned out to be at least tolerable. When my shot at the North Country came, when the right job appeared, I'd make a graceful exit. I'd thank Scanlon, say I was sorry and explain as best I could.

I was at my desk in the lab, crunching data on shore bird fecal matter contaminant rates, when a knock came on the door. So few visitors came to the small lab room at the back of the building where the DEP had stashed me that I startled as I looked up. Jasper's grinning face filled the narrow rectangle of glass in the door. He opened it.

"Who'd they send you down here to sue?" I said.

"Wow, they've got you hidden away, don't they? Who's embarrassed of whom here?" Jasper crossed the room, tapping the licorice black microscope on the lab station table and running his finger along a stand of empty test tubes. "You get all the neat toys," he said. He was walking well, barely leaning on the cane in his right hand.

"To what do I owe the pleasure of this visit?" I said.

"I'm not disturbing you, am I?" Jasper said. "Not delaying any great bird shit discoveries?"

"Yeah, ha-ha. Take a load off." I tapped the chair alongside my desk and he lowered himself, a little cautious on the descent.

"I spent the morning over in New London on a regulatory thing," he said. "I don't want to bore you. How is the research going?"

"Did you know that the birds around here seem to ingest a lot of aluminum?"

"No, I have to say I did not know that."

"Interesting, huh?"

"The things you learn."

Jasper wore a charcoal gray suit and an electric blue tie under his black topcoat. The coat and the cane, the flash of color, gave him a dandyish air. I was wearing ski pants and a sweater for the beach hike I planned later that day to collect water samples.

"How's Bet?" I said.

"Finally starting to sleep through the night—sometimes. I can't tell you how tired I am most days, and it's worse for Chloe. I sneak into the guestroom the really tough nights, when Bet's awake practically ALL night. I don't know how Chloe handles it. I hope to God Bet's sleeping reliably by the time Chloe heads back to work."

"When's that?"

"Spring, May I think. She negotiated a long leave. But, hey, guess who wants to babysit for us? Keeps asking and asking, practically stalking me around the office. Guess who."

"I dunno. Scanlon?"

"Are you nuts? No. Not Scanlon. Glenda Jones."

"Really?" I said. "Well, she's a nice woman."

"And apparently she's a terrific babysitter. Glenda is one of the only people Chloe will leave Bet with. Glenda and her mother. Sometimes my mother."

"Protective maternal urge," I said. "Really normal. You find it throughout the mammalian world."

Jasper gave me a blank stare.

"I'd trust Glenda, too," I said. "There's just something, I don't know, *real* about her."

"Speaking of babysitters, Chloe and I have Glenda lined up for New Year's Eve, and we're planning a night out, nothing big, but we thought maybe you and your new girlfriend might like to join us?" Jasper said.

I'd never mentioned Jenna to Jasper. It wasn't like we talked that often, and he'd had a major case of baby-brain since Bet's birth. "Who told you I have a new girlfriend?" I said.

Jasper winked. "My mother. Actually your mother told mine. Holly mentioned it, too. Anyway, I'm happy for you. Moving on— very commendable, old man."

"Yeah, thanks." I put some files back in a drawer. I could see this was going to take a while.

"She's got a kid, huh?"

"Yes, a son. He's six."

"Six? What a great age."

"He's a good kid." What made Jasper such a child authority all of a sudden? Chloe couldn't even sit up yet. How many six-year-olds had Jasper known?

"Well, I'm looking forward to meeting Janet."

"Jenna."

"Oh, sorry. Jenna. The old ladies lose some of the facts in their translation."

"This is, ah, nice of you, Jasp," I said. "I'll have to ask Jenna."

"Sure, sure. Just let us know." Jasper paused. "Listen, Seth, I hope you don't mind me saying, but I just wanted to warn you that with a single mom, you know, you're fishing in deep waters here, right?"

"Yeah, I know. It's okay. I've got it covered." I didn't have it covered, of course. I didn't even have myself covered.

"I just want to pass on to you, younger cousin, the fruits of my newfound knowledge. Once a kid's in the picture, you're in deep. That's something I never understood until I had one. I mean, how could anyone?"

"Well, I've only known Jenna a few months."

"Right, but the kid complicates things."

I nodded.

"You know, if you're, ah, taking this lightly, thinking of a quick exit, a fill-in-the-time-until-you-move-on kind of thing, forget it."

"Good Lord, Jasper."

"Hey, I'm just saying that if you're not certain about this woman, you may want to think twice now. Leaving a kid is a terrible thing."

"Andy's not my kid."

Jasper gave a soft, rueful smile. "I know that, Buddy. But I'm trying to warn you that it may begin to feel that way."

I knew what he was trying to say, but the truth was I had no answer for Jasper. I didn't have one for myself when it came to Jenna and Andy. "Point taken," I said. "And I do appreciate it, Jasp."

Jasper sat back, apparently relieved to have said his piece. He stared out the lab window, which looked out on the bluff above the beach and the churning gray waters of the December sea. "I've been thinking I'd like to do something about what happened back in high school," Jasper said. He turned to me, eyebrows raised. "A commemoration."

"You want to commemorate our high school?" I said.

"Maybe commemorate isn't the right word. I want to honor the memory of Henry Apgar."

There were some words I just never expected to hear in my life—Travis apologizing as if he understood how he'd offended someone,

Delia praising my career savvy instincts, Mother telling us all was well and truly meaning it, and Jasper *honoring* Henry Apgar.

"You didn't even like him," I said.

Jasper gave me a deadpan look.

"I'm just surprised," I said.

"Yeah, well let's not use our seventeen-year-old selves as frames of reference," Jasper said.

"Okay, so what is this about?"

"Henry. His parents. Their loss."

"And what are you, um, thinking of doing to honor him?"

"A scholarship at the high school, a fund we—or anyone—can contribute to that will go to a graduating senior every year. The Henry Apgar Memorial Scholarship."

I pictured Henry shuffling through the school halls. "I don't know, Jasper. Don't you think he'd roll over in his grave?" I said. "I mean, he pretty much hated the school. And we, you and I, have barely spoken about this in years, and now all of a sudden we're launching a scholarship together?"

"Listen, I know this is coming out of left field, and we'll have to work out the details," Jasper said. "We'll have to talk to his parents, of course, get their okay, set it up with the school, establish the criteria. I can handle that part, but I need you to go see his parents with me."

"To go....have you contacted them?"

"Not yet."

It felt like I was falling—or being pushed—off a cliff. "Has it, ah, occurred to you that all we might do is stir up their pain, reminding them of all this?"

"You think they've forgotten?"

I sat back. "No, of course not. I didn't mean that."

"If they're averse to the idea, we'll drop it, okay?"

"Jasper, I just, I'm surprised. I mean, it's a nice idea, but why now?"

Jasper looked down at his hands. "This will sound corny," he said, "but it must be Bet. Becoming a father, I mean. I don't know how to explain. There are just things you can't imagine experiencing and then something changes in your own life and you kind of can imagine them a little bit, and you realize that you never really understood."

I didn't press it any further. The thought of meeting the Apgars, of coming face-to-face with the hollow eyes I remembered, set my heart racing. But how could I let Jasper down, after all he'd done for me?

"Okay, set it up," I said. "Give his folks a call or send them a letter, or whatever it is you lawyers do."

Jasper smiled. "I know this is weird, coming from me. But what can I say? Having a baby changes things, Buddy. It really does."

"I'll take your word for it."

TWENTY-TWO

....

Holly was spending Christmas Eve with Michael Jordan in Middletown that year. "Our first holiday together," she trilled. Mother decided to volunteer at a soup kitchen in New London, and Travis and Rosemary and the twins were in Pennsylvania with Rosemary's parents.

I'd never been real big on Christmas. Not that I didn't enjoy the perks—the festivity, the food and gifts, the lights everywhere—but I detected a hollow something at the core of the holiday. An insidious "is this all there is?" feeling began in my late teen years. Maybe that was why I always went to church on Christmas Eve. I kept expecting a moment of clarity, of breakthrough, of something. In the pews, especially during the final carol hymn, when they dimmed the lights and everyone held candles, I did feel something. The voices rose all around, melding into one resounding hum, a hopeful persistence ringing up into the rafters. And it seemed possible then that maybe there was *something* going on right beneath the surface, something that I just couldn't see.

I went to Christmas Eve service that year with Jenna and Andy. I thought that maybe Andy would enjoy the music.

"He'll love it," Jenna said. "I try to take him to church when I can. You know, it's tough. Sunday's the only day I get to sleep in."

Jenna was spending Christmas day with her family. Holly and I would be with Mother at the house. Mother was making dinner.

In church, Andy belted out the carols he knew and hummed along to the ones he didn't. "What about Frosty?" he whispered to Jenna, and she said, "That's not a church-type carol, honey."

Jenna looked terrific in this long, red, turtleneck dress that hugged her body. She wore black boots and a green scarf draped over her shoulders. Andy wore a red bowtie, his floppy hair slicked down and away from his face.

"Can we come to church more?" he said.

"Ssshh," Jenna said.

"Will you take me, Seth?"

"We'll see." I'd learned the golden rule of kiddom already: Don't promise what you're not sure you can deliver.

Jenna took my hand in hers. "Hey," she whispered, "thanks for bringing us tonight."

"Thanks for coming. I had no one else to bring." Delia would have crucified me for a comment like that. It hadn't come out the way I intended. I'd made at least a dozen incredibly stupid, insensitive remarks like that in the time I'd been with Jenna. But she seemed to understand. She gave me the benefit of the doubt. Still, for good measure, I added, "Of course you and Andy were the only ones I wanted to bring tonight."

Jenna smiled, and I squeezed her hand as the hymn finished and we all sat back down. The church was packed. It always was on Christmas Eve. I'd attended this church as a child, irregularly, but always on the big holidays: Christmas and Easter, with my parents and Holly and Travis. My father was not a man of faith, but he enjoyed the ambiance. When I tried to boycott Easter service at fifteen, he told me, "Some traditions have merit, if for no other reason, the way they remind us of who we are and perhaps more importantly, who we are not."

As the pastor stepped up to the lectern, I rested against the pew back. Maybe the new year would be my year of redemption.

Atlanta was receding more each day. A few ghosts still flitted about, but here I was, standing in church with the December night dark beyond the candlelit windows. This time next year I could be attending church somewhere up in the North Country, though the thought pained me when Jenna smiled over at me.

When the service was over, we shook the pastor's hand, filing out of the sanctuary to a bright foyer where a towering evergreen filled one corner, and then out into the black, velvet night. Diamond pinpoint stars studded the sky, the kind of stars you'd expect to see on Christmas Eve.

I drove Jenna and Andy home, but I didn't spend the night. It was too soon, Jenna said, for me to be waking up there Christmas morning. At first I was surprised, but I knew she was right. Jasper would have approved. I placed their wrapped gifts beneath the little tree in the living room. It was a tabletop, three-footer. A tinsel star Andy made in school decorated the top, and a string of white lights snaked around it.

"Ma's got a huge tree at her house with the manger scene and the train tracks and the whole deal," Jenna said. "We'll be over there all day tomorrow, so I figured this was enough. Simplify, you know? That's what my new year is going to be about. Simplification."

"Hey, it's more than I've done," I said. There wasn't so much as a wreath on my front door.

"Next year, you're getting a tree, Grinch," Jenna teased, poking me in the ribs.

"Yeah, Grinch!" Andy chimed in. "Did you know that my grandma has like ten presents for me? Seth? Did you know?"

"Wow, Buddy. No, I didn't know that. You're pretty lucky, huh?"

He gave me a giddy grin. "Plus more from my Mom and Santa."

"Andy, that's enough," Jenna said.

He whooped and ran around in circles.

"Kids are shameless," Jenna said.

"We were, too," I said.

Andy came to a sudden stop. "But, Seth, maybe your present is the best of all?" he said.

"Maybe," I said. "You'll know tomorrow." His gift was a microscope set, a small kid set, of course, but with a real working lens and slides. For Jenna, I'd bought a briefcase. She hauled her stuff around in a beaten-up blue backpack with coffee stains. The new one was expandable with file organizers and a pocket for her cell phone. That'd help her simplify.

The wrapped package she handed me before I left was a book, but I promised not to peek until morning. We said goodnight on the stoop. The storage facility's gates were locked for the holidays. Jenna had to punch a code into the box in the office to let me out.

"People stop in and pick up the darnedest things," she said. "I need this lamp. I need this bowl. I need this coat hanger. You'd think they'd keep what they need with them."

I pulled her closer, wrapping my arms around her waist. "But isn't that how you met me?" I said. "What if I'd never stopped in that afternoon?" When I bent to kiss her, the quivery warmth of her flooded my face and ran down my body. "Maybe tomorrow night?" I said.

She groaned. "I can't promise. Escaping my mother's on a holiday is like getting off Alcatraz."

"Then I'll come there." I kissed the velvety spot beneath her ear.

"Don't you dare. She'll sink her hooks into you good."

"A small price to pay." I buried my nose in her dark hair.

She groaned. "Listen..."

"I wish I weren't leaving tonight."

"Seth, listen." She stepped back. "I want to tell you something. Maybe I shouldn't, but you know I've always believed in striking when the spirit moves, even though it hasn't always worked out in the past. Anyway I feel like now is the time to..."

She looked like a twittery bird getting ready to chirp her heart out.

"Jenna," I said. She was getting carried away. We were getting carried away, making out like teenagers on the stoop on a freezing night.

"Seth, I love…"

"Ssshhh." I placed my finger on her lips. "I know."

"Oh." She stepped back into my arms and laid her head on my shoulder.

I wished she hadn't said it. I couldn't say it back. I didn't even know what it meant anymore. I stroked Jenna's hair, and when she shivered, I held her a little tighter. "I'll call you tomorrow," I said.

"I don't care that I said it first," she said. "I said what I felt, and that's simplification. Right?"

"Yes, it is. It's fine that you said it."

"It is?"

"Yes."

"Really?"

"Really." I cleared my throat. "And you know that I care about you, Jenna, and Andy, right? It's just that I…I don't, ah, really know where, I mean I'm not sure where my, ah, life is going right now, and…"

She mercifully put her finger on my lips. "Merry Christmas," she said and, with a quick peck on my cheek, she was gone.

* * *

When I woke Christmas morning, the sun had already filled my rooms above the river. I pulled on my red flannel bathrobe, an old Christmas gift from Delia. In the kitchen, I flipped on the coffee-maker. Its sputtering clicks brought the aroma of fresh, hot brew to the air. The tile was cold beneath my bare feet. I stepped onto the rug beneath the window. The half-frozen river still flowed below, though its banks were encased in glassy ice. I poured my coffee and headed into the living room.

I settled on the couch, mug in hand. Jenna's gift sat on the coffee table. I took it and unwrapped the shiny red paper, setting aside the silver bow she'd taped in the center. Darwin's *The Origin of Species* was in my hands. It was a beautiful hardback edition, bound in chocolate-brown leather with the title in gold leaf across the front. How had she found such a nice edition? I'd read it already of course. Travis pushed it on me in high school. At eighteen, Travis fell in love with *The Origin of Species*. "It explains everything," he'd told me.

"Everything?" I said.

"Well, everything you *need* to know. The rest is just window dressing."

I thumbed through the pages. The Peabody Museum. That was when I'd mentioned the book to Jenna. Our conversation about the bird eggs and camouflage and natural selection. She'd been listening. I stroked the smooth leather cover. It would have been nice to have Jenna here now, curled up on the couch, wearing one of my oversized t-shirts, her hair pulled back in a curly ponytail. It was too early to call and thank her for the book, so I took a shower and made myself scrambled eggs and another cup of coffee. I usually skipped breakfast or ate at the lab, but this morning I had plenty of time. I wasn't due at Mother's until one.

Back in the living room, I snapped on the stereo. A local radio station was playing jazzy interpretations of Christmas carols. *God Rest Ye, Merry Gentlemen, O Holy Night, It Came Upon a Midnight Clear*—all mellowed out with smoky saxes and piano soft as rainfall on the roof. I kicked back on the couch and watched the shimmering flashes of the river reflect on the ceiling. This time last year I was in Atlanta. We'd stayed in town, having traveled to Connecticut for Thanksgiving. My father was still alive, and no one knew the end was coming so quickly. I picked up The *Origin of Species* and flipped randomly to *Chapter 3: Struggle for Existence.* Scanning the first paragraph, I remembered bits and pieces:

"In looking at Nature, it is most necessary to keep the foregoing considerations always in mind never to forget that every single organic being around us may be said to be striving to the utmost to increase in numbers; that each lives by a struggle at some period of its life; that heavy destruction inevitably falls either on the young or old, during each generation or at recurrent intervals."

Travis found some sort of comfort in this at eighteen. I had found it sadly touching, regrettable even, at fifteen. Reading on, I saw Darwin must have felt something similar:

"When we reflect on this struggle, we may console ourselves with the full belief, that the war of nature is not incessant, that no fear is felt, that death is generally prompt, and that the vigorous, the healthy, and the happy survive and multiply."

I laid Darwin on the coffee table, stretched out on the couch and closed my eyes. A lilting *O, Christmas Tree* floated from the stereo. Little had been said about this being the first Christmas without my father. Mother seemed to have grown more distant lately, skittering from one newfound cause to another. She'd recently described wind power as the "breath of the angels saving the planet from its human destructors." She'd declared Ralph Nader, Connecticut's crusading consumer advocate and perennial presidential candidate, "a model for humanity," swearing she would work tirelessly if Nader sought election again. "It's a cause I can get my arms around," she said.

I stretched my toes and yawned. I really had come pretty far in a short time, and from this point forward, I would live in the present, in the here-and-now, guided only by the concrete realities before me. The past was gone. *O, Little Town of Bethlehem* filled the room, as the sun rose higher outside, and I closed my eyes.

Then the past called. My cell buzzed on the coffee table, and I groped for it.

"Seth?"

And I was back in Atlanta. The voice, unmistakable even after all these months. "Seth? Merry Christmas," Delia said.

"Uh, hello," I said.

"It's Delia."

Two beats of silence. "Merry Christmas," I said.

"I guess you're a little surprised to hear from me? I hope I'm not interrupting anything. I just wanted to wish you a happy holiday, and...You sound surprised."

"No, no, I'm not." Why do we feel compelled to lie at such moments? I sat up, stomach lurching as I rose. "It's fine, really."

"I wanted to check in," she said.

Check in. One of her expressions. When she was out on assignment, covering a house fire all night or a shooting or election headquarters, she would call to check in. I'd be home, reading or puttering, and she'd call just to say, "Hi." There was a time when we really loved each other.

"How are you?" she said.

"Good. Fine. Doing great. I'm in Norwich now. I have a place."

"Oh..."

"Where, ah, are you?"

"At my parents'. I decided to come up for the holidays. You know." She laughed. A tad nervously, I thought.

"How was the drive?"

"I flew."

Of course she did. Probably with her new boyfriend. She had to have one by now. Delia was a very pretty girl. She probably had some guy with deep pockets springing for the plane tickets and a rental car. She wasn't drag-assing up Ninety-five with me anymore.

"Good idea," I said. Then there was a truly tortured moment of silence until Delia finally said, "I'd like to see you."

"I, uh, you would?"

"Yes."

"Is that, um, a good idea?"

"I'd like to talk," she said.

"Haven't we talked enough?"

A pause. "It's just that I regret, you know, the way things ended. I haven't been fair to you, Seth. It all got a little too heated, a little too crazy, you know? I feel I owe you..."

"Delia, you don't owe me anything."

"That's not what I mean. I'm sorry things had to end so badly."

"Things always end badly, otherwise they wouldn't end."

She sighed. "I'm here until New Year's. I can meet you down there, or..."

"Why don't we just talk now?" I said. "We can wrap it up. There's no need to go driving all over the state."

"Seth, please."

I closed my eyes. "You're in Farmington?" I said. "I'll meet you half-way, say Hartford?"

"Parking's a hassle. How about Middletown?"

"Sure."

"Is Holly still living there?"

"Yes."

"How is she?"

"She's fine, Delia. E-mail me some times that work for you, okay?"

"I can tell you now, seven o'clock on, say, the 27th?"

"Fine, good, that works."

"Seth? Merry Christmas, okay? Tell everyone I said hi."

"I will. And you, too, Dee. Merry Christmas. Bye."

I hung up, feeling the old pull, that urge to meet Delia half-way, or even go the whole way, just to make things right between us. But there was no "right" now. It had been erased. I sat up and took the pen and small scratch pad I kept on the coffee table and scrawled, "Delia, 27th, 7 p.m., Japanese place M-town." As if I'd forget.

TWENTY-THREE

....

Mother wanted to talk about Nazis. They were on her mind that Christmas Day. "There has been no true reparation for their crimes," she said. "That's the part that bothers me most."

"Not the six million innocents slaughtered?" Holly said.

Mother waved her hand. "That goes without saying. Don't state the obvious, dear." She was in high spirits, her face alive with ideas, though she had a tendency towards momentary distraction, pausing in mid-sentence to gaze out a window or focusing for an instant on the painting of the weathered, red barn hanging over the fireplace, where a comfortable fire cracked and popped. We began Christmas dinner that year, as we always had, with drinks and hors d'oeuvres—brie and water crackers, olives and grapes—in front of the fire before moving into the dining room.

No twinkling evergreen filled the corner next to the bookcase, the way it always had. True to her word, Mother had hung bulbs on her memorial saplings in the backyard. They looked sort of ridiculous. Last Christmas Father's portable hospital bed stood by the fire, so he could enjoy the tree. Towards the end, he was cold all the time. "Fluctuating body temperature, very common at this stage," Travis observed.

Holly and I indulged Mother's every wish that Christmas because it seemed the right thing to do. Mother had cooked, and

Holly brought side dishes: glazed carrots *with dill*, rice pilaf, mashed potatoes and creamed corn. I picked up two pies, apple and pumpkin, at the good bakery in Groton.

"The thing is," Mother said, spearing a little chunk of cheese with a toothpick, "I cannot abide injustice." She lifted the toothpick and studied the cheese. "In all its forms," she said.

"Mom, thanks again for the sweater," Holly said. "It really is perfect." In keeping with Holly's newfound lady-of-substance persona, Mother had given her a gray sweater—"a cashmere cardigan!" Holly had exclaimed—with little pearly buttons. Holly's outfit that day consisted of an ankle-length, black skirt and a fuzzy green Christmas sweater with a beaded snowman on the front. She looked like my third grade teacher.

"Darling, it will be adorable. I must say, Holly, your new 'look' suits you," Mother said.

"Thanks, Mom."

"Yes, and I will delve into my new book tonight. I am hungering for context these days," Mother said.

Holly had given Mother "The Rise and Fall of the Third Reich," a heavy, hardback tome wrapped in Rudolph the Red-nosed Reindeer paper. I gave Mother a gift certificate to this organic, very expensive grocery shop that had just opened in Mystic. Mother gave me a shiny, silver French coffee press. She knew Delia kept the one we'd had in Atlanta.

"I placed a fresh wreath at the cemetery yesterday," Mother said. "So many of the other plots are decorated—poinsettia, flower boxes, even tiny, potted evergreens—I didn't want your father's bare."

"I think it looks lovely," Holly said. "And just remember what Rosemary says, 'Jesus is the reason for the season.'" She winked at me.

Mother chuckled. "This year we embrace the pagan," she said.

"Did you go to service last night, Seth?" Holly said.

"Yep."

"I did, too. Michael goes. His whole family goes together every year. Episcopalians, you know."

"Ah, the elite. In my day we called them 'God's frozen people,'" Mother said.

I laughed.

"It's not like that anymore, Mom," Holly said. "This was really lovely. A full choir in robes, live manger scene out front, a children's pageant with the kids draped in white shepherd robes."

"Seth, with whom did you attend service?" Mother said.

"Jenna and her son."

"Really? My goodness, your relationship has certainly progressed."

"We're good friends."

"I would think you'd like your mother to meet the young lady, if you're becoming serious."

"I didn't say, 'serious,' Mom."

"Let's arrange a meeting," said Holly, who was dying to get a look at Jenna. "Michael and me, Jenna and you, Seth, dinner here on the coast with Ma. Maybe we can eat out somewhere?"

"Well, as I understand from Linda, Jasper and Chloe have beaten us to the punch. New Year's Eve?" Mother said.

"Yeah, we're all going to the casino—Jasper's invitation," I said.

"No one invited me. It's a good thing I'm not thin-skinned," Holly said. "Michael and I have plans anyway. He belongs to the Harvard Club, up in Boston. He's a grad..."

"Of course he is," I said.

"...and we're going to the dinner/dance they have every year. You've got to see the dress I bought."

"I can hardly wait," I said, but my sarcasm bounced off Holly. She was apparently above petty comments, and above Mother's needling. Holly was in love. It was all over. And it wasn't just the revamped clothes and hairstyle. It was her air of serenity, a quiet confidence, the ease of someone who is certain that only more good lay ahead. Holly was in love, and Michael Jordan must have been, too.

"Michael's the *one*, Seth," Holly whispered after Mother had gone out to the kitchen to check the turkey. "This is different than any relationship I've ever had."

"Any guy who can get you wearing granny Christmas sweaters has got my vote," I said.

She laughed, a good-natured chuckle. In the old days, she'd have told me to take a flying leap. But I had to wonder if the lady-in-cultured-pearls routine was just another in Holly's parade of identities? Maybe, only this time something rang true. Holly *was* a person of substance, her own kind of substance, this ability to step back and size things up, and move on again. If that wasn't substance, what was?

"Is Jenna?" she said.

"Is Jenna what?"

She poked my shoulder. "The one. Your one."

"My...Why do you have to front-load everything? I'm not looking at this like that," I said.

"Like what?"

"Like something I have to nail down right now. We're friends, okay? Good friends. We enjoy each other's company. Let's leave it at that. My future plans are up in the air."

"Do you love her?"

"Come on, Holly. What did I just say?"

She smiled. "The gentleman doth protest too much, me thinks," she said.

"Is Michael a Shakespeare fan, too?"

"He minored in English lit."

"A real Renaissance man."

Holly giggled.

I glanced at the doorway to be sure Mother's head wasn't poking around the corner. "Holly listen," I said. "There's something I want to talk to you about. Delia called me this morning."

Holly's blue eyes widened. "She always had interesting timing."

"More interesting than you know, believe me."

"What did she want?"

"To get together and talk. She says she 'owes me.'"

"Owes you? Hmm." Holly rubbed her chin, pursing her mouth, like she was Sigmund Freud or something. "Guilty conscience," she said.

"I don't think that's it, and anyway, isn't it a little late now?"

"Guilt knows no expiration."

The room seemed to press in on me. In the kitchen, the oven door creaked open. "My goodness," Mother said. "Now that's a crispy, golden skin."

"I really don't need to see her," I said. "I think we've said all there is to say. I don't need any more explanations. It's just over."

Holly clucked her tongue. "You're just scared. Listen, I can appreciate where you are. You know what Michael says?"

"No, but why don't you tell me?"

"Practice good emotional hygiene. You know, keep it clean."

"Keep it clean, right. Exactly what does that mean?" I stood, and we started for the kitchen. Then Holly whirled around to face me.

"Oh, but do tell Jenna if you decide to see Delia," she said. "Because you do *owe* Jenna that."

At the table, Mother grew contemplative. Father's empty seat at the head must have started her. Holly had placed a big basket of dinner rolls in the spot that would have been his place setting. Still the table felt a bit too vacant, a bit too spacious. We chitchatted through the meal, then sat back, sipping wine when we were done.

"The turkey was excellent, Mom," Holly said.

"Couldn't have been juicier," I said.

A bare branch, its spindly fingers encased in ice, scraped the dining room window. The wind was kicking up. The sky was slate gray.

"Remember the year Travis totally dried out the bird?" Holly said. "He'd concocted that method to ensure the perfect roast? That turkey must have had seven thermometers stuck in it, all in strategic spots. Remember? One in the breast, the drumstick, the thigh. I think the wing even had one."

Mother seemed not to have heard. "There was a time when this house bubbled with activity," she said. "It overflowed with life." Her gaze drifted out the window. "Now here we are: two unmarried adult children and their widowed mother."

The branch rattled the window.

"Of course, you two will eventually go on to scale new mountains. But I've peaked. This is it," Mother said. "Unless I can find a new way to become useful in this world."

"Mom, we knew the holidays would be rough," Holly said. "Everyone says the first holiday after a major loss is so..."

"Yes, yes, I know." She sighed. "I know all the psychobabble. People try to break these things down, to organize them so they make sense, to make them acceptable." For a moment, it looked as if she might cry. "But what these doctors—what these experts—can't explain is this: Things you don't believe possible one day do come to pass. It happens all the time, and to everyone. The unimaginable strikes. Look at Auschwitz. Look at all the atrocities, all the *losses* of history. It just goes on and on until one day you don't even recognize your world anymore."

Holly cleared her throat. "Mom, you will work through this. I know you will. And listen, you know we're here for you, right? Mom?"

"Of course we are," I said.

Mother nodded. "Thank you," she said. "I'm...it's Christmas...I didn't mean to bring all this up. I hope I haven't ruined..."

"Of course you haven't," I said. "Dinner was fantastic, first-rate, Mom."

"How about some coffee?" Holly said. "Some dessert?"

"Dessert?" Mother said. "Yes, of course. Seth's lovely pies. Let me help you, dear."

"Mom, I'll clear the table," I said.

"The pies look scrumptious," she called from the kitchen.

I spent Christmas night with Mother. Holly was meeting Michael Jordan early the next morning. She had to get home to "prepare." I walked her out to her car.

The wind had died down. Holly fished through her purse and pulled out a small, white box with a green bow. "For you," she said.

"Holly, what..."

"I know we usually don't, but when I saw this, it just said, 'Seth,' to me."

I lifted the cover. A shiny, silver compass, pocked-sized, its crystal face a clear pane with black lettering beneath: N, S, E, W.

"I...Holly...it's really..."

"For hiking," she said, "and whenever else you need a little help finding your way."

I couldn't answer. I swallowed. "Thanks," I said.

"Not exactly a GPS," she said.

"But it does the trick," I said. I gave Holly a stiff-armed brother hug. Our breath turned to frozen clouds.

"You've got a big year ahead," she said. Then she giggled. "From one unmarried, adult child to another."

* * *

I did not take Holly's advice. I slid into bed next to Jenna the following night in her bedroom with I-95 humming in the background and pulled her close to me, without a word about Delia. Jenna's bare toes brushed my leg.

"Your feet are freezing," I said, burying my nose in her dark, spiraling hair.

"Then warm them up," she said, and her mouth was on mine. When she slid on top of me, her body moving like a rising wave, Delia no longer existed.

* * *

Delia's mother, Nancy, never liked me. She didn't dislike me, but I gleaned pretty early on that she thought me a disappointing match for her prized, only daughter. Nancy was as set on Delia becoming a network anchor as Delia was. It was difficult to tell sometimes just whose dream it was, though it was clear enough that in Nancy's mind the dream did not include me.

She was pleasant to my face. She didn't know that I knew she referred to me as "Bog-boy." One Friday night in the first year of our relationship, Delia and I had returned to her apartment near the UConn campus after dinner. Snapping on the light, Delia reflexively pressed the button on her answering machine. I was shaking off my coat in the kitchen.

"Hi Honey, Mom here..." Nancy's tinny voice came from the machine. "I was hoping to catch you in. I wanted to ask how your video editing midterm project is going. But it's Friday night, which means you're probably out with Bog-boy somewhere. Call me in the morning. Kisses."

Click.

Delia opened the refrigerator and buried her head in it, pretending to look for something.

"Bog-boy?" I said. I was doing field research for my Canada goose thesis then and spending a lot of time in the boggy wetlands the geese use in their migration. Nancy had seemed genuinely interested when I told her.

"*That's* what she calls me?" I said to Delia.

Delia giggled a little too loudly. "It's a term of endearment, a little name she's coined for you."

"Yeah, right." I didn't say anything more, but something inside me warned that possible trouble lay ahead. At the time, I was too in love, too bowled over by Delia—her throaty laugh, the thrilling curve where her hip met her leg—to make an issue of it.

Bog-boy became a secret Delia and I shared, our private joke. As Delia and I fused more tightly together, Nancy's authority diminished. Delia and I were the insiders. That was what I believed those first years when Delia's love rescued me from the lonely grief of my adolescence. It was what I chose to keep believing as the years passed and what I finally realized was no longer true when Delia, her face tear-streaked, told me she'd had an abortion and she wanted to end our relationship.

"This was an awful decision for me, Seth," she'd said. She was huddled in a corner of our couch in Atlanta, a blanket from the bed tucked around her like a tent. "I went back and forth, back and forth. It's been hell."

"But how could you not tell me?" I said. The room was spinning around me, the dream of the baby collapsing and whirling away into darkness. I'd just returned from a weekend research trip on the coast. Delia had the abortion while I was gone.

She twitched. "My mother says I did the right thing," she said, her voice cracking. A soft sob came from her. "She said it was my *only* choice."

It felt like someone had clubbed me over the head. "Your mother?" I said. "You talked this over with her, but not me?"

Delia jumped off the couch and almost collided with me, running to our bedroom.

I stayed on the couch. My hands were shaking. The baby was gone. My father had been dead six weeks. I dreamed about him every night. I caught glimpses of people who looked like him on the street. I occasionally wondered if a mistake had been made and I would perhaps find him in some unexpected place.

* * *

The streets of Middletown were quiet in that mellow lull between Christmas and New Year's Eve. I drove down Main Street, lined with twinkling lights and evergreen wreaths hanging suspended from wires over the road. A few pedestrians, bundled in ski caps and overcoats, dotted the sidewalks. Delia and I were meeting at a sushi place behind Main Street. It was small and dimly lit with that hushed air good Japanese places have.

I wanted to arrive first, so I could get situated, but as I approached the hostess, something told me Delia was already here. I *felt* it. Jenna and Holly would have been proud of me for feeling something imminent. Maybe it was the room. The low light, the cool undertones of the pale blue walls and dark carpet underfoot announced Delia. They recalled her cool poise on camera, the icy, diamond earrings Nancy gave her gleaming on her earlobes, her brilliant-white, TV newscaster teeth. She was smart and beautiful, no doubt about that.

Delia had selected a booth in back. Halfway across the room, I saw her and she saw me. A smile flittered across her face.

"Didn't think I'd show?" I said.

"I knew you would," she said. She smiled up at me, and I felt for an instant the good times. We had been friends. Underneath it all, we were once friends. I leaned to kiss her cheek, and she rested her hand on my shoulder.

"It's good to see you," I said, surprising myself, sliding into the booth opposite her. Delia wore a black turtleneck sweater. She'd cut her hair, shorter than I'd ever seen, so that it sort of just brushed her chin in a shiny sweep.

"I like your hair," I said.

She touched it with both hands, tucking it behind her ears. "Do you?" She grimaced. "The station's request," she said. "They're spiffing me up. Grooming me for a 'new role' was how they put it."

"Well, it suits you."

"Thanks. You look good, too, Seth. This—Connecticut—must have been a good move for you?" Her voice rose faintly on the last word, as if in doubt.

"There's no place like home," I said.

She laughed. "Yes, well."

"Work is going great," I said. "I have a new position with the state Department of Environmental Protection. It's fantastic, so much better than the backroom, short shrift my team got at Emory. Wow, what a difference."

Delia raised her groomed eyebrows. They were skinnier, pointier at the ends than they used to be. They gave her face a sharp, subtle ferocity that I found unnerving. Some producer must have really given her a makeover.

"I wouldn't have taken you for a state guy," she said.

"No, huh? The things you learn."

"But it's great," Delia rushed on. "Really terrific. I'm so happy for you, Seth."

I cleared my throat. The waitress, a petite, Japanese girl as pretty as a doll, came and filled our water glasses. "Ready to order now?" she said, the words in her whispery accent barely recognizable. I nodded. Delia caught my eye and glanced down at the menu.

"The sashimi roll," she said, "and miso soup, please."

The waitress turned to me, smiling. Her eyes were a deep, soft brown like mocha coffee. My breathing slowed, and it seemed suddenly that everything would be all right. I was all right. "The vegetable roll, please," I said, "and miso soup."

"Thank you, Sir."

Delia sipped her water. "So," she said, "thanks for coming tonight. I'm sure you have a lot going on with the holidays and all, and I appreciate you making the time for me, Seth. I really do."

"Of course," I said. "I'm sorry if I sounded a bit, ah, testy on the phone. I do have a lot going on, but I'm glad you called." Delia and I had spent six years of our lives together. We'd launched our careers. She watched my father's coffin lowered into the ground. Maybe I did owe her an opportunity to say her piece. And watching her sitting across from me, I was overcome with a flash of desperate, crazy hope that what she said next would magically erase what had happened and make things right between us again. That I would be restored. I swallowed hard.

Delia must have been reading my mind, because next she said, "I know I've made a lot of mistakes."

I nodded. "We both did."

"But I never stopped loving you, Seth. I just realized we couldn't stay together. *It* made me realize we couldn't stay together."

"It?"

"What happened."

"The baby?"

"Yes." She looked down at her fingers resting on the table. "I'm sorry it had to happen this way, Seth. That's what I wanted to tell you," she said.

My shoulders dropped. She sounded sincere. "I'm sorry, too," I said.

Delia shook her head. "I was wrong not to tell you before I did it. You should have known." She looked me in the eye. "I panicked. I freaked out, and I wasn't thinking straight."

I understood how it could happen that way. I believed her. Then I remembered Baby's 1ˢᵗ Bear in my car trunk. *The baby.* The baby had reached through the fog of my father's death with the promise of something new, something to hold onto. Then the baby was gone, and Delia was too. Everything disappeared, even Emory.

"Delia, listen, I know you were in a tight spot," I said. "But we were in it together. Maybe we could have gotten out together."

A strange cold crept up my body then. It closed my mouth. It filled my ears with a wary whisper: *You have crossed over into a new place now and there is no way back.* I swallowed hard again. I forced my hands off the table and into my lap. The point of no return: That was one of my father's favorite expressions. I saw the slow nod of his head, the forgiving, almost airy, way he sometimes urged me to be still.

I looked at Delia. "We did the best we could," I said.

She threw me a tired smile. That was when I realized how Delia had changed: She looked older. And it wasn't the just the new hair and eyebrows. It had only been seven or eight months since I'd seen her, but something in her face, an incipient hardness, had begun to surface. This was a face that had suffered.

"You did what you thought was right," I said. "It's all water under the bridge now." Was she tearing up? "Delia? Hey, Dee, it's all right, okay? Let's just...we'll put it behind us, okay?"

She sniffed. "I should have told you before I told my mother, okay? That was wrong. There were too many things coming at me at once, Seth, and..."

"I know," I said. "I understand, and it's okay now." Her tears made her seem accessible, as if there were still secret, tender things between us. I quashed an urge to draw her close, to blot out what had happened.

The waitress returned, bowing and smiling, placing the plates and little, black soup bowls before us.

"Thank you," I said.

Delia dabbed at her eyes with a napkin. She sniffed again and sat up straight. "Sorry is only part of what I want to say," she said.

Then I knew things were coming that I didn't want to hear.

"I knew you weren't ready, Seth. You have to understand." She lowered her voice. "Things weren't right between us. They hadn't been for a long time."

"You don't have to tell me."

"You were aware?"

"Painfully so.

"I couldn't tell if you were or not. But I knew—I mean *knew*—a baby was out of the question. You weren't ready."

I leaned forward. "But you were ready?" I said.

"Okay, we weren't ready." Delia sipped her water. The cubes in her glass clinked, and I saw her hand was trembling. "Seth, you weren't really *there* with me."

"What are you talking about? I was always there."

"Physically, yes. In your mind, you were somewhere else—tracking bear in the Smokies, making mental notes of every bird you saw in Atlanta so you could add them to that crazy list..."

"They were species native to the American Southeast. I didn't want to forget any."

"Of course not, and it could never wait. Always a sense of distance, always that need to wander off. Remember that dinner at my producer's house? You recited that bird list..."

"Yes, they enjoyed it."

"One hundred and twelve birds, Seth. No one wants to hear that."

"Everyone listened."

"They were being polite. Couldn't you see that? The problem is you just can't imagine anyone not loving what you love."

"And that makes me so awful?" I said.

Delia's lips parted. She gave a stunned blink. "I never said you were awful." She brought a spoonful of miso soup to her lips. The spoon shook in her hand. There were hard things she wasn't looking at. There were pieces of the story she was leaving out. And there was a time when I would have mentioned them, when I would have trotted out my laundry list of grievances.

"How's the soup?" I said.

She nodded. A tear tiny as a pinprick of light glistened in the corner of her eye.

I lifted my spoon. Delia caught my eye for just a second, and we exchanged a smile. She had brought me back to life in the years after Henry's death. She had reached through the isolating clouds and drawn me back into the world of people with all its secrets and strife, its intimate burdens and comforts. I wanted to tell her this, but I didn't trust myself to get it out right. Maybe some of what Delia said about me was true. Navigating the world of people had never been my forte. Holly once said that I would have made a good monk, a monk cut off from the world, a cloistered monk training dogs or making jam, if only I believed for certain in God, in any God.

After Delia moved out and I was living alone in my half-empty condo, Travis called one night. Holly had filled him in. He called on the landline, which sat on the kitchen floor, because Delia had taken the little table we used to keep it on. I lay down on my back on the cold tile, talking to him.

"Remember this," Travis said. "Nothing is without precedent. All events have manifest before. You are not in unknown territory." It was his way of comforting me, and I loved him for it—bumbling Travis reaching out, offering what he could.

Delia and I left the Japanese restaurant together that night. I paid, because it seemed the right thing to do. On the street, in the sharp December air with a new year only days away, we turned to each other. "Some woman is going to snap you up so fast, if she hasn't already," Delia said.

She was fishing for information, but I just smiled. "I'll see you on CNN," I said.

Then Delia kissed me, brushing her lips feather-soft across my cheek. A rush roared in my ears. The dull edge of the old knife that twisted in my gut after she left turned one more notch. "Good luck then," I said.

"Take care of yourself," Delia said. She squeezed my hand and turned to stride up the sidewalk, her shiny hair catching the street-light. It was like watching a piece of my life walk away.

TWENTY-FOUR

....

When the Foxwoods Casino Resort opened in our town, transforming a hilly pocket of farm fields and woods into a hopping hot spot, people spoke of nothing else. With its turquoise rooftops and glittering windows, the casino looked like the City of Oz rising out of the earth, unconnected to anything around it, as if plunked down by an alien space ship.

Then the casino added a skyscraper—by Ledyard standards—a hotel and spa, entertainment arenas, restaurants, more gaming tables and slot machines that rang out their endless chiming drone around the clock. Limousines came up 95 from New York City and down 95 from Boston. Big business, albeit termed "dirty business" by Grandma Hingham, had come to Ledyard. It brought a huge influx of money and jobs, and most people were willing to put up with a little "dirty" for that.

Over on our side of town, Travis, then thirteen, became obsessed with slot machines, or more specifically with calculating the mathematical odds of winning on slots. He couldn't have cared less about the game. He worked tirelessly to crack the machines' codes. He said he wanted to prove "that even randomness has reason, if only we can distill it." Our parents had no interest in gambling. "Might as well just open your wallet and dump your cash on their floor," Father said. Mr. Apgar used to play the slots occasionally—he won $1,000 once—and Henry would tell fantastic stories about the "weirdoes" and "gangsters" his dad saw on the casino floors. "And hookers," he whispered to me once in our fifth grade classroom.

For New Year's Eve, Jasper had made reservations at the up-scale restaurant on top of the tower, the place where the high-roll-ers dined. It had a circular dining floor with wraparound windows looking out over a countryside bordered by the ribbons of moving light that marked the distant highway. I was dressing for dinner, breaking out my navy blue suit, which I hadn't worn since my interview with Scanlon. I was due to pick up Jenna at her mother's in an hour. Dorothy was keeping Andy overnight. It was going to be a somewhat early night, on account of Chloe needing to get home to breastfeed. Jenna and I had planned an early morning New Year's Day hike at Bluff Point.

My cell phone rang when I was tying my cornflower yellow tie, a nice counterpoint to the navy suit and white shirt, I thought.

"Seth? Listen, I've got to talk to you." Heavy breathing, a few sniffles.

"Holly? Uh, okay. What's the...are you alright?"

A big sniff. "Me? Oh, yeah. I'm fine, just dandy. It's Michael who's in deep shit. I'm just so pissed off, I can hardly see straight."

"I guess the honeymoon's over then?"

"Ha-ha. Make jokes when I'm calling for help."

"Sorry. What happened?" Whatever help Holly needed, I hoped she didn't need it tonight. Jenna was spending the night. I sat down on my bed.

Holly cleared her throat. "You've known me all my life, right?"

"I sure have."

"So, you've seen how I do a lot for the men in my life, right?"

"Right."

"I've done a lot for Michael."

"What do you mean, 'done a lot?'"

"I mean, I've grown. I've accommodated him. I've changed—the hair, the clothes. I'm learning about jazz. I signed up for flying lessons—me, with a fear of heights—because he's an amateur pilot, you know."

"I guess he would be—working at Pratt and all."

"I have a *Military Aircraft of World War I* coffee table book in my living room."

"Are you kidding me?"

"That's what I'm saying. I've *changed* for him."

"But, Hol, isn't this what you always end up..."

"...only now it's gone too far. He's gone too far. This, New Year's Eve at the Harvard Club, has turned into a nightmare."

"I thought you were raring to go?"

"I was. Until I tried to invite some guests. See, we can bring along another couple, and I thought Crystal and Steve would be perfect."

Crystal and Steve? My mind raced. Oh yes, Crystal Lindstrom, that nutcase, and her motorcycle-man boyfriend, Steve. Holly had latched onto those two during her own biker-dude romance. She lost the boyfriend, but she held onto Crystal and Steve.

"Crystal has become a really good friend. I know she's a little unusual in some ways, especially to conventional minds, but..."

Crystal had a metal stud in her tongue, a ring in her nose and a "tramp-stamp" tattoo just above her ass that read, "Sweet Stuff." I saw her in a bikini once, when Holly and Crystal went to the beach with Delia and me.

"So what's the problem? Bring them," I said.

"Michael. Michael's the problem. He says they'll stick out like, and I quote, 'freakazoids from Mars.' My friends embarrass him, Seth. That's the problem."

To be honest, I kind of saw Michael's point. "All your friends or just Crystal?" I said.

"Just Crystal. Are you listening?"

"Yes, Holly. I'm listening. I've got to pick up Jenna in half an hour, so can you cut to the chase here?"

"The *point* is Crystal is my friend, and she's a good person. If Michael cares about me, he'll tolerate her, right?"

"I guess so."

"But you know what hit me, Seth? What I finally see now?"

"Tell me." I glanced at my watch.

"Why am I always the one accommodating the men? Why don't they accommodate me?"

"That's a good question, Holly. I wish I could answer it for you."

"When Michael called Crystal 'a black hole,' it hit me: I've done enough. I'm finished. It's high-time the men in my life make a little room for me."

Holly was having a New Year's Eve epiphany.

"I have certain characteristics, certain qualities that make me, me, right? Am I right?" she said.

"You're right."

"And damn it, it's time somebody honored them. I'm an artistic person, so is Crystal. Her macramé is amazing. Bet you didn't know that."

"No, I did not know that."

"Maybe it's Michael who just needs to look a little deeper..."

"Maybe."

"...he needs to make a few mental adjustments." Holly fell quiet a moment. "Otherwise Seth, what the hell am I doing to myself?" she said.

"I'm proud of you, Hol," I said.

"You are?"

"Mr. Harvard's damn lucky to have you in his life—even with Crystal."

"He is, isn't he?"

"Yep."

"But how are you supposed to know when to push it and when to back off?" Holly said. "I mean, no one teaches you this. They say, 'Fall in love, fall in love.' No one tells you about the little dances that come after."

"You're asking me?" I said. "I guess it's all trial and error. So is Crystal coming? Don't' you have to get going?"

"Yeah, she and Steve are on their way. They're taking their own car. Michael is livid. I've never heard him so pissed. He's on his way over here right now. Oughta be a fun ride to Boston, huh?"

"Happy New Year," I said. "Fill me in later. I gotta go."

I shared Holly's dilemma with Jenna on the way to Foxwoods. When I picked Jenna up at her mother's, Dorothy gave me a bear hug and planted a kiss on my cheek. "Still hanging in there, huh?" she said. "My, my, my."

"How are you, Dorothy?" I said.

"You're either very, very nice or you're falling in love, Pal. I can't tell which," she said. Another hug and her cackling laughter. She smelled like sugar and vanilla.

My face warmed. I cleared my throat.

"Me and Grandma are making cookies tonight and then later watching the ball drop on TV," Andy said, racing into my legs.

"Don't get flour on Seth," Jenna called from the kitchen. "Honey, wash your hands first."

"I'll save some cookies for you, Seth," Andy said. He wore blue, footed pajamas and a Red Sox cap.

"The Sox are gonna take it in the new year, Andy, right?" I said, as Jenna walked into the room. She wore a short, snug, emerald green dress and these black sandals that must have had 3-inch heels. She was such a tiny woman—only five-foot-one—and the sudden rise in her height, the way she tilted her back ever so slightly to kiss me, really got to me.

Andy raised a fist overhead and pumped it. "They're going all the way," he crowed. We all laughed.

In the car Jenna said, "More power to Holly. Give me her my e-mail? I want to tell her congratulations."

"The power of the sisterhood," I said.

"You got it," Jenna said. "Every woman reaches the point Holly has. You wake up one day and say, 'What the hell?'"

"Don't you at least want to hear Michael's side of the story? Crystal is pretty out-there. I've met her."

"Unless she's barking-dog crazy, he has to respect the fact that she's Holly's friend and was in Holly's life long before he was."

I flicked on my turn signal. Foxwoods loomed ahead like a twinkling castle. "Women stick together," I said. "I bet my ex tells stories about me...and not all flattering."

"Yeah, well..." Jenna said, sliding closer to me. "She was a fool. We already know that." She rested her hand on my leg.

Maybe *this* was what I needed now. This new reality, this fresh start, not some far-flung dream of life in the North Country. "Hey, you look amazing tonight," I said, as we wound our way higher and higher in the packed Foxwoods parking garage until I found an empty space. I parked, then reached over and ran my hand down Jenna's strangely sleek and shiny hair. "Where are the curls?" I said. "How did you get it so straight?"

"How? God, torture, that's how. I beat every last curl out with a straightening iron. It took forever."

"Well, it was worth it."

"I wanted something different and kind of sophisticated tonight to meet your cousin."

"Jasper? Don't worry about impressing him."

Jenna snapped open her black beaded purse and said, "Look what Dorothy gave me. She comes into the bathroom, as I'm putting on lipstick, and sticks these in my purse." Jenna pulled out a couple of Trojans in their square orange wrappers.

"From your mother?" I said.

"She said, 'Be careful tonight. I know you'll all be drinking. Don't screw up, or you'll send this one running for the hills.' "

I couldn't respond right away, but Jenna read my thoughts. "Yeah, I know," she said. "Who should feel more insulted—you or me? You, because she thinks you're the kind of guy who'd just take off, or me, because she actually thinks I'm stupid enough to get pregnant on accident again?"

"Me, I think," I said. "Dorothy really has a way of cutting close to the bone, doesn't she?"

Jenna waved her hand. "She invented the cut."

Foxwoods was determined to ring in a happy new year. Splashes of gold and silver sparkled everywhere. An enormous evergreen wreath hung over one of the gaming floors, suspended on wires draped with silver tinsel. Muffled strains of holiday music came from somewhere, and champagne appeared to be flowing in every restaurant window we passed, elegant bottles and crystal flutes sitting on tables.

Jenna tap-tapped along next to me in her heels. I took her hand. "Wanna shoot some craps?" I said.

"After this dress and shoes, I can't afford to lose another dime," she said. "I'll just cheer you on."

We stopped at the elevator banks. I slipped an arm around Jenna's waist. She was so easy to be with. Jenna was a sort of judgment-free zone. It could be incredibly exhilarating. "Let's skip dinner," I said. "Let's check into the hotel instead."

"Fat chance," Jenna said. The elevator bell dinged, and the doors slid open. "You're buying me a meal first."

Jasper and Chloe were waiting at the bar—a corner bar of gleaming, dark wood with black, leather-top stools and rows of silent, glinting bottles giving off a dignified glow.

Jasper waved us over. He grabbed my hand as if he hadn't seen me in ages and clapped me on the shoulder. "You made it, old man," he said.

"Wouldn't have missed it," I said. "Jasper, Chloe, this is Jenna Avacoli."

Jenna smiled. "Thanks for asking us out tonight. I've been sooo looking forward to this. It isn't often I get a kid-free night and a fancy dinner, to boot."

Chloe laughed, and Jasper took Jenna's hand. "So you're the mystery woman," he said. "It is so nice to finally meet you."

Jenna fidgeted and gave a twittery little laugh.

When we were seated at our table, Jasper said, "Good thing we didn't try to get rooms tonight. I hear the hotel's completely booked."

"Really?" Jenna said. "Imagine all these people saying, 'Let's go to Ledyard for New Year's Eve.' How weird is that? I mean, I'm sure they said, 'Foxwoods,' not 'Ledyard.' But you know what I mean, right? No one ever came here before the casino."

"As long as they bring their money and keep pumping it into the state, who cares?" Jasper said, giving Jenna his best charming lawyer smile.

"That's exactly how I see it," Jenna said, clearly pleased to have directed the conversation.

"We couldn't have stayed in the hotel anyway," Chloe said. "With Bet—we have a three-month-old," she told Jenna.

"Yes, Seth told me. Congratulations."

"Thanks. We've got to be home by one. I promised the babysitter. Absolutely by one." Chloe caught Jasper's eye. "I love our babysitter," she said, "But I think five hours, counting the drive-time, is plenty for us to be away from Bet."

"Of course," Jenna said.

The drinks came. "Here's to five sacred hours," Jasper said, raising his glass.

"That is what we agreed to, five hours. A nice little break," Chloe said.

"Amen," Jasper mumbled.

"So, how'd you like that UConn-Vermont matchup?" I said.

Chloe placed her Blackberry phone on the table next to her plate. "I have to be available. Sorry. I told the babysitter to text me, if need be," she said. "The ringer's off." She smiled, shaking her head. "We promised ourselves we weren't going to turn into parents who obsess over their kid."

"Yes, we did," Jasper said.

"But Bet's not a kid yet. She's still a baby," Jenna said. "You've got to be obsessive about them at this age."

Chloe turned to her with wide-eyed gratitude.

"When Andy was tiny, I couldn't bear to let other people hold him," Jenna said.

"Because people don't wash their hands," Chloe said. "They pick up infants—or worse kiss them—covered in germs. It's disgusting. I never realized before how dirty people are."

"Shall we look at our menus," Jasper said. "I'm thinking the chateaubriand."

"I'm with you, Jasp," I said. "I haven't had a nice steak in ages."

Jenna looked at the windows. "This place reminds me of the World Trade Center," she said. "Of that restaurant on top?"

"Windows on the World," Jasper said.

"I had lunch there once, before Andy was born. Of course that was so much higher up than this, and all those poor people died up there that day..."

Baby anxieties, 9/11, this night was heading downhill fast. "How about we choose some appetizers for the table?" I said.

"You two order," Chloe said. "Jenna, ladies room?"

"Yes, definitely."

Jasper and I stood as Chloe and Jenna passed. "I'm impressed, old man," Jasper said, watching them walk off. "I do believe you've landed on your feet."

"Jenna? Yeah, she's pretty, ah, special."

"And you like her boy? You get along with the kid?"

"Sure."

"It's a lot to take on, let me tell you..."

"Jasper, not tonight."

He raised his wine glass. "Fair enough," he said. "Cheers."

We clinked glasses and swallowed. Then Jasper said, "So I've given some thought to our Henry Apgar project."

"Our project? It's a project now?"

"The scholarship fund."

"Listen, can we maybe shelve that for the evening, too? I'd like to relax tonight."

"You're right," Jasper said. "You're absolutely right. No heavy lifting tonight." When Jenna and Chloe returned, Jasper ordered for the table. Appetizers arrived, piping hot pastry puffs filled with crab and little toast squares smeared with glistening black caviar. Then the steaks came. A tuxedoed pianist arrived and sat at the black grand piano tucked in a corner off the bar. The ripe, resonant tones of the old romantic standards, punctuated by the occasional Christmas carol, drifted through the room and over the tiny dance floor.

Jenna's dangling pearl earrings caught the flicker of the candle on our table. She was beautiful. In her own way, with the slender stem of a wine glass in her hand, Jenna Avacoli was beautiful. Her beauty was not Delia's polished poise or sleek confidence. It was warmer, pulsating, filling the air around her.

When the coffee came at around ten-thirty, the piano trilled out, "The Way You Look Tonight." Jasper's eyes met Chloe's.

"Ah," he said. "They must have known we were coming."

"How's that?" Jenna said.

"This was our wedding song," Chloe said. "Whenever we hear it, we always dance, no matter where we are."

"Tonight will be no exception," Jasper said, standing and offering Chloe his hand. She took it, and forgetting her cell phone, followed him to the dance floor, where they wrapped themselves in each other and began swaying to the lilting tune. Lights winked in the darkness beyond the windows.

"Oh," Jenna said, "I guess marriage does work out for some people."

"I was at their wedding," I said. "That feels like a hundred years ago now."

"Was your ex there?"

"Delia? No, this was before her. Jasper got married pretty young. He went from law school straight to the altar."

"He's a good man," Jenna said. "I can see that. He has a good heart."

"He somehow appears to have grown one. You should have seen him as a kid."

"Who says people can't change?" Jenna said.

I hated dancing maybe more than anything. Lumbering around to music while people watched—I always felt ridiculous and ungainly. But I had to ask Jenna, just in case she was hoping I would.

"Do you, ah, want to dance?"

"Dance? No way. Last time I danced was my senior prom. I can't stand dancing. In public, I mean. I always feel so foolish. And in these shoes—forget it."

It was as if Jenna had broken a spell, and I saw how incredibly lucky I was to have found her. Thank God for that storage unit. Thank God for that Dunkin Donuts where she almost ran me down.

When Jasper and Chloe returned from the dance floor, they dropped into their seats, silly and relaxed. "You two take a spin," Jasper said.

"Maybe later," I said, catching Jenna's eye.

She smiled. "We were just saying what bad dancers we are," she said. "But you guys cut a beautiful figure out there."

"For an old married couple," Jasper said.

"Speak for yourself," Chloe said, then she glanced at her cell phone. "Hey, it's almost midnight," she said. When the clock struck twelve, the piano peeled out "Auld Lang Syne." Jasper and Chloe kissed. I made my way around the table to Jenna.

"Happy New Year, Seth Hingham," she said.

"The same to you, Jenna Avacoli," I said. I drew her near. "Jenna," I whispered in her ear, "this has been one of the worst years of my life, one of the hardest...and then you...I'm so lucky to...I mean thank you..."

Jenna put her finger to my lips to silence me. "Ssshh," she said. "This is when we kiss."

And we did. I closed my eyes and for a moment, everything else fell away. For a moment, I felt only Jenna. Nothing else seemed real. There was just us.

When I opened my eyes, Chloe was on her cell phone. "You've got to rock her a little longer and put the music on softly, very softly. That's the key," she said. The phone was clapped to her ear, and she held her hand over her other ear.

"We're lucky we made it to midnight," Jasper said. "Time to get the coats." I went with him to the coat closet and got Jenna's and mine.

"Hey, happy new year, chief," I said. "Get home safe."

"We'll have to, ah, get together again," he said. "I'll get back to you on the other stuff."

"Other stuff?"

"The scholarship?"

"Sure, of course."

When we returned to the table, Chloe was still gripping her phone. "Try the other CD," she said. "What? No, not that one. That one riles her up. The *other* one, the one with Winnie-the-Pooh on the cover. It's on the top shelf, behind the..."

Jenna and I went back to my place. "A nightcap?" I said, as she kicked off her shoes and settled onto the living room couch. It was only a little after twelve-thirty, but the building was dead quiet, and the streets outside were empty.

"Why not?" Jenna said. "We're home safe and sound. Dorothy made a big thing of warning me to be careful on the road tonight. All the...."

"...lunatics are out driving?" I called from the kitchen where I was pouring two glasses of cabernet.

"Yes!" Jenna laughed.

"She sounds just like my mother." I pushed the cork back into the wine bottle, shrugged off my blazer and hung it on a chair back. The rest of the night was ours. No Andy, no work in the morning. I muted my cell phone ringer. We could always push the hike back later in the day if we wanted to sleep in. Jenna could decide.

"Hey," I said, walking over to the couch and settling down next to her, "you sure you're up for an early morning hike tomorrow? We could always...Jenna, what?"

She was holding a small pad of paper in her hand, frowning at it.

"What is it?" I said.

"Yours?" she held the pad out to me, my little scratch pad from the table. I placed the wineglasses down and took the pad. There in my hasty, blue ink scrawl was "*Delia, 27th, 7 p.m., Japanese place M-town.*" Jenna was staring at my face. Something must have crossed it, some flicker that she immediately understood.

"You saw Delia? Did you have dinner with her?" Jenna said.

"I...yes, I did. We did. Jenna, I, um, met Delia for dinner a couple of nights ago. We, I mean she, wanted to, um, tie up a few loose ends."

"On the 27th? Where?"

"Ah, Middletown."

"Really?" Jenna slid to the edge of the couch. The light caught her sleek hair. Her face was a startled, unblinking mask.

"We went to dinner in Middletown, Jen. It was no big deal. It was kind of strange actually. I realized I still have feelings for Delia—you know what I mean—I still care about her, and it's...it's too bad things ended the way they did, or that they had to end at all, but they did have to end and I need to move on. I know that now."

The color seemed to have drained from Jenna's face, so that her painted lips stood out in stunned slashes of lipstick red.

"Hey, you're not upset, are you?" I said.

"Why didn't you tell me?" she said.

Then I made that stupid, evasive comment all guys make. "I'm telling you now," I said. "Anyway there isn't much to tell. We had dinner. She wanted to tie up a few loose ends, wish me well, you know. That was it."

"*That* was it?"

Wrong answer. "Jenna, it was nothing. It was just..."

"Excuse me, but were you or were you not in my bed the night after Christmas?"

"Jenna, please listen."

"Did we not have sex, as I recall, a couple of times?"

"Jenna, please..."

"Now you sit here and tell me you just realized that you still *care* about Delia. You have feelings for her. So where were these feelings when you were in my bed, Seth? How is this supposed to make me feel?"

"But I'm ready to move on. That's the main point. I'm not—this isn't coming out right—wondering about it anymore."

"Or so you say. And exactly what did Delia want?"

"To apologize for the way things ended and explain herself a little. That was all. We wished each other well. We said goodbye. Look, Jenna, I didn't tell you before because I didn't want to risk upsetting you, which I can now see that I've done," I said. "I'm sorry you found out this way."

Jenna swallowed and turned fully to me. "Every alarm bell I know is going off in my head right now, Seth. Every one," she said. "I don't care about you having dinner with your old girlfriend. I don't care about her 'loose ends.' But I do care about you hiding this from me."

"Hiding this?"

"And that's not the worst part. The worst part is I don't really think you know what the hell you're doing with me. You can't really decide if you want me or not, right? If I'm good enough or not."

"This has got nothing to do with 'good enough.' I never said that."

"Look, your ex coming into town and you two pouring out your hearts over dinner is not the kind of thing you hide from your new girlfriend." Jenna sniffed. "That is, if I am your girl-friend. Am I?"

"Uh, of course. I mean, I've never been into labels. But at this point I would call you that."

Fiery pink splotches flamed on Jenna's cheeks. "*At this point* you would call me that? You've been coming to my home for months. You eat at my table. You sleep in my bed. You befriend my son, give him presents, make him think he matters to you—and at this point you would call me your girlfriend."

"No, I wouldn't...Yes, I mean, you have been. You've been my girlfriend..."

"I'm not your transitional screw," Jenna said.

"My what?"

"The woman you hang around with until something better comes along."

"Yes. I mean, no, no, you're..."

"I've moved heaven and earth to make things right for Andy and me and to fix what went wrong. I've paid a heavy price, let me tell you. And you are not going to crash in here now and tear it all down. You're just not. I won't let you."

"Tear it down? Why would I..."

"Andy and I deserve more. For once. For the first time. We're not second-rate..."

"No, no of course..."

"I know what people think. *Oh, it's just Jenna. She should be happy with anything, any scrap or handout that comes her way. She can suck up the crumbs...*"

"My God, Jenna, please. Where is this coming from?" My heart was racing.

"I'm not signing up for the shaft again," she said. "You owe me some basic consideration. At the very least, Seth."

"Yes, I do. I do."

"I told you, a new future is beginning for me. For Andy and me, and this," she lowered her voice to a hiss, "behavior isn't going to be part of it. I've eaten enough shit in my life. I'm full."

"Jenna, I was wrong, okay?"

"Did you hide things from Delia? Things that mattered?"

I had to say, "No."

Jenna looked down at her hands a moment, blinking rapidly.

"Jen," I said, "come on. Let's just calm down. This will all make sense when..."

But she seemed not to have heard me. "Maybe you just need to figure yourself out, Seth," she said.

"Well maybe so, but that doesn't mean..."

Jenna stood. "I'm going to head home," she said.

"What? It's New Year's Eve. Jenna, please don't do this. I'm sorry, okay? I never wanted this to happen. It just..."

She held up her hand. "Please don't make this more difficult." I saw the tears about to spill over her eyes.

"Can't you stay tonight?" I said. "Let me make it up to you?"

"It's not like that. You don't need to 'make anything up' to me. I just...I need to think. I mean, get some perspective."

"You won't stay?"

"I can't."

I drove her back to the storage units, the two of us side-by-side in quivering silence. "Jenna," I said at one point, "I am really sorry."

"I know," she said.

My mind scrambled but I couldn't come up with another good thing to tell her, with anything to say that might turn this disaster around.

At the storage center, Jenna opened the car door, murmuring, "Good night." Then she closed the door and strode off to her little apartment at the top of the rickety wooden staircase that I had hammered a few nails into just a couple of weeks ago. She tottered a bit in her high heels, passing beneath the street lamp in the parking lot. She did not look back.

TWENTY-FIVE

....

On New Year's Day, the river beneath my bedroom window lay so still, almost as if it weren't moving at all. At Bluff Point, the frigid air hung still, too. Every twig snapping underfoot, every squirrel scrambling along a bare branch, echoed in the quiet woods. I made my way along a well trampled path that led through the wooded pockets and out to a rocky beach on the Sound. Arriving that morning, I half-expected to find Jenna waiting for me in the parking lot. I sat in my car for fifteen minutes, in case she showed up late. I imagined her pulling into the lot, springing from her car and, with a laugh, assuring me that the night before had been a misunderstanding. She had overreacted, and I had acted without thinking. I'd been thoughtless. I needed to reassure her that I would never hide anything from her again, that Delia was gone for good and that, whether I wanted to admit it to myself or not, Jenna mattered a great deal to me now.

Only Jenna didn't show and the quiet of the forest, always so reassuring, seemed only hollow now. Deep in the heart of the Bluff Point preserve, I walked a trail bordered by thin strips of sandy soil and carpeted with rusty pine needles. The breath left my body in cloudy puffs. At a bend on the trail, I stopped for a minute and closed my eyes. A branch creaked overhead. A distant crow gave its raspy call, and an icy breeze slipped through the trees. I opened my eyes and saw the empty sky soaring above.

Later as I stood on the beach, watching the white caps peak and disappear in the choppy sea, something within me sunk lower. Grandma Hingham used to say, "Follow a river long enough, and you will pass by all mankind's follies." I've always been drawn to water, from the delicate trickle of the spring-fed streams that spread like a living web through New England's forests to the majesty of the major rivers along whose banks I've hiked—the Mississippi threading deftly into the deltas and marshlands of the Gulf of Mexico, the Colorado cutting like a flowing mirage through the Arizona desert, and Idaho's Salmon River, whose pristine rapids feed the great mountains and plains of the West. The flow of water has always carried me, reassuringly, to an inevitable destination, to the place I need to be. So was this my destination?

A black-backed gull swooped low over the sea, its piercing cry cutting the air. I saw Delia striding away beneath the streetlight and Jenna tottering across the parking lot. I stamped the cold from my feet. I could call Jenna. I could say again what I'd said the night before: I'm sorry. I made a mistake. Let me explain. Delia's face, those fiercely arched eyebrows, flashed before me. *You were never there.*

Afterwards back in the Bluff Point parking lot, the Civic had trouble starting. The ignition caught and sputtered. I tried again. The grinding engine whirred, trying to kick in. I turned it off. Maybe it needed a minute to warm up. I'd never had this problem with the Civic before. I sighed. Maybe I'd swing by Dunkin Donuts on the way home, get some coffee and pick up the paper. I had time to kill today. I turned the key again. Whir, sputter, and it caught.

The roads were mostly empty, and there was no line at the Dunkin Donuts drive thru. A teenage girl with a gold-capped front tooth handed me my coffee and smiled. "Happy New Year," she said, sort of lisping around the tooth. Her hair was pulled back in these pigtails that stuck out from her head, and a bold band of freckles paraded across her nose.

"Thanks," I said. "You, too."

Back in the condo, the afternoon crawled by, and the old restlessness took hold. I flipped through some magazines, checked my e-mail and called Mother to wish her a happy new year. She wasn't home. I left a message on her machine. She had changed the long-standing greeting, "This is the Hinghams. We're not home now, but please leave a message after the beep," to a new one: "This is Millicent Hingham. I'm out and about and sorry to miss your call. Please leave the essentials of your story. Beep."

I made an omelet and scanned the paper again. I watched half of a football game. When the sun disappeared, I lay down in bed. Jenna's "Origin of Species" sat on the nightstand. It did not hold, as the teenage Travis had declared, "everything you need to know." It must have amused my father to hear Travis make such statements and to watch me consider them. Father would typically listen, offer a couple of alternate views and leave us to our own devising. Last New Year's Eve, he had raised a glass with a thimbleful of champagne inside, not enough to conflict with his meds, and said, "To what the future holds."

My bedroom was nearly dark. The last streaks of daylight must have been disappearing over the Sound at Bluff Point. I knew what it would look like. I'd stood on that beach at sunset in winter, spring, summer and fall. New Year's Day was almost over. I took my cell phone from the nightstand and dialed Jenna's number.

One ring, two, three, click: "You've reached Jenna and Andy. Please leave a message," came Jenna's voice, followed by a cheery "Bye!" delivered by Andy and her in unison.

"Jenna, it's me. Give me a call, okay? Let's, um, talk." I paused. My heart beat a sickening thud I could feel in my throat. "Hope you guys had a good day," I said and hung up.

Evening set in. I opened up one of the contaminant spread-sheets on my laptop and started inputting new data from some field tests I'd finished just before Christmas. When the phone rang around eight o'clock, I grabbed it.

"Hey," I said, trying to sound nonchalant and not bothering to glance at the caller I.D.

"So you wanna hear the rest of the story?" a woman's voice said.

"What? Hello?"

"Seth?"

"Holly?"

"Hey, Happy New Year!"

I dropped back against my pillows.

"What's wrong?" Holly said.

"Nothing. I thought you were someone else."

"Who?"

"Never mind."

"Mmmm. Want to hear how last night went?"

She was obviously dying to tell me. "Sure. What happened?"

"Nothing," Holly said and chuckled. "I was totally vindicated. I mean, totally."

"Vindicated?"

"Yeah. Crystal and Steve were fine at the Harvard Club, better than fine. We all had a lovely time."

"Even Michael?"

"Yes, after he took the stick out of his ass and loosened up."

"Gee, Holly. Correct me if I'm wrong, but it sounds like the bloom is coming off the rose here, huh?"

"No," she said. "It's more like I'm finally getting real with myself. Michael agreed that he'd been a little too quick to judge Crystal and Steve. So I said to him, 'Well, maybe you need to give me a little more credit. You know, trust my judgment a bit more.'"

"What did he say?"

"He totally agreed. Backed down all the way. We ended up getting a hotel room outside of Boston for the night. We had the best time—hot tub, champagne. He surprised me with this new nightgown, black lace, very classy, and..."

"Hey, hey, Holly. Slow down, okay? Too much information. I get the picture."

She giggled. "Anyway all's well that ends well," she said. "Now who are you waiting to hear from? Jenna? Is something wrong?"

"Yeah, Jenna. We had a little misunderstanding."

"About Delia, right? About you seeing Delia that night. You didn't tell her? I told you to tell her, Seth, didn't I?"

"Yeah, yeah. Touché, okay?"

"I don't blame Jenna one bit."

"I knew you wouldn't."

"So how'd she find out?"

"She saw some notes on a pad in my apartment, the time and date I wrote down to meet Delia."

Holly took a deep breath. There was no way to put this little blonde bloodhound off the trail now. "So you dropped a bomb on her, and now she's not sure how things stand, not sure she can trust you," she said. "Who is this *Seth Hingham*, she's asking herself. And what does he want with me?"

"Could you possibly be more dramatic?" I said.

"You're going to have to get to work," Holly said. "You've got to regain her trust. You've got to prove to her..."

"This is such a small thing," I said. "A mountain has been made of such a mole hill here. I tried to tell Jenna what happened. I tried to explain the way it felt seeing Delia again. That's all. Jenna has blown this out of all proportion, and that makes *me* the bad guy."

"How *did* it feel seeing Delia?"

"Sort of disarming. I felt kind of torn. Not torn, but sad."

"Torn? You told Jenna, 'torn?' "

"Was I supposed to lie to her?"

Holly hesitated. "No, Brother Dear, but you are supposed to get your own head straight before you jump into a new woman's life." Holly sighed. "Look," she said, "my insights are impartial. That's what makes them so valuable."

She must have picked up that line from Michael Jordan. "This is the problem when you get entangled with people," I said. "Maybe I'm just not up for this again. Trying, screwing up, then back pedaling and missing the mark again. I don't even know where the mark is half the time, Holly. And now where am I? In another damn mess."

Holly was quiet for a minute, and then she said, "Maybe that's what love is—taking on somebody else's mess."

"What a heartening concept."

"But it's kinda true when you think about it. And it doesn't always end badly. You know what Bryce did? He sent me a rope of Buddhist prayer flags for Christmas, well maybe not for Christmas, since he's Buddhist now, but as a sort of good will gift. Wasn't that nice?"

"Especially after I punched him in the face."

"That's my point. He's risen above it all."

"Good for Bryce."

"People do figure things out, sometimes. So cut Jenna a little slack...and maybe cut yourself some, too. You've never been good at that, you know. Let yourself off the hook."

"A New Year's resolution," I said.

"Yeah, write it down," Holly said. "Seriously, take it to heart this time."

Later the phone rang again.

"Hey," Jenna said.

"Hey," I said. Calm now, I was going to let her do the talking, instead of babbling on and running the risk of putting my foot further into my mouth.

"Seth, I'm sorry about last night," she said. Her voice was small and distant, as if she were calling from a remote outpost overseas, somewhere isolated, a place I had never been.

"I am, too," I said. "Jenna, I didn't mean to upset you. I should have told you I was going to see Delia."

"Yes, you should have. But Seth, there's a larger issue. Do you really know where you're going? In your life, I mean."

I flinched.

"Listen, it's okay. You are where you are," Jenna said. "I just can't do this right now."

"Do what?"

"Do us, you and me. See, I've been in this situation before."

"Not with me."

"No, but it feels too familiar—the surprises, the uncertainty, wondering what's a bad sign and what isn't, searching for the tip of the iceberg. I just can't. I'm getting lost. I'm getting ahead of myself. And I have Andy to think about."

My impulse was to reassure her, to coax her back, but her words had stopped me. Did I know what I was looking for? Exactly what was I doing with Jenna and where was I going?

"Andy and I are in a good place now. Things are getting better. I'll have a real job and we'll move to a nicer apartment. Who knows, maybe even buy a little house soon," Jenna said.

I cleared my throat. With each word, I could feel her slipping further away.

"I need time," she said. "I need to take a break."

A dark wave washed over me.

"I'll miss you," Jenna said. "Seth?"

"Yes?"

She exhaled a raggedy breath. "Take care, okay? Maybe we'll touch base in a while," she said.

"Yes, touch base. Yes. Good-bye." I listened until the line went dead. A car passed on the street across the river, tooting its horn. I blinked in the darkness, and silence filled the room.

TWENTY-SIX

....

So much is made of spring. It's the season of beginnings, the time of renewal. The world grows green, and all things cute and furry are celebrated. I like spring, too. But it has always seemed to me that winter is when the real work takes place. The riotous excess of summer and the dazzling kaleidoscope of autumn fade. The bones beneath the surface of things are laid bare. There is clarity in the winter landscape, a luminescence reflected by snow and ice. Cold distills the clamor down to only what is essential, and I learn to see again. This was to be especially true the winter when I was thirty-five.

In the lab at Avery Point, I didn't have to contend with many people. Nodding at students I passed in the halls and waving to professors hurrying across the frozen campus were pretty much the extent of my daily contact. I had reams of data from my fall research to analyze. The lab was warm and cozy, frost etched across the windowpanes. I brought in the French press Mother gave me for Christmas, so I could brew coffee at the lab sink and avoid trips to the dining hall. I usually ate lunch at my desk, scanning the on-line job banks in the North Country.

The only gathering I couldn't get around was the weekly staff meeting in Hartford. Scanlon seemed to have begun the year with a renewed sense of purpose, a zest to "boost morale and communication among the troops" as his e-mail to the staff put it.

So on a brutally cold Tuesday, I followed the local roads out onto the highway under a gray sky full of threat. The forecast called for snow that night, a lot of it, starting in the late afternoon. My plan was to hit the meeting and then hightail it home before the heavy stuff started falling.

Hartford was draped in post-holiday malaise. Cutting through a residential section, I passed Christmas trees abandoned curbside and bulging trash cans awaiting pickup. The towering evergreen downtown in Bushnell Park, festooned with lights at night, stood dark against the moody sky. Glancing at it, I changed lanes a second too late, cutting off the car behind me, which blasted its horn. I looked into my rearview mirror, and the driver, a teenage kid wearing an orange ski cap, mouth open in outrage, flipped me the finger. I parked a block down from the DEP and walked past grim faces on the sidewalk, eyes downcast and bundled against the cold.

In the lobby, Glenda waved me over. "Happy New Year, baby," she said. "You going up to join Scanlon's crew? They all up there already."

"Happy New Year, Glenda," I said. I had an impulse to hug her—not something that comes over me often. Something about Glenda just made you want to hug her and close your eyes — again not a sentiment I had ever shared with anyone except Jenna. I told Jenna about Glenda once, and Jenna called her "the mother we all wish we'd had."

"You looking a bit washed-out, baby," Glenda said. "You coming down with something?" She frowned, wrinkling her heavy brow. She wore a huge, red blazer and gold hoop earrings as big as saucers.

"No, I'm fine," I said.

She squinted at me. "Something else wrong then?"

"No, nothing." I cleared my throat.

"You got a haunted look."

"And it's not even Halloween," I said, smiling.

"Mmm. I know a haunted look when I see one, and I've seen plenty." She nodded. "It's some kind of grieving, oozing up through your skin, out through your pores, something sad on the inside leaking out."

"Glenda, no one gets anything by you, do they? But really I'm just..."

"Fine. That's what you're gonna say, right?"

"You got it."

Glenda shook her head. "You gotta learn to talk more, son. Let it all out. It does the soul good." She sighed. "Head on up then," she said. "I'm here if you need me. And tell your cousin, Jasper, I'm dying to babysit that little girl of his again."

"I will, Glenda." When the elevator doors slid shut, I let out my breath. What was I, walking around with "Just Dumped" stamped across my forehead? Of course I couldn't unburden myself to Glenda, tempting as it had been. I didn't want to wind up as agency gossip.

A jovial Scanlon sat at the head of the conference table. He was deeply tanned and had the sated air of someone who had recently fulfilled his every desire.

"Where have you been, George?" I said, taking a seat at the table, as my colleagues shuffled in.

"Oh, we spent the holiday week sailing off Key West," he said. "What a paradise. My wife loved it, too. We lived on the boat."

"Sounds great," I said.

"Let me tell you, Seth, that's where I'm retiring. Fifteen more years, and I'm gone."

"Send me a postcard," I said.

The staff meeting went smoothly. It seemed I was going to have a lot more lab time as the winter wore on, which was fine. I had to gather some control samples up in the northwest corner in February. If Jenna were still around, I could have done it on a Friday and then headed up into the Berkshires to climb Mt. Greylock with her.

I'd been secretly planning to take her up there for Valentine's Day, to a Bed & Breakfast in Lenox. Greylock would have been fun. The thought of going alone was too depressing, but maybe a solo run to the North Country would help. I could head up for a long weekend and poke around, maybe stumble upon a job lead.

Jasper ambushed me in the hall on my way back to the elevator. He must have been waiting for the meeting to end.

"Big guy," he said, "lunch?"

"Jasp, hey. No can do," I said. "Snow's coming, haven't you heard? I want to make it back to the coast before it hits."

"But the heavy stuff's not due until tonight," Jasper said, motioning me towards his office. "You're turning into a real wuss," he said. "Atlanta softened you up."

I followed his heavily limping figure down the hall. Jasper looked young and vibrant, dashing even in his pinstriped suit, until he walked. It was a bad day for the knee. In his office, he dropped heavily into his chair, popped a couple of pills into his mouth and swallowed them with a sip of water from a glass on his desk. A framed photo of Chloe holding the newborn Bet, swaddled in a pink blanket, sat on the desk corner.

"Is it the cold?" I said, pointing to Jasper's knee.

He rubbed his knee. "Cold doesn't help," he said.

"Can't you go for a replacement or something, Jasp? You hear about athletes getting these knee replacements all the time."

Jasper waived his hand. "No simple fixes here, Buddy. Other bones and structures are involved." He tapped his knee. "The inside of this leg is a complicated place."

"It just seems they ought to be able to do something for you."

"Oh, they can do something," Jasper said. "They can try. It's more an issue of when I'm ready to try. No guarantees on how this will turn out, you know."

"There never are."

"But, hey, come on, give me one hour. You can spare an hour for lunch today."

Of course I went with him. We walked to a corner deli Jasper liked. "It's a short walk," he said, pointing with his cane, "which means a lot on days like today." We sat in a window booth, before a view of the darkening sky and traffic jostling through the intersection. An unshaven guy in military fatigues sat in the booth across from us, scowling and muttering at a newspaper.

Jasper ordered a turkey club, and I got the same. The waitress, her graying hair pulled back from her face and deep lines of resignation etched around her mouth, gave us a bored look and turned away.

"So," Jasper said.

I could feel it coming.

"How's Jenna?"

I wanted to duck and avoid, but then I thought, what was the point.

"We're taking a little break from each other," I said.

Jasper's lips parted. "You are?"

"Yeah, we, ah, thought it best."

"But you looked so happy on New Year's Eve..."

I cleared my throat.

Jasper paused. "What happened, if you don't mind me asking?"

A blue and white transit bus lumbered past the window and stopped at the corner. The doors parted, and an old woman wrapped in a puffy black down coat climbed aboard. I had a crazy impulse to jump up, bolt out of the restaurant, race down the street and disappear into the bus. The doors would slide shut behind me, whisking me away.

"Seth?" Jasper was watching me, eyebrows pulled together in a frown of concern.

"Yes, sorry. We, I mean Jenna became upset over something that happened." I sighed. "I had dinner with Delia, my ex. She was up for the holidays. We got together to tie up a few loose ends, and it really upset Jenna."

"What exactly upset her?"

"Me getting together with Delia."

"Did this dinner involve any, shall we say, rekindling of past affections or activities?" asked Jasper the lawyer.

"No, no, it was nothing like that."

"Well, did you discuss it with Jenna?"

"Yes, afterwards."

Jasper fell silent. Then he said, "I see."

"You see what?"

"Not telling her beforehand was an oversight on your part."

"So I've learned."

Jasper picked at his sandwich. "So now she's not sure she can trust you, she's not sure where your head is."

"That about sums it up," I said. "But maybe we both need a little break anyway. Things were moving too fast."

"Moving where?"

"Moving forward, you know."

"Forward to where?"

"To, you know, a relationship. I mean to the expectation of something more, um, lasting."

"And that's not what you want?"

I gazed back out the window. "To be honest, I really don't know what I want."

When I looked back at Jasper. He was nodding, watching me. "It'll come to you," he said. "Leave all the doors open and it'll walk right in when you least expect it."

"That's what I keep telling myself." I forced a smile. "Hey, how's Bet doing?" I said.

"Bet's great," Jasper said. "Smiling at us, babbling. You wouldn't believe how crazy she goes over the mobile hanging over her crib.

She'll lie beneath that thing, if you turn it on, kicking and giggling for fifteen minutes. You've got to come to the house and see her, huh? Maybe stay for dinner?"

"Sure, yeah. Any time."

Jasper opened his mouth and then quickly shut it. He was about to say, "Bring Jenna." Instead he took a bite of his sandwich, and I did the same. We chewed in silence, until Jasper cleared his throat.

"Actually I do need to nail you down on another date," he said. "I heard from Henry Apgar's parents. They're very receptive to the scholarship idea."

"They're receptive?"

"More like delighted. They wrote me back —or Mrs. Apgar wrote, it was a woman's handwriting—a glowing letter."

"Glowing?"

"How good it was to hear from me, how wonderful that we want to honor Henry's memory this way, etc. etc. They invited us to their home to hash out the details."

"The details," I repeated stupidly. "Such as?" The current was pulling me in and under.

"The legalities," Jasper said. "Where the funds will be deposited, who has access to them, how recipients will be selected."

"Oh, I, um, see. Well great, good. Is this something that we could set up electronically? I mean, through e-mail or regular mail even?"

Jasper sighed and sat back in the booth. "Wouldn't that be a little strange?" he said. "I thought you were on board with this?"

"I am on board, Jasp. I support the idea. I guess I thought, naive-ly maybe, that we could just open a bank account, put some money in it and give it to a graduating kid every year."

A flash of annoyance lit Jasper's dark eyes. "How inappropriate would that be, setting up a memorial scholarship and not inviting the dead boy's family to take part? Not even meeting with them?

What are you afraid of, Seth? They are his parents, for God's sake. We can't leave them out."

"I don't want to leave them out," I said.

Jasper eyed me. "So are you in or are you out?"

"I'm in," I said. "This is a really nice thing to do. You have my full support. I just didn't imagine I'd have to be so *personally* involved. Do you know what I mean?"

"Personally involved? You don't want to be *personally* involved. How else can you be involved in something like this? And, if you don't mind my saying, Seth, aren't you *already* personally involved?"

I looked out the window. No buses to run to now, just a weary caravan of cars floating past, and tiny snow flurries whirling in their wake. "I like to leave the past in the past," I said.

"Really? Well, it seems to me a little trip to the past might do you some good," Jasper said. "And anyway this isn't about resurrecting the past. Don't you see that? It's about creating something good out of what happened in the past. And, Seth, you can't do that from a distance."

"From a distance is where I'm best," I said, flashing Jasper a weak smile.

He grunted. "Keeping tell yourself that, see how far it gets you," he said. "Up close and personal is where you need to be."

"With the Apgars?"

"No, Buddy, with yourself."

Jasper pulled out his wallet and tossed a few bills on the table. "Let me buy you lunch," he said, sliding out of the booth, wincing and rubbing his knee.

"Thanks," I said. "Hey, I'm not trying to be a pain in the ass, okay? This is all just a little sudden. I'm moving as fast as I can. It's been one hell of a year."

Jasper smiled. "You're singing my song, Buddy," he said.

It wasn't that I didn't want to honor Henry's memory. It was just that I couldn't see the point of stirring up the past if you couldn't hope to change the outcome. It never occurred to me that I could change the outcome for myself, that the story I told myself was not set in stone.

The snow was now coming down in sheets of determined flakes as Jasper and I made our way back to the DEP.

"Take your time getting home," Jasper said.

"Tell that to all the other lunatics on the road," I said.

Jasper laughed. "That sounds so much like something your mother would say. That's a true Milllicent-ism."

Driving back to the coast, I wished I could tell Jenna about the Henry Apgar Memorial Scholarship, about how I didn't want to look into the Apgars' faces, about how I was afraid of what I might see there. Jenna would have her own take on the situation, different from mine and from Jasper's. She had more common sense than anyone I knew. "Comes with the single parent trade," she once told me. Jenna would probably want me to go to the Apgars precisely because I was afraid.

Snow was filling the road now, falling from a seemingly endless gray sky. It coated trees and rooftops and the cars navigating the slick streets of Norwich alongside me. I made it to my building, but cruised by the parking lot and got back on the main road instead. I took the connector to Groton, a stupid, dangerous thing to do in what was clearly becoming a blizzard, but something powerful drew me along the slushy road to Jenna's. Was it the memory of Henry as a young boy building a snow fort with me in our yard, my father calling us in for hot chocolate, saying we'd been out long enough; was it Delia walking away on the dark sidewalk in Middletown; or Jasper rubbing his knee? Who could say? All of them maybe.

I slowed, approaching the storage center. A fluffy, white frosting covered the building and apartment on top, collecting in the corners of Jenna's bedroom window. I tapped my brakes, nearing the driveway. A flash of red in the yard—Andy, in a scarlet snowsuit, scooping up armfuls of snow and tossing them in the air. School must have let out early. I idled at the driveway. Andy had his back to me. My mouth went dry. Andy spun in circles, arms reaching wide, whipping around until he dropped to the ground. I stepped on the gas pedal and peeled down the road, skidding at the bend and grabbing the wheel to steady the car.

Back in my apartment, with snow swirling furiously into the river and wind rattling the tree branches, I scanned the online job banks. The University of Maine, of New Hampshire, of Vermont and the smaller, private schools were all up there, strung out like lustrous pearls across the vast and quiet countryside. A life of solitary ease was still within reach, if only I could find the entry, if only I could be sure.

TWENTY-SEVEN

···

J asper scheduled our visit with the Apgars for a Saturday afternoon. Come for coffee, they said, which seemed like the easiest way to handle this—no meal, no big sit-down thing—just a quick coffee, some handshakes and we'd be out of there. Jasper's plan was pretty simple: A bank account into which he and I—and anyone else so inclined—would deposit funds adequate to cover an annual $2,000 college scholarship for a Ledyard High graduating senior.

The issue to be resolved was how recipients would be chosen. Based on their academic standing? Community service? All around good-kid status? The Apgars, Jasper said, needed to dictate this part. It was their call. "This really is for them," he said, which was fine with me. I planned to stay in the background.

The night before our meeting, I made a grocery run. I like to shop late at night. There are no lines at the registers, no little kids pitching fits in the cereal aisle and no one else's cart to bump into. Sometimes I'm the only customer cruising the bright aisles at ten or eleven o'clock.

Only that night the grocery store felt depressingly empty as I dropped the little food I bought into my cart. My life was dead-ended. I hadn't heard from Jenna, or had the nerve to contact her, in a couple of months now, and the North Country hadn't yielded any promising job prospects. I was treading water, going nowhere.

I was in the frozen food section when I turned around and saw Dorothy's cart coming right at me.

"Seth? Is that you?" she called, rolling her jammed-full basket up to mine.

The breath caught in my throat.

"No time to duck out, huh?" Dorothy said, chuckling. "Cornered by the old lady."

"Hello, Dorothy. How, uh, are you?"

"Me? Seems you're the one ought to be answering that question."

"Well, I'm fine. Just getting my, ah, shopping done. I like to go late, beat the crowds."

Never one to mince words, Dorothy was like Jenna that way. "Andy asks about you all the time," she said.

My face grew warm. I unzipped my jacket. "How is he? Tell him I said hi," I said.

Dorothy shrugged. "He's a kid. They bounce back. At least I always thought they did, though looking at my own now, I sometimes wonder." Dorothy must have been coming from a late night at the spa. She wore a long black overcoat and these spiky, high-heeled boots. Her hair was a shiny, stiff beehive, her lips a perfectly painted, arching pink bow. Dark half-moons hung beneath her eyes.

"Listen, I don't want any details," she said.

"That's fine, Dorothy," I said. "But I do want you to know that I'm sorry about the way things turned out."

Dorothy shook her head. "I told Jenna you were a bad bet," she said.

"I'm sorry to hear that, too. Dorothy, can we, ah, just say good night?"

"Not a *bad* bet, mind you. Just an unlikely—let's face it—husband for her."

My jaw clenched. "Dorothy, you don't really know me very well."

She cocked her head. "I know enough," she said. She patted my arm. "Listen, I'm not ragging on you, Seth. I'm agreeing with you."

"Agreeing with what? I haven't said anything."

"You don't have to," she said. "The situation speaks for itself. A single mom, hurting financially, little boy longing for a daddy, and a thirty-five-year-old, never-been-married man reeling from a recent break-up. Not exactly a recipe for stability, don't ya think? The stars were aligned against you."

"Yeah, but you can't count on the stars, Dorothy," I said. "And remember, you don't know the whole story." I angled my cart away from her, trying to give her a hint.

She touched my arm. "And you remember, sometimes the whole story isn't what you think it is. Do you know what I mean?"

"No."

She smiled, sort of a sad little smile. "Oh, I got a feeling you do," she said. "Or you soon will."

"Whatever you say, Dorothy."

"I don't want hard feelings between us. I always liked you, Seth," she said.

"Then we won't have any," I said. "Dorothy, give Andy my best, and Jenna, too."

"That, I can do," she said. "And you can do it yourself, too, you know."

"Good night, Dorothy," I said.

"Seth? The important thing to remember is the story isn't over yet." She raised an eyebrow at me.

I smiled at her and pushed my cart down the aisle.

Later, sitting with a glass of wine on my couch, I almost called Jenna. I could, as Dorothy suggested, wish her well. And Andy, too. I felt a pang, remembering his little hands on the knobs of my microscope, and the glow of pride on his face as he introduced his "animal scientist friend" to his teacher.

I drained my wine glass, stretched out on the couch and closed my eyes. My father would have peeled back a layer and pointed out things here that I hadn't noticed. If only I could dial his number on my cell and hear him pick up, hear him answer my question in a voice of only mild astonishment, as if he were expecting this call, as if he knew I would one day get around to this.

The empty wine glass glowed in the dim light of the living room. It occurred to me then that what my father had done was negotiate the world without losing himself—in his marriage to a difficult woman, in the death of his White Mountains dream, in the stresses and worry his children occasionally brought and finally in the merciless illness that took him from us. My father— with my eyes closed, I could see his face. He had learned the steps to this delicate, treacherous dance. He had mastered the relentless give-and-take, the rising and falling and rising again to face himself and everyone else.

TWENTY-EIGHT

....

Tucked in a corner of the Apgars' sloping backyard years ago was a tree house that Henry and I had dubbed "Command Central." It was where we regrouped to bad-mouth the teachers and kids we didn't like, where we stashed our cap guns, our best comic books and, in fifth grade, a "Playboy" magazine Henry stole from his uncle's house. Henry's dad built Command Central, lugging wooden boards and a can of nails up into the elm at the edge of the yard, when Henry and I were eight. I had my first sleepover in Command Central, waking to the twittering of birds and the bleary light of dawn, Henry snoring next to me.

By junior high school, Command Central had lost its charm. The tyranny of popular kids, the sweaty palms of seventh-grade dances, had begun. There was no place to hide from the changes coming at us, or the ones growing between us.

Standing on the Apgars' stoop on a winter afternoon so many years later, I watched Jasper ring the doorbell and steeled myself for whatever would come my way.

A smiling Mrs. Apgar opened the door. "Hello, boys," she said. "It's so good to see you after all these years."

"Mrs. Apgar, how are you?" Jasper said, with me chiming in on the last few words.

"Please call me Wendy," she said, and when her eyes met mine, they were not the eyes I remembered. They were not dead with grief.

"I'm fine, just fine. Seth," she said, "I almost didn't recognize you. And Jasper, you've both grown up so nice. Come in please."

In the wood-paneled living room, we sat around a glass coffee table. A broad, bay window looked out on the backyard, a rectangular clearing with birch and poplar at its edge and dense woods beyond. I turned to look for the elm. It was still there, gnarled branches bare in the dead of winter. The tree house was gone. Long gone, of course. How ridiculous that I had expected it still to be there. Henry's great-great grandfather had cleared this plot of land. It had been larger once, a working farm including the cornfields across the road, from which the deer had emerged the day Henry died.

On the couch next to his wife, Mr. Apgar was a shadow of his former self. He had been a heavy-set man, a guy at home with a Budweiser in his hand and his beloved Red Sox cap perched on his head. There was something chastened, subdued bout him now. He was, if not exactly lean, no longer robust. He had always been kind and friendly, driving Henry and me to little league and to sleepovers and taking us fishing. He used to tousle my hair and call me "The Hingster." He must have wondered why I disappeared when Henry hit adolescence.

"Boys," he said, "it's been too long, too long. We look a little older, huh, I bet?"

"Don't we all?" said Jasper. His cane was propped between us on the loveseat couch we shared.

"Well, I'm following doctor's orders," Mr. Apgar said. "Had to lop off thirty pounds, get the pressure down, get the cholesterol down, watch every morsel I put in my mouth. You know how it goes. How are all your folks?"

"Fine," Jasper and I said in unison.

"Sorry to hear about your dad, Seth."

"Thanks," I said. "It's been a tough, ah, adjustment, as I'm sure you can, ah, appreciate. I mean, anyone could appreciate. Anyone who's lost someone in the family, which I guess is just about every-one...eventually. We can all, um, appreciate it." I cleared my throat. I could feel Jasper looking at me.

But Mr. Apgar just smiled. "Damn fine man, your father. Good accountant, too. Did our taxes for years."

"Yes," I said.

"Coffee, boys?" Mrs. Apgar said. She wore crisp blue jeans, the kind old ladies wear with the pleat down the front, and a pale pink cardigan sweater over a white turtleneck. A small, gold cross dangled from a fine chain around her neck. "It's fresh ground," she said. Let me just run out and get it." She stood. I did, too, and Jasper rose stiffly, leaning on the couch arm to spare his knee.

"Can we help?" I said.

"Absolutely not," Mrs. Apgar called, heading out to the kitchen. "No need, everything is ready."

"Just take a load off, son," Mr. Apgar said, pointing to Jasper's knee. "Still bothers you, huh?"

Jasper dropped onto the couch. "I have good days and bad days," he said.

Mr. Apgar nodded. "I hear that," he said. We sat in silence for a moment. I exhaled. A photo of Henry at maybe fifteen sat on an end table off the couch across from me. Henry was uncharacteristically (at fifteen, that is) smiling in the shot. I glanced at Jasper.

"You're retired now, Sir?" he asked Mr. Apgar.

"I sure am, retired from the town with a nice little pension. Wendy volunteers two days a week at an old folks' home in Groton. But I don't feel the need. I've been out serving the community, as they say, my whole life. Now I'm staying home. My time is my own."

"Yes," Mrs. Apgar said, coming from the kitchen with a tray of coffee mugs and what looked like a plate of brownies, "and next winter we officially become snowbirds."

"Really, where will you spend the winter?" I said.

"Got a time-share in a condo on a golf course in Naples, Florida. Beautiful place. When I went down there, I said, 'What the hell have I been doing, freezing my behind off all these years?' I'm seventy-two years old, boys, and I've had enough. Icy roads and snow on the roof and power lines down and a freezing house. Lord, almighty, I'm too old."

"The Red Sox hold spring training down near Naples," I said. My old boss at Emory, a transplanted Bostonian, was a huge Red Sox fan and made a spring pilgrimage to Florida every year.

Mr. Apgar winked at me. "Why do you think we went down there in the first place? I plan to hit every game," he said.

"We'll go together, dear," Mrs. Apgar said, settling on the couch so close to him, their legs touched. I didn't recall the Apgars being a real affectionate, or touchy-kissy, couple when we were kids. But then, of course I hadn't really paid much attention. Something about them now though caught me. She patted his hand, passing him his coffee mug. He plumped the pillow behind her before she sat.

"I've brought you the light cream," she said, pointing to a separate, small pitcher on the tray.

"Doctor's orders," he mumbled. "But what does that quack know?"

Mrs. Apgar patted his knee. "You just do as you're told," she said. "Boys, help yourselves."

Jasper and I stirred our coffees. I took a sip—piping hot and then the bold, sharp bite. Warmth spread down my throat. We were here in the Apgars' house, drinking coffee, and it was okay. Everything was okay. A scarlet cardinal landed on a bush in the corner of the bay window. The flutter of red caught my peripheral vision. I turned, and there he was, beady black eyes shining in the cold, beak slightly ajar. He shook his head, and his crown of feathers puffed up like a red mohawk atop his tiny head.

"Good year for cardinals," Mrs. Apgar said, pointing to the window. She'd noticed my gaze. "I've got a few big feeders out there, and the little rascals visit all day. Blue jays, too, and of course black-capped chickadees."

"They're so numerous this time of year," I said.

"Wendy's into her birds now, a real bird-lover," Mr. Apgar said.

Jasper laughed. Mrs. Apgar caught my eye, and we shared a smile. I cleared my throat. My left leg started jiggling. I stopped it.

Jasper leaned forward. "So Seth and I were really glad to hear you're on board with the scholarship," he said.

"It's a lovely, thoughtful way to honor Henry," Mrs. Apgar said. "Let me just say," she glanced at her husband, "how touched we are that you boys want to do this."

"Well, we're a little late out of the gate on this," Jasper said. "I don't really know why it's taken us so long to..."

Mr. Apgar waved his hand. "Some things don't need saying," he said. "There was a lot for you two to wrap your heads around here. Don't think we don't realize it."

"Yes, a lot," said Jasper. His voice trailed off.

My heart thudded. I put my coffee cup down and glanced to the window. The cardinal was still there, eyes partially closed now, basking in the winter sunshine. I exhaled slowly.

"The point is," Mrs. Apgar said, "we're doing it now."

"That's right," Mr. Apgar chimed in. "And it's a damn fine idea, and we're grateful to you for thinking it up."

Jasper clapped his hands. "Good. Well, it looks like we've pretty much worked out the logistics already. We'll use the Coastline Bank here in town. It's local, small, easy to work with..."

"Good as any of 'em," Mr. Apgar said, waving his hand. "Banks—crooks in suits, the whole bunch, if you ask me."

"Yes," Mrs. Apgar said, "but for our purposes, this bank works fine. And you know, Gerard Stillman still works at Coastline."

"Oh, yeah, Gerard. He's okay. Plays bingo with us down at the firehouse from time to time."

"Good," Jasper said. "That's settled then. Seth?" He turned to me.

"Yes?" I sat up straighter. "It works for me, sounds good."

"Local is good," Mr. Apgar said. "None of this online banking and identity theft and all that. You hear about it all the time—people stealing your money through computers. What's next? They grab your paycheck before it ever hits your hand?"

"We'll make personal deposits at the bank," Jasper said. "No online banking."

Mr. Apgar nodded and sipped his coffee. I leaned back. We were heading into the final stretch, and really it hadn't been bad. No ghosts, except the ones I had brought with me. The house was so different, or I remembered it so differently, that I couldn't really picture Henry here anymore.

Mrs. Apgar must have noticed me looking around, because she said, "Eighteen years changes a lot, doesn't it, Seth?"

"It does, Wendy," I said. I had always thought of her as 'Mrs. Apgar,' but for some reason in that moment, I used her name and when I looked again, I saw that her eyes were shaded by something that warmed and deepened them. They were beautiful in a strange way, these glinting, blue mirrors that seemed to see right into me. I was not afraid of them.

"But not everything has changed, I hope," she said.

"No, not everything," I said.

Jasper coughed. "How shall recipients be chosen?" he said. "We felt, Seth and I, that as Andy's parents, you two should decide."

"Sounds reasonable," Mr. Apgar said.

"We've come up with a plan," Wendy said.

"This isn't like other scholarships—going to the kid with the best grades, or the one who's the best athlete or best cheerleader or whatever all else they give 'em out for these days," Mr. Apgar said.

Jasper nodded, and I shifted on the couch.

"What we want is the nicest kid," Mr. Apgar said.

"The nicest?" Jasper said.

"The kindest," Wendy said, "as nominated by the teachers."

They must have read our blank faces, because Wendy said, "It's simple. We want to honor the student who over the four years has stood out as a kind and compassionate soul."

"Think of it as a 'Good Will Scholarship,'" Mr. Apgar said. "That's what we want to recognize. It's what kids need to show each other, right? And it's what Henry would want, if he had a say in this."

"Like the kindness you showed Henry," Wendy said. She was looking at me, but this time I avoided her eyes. My heart thudded a few beats. I looked down at my hands. Then I looked at Wendy. My mouth started moving and out came the words that had been buried in me far too long.

"What kindness?" I said. "I blew him off as we got older and then offered him a ride to his grave. I was the one who invited Henry into the car that afternoon, you know. Not Jasper, it was me. Jasper was driving, but I put the whole thing in motion."

A car passed on the road, its tires hissing over the damp pavement. I stole a glance at Jasper, but he was staring at the floor. Mr. Apgar shifted in his seat. Wendy cleared her throat. I looked back to her. Her brow furrowed for a moment, as she took me in. Then the lines around her mouth softened. She smiled. "Seth," she said, "we know all that. We've always known. But you reached out to Andy with kindness and that's what matters."

I glanced at Mr. Apgar. He was watching me, too, with a dull glint in his eyes, and Mr. Apgar had never been a moist-eyed kind of guy.

"Your kindness is what remains, Seth." Wendy said. "Henry knew it then, and we know it, too."

I swallowed hard over the lump rising in my throat. "What's that expression?" I murmured. "The road to hell is paved with good intentions."

"So is every road worth taking," Wendy said. "The problem is you never know which is which. You never know where you'll end up, so you might as well just get going."

"Good God, Wendy. This sounds like a sermon," Mr. Apgar said. "Don't preach these boys to death. They know there's no one to blame. There never has been. The point is now we want a good kid to get this money simply because he or she is good. End of story. Teachers can nominate the kids, and we'll choose the winner."

Jasper sat back. "What a unique concept," he said. "Those criteria are as good as any."

"Actually they're better," Wendy said, "in the end."

I didn't hear too much of the rest of what was said, the wrap-up chit chat. I couldn't focus. A fog was drifting through my head, pressing behind my eyes, dissipating and shifting the light. Where had I been all this time? Henry's angry, accusing face flashing in my dreams, the pall of the past following me insidiously to UConn, then to Atlanta. All these years I had carried a phantom ache, an accusation lodged beneath my breastbone. I had done something wrong, terribly wrong, and there would be a price to pay. Yet here sat *Henry's mother* honoring my good intentions. She was chuckling now at something Jasper said, her face growing rosy. Jasper and Mr. Apgar were laughing, too. At what, I hadn't heard, but I cracked a smile anyway. It seemed I had been holding onto something that Wendy—and from the looks of it, Mr. Apgar and Jasper, too—had learned to put down. Dr. Haram's intent, bespectacled face came to me. *Without regrets, one has not truly risked, one has not truly lived. In time, one puts them aside. They do not belong to the present, yes?*

When Wendy took my hand in hers, cupping it between her warm palms, saying good-bye, I realized how much I had misunderstood.

"Let's keep in touch," Wendy said, giving my hand a squeeze.

"I'd like that," I said. "And Wendy, thanks for ..." My face grew warm.

Jasper coughed. "We'll set it up so the high school forwards all candidates directly to you," he said, rising from the couch. I handed him his cane.

"Course we want you boys to approve our picks, too," Mr. Apgar said.

Jasper smiled, the lawyer in him oozing out. "We'll all put our heads together," he said.

"Seth, will you be staying in the area?" Wendy said. I ran into your mother a couple of months back, and she said she wasn't sure where you'd end up."

"For now," I said.

"Didn't like Atlanta, huh?" Mr. Apgar said, rising from the couch.

"It's a long story," I said.

"It always is, son," Mr. Apgar said. He turned to Jasper. "And take care of that knee, will you? No sense having that damn thing dog you your whole life."

Outside, late afternoon was drifting into evening. Tattered clouds of gray and pink streaked the horizon. Jasper did not say, "I told you so," as we got into his car. It wouldn't have been true. Jasper had not told me that I would leave the Apgars' house and feel as if I had turned a corner into a place I had never been, though it had been here all along, that a lightness and a freedom—a grace—would fill and silence me. That forgiveness would have the final word.

We rolled down the driveway and turned left onto that narrow strip of pavement where Jasper had lost control so many years ago. A glittery layer of snow covered the cornfield. High above, a few pinpoints of starlight hung in the sky.

"Went well, don't you think?" Jasper said.

I turned to him. "Better than I could have imagined."

When he dropped me off at home, I stood in my kitchen, listening to the clock tick on the wall. The last of the day's light reached through the window in a muted gray glow. I looked out at the river, a dark ribbon flowing between its snowy banks. My cell phone sat in my back pocket. I wanted to call Jenna, to tell her about the stars over the cornfield and the cardinal at the Apgars' feeders, about Wendy's eyes taking me in, exonerating me in a way that I had not believed possible, about the way the world itself seemed a more forgiving place as I stood there in the dying light.

But I didn't call. I placed my cell on the kitchen counter. Jenna had her own journey. There were things she needed from me, and they were things I wasn't sure I knew how to give.

TWENTY-NINE

....

Mother called a week later and asked me to come to the house. I hadn't seen her in a little while. She'd been uncharacteristically quiet. Even Holly hadn't heard much from her.

"She's probably up to her eyeballs in some new cause," Holly said on the phone when I asked her to come visit Mother with me. "She left me a message a few days ago after I called her about ten times and said she was 'in the thick of it' and would get back to me when she had time," Holly said.

So on a Saturday morning in late March when the ground had begun to thaw and the days were growing longer, I drove to the house. Jasper had called me earlier that week, surprising me with an invitation to become Bet's godfather. Her baptism was set for late April.

"Who else would we ask?" Jasper had said. "We've been through it all, you and me, right? And you're solid, Buddy. In the end, you carry through. You're exactly the kind of person Chloe and I want in Bet's life."

Of course I said yes.

On the same day as Jasper's call, a researcher position at the University of New Hampshire popped up on my computer screen. I had signed up for instant notifications. I clicked on the announcement but instead of the usual mounting hope, I felt only an odd detachment as I read the qualifications and duties, all of which fit me to a T. It felt like I was peering through a streaky window at a scene slightly out of focus, an uncertain thing with no clear boundaries.

At Mother's house, the snow layer on the lawn had begun shrinking, creeping back from the edges and revealing the yellow winter grass beneath. Mild hints of spring drifted on the air. Birds called in the treetops. The first anniversary of my father's death was just a few days away. I no longer expected him to be at this house, waiting just inside, ready to greet me.

I walked down the driveway to check the mail for Mother. The mailbox door was stuck. I yanked it open. Empty. The mail probably hadn't run yet. It was only ten o'clock. I glanced up the road, still quiet at this hour. This had always been a quiet road. The people driving it tended to be the same ones living on it. When we were kids, my father could identify the cars going by. "George Driscoll heading home...Anna Cowlby running into town...The Goldsteins probably going out to dinner at this hour."

I turned back to the house. Then something caught my eye. A pile of dark stones had fallen from the wall not far from the mailbox. Winter always took a toll on the stonewall. Every spring Father had set aside an afternoon to repair it, wedging the fallen rocks back in securely and raking away the dead leaves and debris. I crunched over the crusty snow. Four dark stones lay half-buried in the icy rim at the foot of the wall. I squatted down and tugged them free. Then I hoisted them one by one back on top of the wall, fitting them in snugly. It felt good, carrying on something that had been important to my father. I'd come back in a month or so when spring was really under way and do a sweep of the entire wall. Maybe I'd get Travis to help. I brushed off my hands and turned again to the house.

I went in through the garage, which had been left open. Mother's old Volvo sat in one of the parking bays, and the other bay was filled with what looked like pet kennel crates. I walked closer. They were pet crates—a half dozen, all different sizes and colors. They weren't new. The plastic was scuffed on most, and the metal doors rusty. What was she up to now?

"Mom?" I called, stepping into the narrow mudroom off the kitchen. Her rubber boots, smeared with mud, sat drying on newspaper. The kitchen was empty. A deep pot of something simmered on the stove. Pungent garlic and onion, and bubbling tomatoes, filled the air.

"In here, Seth." Her voice came from the living room, where I found her sitting on the floor. Before her was a wooden rabbit hutch, a large elaborate one with an enclosed sleeping box and a roomy open area littered with carrot nubs. Two black-and-white rabbits crouched in the corner, noses twitching.

"Their names are Adam and Steve," Mother said. "Get it? They're both male."

I stared a moment. "You got rabbits?" I said.

Mother smiled up at me. She wore easy looking blue jeans and a white sweatshirt. Her hair was smoothed and pinned back. "Not quite," she said. "I'm fostering them."

"Fostering? When...how did this start?" I squatted down and reached a finger into the cage.

"I drove Mrs. Elmore—you remember her? House at the end of the road? Her husband passed six months ago."

"Mr. Elmore died?"

"The man was nearly ninety, and Mrs. Elmore—she was practically a child bride, you know—is only seventy. Now she's rattling around that big house alone. Her children hardly ever visit; they're scattered across the country. So I told her to get a pet."

"*You* told her to get a pet?"

"Do you know that both you and Travis have the most annoying habit of repeating other people's words?"

"Sorry, Mom. Go on."

"Yes, I told her to get a pet. Animals can be a lifeline for the elderly, you know. We drove over to the shelter in Groton to pick out a cat for her, and suddenly I knew what I needed to do with my life."

"With your life?"

"Oh, that dreadful place was lined with cage after cage of the sweetest, most forlorn little faces I've ever seen, all staring out at me, all pleading for a second chance..."

"Mom..."

"So I decided to give them one." She spread her arms wide. "Welcome to Millicent's foster home for abandoned pets. I'm considering naming it 'Millie's Meadows.' What do you think?"

"You're going to keep the animals here? Those cages in the garage..."

"Yes, another shipment will be coming. I'm devoting the sunroom, the backyard and two bedrooms to house them. Of course they'll only be caged until they're comfortable, the cats and dogs, I mean. The smaller animals live in cages."

"Uh, Mom, how many animals do you plan to keep here?"

"My limit is three dogs, four cats and eight smaller critters at a time. The goal is to adopt them out as quickly as possible."

I stood up. "The rabbits came from the shelter?"

"Mrs. Elmore walked out with an orange tabby, and I left with these two. The cats come next week."

I sat down on my father's old leather recliner. "And dogs, too? This is going to be a lot of work, Mom."

"The dogs will stay outside mostly. I'm having a small kennel installed out back, and I think I'll put up a fence to give them the run of the yard."

A kennel? "But Mom, you don't really like animals. I mean, you never used to. You objected to every pet we had as kids."

Mother got to her knees, and I offered my hand to help her to her feet. One of the rabbits hopped into the sleeping box. "I can see you're against this," Mother said.

"I'm not against it," I said. "I'm just surprised. It's kind of sudden, and I don't know that you've really thought through..."

Mother held up a palm to silence me. Then she brushed off her hands and sat on the couch. In a voice unusually slow and thoughtful, she said, "What you say is true. I haven't always known what I want or which way to go. God knows, your father had his complaints about me, many of them valid. Rest his soul. But I'm at a turning point, Seth. I'm not so far from where Mrs. Elmore is, and I need a plan. I need to move forward in any direction as long as it's forward, or I'm going to stagnate here and be passed by. Do you understand?"

"I think so."

"What I really need is a place to put my energy. Your father would have wanted it. Can't you see him, approving of this foster home? It's something kind and practical. He'd be elated, I think."

"I have to say, I think he would be, Mom."

"And you know, children are not society's most vulnerable members. Animals are. Children can at least speak up for themselves. Animals suffer in silence. It's unconscionable."

"But people do love children more," I said. I didn't know exactly what made me say that, but I thought of Jenna, rushing to meet Andy's school bus and cook him dinner, decorating his bedroom with planets and stars that glowed in the dark, reading to him, curled up in his little bed, wishing him "Good night, my sweet boy," while I waited in her bed across the hall. I thought of Jasper saying he wouldn't be able to go on living if ever he lost Bet.

"I know I haven't been easy to live with this past year, but you know your father and you children were always my center, the place I put all my love," Mother said.

"Mom, when you put it like that, this sounds like a great idea," I said. "But just be sure you know what you're getting yourself into."

"Words to the wise," Mother winked. "But do we ever really know?"

I heard Mrs. Apgar's—Wendy's—voice. *You never know where you'll end up, so you might as well just get going.*

"I'm going to spread the love around a little more, even if I do end up regretting it," Mother said. "And I hate to tell you this, but your room has already been converted to the small animal sanctuary. The Salvation Army came and took the furniture a few days ago."

"That's okay," I said. "I've always been a sucker for the little guys."

"Go take a look," Mother said. "We have some residents I think you'll like, courtesy of Mr. Schmidt at the hardware store who said his son can't keep them anymore. I took them as a thank-you for all the free cages he donated."

I climbed the stairs, as Mother disappeared into the kitchen. She was certainly enthusiastic about this. Maybe she had latched onto something good. Maybe it would be interesting to see where this all led.

Upstairs my old room at the end of the hall was weirdly empty. Dust motes drifted in a beam of sunshine. All the furniture was gone, as was the beige area rug that had covered the slick, wooden floorboards. A thick, black rubber mat covered most of the floor now. The walls were bare. I wondered if the Salvation Army had taken the AC/DC posters, too. A metal table ran the length of one wall. A glass aquarium, full of wood shavings, sat in the middle. The shavings shuddered, and I stepped closer. Something shuffled, and a brown gerbil rose up on its hind legs, pressing its tiny, pink nose against the glass. Another scampered up beside it. I walked over and reached in. The gerbils froze and then ever so cautiously stretched their necks to sniff my hand.

"Mom, gerbils?" I called over my shoulder. "Aren't you afraid you'll catch the plague?"

I stepped back from the aquarium. If Mother could embrace gerbils, it seemed anything was possible. I went to the window. Patches of grass broke through the thin layer of snow covering the back yard. Mother would need help setting up the kennels and getting the doghouses in place. What I would have given for this set-up as a kid—a houseful of animals. What kid wouldn't like it? Andy would explode if he heard about this. He'd beg Jenna to bring him here, to let him help with the animals. I could see him rolling in the grass with a cast-off black lab mix, luxuriating in that intimate, fawning joy only dogs give. Andy could help clean cages and change litter boxes. He could even spend the occasional night in a sleeping bag on the floor of my old room listening to the rustlings and squeaks of the small animals.

Hadn't my father and I listened this same way for my gerbil Teddy, lying side-by-side in our sleeping bags that night so long ago? If I concentrated hard enough, I could feel my father next to me, conjuring Teddy in the dark, luring him with peanut butter and love and stubborn longing. Perhaps my father had been right all along, believing in the best, expecting it sooner or later to show up.

A car horn tooted in the driveway. It must have been Holly. The gerbils were rooting around in their food bowl, knocking the seed-like kibbles out into the shavings. "Good-bye," I said. The words pained me in some small way. "See you later," I said. I left the bedroom door open. Keeping fresh air circulating up here would be important. We could install baby gates to keep the bigger animals out. I paused in the doorway. When gerbils running on wheels and chirping, caged finches filled this room, no one would ever guess that it had once held the stunned grief of a teenage boy who would one day learn that the true power of kindness, and even of love itself, is the power to heal.

Holly's voice met me halfway down the stairs. "No, I don't have a ring, Mother. We've been *discussing* the future, that's all."

"You're not engaged until there's a ring on your finger," Mother said. "It was true in my day, and it's true now, despite all the nonsense young people go on about."

"You're getting married?" I said, joining them in the kitchen. Holly and Mother stood around the center island. The pot on the stove was still simmering.

"No," Holly said. "Wow, that's the last time I open my mouth. I just mentioned a minute ago that Michael and I have been discussing the future." She jerked her thumb at Mother. "Mom took this to mean marriage."

"Oh, come on," Mother said, turning to the stove and lifting the lid off the pot, so a cloud of aroma could escape. "It's understood. When a man and a woman—or two men or two women, you know I'm not prejudiced—talk about the 'future,' it's marriage they mean."

"Actually, Mom, more and more couples are cohabitating these days without getting married. Many of us see marriage as archaic," Holly said.

"Right," Mother said, putting the lid back on the pot. "You just keep telling yourself that. Maybe you'll even believe it one day."

Holly shook her head.

When I chose the ring for Delia, the jeweler in Atlanta shook my hand and congratulated me. "She'll love it, Sir," he said. "You're off to a dazzling start." He wasn't in the store when I slunk back a week later to return the black box with my "dazzling start" tucked untouched inside.

Yet a cautious ease filled me now in Mother's kitchen, the kind of ease you feel after swerving the wheel at the last second to avoid an oncoming car drifting over the line. I had been spared. Not that I deserved the credit. Maybe Delia did. Maybe the universe, God or whoever, spared me. Holly's Great Hum had stepped in and rescued me from my unwitting self. Whatever the case, I was suddenly and hugely grateful.

"We should go for a walk," I said. "It's getting pretty nice out."

"A walk?" Mother turned from the stove. "The stew's nearly done, and then I need you two to help me set up the litter boxes in the basement. I've got forty pounds of cat litter I just can't lug down those stairs."

"Mom, I told you to buy the small bags like I get for Snowy," Holly said.

"Buying in bulk is thriftier, and thrift is going to be key in this endeavor," Mother said. "If your father were here, he'd figure out a way to make this foster home pay for itself. Nobody understood money like that man."

"That's true, Mom," Holly said.

"Travis and the boys are coming tomorrow to help clean the cages in the garage. One thing I do have is lots of free labor," Mother said.

"Travis is cleaning cages?" I said.

Mother chuckled. "I've agreed to sit with the twins, so Rosemary and he can go out to dinner afterwards." She paused. "Fair is fair."

The stew needed a few more minutes, so Holly and I went into the living room. "You knew about this?" I said. "Millie's Meadows?"

Holly squatted down to pet the rabbits. "Yep," she said. "I wanted you to be surprised."

"Well I am."

Holly sat cross-legged. "I think it's a good idea," she said. She dropped her voice to a whisper, "It gives her something to focus on, something new to love, you know."

I walked over to the window. "So *are* you going to marry Michael, Holly?" I said.

She was stroking one of the rabbit's ears. "I hope so," she said. "This is a good thing Michael and I have, a *flexible* thing, and I'm old enough to know that's not easy to find."

"Sounds like you've got it all figured out," I said.

"Maybe just a little bit of it," Holly said. She wasn't done up like a lady of the manor today. She wore black jeans and a blue sweater that turned her eyes a rich, peacock blue. Holly looked like herself.

"Hey, there's a job opening at the University of New Hampshire that's right up my alley," I said.

Holly wrinkled her nose. "It's so cold up there. Why in the world would you want to move up there?"

"It's beautiful," I said.

"It's beautiful here, too," Holly said. Then she spread her arms. "And besides you'd miss out on all this."

"The launching of Millie's Meadows?" I said. "Maybe Travis can drop off his discarded lab mice."

Holly laughed. "Seriously, don't go to New Hampshire," she said. "You don't belong there."

"I don't...how do you know?"

Holly smiled. "Just a feeling."

"Oh boy, here come the feelings again."

Mother clanked some bowls in the kitchen. "This stew is a masterpiece," she called. "I've outdone myself."

"So you're gonna be Bet's godfather, huh?" Holly said.

"Word travels fast in this family."

"Nice of Jasper to ask you."

"Kind of surprising though. He said he wants me to play a role in her 'spiritual development.' Imagine that."

"Yes, I can."

"You can?"

"Sure, why not?"

"How about I don't know anything about spiritual development?" I said. In truth, I barely understood my own, though maybe I was beginning to.

"Spiritual doesn't just mean church, you know, or even religion," Holly said. "I'd say you're a very spiritual guy, in your own way. You're a seeker."

That sounded like something my father would have said. Maybe he'd been a seeker, too. Father, who had given us the best of himself and who, like Grandma Hingham before him, expected no less in return. What I could now tell my father and Grandma Hingham, too, was that the clear open country we had all longed for, that wordless grace, so unobtainable in the crush of daily life, had been with me all along if only I had stopped and reached deeply enough inside to claim it. Perhaps that was what my father understood so long ago. That was the secret of his ease in the world.

"Hey," Holly said, her peacock eyes riveted on my face. "You'll need to bring a date to the baptism, right? To the party at Jasper's afterwards?"

"I hadn't thought of that," I said.

"I'm bringing Michael," Holly said. "Everyone will get to meet him."

"Finally," I said, "the great unveiling."

"You won't be disappointed," Holly said.

"I never am with you, Hol."

Mother's stew was surprisingly good. We sat before the dining room windows, looking over the soon-to-be-fenced yard. Mother pointed to the corner where she planned to set up the doghouses and runs. She sat in Father's old chair at the head of the table. It gave her the best view of the yard.

"When the ground thaws, we'll stake out the fence line, and I'm sure Mr. Schmidt from the hardware store can suggest a crew to do the work. Will you help, Seth?" she said.

"Sure, of course." I caught Holly's eye.

"It's good to know you children are behind this," Mother said, "because I'm in it for the long haul, you know. You can't just walk away once you get started on something like this. There will always be another animal that needs you. The shelter man warned me. Once you get started, there's no turning back. Seth, why are you smiling?"

"Huh? Oh nothing. It's just that Jasper recently said almost the same thing. Only he was talking about Bet, about becoming a parent."

"Yes, I guess he's discovered that now," Mother said. "And he's absolutely right. Children are the ultimate commitment, and certainly the ultimate love." She stood to carry her bowl into the kitchen. "Now I'd like to see you two catch up with Jasper. I would like to die with more than two grandchildren to my name if possible," she said, disappearing through the doorway.

"Bet has inspired her," Holly whispered. "The grandchild campaign is underway. Travis is in the clear of course, but you and I need to look out."

It was touching, Mother wanting more grandchildren. She'd had such a nervous run with her own children. A reduced role actually could be the perfect fit for her. After we cleaned up, I promised her I'd be back the next weekend. I kissed her cheek good-bye. She stopped short when I did that, standing in the garage amid the cages. She looked into my face for a wondering moment. "So much to do," she said, throwing up her hands.

"Yes," I said. "There is."

Then I headed to Norwich. I could almost hear Dorothy's throaty cackle: *I knew it, Seth Hingham. I knew it before you did. You are not so different from the rest of us.*

The storage center gates were open. I parked next to the office. Jenna's car sat in the last spot. I walked around back and climbed the wooden stairs to her apartment. Had she already heard me? Would she be glad to see me? I took a deep breath and knocked. It took a minute and then she appeared, Jenna in a blue sweater, her curly hair piled on top of her head, a cautious look in her dark eyes.

"Seth?" she said, opening the creaky door.

My heart was thudding so hard, I could feel it in my throat. "Hi, Jenna," I said. "I, um, wanted to stop by to, ah, see if we could talk. Maybe. That is, if you want to."

Jenna raised a quizzical eyebrow. "Come in," she said.

I followed her into the kitchen. "Andy?" I said.

"At my mom's."

"Ah."

We sat at the little table. "Listen, Jenna, I, ah, want to tell you about some things that have been going on lately and about some stuff I've been thinking about." The words never come easily when you need them to most. "No big deal, okay?" I said, because her lips were set in a tight line. "Just hear me out. You're so good at listening, Jenna. Did I ever tell you that?"

"Just right now," she said. "Go ahead."

And so for perhaps the first time in my life, my mouth ran on and on, and I didn't regret it. Not a word. Out it all came: the Henry Apgar Memorial Scholarship Fund and the dry warmth of Wendy's hand in mine; Jasper saying he loved Bet so much he couldn't live without her; Mother's rabbits peering cautiously from their pen; Holly finding her 'flexible' love; my father and Grandma Hingham and the magical lure of the North Country; and even Delia and how I now realized that, as Mr. Apgar—and my father before him—had put it, "there's no one to blame. There never has been."

Jenna listened, sometimes frowning, sometimes nodding and once closing her teary eyes. When I reached to take her hand, she gave me a playful punch on the shoulder and then cupped my face with her soft, lovely hands.

We decided to take things slowly. Real slowly. "One step at a time," Jenna said. "We look before we leap."

I agreed, but by then of course I had learned that leaping is not a thing you do with your eyes open. You can keep them open right until the moment of takeoff, but in the end you can't really see where you're going to land.

Following the river home alone later, I thought of all the hikes I could take with Andy and Jenna. Only I wasn't going to cajole Jenna the way I had Delia. It would be up to her. Maybe we could start out in the valleys, along the riverbanks where the ground is soft and flat and the going is easy. We'd build up to the harder stuff—the scrambles along steep, rocky trails, the step-by-step trudge up the sloping shoulder of one of New England's merciless little mountains. We could camp out on a rocky summit, watching the dark mystery that night, and perhaps God above, usher in, listening for the chant of the insects and the scuffle of the wild creatures searching endlessly for the things they need.

ABOUT THE AUTHOR

Karen Guzman has published fiction in literary journals including *Melusine, Words & Images, Main Street Rag* and Many Mountains Moving Press. She has worked as a journalist at the *Hartford Courant* in Hartford, CT, and at the *News & Observer* in Raleigh, N.C. She is one of the writers behind the blog WriteDespite.org. She has an MFA degree from George Mason University, as well as a journalism degree from Boston University. She works as a writer for the Yale School of Management.

CPSIA information can be obtained at www.ICGtesting.com
Printed in the USA
BVOW08s1751130515

400260BV00001B/8/P